Madness Unbound

Book 2 in the Madness of Kanaan Trilogy

Karina Fabian

I0634083

LASER COW PRESS

Laser Cow Press

MERRITT ISLAND, FL

Laser Cow Press
Merritt Island, FL
https://fabianspace.com

Publisher's Note: This is a work of fiction. Names, characters, places, and incidents are a product of the author's imagination. Locales and public names are sometimes used for atmospheric purposes. Any resemblance to actual people, living or dead, or to businesses, companies, events, institutions, or locales is completely coincidental.

Cover art by 100Covers
Laser Cow Logo by Allen Oaks

Book Layout © 2017 BookDesignTemplates.com

Madness Unbound/Karina Fabian -- 1st ed.
Print ISBN 978-1-956489-19-4

Dedication

To my husband, Rob, whose love is one of the steadfast
Truths in my life.

2025 Dedication

To Rebecca Martin for believing in these books and being
a steadfast friend.

Contents

Chapter One

"Get up, O Great Ydrel! Dr. Malachai wants to see you."

Don't call me that. Deryl Stephens rolled over in bed and cracked his eyes open just long enough to see the orderly looming over him.

"Thought you got fired," he muttered and started to pull the covers back over his head. He surreptitiously pushed his old stuffed bear, Descartes, under the pillow.

Roger yanked the covers off roughly. "Only in your fantasies. Sleeping in your clothes now? Thinking about escaping?"

Deryl ignored the taunts and sat up, yawning and running his fingers through his hair. He glanced at the clock: 5:05. Just as well; he was having weird dreams, anyway. He was in a park in his hospital gown, about to kiss Clarissa, when Tasmae spun him around and demanded to know what was wrong with her uniform. He'd looked over the red outfit that hugged her curves and could only think that the color was stupid. Then she'd swung a sword at him just as a piece of the moon fell out of the sky...

He shook his head.

"What?" Roger demanded.

"Nothing. I just knew Malachai would come into work early," he replied blandly.

"Because you're psychic?" Roger sneered.

"Because Malachai's ticked about Joshua proposing to Sachiko—and even more so about her accepting. Bet he didn't sleep at all. I figured he'd want to take it out on...work."

He almost said "on me," but he wouldn't give Roger a reason to report him for paranoid fantasies, not when he was this close to convincing the staff that he could make it in the world outside the asylum doors. Besides, his new approach of not reacting to Roger was raising the man's frustration level in a most satisfactory way.

He put on his sneakers, carefully because the incision site from his appendectomy was a little sore, and followed the orderly placidly to the chief psychiatrist's office.

He felt tired and a little shaky as they made their way down the long hallway. He wondered if he had a fever again. If so, this time he'd actually tell one of the duty nurses. Last time, he'd let fear stop him: The Master had invaded his dreams and forced him to fight, and when he refused, had punished him with Netherworld wounds that left real bruises. The Master's demons had probably slaughtered his appendix, he suddenly realized.

And I was so afraid if I said anything, the staff would think I was delusional. Of course, I blew that when the demons followed me into the waking world. I wonder if that happened because I was feverish. Thank goodness Joshua was there to stop me before I really hurt someone.

"It was freaky," Joshua had told him in the hospital later. "You threw things around with your brain."

And yet, only Malachai and Joshua believe I'm psychic. Deryl snorted to himself.

Madness Unbound ⬡ 5

"What's your problem?" Roger snarled.

Quickly, Deryl grabbed something from Roger's thoughts. "Just thinking how it probably cost more to decorate this hallway than it would to repaint your entire apartment."

"Hurry up, you little shit." Roger stormed down the tasteful hall with its heavy mahogany doors.

A wave of weariness swept over Deryl. He was definitely going to mention this in the morning—or maybe to Sachiko in the afternoon, if sleeping in didn't help. In the meantime, he didn't think he had the strength to keep up his mental shields and deal with the chief psychiatrist. He reached out psychically for a ley line and pulled in its energy. Thus fortified, he marched smartly to the office door with the gold lettering that proudly proclaimed, "D. Randall Malachai, Chief of Psychiatric Services" along with a slew of designations, both honorary and earned.

As soon as Roger left, closing the door behind him, Malachai spoke. "You honestly think you will be leaving our institution soon, don't you, Deryl?"

Deryl smirked and crossed his arms. He didn't think it; he knew it. Thanks to Joshua and his unique way of helping Deryl tackle his "issues," he'd learned to control his powers and shield his mind from others—even the Master.

Even Tasmae, but he couldn't think about that now. Not if he was going to have to prove his sanity.

"I agree," Malachai affirmed.

Deryl forced his jaw not to drop at the chief psychiatrist's statement. He didn't trust himself to speak.

Malachai continued, "You need to keep one thing in mind, however: Our star intern has made remarkable progress with you, but Joshua will be gone at the end of the summer, either finishing his degree or pursuing that music career he's so set on. Meanwhile, I remain the ultimate authority at South Kingston Mental Wellness Center. Further, your family has trusted my judgment for years."

He paused, letting Deryl draw his own conclusions.

Deryl stomped to the chair in front of the desk and sat down. "What do you want?"

"What I've always wanted, Deryl. To better understand your unique abilities."

Deryl bit back an angry reply, but nonetheless countered, "You told everyone Tasmae wasn't real. That I couldn't telepathically communicate with anyone, much less an alien, and that she was a figment of my imagination I had to give up. Changing your story now?"

"Interesting that you mention her and not your telekinesis. Are you still in contact with her?"

I told her to go away. I shoved her out of my mind. She was so scared when I told I'd almost died from my appendix, and I made her go away. He felt a stab of guilt and loneliness but squashed it before it showed on his face. *But I have to get better, get out of here. Then, then I can figure out what she means to me.*

When Deryl didn't answer except to glare his challenge, Malachai shrugged. "Thanks to your... demonstration...while delirious during your appendicitis, I believe it's safe now to admit you do have some unexplainable talents, and that they may indeed be a factor in your emotional stability. Quite a breakthrough, if you think about it."

He leaned his elbows on his desk, hands clasped, and regarded Deryl with a not-quite smug smile.

Deryl seethed inside, but forced himself to mimic the psychiatrist's posture. He was getting out of this place, one way or another. "So?"

Malachai raised a brow, and the fullness of the plan pressed into Deryl's mind even before he felt the invitation. The Chief Psychiatrist waited expectantly.

Still, Deryl squinted, making a show of concentration. No way would he let Malachai know the extent of his abilities. He'd always had a hard time reading the chief psychiatrist—now was his chance to take advantage of Malachai's openness. Besides, he needed time to think.

Malachai's name on respected psychiatric journals. No more articles in rag-mags like Psychic Living Now!

"You want to study my abilities openly..." Deryl spoke slowly.

Malachai on the podium at international symposiums, presenting his findings to his peers, video of Deryl in an MRI chamber performing tricks while the results of his brain scan played on a separate screen.

Malachai nodded. "In return, I will arrange for you to have outpatient status."

Deryl being called to his side, like a faithful dog, and told to perform similar tricks for Malachai's audience.

Malachai pointed to the EEG machine in the corner. That surprised Deryl; usually, it remained discreetly behind the cabinet doors until he had Deryl's cooperation. "It's the best we have at the moment, but enough for a start. We'll do a simple telekinesis exercise and get some preliminary readings. Monday, I'll use that data to arrange for more precise instruments. This is your chance at a normal life..."

Malachai with his own private institute, combing the country for other psychics. A team of scientists under Malachai's direction, drawing blood, administering drugs—playing with Deryl's body chemistry to determine the cause of his abilities. Seeking a way to replicate them in others.

A normal life? Deryl shivered. "And if I refuse?"

A barrier clamped down so hard on Malachai's thoughts that Deryl flinched.

"I think neither of us wants to investigate that possibility," he replied, but Deryl felt the threat in his bland words.

Deryl held his jaw so tightly, it hurt to nod, but nod he did. Malachai had just made it startlingly clear that he could not gain his freedom by, as Joshua said, "Shamoozing the staff." Still, he needed time: time to think, time to plan.

By the time Malachai had finished applying gel and placing the last sticky circle to the base of his skull, Deryl had decided his best course of action was to play along until he could get out of the facility on his own— one way or another, but nonetheless far enough away that Malachai couldn't drag him back.

He had a fake ID and control of his inheritance, even some cash to get started, all hidden in his bear. He just needed a way out. He imagined just wishing himself away, like a psychic Houdini. If only he knew how!

Malachai switched on the equipment and took a seat in the leather chair, setting a baseball on the coffee table between them. Across the room, the small butler's table held a catcher's mitt—Malachai's idea of a clever joke, apparently.

"This should be a simple enough exercise."

"Fine. You do it." Deryl crossed his arms. He couldn't make it look like he thought it was easy.

"Now, let's not be difficult. You've demonstrated the ability to move objects. Try to relive what you experienced that day."

Deryl shook his head. Stalked by demons only he could see, his gut on fire, too terrified to ask for help, flinging whatever he saw at his attackers, only to have the objects pass through them, but their own blows landing with painful accuracy? He never wanted to relive that day.

"I don't remember. I was delirious."

The psychiatrist shrugged. "You thought yourself in danger—attacked by monsters, correct? Why not imagine a monster in the direction of that mitt, and hurl the ball at it?"

I expelled those monsters, same as I've expelled the Master and Tasmae. The only monster here is you. For a wild moment, he thought about flinging something at Malachai, knocking him out, and running. Behind his arms, his hands clenched with the desire. He forced them to relax and set them on his lap.

And go where? I have to get far away—the farther, the better. Roger's outside the door. Running won't work, and I'd have to grab Descartes first. Even if I got off the grounds, then what? I can't drive.

"I'll try." He sighed and pretended to concentrate.

In reality, he'd been surreptitiously moving things around for weeks. He could almost do it without thinking. Now, he strained to keep the ball from simply zooming across the room to land smack in the center of the mitt. He focused on distractions: how the electrodes itched, that the equipment's sounds resembled breathing, what Roger might have done had he found Descartes...

Malachai's impatience morphed to greed when, despite his best efforts, Deryl caused the ball to shake a bit on the table.

"Yes, come on, Deryl. You can do this." Malachai's expression turned salacious, and Deryl could feel an almost lustful possessiveness coming from him. It made his skin crawl.

How long could he keep up the charade? How hard would Malachai push? He couldn't give him what he wanted. He wouldn't! He had to get away. Without thinking, he pulled power from around him, letting it envelope him like a cloak, even as he protested, "I can't."

"Try harder. Want it to move."

I want to get out of here, Deryl thought. He felt the power growing around him; it took effort now not to direct it toward the ball. "I am trying. This isn't as easy as it looks."

Escaping wouldn't be easy, either. Malachai would search for him; all the running in the world wouldn't stop him. Malachai leaned forward, and his will pressed against Deryl's shields. Deryl shivered, and the ball with him.

"Do it! Want the ball to move."

"Back off!" He leaned away from Malachai. The psychiatrist's greed flowed over him, repulsive and terrifying. He hadn't felt like that since he was a child and—

I have to get out of here! He trembled against the urge to run.

"Into the mitt! Do it! Want it!" Malachai reached out to grab his arm.

I want to get away from you!

The power surged through him.

A sudden, terrible wrenching.

Then blackness.

Awareness returned with a shock. His head buzzed, both psychically and physically. He felt groggy, his muscles as weak as when he'd awakened from the anesthetic after his operation. Dimly, he noted the baseball in his hand.

He lay on the shattered remains of the table that had held the mitt.

He forced himself to concentrate, his eyes to focus on the other side of the room—the part of the room where he'd been only moments before.

It was a shambles. The equipment tilted against the toppled chair, the needles bent and its casing dented. The wires that led to the electrodes were yanked out, and he reached up to touch the sensors still attached to his head. The table had broken in two, the halves caved in toward each other. Malachai lay draped over it.

Malachai groaned and pushed himself up. His lip bled from having bitten it, and a long bruise was forming under his jaw. Nonetheless, the expression on his face as he groped for a tissue and examined the scene was one of calculation and regret.

Deryl shuddered, fighting the waves of dizziness that came with the motion. Malachai's favorite lab rat had gone too far.

"I swear, I don't know what happened!" Deryl pleaded, but he knew. He'd wanted to get away. His mind had been on the ball and the mitt, but his desire had been to get away.

He'd teleported. With a little concentration, he could do it again to anywhere he could picture. He knew he could.

Malachai knew it, too.

As Deryl watched in helpless horror, the chief psychiatrist walked to his desk and pulled a syringe from the drawer. It was already full. He tapped it, removing the air.

Deryl struggled to sit up, to scramble away.

"We both knew this day would come," Malachai said, almost wistfully. "I had hoped it wouldn't be for a while, yet. You were making such wonderful progress."

Run! Deryl tried to teleport, but he didn't have the energy.

Fight! He remembered the baseball in his hand. He threw it.

Malachai howled as it hit him. He brought his hands to his face, mindful of the syringe he held.

Run! With sheer force of will, Deryl shoved himself up and tried to dash past. If he could just get out of the office, maybe Malachai wouldn't—

His weakness and disorientation undid him. He stumbled over the mitt and fell into Malachai. They landed in a tangled heap, and he punched Malachai in the face as he scrambled for the door. A sharp pain in his side told him he'd torn some stitches. He ignored it and lurched to his feet.

Calling for the orderly, Malachai grabbed his ankle, and again, he fell. He felt a sharp prick in his calf.

Run! Fight!

As blackness overcame him, all he could do was whimper.

Tasmae, the Miscria, Protector of Kanaan and its peoples, raised her sword in a front block then heaved, forcing her opponent's weapon aside. She followed with a kick that Salgoud jumped back to avoid. All the while, she continued to share her frustrations, letting her ire show through their telepathic conversation.

The Ydrel confuses. The Ydrel refuses. The Ydrel makes demands: "Call me Deryl. Show me your face. Show me your world." And now, he has rejected me altogether!

In her fury, she let loose with a series of swings that drove him back.

You are certain this Deryl is the Ydrel? he asked with complete calm.

Surprise at the thought made her drop her guard, and he lunged. Ignoring the tear he'd put in her armor, she spun and slashed, just missing his leg. He grabbed her sword arm with one hand while wrapping his arm around her neck. He squeezed hard with both.

Of course, it is the Ydrel. My mentor told me. She let herself go slack, making him bear her weight, then lashed back with her foot. She felt his shock of pain as it connected, and pushed away, swinging.

He blocked. *Your mentor died before the Ydrel began acting strangely. Could this be an imposter?*

He limped slightly, but advanced with his own whirlwind blows that made her step back as she considered his words.

No, she replied. *I would know. It is the Ydrel. Something has changed.*

Has he ever communicated to a Miscria this way? He had driven her to the edge of the trees.

I don't know! She leaped forward, swinging toward his good leg to make him pull back and place his weight on the sore one. *I've not experienced all the Remembrances of the Miscria who contacted the Ydrel. You know that.*

He retaliated with an upward swing, then pushed forward again, as relentless in his attacks as in his thoughts, again driving her toward the trees. *There were five—you have experienced the memories of two, and even those not in their entirety. You are not a fully trained Miscria. If you are so certain he is the Ydrel, then perhaps it is something you have done?*

The flat of his sword connected with her sore wrist, and she released her grip. Before she could get her balance on the sword one-handed, he kicked out, sweeping her legs from under her.

She called upon her power over Kanaan.

The ground rumbled beneath him, and the ivy twined around one tree whipped out and captured his arms and legs, and yanked him off the ground.

Good! Salgoud called, but she had sat up, sword discarded beside her, and hugged herself, shivering.

She could see Deryl, in the Netherworld that he'd insisted she make look like her own Kanaan. She realized now how pale he looked, but at the time, she'd only been angry. She had questions for him—questions about strategies he'd given her that she only half-understood, despite her warrior training. Urgency had fed her frustration—she had to teach the others, but he'd disappeared for weeks, refusing her Callings. It shouldn't have worked that way: she, the Miscria called to the Ydrel, asked her questions, received her answers. Ydrel Mentor, Ydrel Guide. Why wasn't he doing his duty?

Then he'd snapped at her that he'd been sick, had almost died.

She'd panicked. She'd lost faith—in herself, in him. Was that why he denied her now?

He said he almost died. Her admission came as a whisper.

Gently the tree lowered Salgoud, and he sat down beside her. *Can an oracle die?*

I followed the rituals, she thought. *I did as I was trained. He insisted on doing things differently. Could I have hurt him?*

Salgoud wrapped his arm around her and pulled her close. *Let Leinad bring the Remembrances here. Finish your training.*

She shook her head. *The war—*

—will not begin for months. He glanced up at the small planet that shone like a star in the daytime sky. *Even an old warrior like me knows Barin has not come close enough to loose its vermin on us.*

She followed his gaze, but she felt overwhelming dread. *Salgoud, this has to be the last war. I don't know why, but I can feel it. We can't just repel the Barin this time; we have to make sure they never come back.*

Such dreams are for children, he replied. *How would you make this real?*

I don't know. But the Ydrel does. He has to teach me. I will not let him abandon us!

Of course not. You are Tasmae, the most stubborn student I've ever trained. Had you not become Miscria, I would have let you take my place in leading our warriors. But you are the Miscria, and you need to train.

And, he concluded, pointing at a rider thundering toward them, *I think you shall not have a choice.*

Tasmae followed his gaze. *Leinad!*

Chapter Two

Joshua leaned into the curve as Sachiko guided her Harley into the parking lot of South Kingston Mental Wellness Center. Riding to work on the back of her bike was one of the many things he could get used to.

I love this summer! He leaned into his fiancée's curves.

She pulled up next to his car, but didn't shut off the engine. Reluctantly, he released her and dismounted. He stowed his helmet in her saddlebags, then stuffed his jacket around it. By then, she'd removed her helmet so he could kiss her good-bye.

"See you in a couple of hours," she said when he pulled away.

"Swing shift can't come soon enough."

She snorted. "Oh, I'm sure it will go by fast, since you'll probably be telling everyone the story of your proposing. Just try not to embellish, okay?"

He did his best to look affronted. "I'm a songwriter, not an author."

"You're a romantic," she countered, then added, "and an intern, so once you're through those doors, you'd better have your professional face on. You're already on thin ice with Dr. Malachai."

Joshua sighed. "Don't I know it." His rather showy at-work proposal, which included a song he'd written just for her, had drawn an audience. The chief psychiatrist had decided it would be "impolitic" to fire him, but had also warned him that one more display of un-professional behavior, and Joshua would spend the rest of his summer bussing tables for Sachiko's parents and busking in the streets for extra coins. He hadn't liked the idea of a 19-year-old intern, anyway, and Joshua's romance with Sachiko seemed to really put him on edge.

"I'll be good," he promised. "I won't make any waves. It'll be a boring, ordinary day."

She raised a brow, as if she didn't believe he was ca-pable of ordinary days, and he felt his heart skip. "I love you."

He would never tire of those words. "And I love you."

He leaned against his car and watched her pull out of the parking lot. His thumb rubbed against his great-great-grandfather's ring, now back on his finger. He'd given it to her Friday night when he'd proposed, but Saturday, they'd bought her a simple marquise.

Best weekend ever! Only one thing could have made it better, but that would wait for the honeymoon. They both had some issues to work out first.

He sighed. He was going to have to tell her about Lattie soon. There hadn't been opportunity this week-end, not really. They were with her parents or out doing stuff...

Please, a part of him countered, *you chickened out.*

How did I ever think I was in love with LaTisha? He imagined himself explaining it to Sachiko: I was an idiot. I mistook lust for love. I let it blind me. I didn't even know she was pregnant until after she'd "taken care of the problem." I didn't even realize she was the kind of woman who could do that. And I am so sorry!

God, I am so sorry!

He shook himself. Tonight, after work. Before he chickened out again. In the meantime, there was no point going home now. He'd just brood. He had a spare set of clothes in his locker; he could change, start work early. That would make Malachai happy. Besides, the cafeteria made great breakfasts. He'd check on Deryl, too; no doubt he'd want to know all the details of their weekend with Sachiko's parents.

Joshua slowed to a stop when he saw Deryl slouched over his breakfast in the cafeteria, motionless, robe askew.

At least, he thought it was Deryl. The shoulder-length blond hair, though dirty and tangled, was unmistakable, but nothing else resembled the young man who'd so cheerfully hugged him in congratulations the Friday before. With a sinking feeling in his stomach, he made his way to the coffee machine, watching Deryl as he went. He couldn't see his expression, but the slack-jawed way he regarded his waffles spelled trouble.

He decided on an oblique approach. He got his coffee and sat down next to the patient. "So, Deryl, how was your weekend?"

For a moment, Deryl didn't seem to hear him; then he turned slowly, blinked owlishly, and smiled. "Oh, hi, Josh." He paused between each word, as if fighting to remember how to say them. His pupils were...pulsating, very slightly. Joshua had seen them contract before, usually when he was fighting someone else's thoughts. This gentle, rhythmic pulsing, however, was new, and a little disturbing.

What's he on? What happened? "How was your weekend?"

Deryl picked up the syrup bottle and without looking at it, began to pour it on his waffles in careless, swirling motions. Joshua watched.

HELP

Joshua glanced sharply at the young client. "Deryl, what's going on?"

Deryl stuck his fingers in the syrup and erased the letters with a lazy sweep of his hand.

Gently, Joshua took him by the chin and turned his face toward his. "Deryl, focus. What—" He stopped as the young client's eyes looked past him. Joshua turned around.

Dr. Malachai stood behind him, regarding them with resigned patience. He had a black eye and wore a bandage on his nose and one on his lip; beneath it, it looked like he'd had stitches. "Don't you think you should use a fork instead?"

Like a child, Deryl stuck his sticky fingers in his mouth.

Malachai signaled an orderly to help the young man eat. "Come with me, Mr. Lawson," he said, and headed back to his office without bothering to see if Joshua was following.

Malachai allowed him to enter the office first, no doubt to let him take in the cheap table that replaced his lustrous cherry wood one, the broken equipment set against the wall, the blood stains that had not yet been shampooed out of the carpet.

Joshua looked from the room to him, opened his mouth, found he had no idea what to say, and closed it.

"Deryl attacked me Saturday morning," Malachai explained as he pointed Joshua to a chair. He leaned on his still-immaculate desk. "I had brought him in with the intention of running an EEG. Deryl's recent behavior warrants further study, I'm sure you'd agree. When he saw the equipment, he laughed and said you had taught him enough that he could use his powers to force me to release him."

"What?" Joshua gaped. *Of all the ridiculous—!*

Malachai sighed. "Perhaps this is my fault for challenging him. When he could not 'psychically' bend my will to his, he became physically violent. He struck me, threw me onto the coffee table and broke an extremely expensive piece of equipment. Luckily, we were able to sedate him, before..." Malachai paused.

I don't believe this, Joshua thought, but the evidence was before him. He tried to study the chief psychiatrist, to use his skills to see if he was lying, but he couldn't focus past the bruises and bandages.

His boss continued. "He was quite delirious, saying that you were his only protection, yet you were leaving soon—and taking his only other friend away from him. That he knew we feared him for his power, and he would have to escape. That you had shown him how."

His gaze narrowed on Joshua.

"Why is he drugged to the gills?" Joshua challenged, but he looked at the carpet, the equipment, the walls, anywhere but at the psychiatrist's battered face. Could Deryl really have done this?

Malachai answered with patronizing patience. "We decided it was a more humane way to control him than placing him in restraints and putting him in an increased intensity ward, of which he has a most particular dread, as you know. His aunt and uncle are coming this evening to discuss his future treatment. This may be his last day with us at the South Kingston."

Now, Joshua met his eyes. "What?"

"I know you've become quite attached to him—that was our error, asking you to befriend him so. You did a fine job. Things seemed so hopeful... I'd like you to spend today with him, not as a psychologist, but as a friend." He rose.

Joshua followed suit. "Um, yeah, sure."

Malachai reached out and placed a fatherly hand on his shoulder. "Go get one of those lattes you're so fond of and take a few minutes to get yourself together. And keep in mind that Sachiko is also particularly close to Deryl. This is going to be a blow for your fiancée, and she's going to need your strength."

Again, Joshua looked over the room, the chief psychiatrist's wounds.

"It doesn't make sense," he muttered.

"Sometimes, we cannot predict a client's reaction to certain treatments or stimuli. It's a difficult lesson, and I'm sorry you had to learn it before your career had even begun. Now go on. I suspect if Deryl isn't already in his room, he will be shortly."

Mutely, Joshua left.

Run. Fight.

The drugs they had given Deryl had split his mind in three.

A part of himself lay curled up in a corner of his mind, gibbering, assailed by outside thoughts he could not shield against. Occasionally, he cried for Tasmae, calling her Miscria, the title she had used when she first came to him; sometimes, he begged for his guardian angel.

A second part, the part that was in control of his body, lay slumped and smiling, wrapped in a warm, fuzzy, comfortable uncaring. Everything was okay. And if it got less okay, they'd come and give him something to make it better. He just had to do what they said, and he could bask in the nice, comfy nothing.

The third part of his mind, he managed to shield from the effects of the drugs: the conscious, panicked, thinking Deryl. He had railed against his other selves, tried to pull them into rationality, but the drugs were too strong. He could not make his body move, though it responded easily enough to routine and the suggestions of the staff. He was barely able to gather psychic energy; it came in slow, thick drips, like the last drops of honey from a jar.

So he waited, fighting the terror that would leave him curled up like his other self, and trying to push back a longing to join Tasmae in the Netherworld. Confusing as his times with her had been, at least he'd felt safe with her. Nonetheless, that kind of escape might ease his mind, but it wouldn't help his situation.

Joshua will help me. I just have to hang on. He thought he'd managed to send him a message, to sneak the movements past his too-amiable self. Then, Malachai appeared and whisked him off, leaving Deryl in the care of an orderly who escorted him to his room and told him to stay there. Just as he was to leave, Deryl had managed one desperate thought command.

The orderly, Paulie, sighed with exasperation.

"Don't just sit there like an idiot. Draw or something. You like to draw." He thrust paper and pencil in his hands and left.

Deryl's compliant self sketched obediently, without awareness of his subject.

Inside, however, thinking Deryl smiled in victory.

"Hey, Deryl, how're you doing?" Joshua pushed the door fully open and walked in slowly, as if approaching a shy child. He knew he was the one feeling insecure, and he hated himself for it.

"Oh, hi." Deryl sat cross-legged on his bed, still wearing the same blank, goofy grin he'd had at breakfast, his eyes unfocused and roaming. His hands, however, were busy at work drawing on the sketchpad in his lap.

"What are you drawing? May I see it?" Deryl looked down as if seeing the paper for the first time. He didn't object as the intern took the pad from him.

Joshua's eyes widened at the cacophony of images. A large syringe dominated the lower right. At the top left, a baseball. To the middle was a ring of fire, or lava, or water standing vertical. It reminded Joshua of the stargate on the television show. Across the page Deryl had drawn images of himself—tied to a machine; sitting on the floor, a shattered table beneath him, a baseball in his hand; wrestling with Dr. Malachai. Of the chief psychiatrist, he had drawn a portrait of him leering. It was a disturbing—and disturbed—mural. Joshua looked up to ask him about it.

Deryl had folded over like a rag doll and was clawing at his hair, pulling it up over his head and across his face.

"You itchy?" The patient didn't answer. "Never mind. Your aunt and uncle shouldn't see you like this."

Joshua made him dress in a T-shirt and jeans, then rolled up his own sleeves and had the teen lean over the tub to shampoo his hair. He noted the dried flakes of gel. Hadn't Malachai said he'd destroyed the EEG machine *before* they'd started any tests? Joshua scrubbed them out, then combed and braided Deryl's long hair. He thought about Rique teasing him about playing with Sabrina's hair and wished his best friend were there to bounce his thoughts off of. Despite Joshua's skills of observation, Rique's BS meter was better than his.

Deryl padded docilely back to his bed, sat obediently while Joshua helped him put on shoes, and then lay back on the covers and fell asleep. Joshua turned the desk chair toward the bed, picked up the sketchbook, and flipped a page.

He found the beautifully detailed pencil drawing of Joshua proposing to Sachiko that Deryl had refused to show them Friday night, claiming it wasn't finished. Deryl must have worked on it for hours. It said, "To 'Ko and Josh. I'll be there. Promise."

Afraid of our leaving, huh? Joshua decided he didn't need someone else to tell him something stunk. He grabbed the notebook and headed to Edith's office.

No! Tasmae slammed her hand on the table, making the plant in the center bounce. *I am not doing this. Not now.*

The plant, which held the memories of Gardianju, the first Miscria to contact the Ydrel, uncurled a leaf in her direction. She shuddered. It was the most dangerous of all the Remembrances, for Gardianju's sanity had been ripped from her with the coming of the Second Sun. Though she had protected their world, even though some miracle had chased the invading star from their sky, all had feared her then and in generations to come. Only a few Miscria—those chosen to communicate with the Ydrel—ever experienced the Remembrance. No one touched her memories and came away unchanged.

Salgoud sided with her. So close to the war, they could not lose her or her abilities.

She will not lose her abilities, Leinad countered, although she felt his hesitancy.

Perhaps not her abilities, then, but what about her sanity?

Leinad offered no false reassurances, only an urgency. When the Remembrance demanded to be experienced, one had to comply.

I've not even experienced the memories of the Miscria from after they encountered Gardianju's Remembrance, she argued. *I agree that I need to finish my training, but there are other Remembrances I should experience first. Why would you bring me this, now?*

Leinad sighed and sent them a confusion of images:

—Kanaan and Barin, racing toward each other, each shearing off pieces of itself to hurl at the other—

—A young man with blond hair and incredibly blue eyes. Tasmae calls him Deryl, but all Miscria call him the Ydrel—

—The traitor Alugiac laughs, calls the Ydrel to him. The Ydrel kneels before him, and his eyes fill with tears and longing, and his wrists bleed freely—

—Gardianju, the first Miscria, cradles the Ydrel, rocking him as both scream in agony—

—Tasmae wraps her arms around the Ydrel and he becomes Deryl. She brushes her lips against his, then falls to the ground as seizures take her—

—Another Miscria, Gardianju's apprentice, also on the ground, thrashing and shrieking—

—*None shall know the Ydrel as I have. It is too dangerous*—

—Tasmae, deep in concentration, calling the power to her as Miscria have for centuries. But instead of power, pain lances through her. Deryl takes her hands, touches his lips to hers, removes the pain. She sighs, and sleeps in his arms—

—The Ydrel, larger than the sky. He holds Kanaan and Barin in hands bloodied from the slashes on his wrists. He laughs—

—Tasmae's hands, slick with blood, as she clutches her belly—

—Kanaan trembles—

—Tasmae dances with Gardianju and they laugh. *I am the Queen of Riddles!*—

The images vanished as abruptly as they appeared. Tasmae sagged against the table, nonetheless careful not to touch the Remembrance.

But they were of Deryl—and me. She shook her head. *That doesn't make any sense. How could Gardianju know about Deryl and me?*

Which is why I have come, Leinad insisted. *You must experience this Remembrance. You must learn its secrets.*

Tasmae shook her head. She could not give her mind to...that. Not now, not so close to the war—

You would rather wait until we are in the war? Leinad countered.

I saw myself, she told him. *How can I see myself in the memories of a woman dead five thousand years?*

She felt his confusion. He, too, had seen her, clearly her, in the few visions the Remembrance shared with him. He could not explain it any better than she.

No, she thought. But she knew who could.

She pushed away from the table and, ignoring the protests of Leinad and Salgoud, stormed out of the fortress where they were staying. Once out of its protective walls, she ran to the clearing where she would Call the Ydrel.

The Ydrel would have the answers, and she would *make* him tell her!

"I don't know why, Edith, but I can see that Dr. Malachai is not being totally forthcoming with us." Joshua forced himself to use formal language and curb his growing temper. When he'd met Dr. Sellars in her office, feeling as low as he'd felt earlier, and heard the story Malachai had given her, it took all his control not to scream, "That jerk set us both up!"

"Joshua, I know you're upset—"

"No, I *was* upset. Now, I'm suspicious. Why, if Deryl was as agitated as Dr. Malachai told you he was, did he sit still for the EEG? Malachai told me he got violent *before* that. Why, if he's been having paranoid fantasies about Sachiko and me no longer 'protecting' him, would he have spent Friday drawing this for us?"

Edith looked at the sketch again, without really looking. He turned it to the most recent sketches.

"Why today is he drawing baseballs and Stargates? For that matter, has he ever talked about being protected by anyone? And why does he have to be so drugged he can't put three words together?"

"He needs to be controlled."

"He's a zombie. If his aunt and uncle see him like this, of course they're going to think he's gone off the deep end."

"Well, what do you want me to do?" Edith finally snapped. "Do you have any *professional* suggestions?"

"Matter of fact. Give him a blood test. Make sure he doesn't have too much junk in his system. Better yet, cut the meds, even if it means putting him in a straitjacket and tying him to his own bed. Then we could get his side of the story."

She placed a hand on his forehead, and he knew she was fighting between the desire to follow his suggestion and to throw him out. She'd taken a chance on hiring him, specifically to befriend Deryl. She'd given him a lot of leeway with the troubled patient, and suddenly, everything pointed to her having been disastrously wrong. He felt sorry for her, but his anger far outmatched his sympathy. He waited, stance determined, gaze strong and expectant.

"All right. I'll approve the blood test. But the other I'd have to run past Randall, and I think we know what his answer will be."

Run. Fight.

Deryl lay quietly on his bed. Behind closed eyes, his mind worked furiously. Earlier, Joshua had come in with one of the nurses and explained that they were going to draw some blood to check that he wasn't overmedicated. That gentle suggestion was all Deryl needed; he used what energy he had to force the drugs still in his blood to the artery and out the piercing needle. He wasn't sure it would work, but to his surprise, he felt his head clearing. The gibbering part of him still lay curled up, fearful, assailed by thoughts and senses that weren't his, but the dazed, pliable part of himself began to fade away, leaving him in control.

His body felt sluggish and sore, and he didn't dare try to move except with the same drugged lethargy. Psychically, however, he had more freedom. He gathered energy from the ley line.

If I can just teleport out of here, I can hole up somewhere, sleep off the rest of the effects, figure out some kind of real plan—

A familiar calling broke his thoughts.

I am the Miscria.

No! His conscious mind rebelled, but his fearful self latched onto the Call like a lifeline. As he struggled to keep control, his sense of the outside world faded—until a sharp prick on his arm brought him completely awake with a panicked start.

His eyes snapped open to see Sachiko, a pained expression on her face, pulling a needle out of his arm. Joshua stood beside his bed, speaking something reassuring, but he felt his friend's suppressed fury. Behind him, Dr. Malachai stood: calm, controlled. Victorious.

I am the Miscria.

Run! Fight!

"No!" Deryl stood and lashed out with his mind, shattering the bathroom mirror. A shard flew to him. He caught it, at the same time half-psychically, half-physically grabbing Joshua and spinning him around. He held the broken glass against his friend's neck.

"I'm sorry," he whispered, then louder: "Everyone get out of this room! Leave me alone!"

"Deryl!" Sachiko shrieked.

Malachai smiled an I-Told-You-So smile, and with a twitch of his hand, waved in the orderlies waiting outside. "Put that down, Deryl. You wouldn't hurt Joshua. He's your best friend."

His fearful self yearned toward the Miscria. Toward Tasmae.

"Shut up! Get them out of here! I want two minutes alone." He fought to keep his voice steady. His legs felt like jelly; if he hadn't been leaning on Joshua, who was frozen with fear, he wouldn't stay standing.

"Deryl, don't," his friend breathed.

Sachiko started to back up, but Malachai held his ground. "Stay there, nurse. Deryl, we're only—"

"Randall!" Sachiko interrupted.

Joshua's fright was as sharp against his mind as the glass cutting into his palm. Deryl tried to call the energy, to concentrate beyond his senses. The situation would not get better. He had to leave. He chanted, "I want to go someplace safe. I want to go someplace where I'm free. I want—"

"But that's what we all want for you, Deryl," Malachai's smooth voice cut across his thoughts.

I am the Miscria. I call the Ydrel.

"Shut up!" He pressed the glass shard a little tighter against Josh's neck. He could feel the glass cut into his hands, could smell the warm blood. His, not his friend's, but they didn't know that.

Sachiko fought back a second scream and turned on Malachai. "Dolfus Randall Malachai, let's go!"

"Now, Sachiko, this is not the time to panic."

Josh whispered, "Deryl, please, man."

Concentrate! "......where people believe me. Someplace where I'm accepted. I want—"

Ydrel Mentor, Ydrel Guide...

Sachiko and Malachai arguing.

The orderly asking for instructions.

The drug taking effect. Things getting hazy.

"I want—"

Joshua's fear as loud as if he were shouting.

Come to me!

"I want to go home!"

A great surge of energy. A pull like the vacuum of space yanking him from reality. Then nothing.

Chapter Three

Joshua returned to consciousness fully expecting to be in a hospital bed, his slashed throat swathed in bandages, his singing career over before it had started. His hands moved to his throat and found it bare and intact. He breathed a prayer of thanks before opening his eyes.

He found himself on his back in a small, tree-lined meadow, but he didn't recognize the trees.

He sat up slowly, more disoriented than dizzy. Had he had amnesia?

"Sachiko?" he called. "Mom? Dad? Anyone?"

He saw Deryl lying on his side, unconscious. Not far from him, near a break in the tree line, stood—

Joshua gulped.

A unicorn!

...or something like a unicorn. Its rhinoceros-like horn and thick neck and shoulders made it a far scarier version than any Joshua had read about in fantasy novels. It stared straight at them.

Joshua licked dry lips. "Easy fella," he soothed, and reached over to shake his friend. "Deryl, time to wake up."

Part of Joshua's mind gibbered that Deryl was really psychic, that he'd teleported them to an alien planet. Another part argued that he was dreaming or had gone insane himself. He told them both to shut up, but he couldn't stop his breathing from accelerating or his hands from trembling as he shook his friend. "Deryl!"

Deryl's eyelids fluttered, then closed.

He's drugged. Malachai's zombified him again, and we're stuck on another world!

He tore his gaze from the not-quite-unicorn and shook his friend harder. "Come on, man! Don't do this to me. Wake up!"

Joshua heard hoof beats and turned in time to see several unicorns with red-clad riders approach from the trail. He vaguely noted they looked human, then his eyes focused on the swords they drew.

He did the only thing he could think of. He raised his arms, palms open, and said, "We come in peace!"

The warrior he faced, a scowling man with a narrow head, wide-set eyes, and a pocked and scarred face, didn't understand him or didn't care. He arched his sword toward Joshua.

Joshua covered his head with his arms and ducked.

He heard a loud clang of steel against steel.

When he risked a glance up, he saw the warrior's sword blocked by one held by a young woman with powerful arms. They strained together a moment, then the man backed off.

The woman from Deryl's sketches!

"Tasmae! Oh, please be Tasmae. Look! This is Deryl. The Ydrel!"

He propped up his unconscious friend toward her. Deryl flopped like a rag doll in his grip.

"C'mon, please recognize him. Please, please understand me! It's the Ydrel—your friend..." He was babbling and knew it, but couldn't stop himself. "He's drugged, um, poisoned? Sick! Please understand sick. We need your help. Please understand me."

When she knelt down to examine Deryl, the young man roused himself enough to smile at her in recognition. Joshua almost cheered with relief.

A warrior lifted Deryl and settled him on a unicorn, where he slumped, unconscious again. Tasmae mounted behind him to hold him steady. Another warrior directed Joshua to a ride of his own. For a moment he hesitated, wondering if there was going to be a problem—this was a unicorn, and he was no virgin—but the mare neither threatened nor shied away. Nonetheless, he approached her slowly despite the swords at his back and spoke to her in gentle tones as he mounted, careful of the odd folds of skin connecting her forelegs to her underbelly.

He glanced at Deryl as the unicorns moved toward the forest, and prayed they were doing the right thing leaving the glen. Tasmae would take care of them until Deryl was awake and clear-headed enough to return them home, wouldn't she?

Despite the mare's stiff-legged gait, she moved like a regular horse, for which Joshua was grateful. He was glad, too, that he'd done a lot of bareback riding back home.

They passed through the hilly meadow, green and lush and carpeted with delicate purple flowers that gave off a gentle sweet scent as the unicorns' hooves crushed them, and entered a second thick wood of trees that seemed teasingly familiar. He ducked a low branch of what looked like an oak. He relaxed just a bit.

Then, the woods morphed into a cultivated forest of the most amazing trees Joshua had ever seen. Dark trunks held sturdy branches frosted with silver, like a sudden freeze had shrouded the trees in thin ice. It was much too warm, however, for frost. And the leaves! Though rounded like aspens, they bore no resemblance to any terrestrial foliage. Most were larger than his hand—and transparent. He reached out to touch one.

"Yeow!" He jerked back his hand and sucked on his sliced finger.

The unicorn snorted, and he caught Tasmae, who had apparently been watching him more closely than he'd realized, rolling her eyes. Her expression mimicked Deryl's when he found something stupid.

They cleared the grove and paused at the edge of a cliff. Joshua's hand lowered slowly as he gaped at the magnificent view. He whistled.

A gorge cut through the plateau, but he didn't think any river had carved it. For one thing, he saw no river or stream, despite the lush vegetation. The cliff walls themselves were craggy and bare, and he spied shadows that made him suspect caves. To his left, the canyon curved sharply; to his right, it opened about a mile away, the cliffs curling away without losing their height. Were they on some gigantic mesa? He turned his body slightly and leaned back, trying to look past the soldiers to follow the edge of the land.

He felt his unicorn bunch her muscles, and reflexively grabbed her mane as the animal threw herself over the cliff.

Joshua screamed.

His shout of terror turned to a cry of surprise, then a great whoop of delight as the unicorn shifted her shoulders and in an un-equine feat of double-jointedness, spread her legs sideways from her body. The folds of flesh attached to her legs and side unfurled into great gliding wings. She banked and soared into the canyon, landing just before it curved to the right. Two of the warriors, then Tasmae, landed beside him.

"That was way cool," he gasped, then said to Tasmae, "but how about some warning next time?"

She glared at him before retaking the lead.

"Hey, can you understand me? I know you talk with Deryl," he called after her, but she didn't so much as turn to acknowledge him.

Joshua clicked his tongue and signaled the unicorn with his legs like he would a horse back home, but the beast merely turned her head to give him a You've-Got-to-be-Kidding look before filing in placidly behind Tasmae. The warriors on their rides surrounded him.

It took several minutes longer than Joshua expected before they rounded the curve he'd seen from above. A large wall of intertwined vines and branches ranged from one cliff wall to another, blocking the path.

As they approached, the branches and vines twisted and unwound, creating a gap just big enough for them to pass through single file.

The weird wall was almost as thick as his mount was long, its interior the same woven tangle of branches as the outer edges. Joshua shivered, thinking of all the stories in which vines reached out and snatched unwary victims. His hands coiled more firmly in the unicorn's mane. When they were through, he glanced back and saw the wall shift closed. Creepy.

They rode on in silence.

Joshua gathered his courage. "Tasmae? It'd really help if you'd tell me what's going on."

The woman didn't reply, but she did turn at the sound of her name.

Joshua clenched his teeth against a sudden anger that welled within him. Deryl had been telling the truth all along. He was psychic. He could move objects with his mind. He could *teleport*. He'd even been in psychic contact with an alien named Tasmae. Thinking back on Malachai's behavior, Joshua bet he'd known it all along, too.

And I got called on the carpet for practicing psychology without a license, he grumbled. With the philosophy learned from his Neuro Linguistic Programming training, Joshua had taken Deryl at his word and had tried to teach him to control his abilities. He'd been more concerned about the alleged telepathy that Deryl said left him prey to the thoughts and emotions around him. Now, he wondered how much Malachai had told him today was true. Had he inadvertently given Deryl the means to escape?

Doesn't matter. He got us here. He'll get us home. I just have to wait out the drugs. Patience. Firmly he pushed his mind away from negative thoughts and back to the world around him.

It was too quiet. Why hadn't they seen any wildlife? He looked around, trying to find some animal sign, but the grass grew smooth until the shadow of the canyon caused it to become sparse before stopping altogether. There may have been creatures in the shrubby trees and tangled vines along the base of the cliff walls, but he hadn't seen any yet. Nor had he heard birdsong, no call of an animal seeking a mate or warning off a rival— just the muffled footsteps of their mounts. He felt himself getting creeped out again.

He heard a sharp cry like that of a hawk, and looked up. Despite himself, he smiled with wonder as he saw an everyn, one of the small dragons Deryl had drawn in art therapy, when they'd had a very strange conversation about this world. Deryl had said they were friendly and worked with the Miscria's people. This everyn, however, showed no inclination to join their group, though it circled overhead for a minute or two before heading back down the canyon.

They rode on. The sun had moved to the other side of the canyon, though that didn't mean much to him. He glanced at his watch. Six p.m.! Sachiko must be frantic by now. Had anyone contacted his parents? He stifled a groan. They'd go ape. Certainly by now, the police were out searching for him and Deryl, not that they'd be anywhere to find.

Would Malachai call the police? He wouldn't put it past the chief psychiatrist to find some way to cover his own butt while making Deryl—*and me, for that matter*—the villains. He could almost hear Malachai talking to his parents, blaming himself for letting their brilliant but young and inexperienced son get too close to a patient. *"Edith had wanted Joshua to befriend Deryl, but we had no idea how seriously he'd take that charge. Who knows how long they'd been planning this dramatic escape?"*

Don't be paranoid, he scolded himself. *Even if Malachai was stupid or arrogant enough to try that, Mom and Dad would know it was BS. He probably thinks I'm a typical teenager who doesn't talk to his parents.*

In fact, Joshua talked to his parents about everything, from the glass of wine he'd had at Sachiko's dinner party to his troubles with Malachai. In fact, there was only one thing he never talked with his parents about—Lattie. He wished he had. They probably could have helped him avoid that disaster.

At least he'd learned from his mistake. He'd told them about his feelings for Sachiko, and about Deryl. They knew full well that he considered Deryl a friend, but also that Joshua was helping the teenage client learn enough coping skills to make it in the real world—and to convince the staff that he could live sanely on his own. That was the only "escape plan."

So, how'd that work out? He stifled a moan.

Joshua and his guards, and Tasmae with the still-unconscious Deryl in front of her, arrived at the end of the gorge and faced a dead end. Joshua barely had time to wonder what was going on when the unicorns reared, unfurled their wings and half-flew, half-leaped to a huge overhang about halfway up the cliff. He hung on for dear life, and only when they at last reached a level point, did he chance a look around.

Again, the view surprised him. The "outcropping" they stood upon could hold a large campsite, yet he hadn't been able to see it when looking at it from the cliff top. They passed through another of those bizarre living walls, and stopped.

"Whoa!" He gasped as he looked at the incredible plant that twined itself over the outcropping and up the cliff. "Gigantic" didn't do it justice. The branches, some as thick as ancient redwoods, twisted in a complex pattern that rose over three stories high. A few smaller but still substantial branches stretched toward the fence, ending in nest-like platforms with low walls of twining branches and leaves. Among the brown and green foliage, some spots sparkled in the fading light.

"What is that?" he asked Tasmae.

As usual, she didn't answer.

New warriors pulled Deryl from the unicorn. One of them started to carry him, still unconscious, toward the strange plant.

"Hey!" Joshua jumped off his ride and ran after them. Two warriors grabbed him.

"Hey!" he shouted and struggled. "No way! Don't separate us! C'mon! You can't do this! No!"

He nearly broke away, and one of the warriors pulled out a dagger and pressed it against his throat so that he could feel his pulse against the blade. Unlike Deryl, he had no doubt this person would not hesitate to slit his throat.

These guys didn't know him from Adam and could probably kill him without breaking a sweat. Seething, wild with panic, he nonetheless stilled, and stayed passive even when the pressure eased. Helplessly, he watched as they took Deryl inside the plant.

He felt a point against his back, more of a nudge, and he obeyed, following one of the warriors quietly. He, too, went into the plant, though he didn't marvel at the thought, so intent was he on trying to spot Deryl. Soon, he gave up looking; even if he had seen which way they'd taken him, the corridors twisted and branched so much he quickly lost his sense of direction. In a few minutes that seemed to last forever, they came to a large, leaf-shaped curtain. It folded away as if pushed by a gentle breeze.

The guards shoved him into the room beyond.

Chapter Four

Deryl awoke to comfort and an incredible stillness. He couldn't define it, so he lay quietly, eyes closed, feigning sleep and basking in the peacefulness while trying to figure it out.

There was sound, but not the institutional noises of the asylum where he'd lived the last five years of his life, nor those of the hospital where he'd spent a brief week of freedom after his appendectomy. No sounds of rubber soles of nurses' shoes squeaking slightly on the tile, no metallic roll of a cart, none of the occasional moans or cries of patients—only birdsong and a voice raised in wordless accompaniment.

Not vocal. Psychic.

Deryl sat up, eyes opening in shock.

A dark-haired man in a green tunic with a red sash regarded him without surprise. He spoke directly to Deryl's mind, not in words per se, but Deryl understood him, nonetheless.

I cannot tell you if you are home, but you are safe, came the message, with a flash of wry humor and a gentle reassurance that then turned to subtle warning. *That is, as long as you mean no threat to us.*

While trying not to be obvious about it, Deryl shielded his thoughts. He didn't know what this healer had learned from him in his drugged state, but until he knew more about these people, the less he told them about his past, the better. He merely reassured the healer that he felt fine and held no evil intent toward him or anyone.

Nonetheless, the healer rearranged the pillows so he could sit more comfortably, gave him something resembling vegetable soup, and watched as he ate. Deryl sipped slowly, trying not to stare, trying even harder not to let his growing panic show. Where was he? Was any of this even real?

Real or not, the soup tasted wonderful, and he finished it before he'd realized how hungry he was. The healer took the bowl with a smile.

That's enough for now, or you may regret it later. The thought entered Deryl's mind with ease. *Someone wishes to see you. Wait here.*

Deryl waited until the odd door folded shut, then let himself feel his panic.

How had that man communicated with him like that? Quickly, he checked his shields, mental barriers he'd learned to forge over the years and had perfected with Joshua's tutelage over the past month. They were battered and worn down from the horrific weekend during which Dr. Malachai had kept him drugged. He shuddered. Anything could get through them now.

So why wasn't he being bombarded with the thoughts and feelings of others? Why hadn't they overwhelmed him? Why was he still, well, sane?

Or was he?

He recognized the uniform the man had worn—a warrior-healer, a specialty developed by the Miscria, using Earth's knowledge of triage and army medical techniques. Knowledge she'd taken from his mind by "Calling" him out of reality and pestering him with questions he was compelled to answer—just one of the reasons he'd been admitted to SK-Mental, and one of the "delusions" that had kept him there for five long years.

I banished her from my mind. Told her I was no longer the Ydrel, the Great Oracle come to save her with my wisdom. So why am I seeing her people? He threw off the covers, discovering he still wore the jeans and T-shirt Joshua had helped him put on. How long had he been unconscious?

What did Malachai give me, anyway? I'm hallucinating. Or maybe dreaming? Come on, Deryl, wake up!

He shut his eyes tightly, telling himself that when he opened them again, he would see the comforting blue and white walls of his room at the institution. Comforting! Despite himself, he laughed at the thought, but right now, even the padded pink room of the high-intensity ward would comfort him. Anything with straight lines, right angles, and familiar, human, non-psychic people. He fixed the sight, the sounds, the impressions, in his mind, then opened his eyes.

Gently curved walls of a light greenish brown. A thick mat on the floor that served as a bed. A small chest that, despite its flat top, didn't have a sharp angle anywhere. A leaf-shaped window whose "glass" pane sported translucent veins. No sounds, no psychic buzz of staff and patients.

"Joshua?" His voice sounded small and plaintive to his ears, and he bit down on his lips to prevent a panicked sob from escaping. Of all the staff at the SK, he trusted Joshua the most. If this was all fake, he'd help Deryl see it. And if it was real...

If this is real, I have escaped and am on another planet, and Joshua... Again, he saw himself holding a piece of broken glass to his friend's throat. Then that wrenching. If this was real, where was Joshua? Had he hurt him?

Deryl realized he had wrapped his arms around himself and was rocking slightly. Was he doing it because, in reality, he wore a straitjacket? Is that what he wanted?

He shook himself and stood. Barefooted, he walked to the open window. The floor felt smooth and a little soft, like no tile or dead wood could feel. He pulled open the strange window and leaned out, turning his head, wishing for the brick-and-mortar of the stately building of the asylum, with the well-manicured lawns of the courtyard just outside.

Instead, he found himself on the second floor of a building like none he'd ever seen before. It seemed to be covered in a rough bark and decorated with large leaves...unless...were they growing on the walls? Or *were* they the walls? He looked past the grassy field to the tall walls that surrounded the complex and gulped.

He knew those walls: how thick they were, the narrow passages between and inside them, the secret entrances. He knew, too, what defenses lay beyond, and even within the city, if there was one here. The Miscria had designed this keep using her knowledge of Earth battle defenses and medieval fortress construction.

He'd spent a year studying medieval architecture and history as well as defense strategies to satisfy her curiosity.

Can this be true? He ran his hand on the window-sill—rough on the outside, but smooth indoors, and a little warm. Alive. Real.

Yet he could hear Dr. Malachai speaking to him in calm, reasonable tones. "Perhaps it was not the best of ideas to let our young intern try his Neuro Linguistic Programming tricks with you. With his one-size-fits-all-psychoses brand of psychology, he may likely believe that it makes no difference if your Miscria is real, as long as it allows you to...function...in polite society. But we do know better, don't we, Deryl? You'll never be truly sane until you accept this Miscria for the illusion it is. Yet, after a few short weeks with Joshua, your 'it' has a gender..."

More than a gender. He shivered as he regarded the peaceful scene before him. *A city. Inhabitants. Infra-structure—*

"Ydrel?"

A voice?

He whirled and gaped at the stern young woman standing at the doorway.

The Miscria!

He backed up so fast his elbow slipped on the windowsill. If it was a windowsill.

Of course, it's a windowsill, a voice answered in his mind. *Or are you back to disbelieving I'm real?*

When he didn't answer, her exasperation turned to concern, and she spoke to him aloud. "Ydrel. Deryl. It is I, the Miscria. Tasmae, remember? It's all right. You are safe here."

She moved toward him slowly, murmuring gentle reassurances and projecting concern, and he let her take him by the arm and lead him back to the bed. He sat down on the low mattress while she got him a drink—water, clearer and purer than any he'd ever known—then sat down on the floor in front of him. She waited until he'd slowly sipped the entire glass.

"I'm sorry," he finally said, surprised to find his voice sounded so steady. "I'm a little...disoriented. I'm really here? On Kanaan?"

"Yes." she said, and smiled, though her eyes held worry. He felt her concern in his mind, but he fought the urge to answer in kind. Not yet.

"How did I get here?"

She shrugged. "Through the Void, I imagine, though how you managed it is a mystery. The storms in the Void are fierce; none can travel them right now. Perhaps that is why your recovery has taken so long. Or is it because of the poison?"

"Probably both," he bluffed. He had started to feel surer of himself, at least enough to think more clearly. He still wasn't ready to believe in this world, in this miracle. It was too much to think he'd escaped Malachai's clutches, that he'd found a world where being psychic was as natural as being able to see, where he wouldn't have to constantly guard against the unwanted thoughts and emotions of others.

For the most part, anyway; he was still very aware of Tasmae's concern.

She watched him in that direct, probing way of hers. He stared back, taking in her features, searching for some clue as to whether or not she was truly real. Her long black hair, in a tight braid that curled around an elaborate headpiece he knew held a sheathed dagger, drank in the light of the room while her eyes, nearly as dark, glowed with intensity.

Her alien features didn't quite meet the human standards for beauty—her face too narrow, her eyes too wideset—but she had the most amazing cheekbones, and her body was attractive enough by Earth standards; at least, as Joshua had once told him, if you like Xena-body-builder types. He wondered for a moment what this Xena's skin color was; Tasmae was a lovely honey brown. He hadn't been able to capture that in the pencil sketches he'd made after taking Joshua's advice and confronting her in the Netherworld.

Do I look as I did in the Netherworld? she asked telepathically.

He nodded, feeling a lightheadedness that had nothing to do with drugs or hunger. Without quite realizing it, he answered with a telepathic affirmation. *Me?*

She sent to him images of the Ydrel she had known in the Netherworld and how he looked to her now. They weren't too different—same shoulder-length blond hair, same sky blue eyes over a slightly sharp nose—but his Netherworld image was at once more ethereal and heroic. He wondered if he disappointed her.

She cocked her head, considering. *Perhaps it was my lack of skill. I have only been to the Netherworld to communicate with you, and until your suggestion, did not know it could be a place with scenery, objects, and people.*

And we're not in the Netherworld now? he pressed, seeking some way to reconcile what he thought he was experiencing with what he thought should be reality. Perhaps what he'd felt was just her Calling him from consciousness.

Madness Unbound ⊕ 49

He sensed her negation, along with a detailed description of the keep where they'd brought him and what had happened.

So, he *was* on Kanaan, physically as well as mentally—and he had traveled there by his own psychic power?

She nodded. *And you brought another—*

"Joshua?" he gasped in surprise. "He's here? He's all right?"

"He's here," she responded, following his lead in switching to spoken tongue. "Though I cannot if say he's all right. His behavior is most...odd."

"Take me to him!" Deryl found his shoes and slipped them on, trying to quiet the thundering of his heart. If anyone could help him figure all this out, it was Joshua.

But Tasmae did not move, nor acknowledge his demand. *Why are you here?*

He felt the force of her will against his weary shields, and strengthened them against her, meeting her will with his own stubbornness. *After I see Joshua.*

She met his stubbornness with her own. He didn't care. He concentrated on his friend as he walked to the door, hoping to sense his way to him if necessary.

He had to see Joshua. Somehow he knew that the intern held the key to keeping his sanity.

Chapter Five

Joshua lay on a bed too comfortable for a jail cell and stared at a wall too alien for comfort. Still, he preferred it to getting up and looking out the window. Through it, he had seen a hallway-sized branch that grew out of the side of the building, "blossoming" out into a low-walled platform that looked past the compound walls. In the dusty area below it, human-enough-looking aliens wearing thick, skin-hugging red outfits practiced sword-fighting skills with a seriousness that said it was no SCA get-together. Even now, he heard grunts and the occasional yelp, but no commands, no words at all, not in any language, and that struck Joshua as the most alien thing of all.

I am not going crazy, he told himself again. Still, the psychiatric part of his mind warned him that if he didn't do something, he might fall into depression.

What could he do? Panic? He'd already done that, throwing himself against the leaf-like curtain, which was now as solid as any door back home. He'd pounded on it and shouted until his fists were sore and his throat raw. He didn't know if anyone had noticed, though once he'd calmed down, a warrior had come with food and two pitchers of water. With signs, he told him one was for washing only.

What could he do, cry? He'd done that, too, as soon as the warrior had left him alone. It had released his stress, but otherwise done no good.

Pray? He'd never prayed so hard in his life, starting with desperate pleas, gradually moving toward familiar prayers he'd learned in years of Catholic religious education. It had calmed him some, and he had begun to sing some of the prayers, comforting himself with the music, moving on to other hymns, then popular songs.

He'd stopped when he found himself singing one Rique had written for Chipotle. Would he ever see his friends again? And what if he did get back, but too late for their audition?

He'd reverted back to prayer before finally falling into an exhausted sleep. He didn't know how long he'd slept, but he woke lethargic, depressed, and hungry. Food waited for him on the table along with a jug of water and a basin of wash water, but he hesitated to eat or drink. He had put his hands into the wash water and it had frothed like peroxide. Could he trust the food? He checked his watch, idly glanced at the angle of light coming in from the windows. This planet's days were a couple of hours longer than Earth's, he figured. He'd already been missing for twenty-six hours.

Where was Deryl? he wondered again. He shivered as he remembered his fiancée arguing with the chief psychiatrist. *What if Sachiko was right and Deryl's meds were too high? What if he's OD'd?*

He was going to throw up thinking about it. He had to do something.

He could try one thing, ridiculous as it seemed. He shut his eyes and thought as hard as he could: *Deryl? Where are you? Can you hear me?*

"You don't have to shout."

Joshua yelped and sat up. At the door stood Deryl, his long blond hair a little disheveled, his blue eyes a little wild, but otherwise healthy and whole. Joshua froze, torn between the desire to hug his friend in relief and the urge to throttle him for getting him into this mess.

"Oh, thank God!" Deryl exclaimed. "You need a shave!"

Joshua blinked. Then he laughed, short barks that grew into whooping gales until he hunched over, clutching his side.

"Joshua?"

"A shave?" Joshua managed to burst out. The psychologist part of him warned that he was bordering on hysteria, but he didn't care. It felt so good to laugh! "Thank God I need a shave?"

A smile quirked Deryl's lips, but he spoke earnestly. "You don't understand. When I woke up, here, I thought—I thought I'd really gone crazy—"

"Yeah? Join the club!"

"Well... they said your behavior has been kind of erratic..."

Suddenly, Joshua realized they'd kept him under surveillance. Somehow, that made it funnier. He fell back against his sleeping pallet, rolling. Soon Deryl was laughing too.

"'We come in peace' didn't work!" Joshua sputtered.

"You're so scruffy! I never would have hallucinated you with two day's growth of beard!"

"I'd have never hallucinated being a prisoner in a mandrake on steroids!"

"A what on *what*?"

Then neither could talk for their laughter.

Finally, Joshua sat up, still chuckling, and wiped his eyes with the heel of his hand. "Whew! Deryl, I am so glad to see you. Now, let's go home, man."

"We can't."

The words bathed Joshua in ice water. The panic came back. "What do you mean, 'We can't'?"

Deryl took a deep breath to calm the last of his giggles. "Joshua, I'm not even sure how we got here. Tasmae—Josh, she's here! She's real!—she said that no one can teleport right now. There are 'storms.' I don't know, maybe you'd call them 'anomalies in the space-time continuum'? I think the only reason we got here was because she was Calling me when I was trying to escape—"

The urge to throttle his friend returned with a vengeance. "Deryl, I want to go *home*!"

"Yes. Okay. I know. Josh, I'm so sorry. I never meant to drag you into this. I just—I freaked. Malachai drugged me. He was going to convince my aunt and uncle that I was beyond help and I don't-know-what and..."

He took a deep breath and released it slowly. "I'm sorry. I'll talk to Tasmae. I'll figure out what I did and how to get you home. I promise."

"Yeah, all right." It was the best Deryl could do at the moment, and Joshua knew it. He leaned back against the wall—it gave slightly, as if thinly cushioned—and shut his eyes. He felt weary again, but a better weariness than the malaise of earlier. However, the headache that had been dogging him since yesterday made itself known in force.

With one hand, he rubbed his temples. "So, what do we do in the meantime?"

"Well, Tasmae's convinced you're harmless—"

"'Mostly harmless.'" Joshua smirked, but fought back another bout of laughter.

"What?"

"Never mind." He hadn't lent Deryl a copy of *Hitchhiker's Guide to the Galaxy* yet. In the story, a researcher for the guide spent fifteen years studying Earth before changing its entry from "Harmless" to "Mostly Harmless." "So?"

"So we're guests now. I'm going to take the room next to yours—"

"This isn't a cell?"

Deryl rolled his eyes, and it again struck Joshua how he and Tasmae both had that expression. "I'll have to be your interpreter until some of the others learn English. Tasmae, of course, already knows it from me."

"Could've fooled me. She never said a word."

Deryl shrugged. "This isn't an actual town. It's sort of a keep—a fallback if one of the nearby cities gets overrun by the Barins—that's their enemy—"

"We're in a *war zone*?"

"No. Calm down. The Barins—didn't I tell you this at SK-Mental?—they're from another planet, and for whatever reason, they only attack in waves with a long time—months, even years—in between. The Kanaan call it the Season of War. This is the Season of Preparation, so they're here checking the defenses, doing military exercises, and making sure the keep is ready just in case. Anyway, the point is, there aren't very many people here right now. They're only using the outer areas."

"The part that's a plant? We're inside a plant?"

Deryl's face split into a grin. "Cool, huh? No wonder I had such a tough time explaining mortar to them. Would you try to make a daisy chain with cement? I think we need to just lay low and follow Tasmae's lead. There are mostly warriors here, with some support staff, and some of them are having problems believing I'm the Ydrel. And nobody knows what to think of you. Hey, you don't look so good."

The headache had him full in its grip. "Caffeine deprivation, probably. Dehydration. Hunger. Stress. What I wouldn't give for a D.C."

"No Diet Cokes here, I'm afraid, but let's see what we can do about the rest."

"They didn't feed you?"

"I wouldn't eat. Alien planet? Prisoner? I didn't know what to trust."

Deryl nodded, grimacing. "Yeah, I get it. But the food's fine—pretty good, actually. Come on. Let's find a healer for your headache first."

Joshua didn't even bother to argue or nod, just stood—slowly, as the vise around his head tightened at the change in altitude—and followed him.

The door, which resembled a violet petal but had proved sturdy enough when he'd been banging his fists against it, folded up and out of the way, and they passed through to the smooth light brown corridors that he vaguely remembered going through two days before. Deryl walked with complete confidence, and Joshua followed. After the third turn, however, his curiosity got the better of him. "Do you know where we're going?"

"Obviously."

"And you've been awake and about for...?"

"An hour or so." The corridors forked, and Deryl took the left one.

"So how do you know?"

"Tasmae. I guess you could say she, uh, 'flashed' into my mind a map of the outpost." Deryl looked at his friend thoughtfully. "Well, not a map, exactly. Everybody here communicates telepathically. I think you've figured that much out, right? So she didn't tell me or even show me—she shared her understanding of the outpost."

"So you know everything she knows about it?"

"Everything she wanted to share with me. Psychic communication is like verbal communication; when you communicate telepathically, you can usually share just what you want the other person to know. Does that make any sense?"

"No. But maybe it will when my head stops pounding. In the meantime, we ought to come up with a name for telepathic talk. It's awfully awkward saying 'psychic communication' or 'communicating telepathically.' And let's not even get into Tasmae 'flashing' you."

Deryl snorted. "You can't be too sick, if you can make puns. Not illness sick, anyway. Any ideas?"

"Ask me after the local equivalent of ibuprofen kicks in." Joshua groaned.

"Hang on, we're almost there."

They passed through another, sturdier door. At first, Joshua thought Deryl must have made a wrong turn and ended up in a dormitory. It held none of the usual things he associated with an infirmary—no equipment, no charts hanging on the beds, not even privacy curtains. Just two men in green tunics and slacks sitting beside one bed, leaning in concentration over the leg of a young woman dressed in the same thick, skin-tight red outfit that passed for uniforms here. Sweat beaded on her pale face, and when one healer shifted slightly, Joshua saw why. A huge gash cut through her calf so that a meaty flap of skin and muscle hung loosely.

The sight of it, combined with his headache, brought bile to his throat. He sat down on the nearest bed with his head in his hands, trying not to gag. He felt the bed give slightly as Deryl sat beside him.

Then he felt...something. He couldn't define it, but it teased at him through the pain of his headache, and he tried to concentrate on it instead. It was almost sound, almost touch, and it suggested comfort, like a soft pillow and low peaceful music did whenever he was sick with the flu. But just like when his mother turned the music too low, he strained to make out what it was.

Deryl nudged him, and he looked up, moving his head as little as possible. The young woman was standing, balanced by the men in green as she put weight on her leg. She hesitated a moment, then nodded, smiling. They released her and she stood on her own, turning to give each one a quick hug. As she strode out of the room, Joshua took a good hard look at her leg. Where her flesh had been cleaved in two, there was now only a slightly pink area on her lovely skin. His jaw dropped.

Deryl snickered.

"Oh? Can *you* do that?" Joshua snapped at his friend.

"No, but he can."

Joshua turned just in time to see a pair of hands move toward his face, and the sensation he'd only vaguely felt earlier flooded his awareness. If what he had sensed before had been quiet music, this was like standing in front of the speakers at a major concert. He could feel the power of the healer, beating in time with his heart, his very cells joining in the harmony. His headache washed away in glory.

A momentary prickling in the back of his skull, and as suddenly as it had engulfed him, the sensation of power vanished. He swayed in its absence.

"Whoa."

Deryl and the healer steadied him. "Are you okay?" Deryl asked.

"Yeah. Great. What a rush. Can we do it again?" He felt giddy and unfocused.

The healer laughed. "You are surprisingly sensitive to healing power. You are a healer in your world, then?"

"No way, not like that!" But then he stopped, considering. His mother's friend, a local Reiki master, insisted Joshua had power and had invited him to train with her. He recalled, too, just how deeply he'd gotten inside Deryl's head when circumstances had driven the psychic client into catatonia. "Well, maybe?"

The healer sat next to Joshua and handed him a drink. He didn't look much older than Deryl or himself. "Well, I can. Drink this. It's safe, and you need the nourishment. You must come back sometime. Perhaps we could teach each other."

"That'd be cool, but I— Hey! When did you learn to speak English?"

"I picked it up from you. *Es más fácil, eh*?"

"*Sí*—but that's Spanish! You picked up both languages from me? Just how long were you in my head?"

"Not long, and I promise, my intention was only to cure your headache. The language is incidental. I did not know your world had two languages. *Que cómico.* You'll have to help me sort them out." Suddenly, he looked up toward the healer who frowned at him from the other side of the room. "*Con permiso*, but I need to perform a cleansing."

"What's that?"

"I expel any parts of your memories or personality that I may have picked up during the healing. It's important especially when dealing with head injuries—or aliens." He smiled. "But I will keep the language. It will be useful for us. *Muchas gracias.*"

"No, thank *you*. I feel terrific." As the healer walked away, Joshua stood and stretched. "What's next?" he asked Deryl.

"Let's go." His friend scowled and left without checking to see if Joshua followed.

"Hey, what's the matter with you?" Joshua asked as the door closed behind them and they were alone in the halls. It struck him as kind of eerie how empty the hallways were.

"How can you sense the power in that room?" Deryl demanded crossly.

"You got me. Why, jealous?" Deryl didn't answer, just upped his pace. Joshua grabbed him by the shoulder, making him stop and face him. "Listen, I'm not psychic. I can't telep."

"Telep?"

"Yeah. Speak telepathically? Telep? I made it up just now. The point is, you've got to tell me what's going on, okay? This place is even more bizarre to me than it is to you, and you're about the closest thing to normal

I've got—and that's not saying much." He hoped Deryl would take that as the joke he'd intended and felt relieved when his friend gave him a sardonic grin. Deryl had come a long way since the beginning of the summer, when he couldn't even say the word "crazy." "You seemed pretty happy to be here until just a minute ago. So what happened?"

"It's nothing," he hedged, but Joshua pinned him with his stare until he added, "It's just... The healers didn't do anything for me."

"Oh? What about your hand?"

Deryl looked at his hand as if remembering it for the first time. Rather than a nasty, scabbed cut, a narrow, jagged scar cut across his palm.

"Fine," he acquiesced. "But what about the rest? I was out for almost a whole day thanks to Malachai's 'cocktail,' and they didn't help me with that. It's like they were scared of me."

Joshua crossed his arms, considering. "The drugs?"

"I asked Tasmae. They know how to expel poisons."

He shrugged. "Then maybe they were afraid. You are the Ydrel."

"So?"

"So, up until a few weeks ago, our weeks, that is, the Ydrel was—as you put it—some kind of cross between an angel and a supercomputer, right? Now you suddenly appear on their world—acting very strangely, I might add. You kind of scared me back at SK-Mental even *before* you freaked out and took me hostage."

"I'm sorry about that." Deryl studied the floor.

"Don't worry about it." Joshua's stomach growled loudly. "Know where we can get some food?"

Again, Deryl led them down a twist of halls that Joshua couldn't keep track of.

"Is there any method to this architectural madness?" he finally complained.

"There are direct routes, if you know how to find them, and if the 'mandrake' as you call it, will let you in. I'm not sure I'm trusted, yet, so we're taking the common public ways everywhere. Certain areas, like the healers' den, are hard to get to on purpose, except when taking someone who's seriously injured there, Then a direct path opens up. Some places are hard to get out of. You can lead the enemy in, trap them, and collapse part of the building on them."

Joshua stopped to examine the walls suspiciously. "Really? That's vicious."

Deryl shrugged. "It was Tasmae's idea, not mine. I did tell you that the invaders tried to kill her in the last war? Well, that was how she destroyed the Traitor's forces after they sneaked inside her city and killed her mentor and about half the people attending her installation ceremony. Let's go. I'm hungry, too."

He hurried ahead.

"Remind me not to get on Tasmae's bad side," Joshua muttered as he hastened to catch up. He shuddered against the feeling that the walls were going to come down on him out of sheer spite.

Soon, the hallways became a little wider and straighter. Just before a turn, Deryl stopped Joshua with his arm and paused with his eyes closed. Joshua heard noises—no words, but movement. People.

"Checking your shields?" Josh asked. Deryl nodded. One of the first things Joshua had helped him learn to do at SK-Mental was to develop multiple layers of shields against the psychic impressions that bombarded his senses. Joshua wondered if he had a tougher time protecting himself here, where everyone had psychic abilities, or on Earth, where no one did but where uncontrolled thoughts projected themselves to Deryl. He filed the question away to ask when they had privacy, like maybe when they got back home..

They crossed the hall and went through a large door which opened into a cafeteria. Like all the rooms they'd seen so far, this one lacked familiar angles and flat surfaces. Everyone ate sitting on cushions at low tables. Otherwise, it looked like a typical cafeteria. About a dozen large round tables dotted the area, half of them full of diners, most of whom wore red uniforms. Servers flowed in and out through a door in the back, bringing plates of steaming dishes or platters of exotic fruit, which they set in the middle of the tables. Now that he'd had some reassurance that he could safely eat, Joshua's stomach growled again.

One of the servers noticed them and stopped in her tracks. Everyone turned toward them. Caught under the stare of forty-odd warriors, Joshua wondered if he shouldn't have remained in his cell, after all.

Chapter Six

Deryl set his face in a neutral, almost haughty, expression, but he held himself as tightly as a guitar string about to snap. His pupils contracted and twitched in a way that worried Joshua. Their appearance had apparently caused some kind of psychic ruckus, and Deryl was caught in the midst of it.

"You okay?" Joshua didn't want to think what would have happened had Deryl not checked his shields beforehand. He'd seen the young psychic react with everything from hysteria to self-induced coma, and he could not afford to lose his only friend, ally, and, for that matter, interpreter. "We could come back later."

Then, from further down the room, Tasmae stood and made her way to them. As she did, others rose in their places. Today, she wore a sleeveless black tunic that tied kimono-like on the sides over loose black pants. Her slippered feet made a swishing noise as she moved smoothly toward them. Deryl turned his focus on her, and his expression gentled.

She stopped in front of him, and, including Joshua with a glance from her obsidian-black eyes, brought her fist first to her heart, then to her forehead. Around the room, others repeated the gesture.

Deryl returned the salute, Joshua a half step behind. With a nod and a smile to them, Tasmae led them to her table.

"Want to tell me what that was all about?" Joshua muttered to Deryl through the side of his mouth. People still stared at them, most without the veiled hostility of before yet with enough with suspicion to make him nervous.

Deryl he kept his aloof smile firmly in place. "Tell you later. Don't worry. Tasmae's got it under control."

Tasmae, who once dropped a building on her enemies' heads. Great.

Nonetheless, once they sat down at her table, Joshua's extreme hunger overcame his milder suspicions, and he concentrated on filling his plate and his stomach. The table held fruits and vegetables cooked in several ways, plus breads, but no meat. They hadn't given him any meat earlier, either, but he'd thought that was because he was a prisoner. *What I wouldn't do for a steak. Are the Kanaans vegetarians or herbivores?*

"Vegan," Deryl said.

Joshua gave a start—had he been thinking that loudly?—but devoted his attention to his meal. He couldn't do much else, really. The telepathic conversation excluded him more effectively than that of Rique's relatives before he'd learned Spanish. At least then, he had the chance of picking up a word or two. Here, he heard some laughter—apparently, some things were universal, literally—and he might be able to guess at the emotions playing across people's faces, but he didn't know who was speaking when. He concentrated on his delicious, if unfamiliar, food.

When Tasmae spoke to him, he almost jumped again. "Pardon?"

"I asked if you are all right." She spoke English with a New England accent, which made sense, since she would have picked it up from Deryl. She seemed to be asking about his wellbeing in general.

"Yeah, I'm fine. Be better if I knew I was going back home to Earth soon, though."

She nodded seriously, her head tilting first one way, then the other. "The ways of God are not always known to us."

Joshua snorted. "Tell me about it."

She apparently understood the idiom—or the sarcasm. "It is so for your people, too? I do not know why God has chosen to bring the Ydrel to us now, nor why you have been sent as well."

She glanced quickly across the table at a scowling man in russet robes, and Joshua sensed that Tasmae may not have things under as much control as Deryl wanted to believe. *Oh, yeah. Really great.*

"Your people don't believe in dumb luck?" he asked Tasmae.

She looked at him uncomprehendingly.

Even better. "Really? So what are you saying? That you're going to keep us here until you figure out what God wants with us?"

Tasmae frowned, and for a moment Joshua worried that he'd stuck his foot in his mouth. She didn't seem upset, however; rather, she looked more like she was searching for the right words.

Deryl jumped in. "What she's trying to say is that it's not really in her control so much as God's."

"Yes. We will not purposely detain you." Again, she glanced at the man in brown. "But it may not be possible for you to leave until your purpose on our world has been fulfilled."

"Really? Ooo-kay. Well, I know what to pray for."

"As do we all," Tasmae concluded. "Until then, once you have finished eating, you will want to bathe." It was as much an order as a question.

"That's a great idea. I'd like to shave, too, if you can get me a razor." Seeing how both Deryl and Tasmae hesitated, he added, "I don't need anything fancy. I can even use one of those old-fashioned blade razors. But I'd really like to get rid of this fuzz. It's not like I'm going to run amok with so many armed guards around."

Some silent consultation, then Deryl turned back to Joshua. "Here's the deal. They don't have razors. They don't need them."

Joshua stole a look at the faces of the men around him. All of them were clean-shaven, but he'd thought it was just the fashion or military regulation. Deryl, he realized, always bore a baby-smooth face, and he'd never seen him shave nor seen a razor in his bathroom. Deryl had once told him he thought his father was an alien. Could he be right? Would explain a lot.

He could not believe he was even thinking that. Nonetheless, the geek part of him wanted to squeal with excitement.

Deryl was saying the metalsmith wasn't especially busy. "So it'll only take a couple of hours, but it'd have to be simple." He hesitated, then added, "You'd have to let me into your mind so I can describe it."

"I thought you didn't like to do that. Made you dizzy or something." For that matter, he didn't like the idea much himself.

"It does. But you want to shave, don't you? And before you ask, drawing a picture isn't going to work unless you know the right dimensions or want to keep cutting yourself on prototypes until you get it right. This isn't going to be like that healer picking up English, either. To get that specific, someone's going to have to get into your personal memory. Tasmae's people won't do it. Humans have too much... contamination, she says. Like emotional baggage. But if I do it, I can telep Tasmae just the information she needs. So?"

Joshua sighed and scratched his chin thoughtfully. Maybe he shouldn't shave; after all, he was supposed to be a kidnap victim. How would he explain it to the authorities if he showed up clean-shaven and unaffected by the experience?

Deryl misread his hesitation and huffed. "Fine. Be scruffy, or shave with a dagger for all I care. But I don't know what you're so uptight about. It's not like you ever really noticed the other times I'd read your mind."

"It's not that. I was just thinking how it'd look if I— What do you mean, 'the other times?'"

"Well, you know," Deryl hedged. "When we first met, and I was trying to prove to you I was psychic..."

With everyone at the table watching them, Deryl maintained a steady, guiltless gaze, but Joshua could see that he'd said more than he'd intended. It occurred to him that they probably shouldn't discuss this now, but he couldn't bring himself to let Deryl off the hook. "You said times. Plural."

"Fine. It was that same evening. We'd just met, and you were gawking at Sachiko."

"Was not!"

Deryl just rolled his eyes. "She was the closest thing to a friend I had. Did you think I was going to trust you after a few minutes' conversation? I just sort of let you daydream about her for an hour or so while I probed your mind and found out what kind of a person you are. Oh, and I drank all that Scotch my uncle smuggled in for my birthday," he added, turning his smile to Tasmae. "Remember that day?"

Joshua watched Tasmae frown and guessed that that must have been when she and Deryl had met face-to-face for the first time in the Netherworld. *Which started the chain of events that led to us being here now. Bet she can't decide whether to be happy or annoyed about it.*

Joshua, however, had no doubts concerning how he felt about Deryl's invasion into his private thoughts. "How many times?" he demanded quietly.

"That fully? Just that evening, promise. Any other time was very surface and not really intentional—kind of reflex. Like how you sometimes change the way you talk to match the person you're talking to. Joshua, I was desperate. I, I had to make sure you wouldn't do anything to hurt Sachiko. Or me. I really did need a friend. I had to know I could trust you, too."

"Yeah, all right." With a long breath, Joshua released his anger. He rubbed his face with his hands. As he brushed over the growth on his cheeks, he remembered why he'd objected to it in the first place. "I'm still not sure it's a good idea that I shave, though. I probably should look like I've been a hostage for a few days. Otherwise, what do I tell the cops?"

"I was 'teleping' with Tasmae about that," Deryl smiled. "Time is both relative and irrelevant—"

"Wrinkle in Time?"

Deryl nodded. "My mom's favorite. Anyway, I'm fairly sure it's true as far as teleportation goes. I think once I've figured out what I did and we can leave, I can get you home within a couple of hours after we'd left."

"Really? I'd better shave, then. So what do I do?"

Tasmae watched, fascinated, as Joshua calmed and Deryl instructed him to think about the curious blade. Only a few Kanaan had the talent of reaching into alien minds on purpose. Was there anything the Ydrel could not do?

They're dangerous. Leinad's assertion slipped into her mind.

Tasmae brushed it off as if it was an irritating insect. He was the Ydrel.

The Ydrel is dangerous. You are not meant to interact with him like this. No one is. The Remembrance was quite clear—

Tasmae cut off his assertion with a mental snort. When had a Remembrance ever been clear about anything?

All the more reason to experience the Remembrance, learn the fullness of its warning, Leinad pressed. *Ydrel or not, they should both be imprisoned.*

The compound knows where they are allowed and where not. Besides, do you truly think two unarmed aliens are a danger to us here? She shared her thoughts—and her amusement—with Salgoud.

The general projected his confidence that, with a thousand soldiers in the maze and here, they could handle the two.

Tasmae teased him with the memory of her dashing in just in time to keep him from "handling" the aliens by lopping their heads off.

Her mirth cut short when she felt a stirring in her gut that had nothing to do with digestion or fear.

I did not know it was the Ydrel, he shrugged laconically, a hint of a smile showing on his scarred face. He rose and left.

If he is the Ydrel, Leinad persisted.

His comment barely registered. Her own talent had alerted her to a disturbance in the earth. She had to find it, contain it if necessary before the earthquake grew to harm others. She pulled deep into herself, sought the shifting plates...

She hardly registered Leinad rising to follow Salgoud.

Deryl and Josh had not noticed the discussion going on around them. Deryl said, "Just relax and just remember the razor. It has to be a memory, not imagining, though. I can get the details from there. I promise I won't go searching about for deep dark secrets."

"Better not," Josh warned as he shut his eyes. He rested his chin on one hand and thought about his grandfather's razor.

It was definitely simple: a straight, long blade that folded out of the handle. For a moment, he saw it, shining and suspended against a black backdrop, then the scene filled in, and it was held in the strong hand of his grandfather, and Joshua was six years old, sitting on the edge of the counter, watching in fascination as his grandfather brought the sharp blade up to his neck and scraped off the hair and shaving cream with deft strokes. It had been one of the happiest days in his life when Grandpa moved in with them.

"This is how real men shave," he said. "Not with that sissy thing your dad uses." He rinsed the blade under the steaming tap and pointed it at his dad's electric razor before bringing the blade to his face again. Joshua snickered at the thought of his dad having a sissy anything. "Told me he has to buy one every couple of years. Throwing good money away on a fancy piece of technology when this is all you need. Now, my pappy gave me this blade back in..." He paused to scrape his lip and never did tell Joshua the exact year. He hadn't known it then, but his grandfather's memory was starting to go, the first symptom of the disease that would take his life. "I was going to war. Lied about my age. Had to— hard enough for a Black to get into the army those days. Not like it is now. You learning your ciphering?"

"Yes, sir. And I can read *Curious George* all by myself."

"Good." He pulled his cheek long and flat, making his words slur. "Your color ain't never gonna be a hindrance, and don't you ever use it as an excuse. Understan'?"

"No."

His grandfather glanced at him, shrugged. "You will. You better, if you want to be a man. You get old enough, I'll teach you to shave like a man."

That time had come far sooner than either had expected. Joshua was only eight years old when the disease that baffled physicians had stolen his grandfather's strength, and he insisted Joshua shave him. He'd been letting Joshua play for months, scraping the fluffy mint-scented shaving cream off his face, first with a covered blade, then with the blunt side, and he had flatly announced to Joshua's mother that the boy was the only one he'd trust with his special blade.

"I'm not using one of those pretty disposables like you ladies use on your legs. I had my first shave with this razor and by God, I'll have my last by this razor. Now you get on out of here, little girl, so's he can take care of me right," he ordered, and Joshua's mother, who had always been the ultimate authority in her home, lowered her eyes and left.

"All right now, Joshua," he said as the door closed behind her. He settled back in his chair and closed his eyes.

Joshua stared at the door. "She didn't even argue!"

"'Course not. I'm her pa. Besides, we both know I'm right. Now go to it, boy."

So Joshua had shaved him, and nearly dropped the blade the first time he nicked the old man's skin. "I'msorryI'msorrryI'msorry," he whispered as he brought a clean towel up to his grandfather's chin. He was so sure his mother would come in, see what he'd done, and take the razor away, never mind what her pa wanted, but his grandfather just pressed the back of one hand against the nick and said calmly, "Ain't nothing I haven't done. You're doing fine. Just trust yourself."

Afterward, he'd looked himself over in the mirror Joshua held up for him, his too-thin and trembling hands running over each cheek. "Not bad, boy. I'm going to expect you to do this for me every couple of days or so, but that blade's yours now. You've earned it. You take care of it like I taught you and you use it.

Remember what I told you. Trust yourself and don't be afraid of the nicks."

He'd died not long after that, and the razor went on a shelf in Josh's room beside a photo of him and his grandfather. The day Joshua decided he was ready to shave, he'd pulled it down, cleaned it up and used it like he'd promised. For a few minutes, it was like his grandfather stood beside him, instructing him on how to angle it, telling him that was how a man shaved. He'd gone downstairs feeling like a man, despite the many band-aids plastered on his face.

His parents had exchanged quick looks, and his mother shrunk behind the book she was reading.

"With all due respect to your grandfather, there are less painful ways," his father remarked blandly while his mother suppressed her snickers.

He'd eventually gotten a "sissy high-technology" shaver, but he kept in practice with his grandfather's old one. It was useful (and kind of impressive) on camping trips, and good for whenever he just wanted to feel close to his grandfather.

He stood by his grandfather's gravesite in Oklahoma, his car, packed to the gills, on the gravel road not too far off. He'd made the side trip on the way to Rhode Island from Colorado, and he brought the blade just to show his grandpa that he still had it. He'd played with it while he talked, feeling the weight, the smoothness of the wooden handle. He'd pulled it open, and ran his finger along the flat of the blade. He tested its sharpness. All the time he talked about his new adventure, his horrible last year, how he wished he'd been around to talk to.

The memory vanished. Joshua blinked at the sudden brightness of the room. "Whoa," he whispered.

Deryl and Tasmae were looking at each other, conversing, he supposed. Everyone else had left. He took the opportunity to breathe in and out slowly, letting the emotions of the memories flow over and away. *So much for surface impressions.*

Tasmae stood. "I'll see about the razor. It seems simple enough to fashion. The baths should not be busy for another couple of hours."

After she left, they picked at their food in silence. Finally, Joshua ventured, "I haven't remembered him that vividly in a long time."

"Yeah, sorry. I was kind of...helping. But I didn't direct your memory. I mean, you remembered what you wanted to—and I wasn't trying to eavesdrop. You've got strong memories. I sort of got caught in the current."

"Yeah, well... Thanks." Joshua shifted position, then stabbed at his food lightly. "You know, I'd forgotten how much I worshiped him."

Deryl toyed with his food. "You're lucky. He was cool. My grandfather—the one I know of, mother and Aunt Kate's father—he barely acknowledged I existed. The first time I met him was at my mother's funeral, and he told Aunt Kate to send me away. Said I was an aberration. That I never should have been allowed to be born."

Joshua nearly dropped his fork. "You're kidding. That's whacked! How could anybody—" He stopped as he noticed Deryl's shocked expression. "Listen, I'm sorry to dis your family, but that's really heinous."

"No, it's not that," Deryl stammered. "It's just—it's in my file. First thing, practically. Edith seemed to find it was particularly enlightening."

Joshua stifled a groan. "I never read your file. Edith wanted me to treat you like a friend. Do you go reading dossiers on your friends?"

Suddenly, Deryl shoved his plate of food away. He thumped his elbows in its place and dug the heels of his hands into his eyes.

"You okay?"

"Don't be nice to me!" Deryl snapped. "You've been nice to me from the very beginning, gave me your trust, tried to take me for who I am and not who everyone said I am. Look how I've repaid you! No, I don't read dossiers on my friends. I just read their *minds*. You ought to be agreeing with my grandfather."

"Well, you're not easy to love," Joshua agreed with a twist of irony in his voice, and Deryl dropped his hands away from his eyes to gape at him. "Not everybody is. That doesn't mean you shouldn't have been born, or that we aren't friends. Besides, I've kind of enjoyed being around you. I've learned a lot, about myself. About the universe."

Again, his voice took on an ironic twist, and he turned his head to take in the alien cafeteria, making Deryl laugh. "Hey, how many friends take their buddy road-tripping to another planet? How phat is that?"

"'Fat'?" As Joshua had intended, the word distracted him.

"Phat, with a P-H. Means cool, but it's kind of old now. When we get back to Earth, you've got some slang to catch up on. Listen, I'll make you a deal." Joshua glanced at the date feature on his watch. "I've got ten days until Chipotle auditions in New York. I miss that, my music career ends before it's begun. Not to mention, Rique will kill me. Figure on two days to handle the fallout of our disappearance. Get us home in a week and things are cool between us. And if you can time-tesser, get us home the day we left, and things are totally phat. Deal?"

"Deal." They shook on it. "You ready to go find the baths?"

Joshua rose. "Oh, yeah. We're both pretty skanky."

"'Skanky?'"

"Hey, that's an old one. My mom uses it all the time."

Chapter Seven

Tasmae left the two brooding over the last of their meals. Leinad would not have approved, but he did not know Deryl like she did. She trusted Deryl, as the Miscria had always trusted the Ydrel. Still, it bothered her that Deryl refused to answer her questions until he'd taken care of his friend. In truth, he seemed as confused about his arrival as they were. Perhaps Leinad was right that the answers could only be found in the Remembrance.

She reached out with her senses, determined where Salgoud and Leinad stood conversing, and headed in that direction. The earthquake had stilled under her care, and she thought she had a few days' respite.

The role of the Ydrel had always been advisor, with the Miscria interpreting his riddles. Now, the Ydrel—Deryl—was here. If he Deryl could advise Salgoud directly on the strategies she had tried to adapt, she could take time to experience the Remembrance. Not that she had a choice, but she would do it on her terms.

She found them, as expected, leaning against a wall in the outer courtyard where many of the warriors busied themselves with sword practice. Salgoud's eyes were on his troops, taking in flaws of step or swing, noting improvements, but even so, he kept his attention on what Leinad was telling him—about the Ydrel and probably her, no doubt. She did not interrupt. She would know what she needed to know soon enough.

Leinad pinned her with his stare. She felt his urgency, the call of the Remembrance—

And I shall, she agreed. *But that is not my only duty now, and I cannot allow it to monopolize me.* She shared with him a hint of the obligations pulling on her: the preparations for war, the increased needs of Kanaan, neither of which she could tend to while under the influence of the Remembrance. Add the sudden, mysterious arrival of the Ydrel—

That is why the Remembrance Calls! he protested.

Salgoud, whom they'd included in their conversation, added that Ocapo and his everyn, Spot, understood their roles well enough that they could do without her for much of the training. *For whatever reason, the Ydrel is here. Let him teach us directly,* Salgoud added.

She projected warmth—how often they thought alike. She told Leinad that she would take time to make the arrangements with Deryl, and then—if Kanaan were still—she would give herself to the memories of Gardianju. She felt his sullen assent, turned to go.

Salgoud shoved her into the middle of a sparring circle. She managed to duck and roll to avoid getting smacked by a practice blade. She came up in a crouch, her short sword out of the scabbard she wore and a dagger from her hairpiece in her other hand. The two sparring warriors hesitated only a moment before turning on her. She ducked below the swing of one, scored on the side of the other, barreled between them, and spun toward Leinad and Salgoud. She swung her sword toward the unarmed Leinad, forcing Salgoud to defend him, while with her other hand, she jabbed her dagger toward the other warrior's gut. He anticipated the move, blocked it, and the three stood, weapons locked, until they broke into snickers.

Leinad, still flat against the wall, gave them the full brunt of his displeasure.

You know what happens when you bring a Remembrance into a 'war' zone; besides, we need to work on your reflexes, she chided lightly as she backed more carefully away from her general and left the practice grounds.

The Ydrel and his friend had had enough privacy, she'd decided. It was time they spoke with her.

She shivered with excitement. Only a few Miscria were ever blessed with the ability to contact the Ydrel. Her mentor hadn't been one of them. Her talent had focused on Kanaan—detecting the changing weather patterns, the unrest caused as the Season of War approached and the planet Barin shone too bright and too large in their sky. No one understood why their world suffered as the other neared.

Perhaps Deryl knew; she would ask now that she'd thought of it. Nonetheless, her mentor had been especially adept at regulating the tides, calming the earthquakes and redirecting Kanaan's life blood so that when the pressures were too high and it sought release through the violent bloodletting of burning stone, it was done in areas where damage to life was minimal. At least she had managed to teach Tasmae that much before she was killed by the traitor the Barins now called Alugiac the Prophet.

Prophet, Tasmae thought, her anger washing away her excitement. The only prophecy he'd brought was one of doom. He had once been Kanaan, a brilliant warrior healer—and her parents' best friend. He had assisted with Tasmae's birth and had tended her along with the other warriors in their group. She remembered him and her father trading amused glances when she would run up to him to demand a healing of some cut or bruise she'd gotten in practice, only to run back to the practice ground to get injured again.

Once a lapse in attention had made her drop her guard and receive a blow that had knocked her senseless. Her mother had scolded her, but Alugiac had come to Tasmae's defense, reminding her mother of the time he had healed her of a concussion.

However, he'd also recognized there was more to Tasmae's "lapse" than carelessness; not long afterward, her Miscria talent overwhelmed her. He had taken her to the elderly Miscria himself.

At least they didn't live to see him change, she consoled herself.

Alugiac had last been seen in the thick of the battle that had killed her parents, healing friend and foe alike. Then he was gone. The Season of War ended, and they scoured the battlefield yet never found him. The next Season of War, he reappeared, leading a Barin army on a sneak attack. Their target: to destroy the Miscria and thus doom Kanaan.

Tasmae frowned. A group of warriors passing her in the hall picked up the grim nature of her reverie and gave her a wide birth, but lost in her memory, she didn't notice. The Barins had killed her mentor, but they hadn't killed her, and they'd paid dearly for their error. Tasmae's talent had come upon her later than it did for most children, and she'd spent the bulk of her childhood learning from her warrior parents. She had a great deal of skill and a natural ability to see beyond what her senses told her, and to use her talents in unique ways.

Seven of her friends had died trying to protect her that day as they fought their way out of the city. When the last Kanaan had dashed out, the door closing on the enemy's outstretched hands, Tasmae had pressed her hands against the building, drew on the power of her world, and sent a command. The building trembled and collapsed in on itself, crushing everyone inside, burying her dead friends and dear mentor.

"These are the baths. Hope you don't have privacy issues," Deryl said.

"Nah. I'm fine," Joshua replied as he surveyed the room. It resembled a locker room—if one grew out of a humongous plant. Josh eyed the walls of hexagonal shelves as he sat on a long, flat mushroom and pulled off his shoes. "Those are kind of weird. Like the honey-comb in a beehive."

"What's the matter? Scared the laundry bees will get you?" Deryl teased as he pulled a towel from a shelf and replaced it with his shirt. He brought the towel to his face. It felt soft as a flower petal, but thick and sturdy. He expected it to smell like lilac, but instead it had a basic non-scent of clean clothes.

"Laundry bees? You're kidding, right?"

Deryl laughed at the trepidation in his friend's voice. "I'm sure they're too busy to bother with you."

Joshua paused, his shirt dangling in one hand. "Did you just *pun*?"

"I don't pun." Deryl said with complete seriousness then murmured, "I'm stung by the accusation."

He felt Josh's surprise, quickly replaced by amusement. "Arrgh! Who are you, and what have you done with my friend?" He finished undressing, and wrapped a towel around his middle. "Wish I had a change of clothes. So, where are the showers?"

"No showers. Communal baths. Like ancient Rome or something. Hope that's not too weird for you."

"Just as long as we don't run into any laundry bees," Joshua quipped as they headed across the room and through the next door.

Two steps out of the doorway, they stopped. Joshua let out an appreciative whistle as they scanned the "baths."

They had passed out of the plant part of the keep and into the part within the mountain. The large cave was illuminated by some kind of phosphorescent moss on the walls, covering everything in a shimmering shade of near-twilight blue. Wide, flat-topped stalagmites served as stools or tables around a deep pool more suited for a gym than a bath. Above it, stalactites hung, condensation dripping off them and into the pool. The sound and the ripples caused by the drops were both peaceful and entrancing. Despite the size of the cavern, it was pleasantly warm and just a little steamy.

"Whoa," Joshua breathed.

"Like their idea of a tub?" Deryl smirked at his friend.

"What? That? It's bigger than the swimming pool at SK-Mental. Where's the soap?"

"Don't need any. There's some kind of microbes or something that eat the dirt and oils."

"Really? Are you sure it's safe?"

Deryl rolled his eyes at him. "Only one way to find out!" He threw off his towel and dove in.

It felt like swimming in Perrier. The bubbles tickled him so that he came up laughing. He took a huge breath and ducked under, rubbing and fluffing his hair with his fingers to get the water all over his scalp, ridding it of the sweat and dirt of the past couple of days. Then he surfaced for a breath, and ducked under again, letting the water drag his hair back.

When he surfaced, he saw Joshua staring doubtfully at the frothy water around him. "Come on!" he laughed. "It's not acid. It's...effervescent!" He swept his arm, splashing his wary friend.

Joshua didn't flinch, but he didn't jump in, either. He stood at the edge and dragged a foot through the water. "How deep is it?"

"I don't know," Deryl replied as he tread water. He'd rather carelessly dived in head first, but hadn't touched the bottom. One stroke had pulled him to the top, but he hadn't tried to dive any deeper. "Eight, ten feet. Maybe more. Why?"

"There a shallow end?"

Deryl started to ask him why it would matter, when it occurred to him. "Oh, right. Boy genius can't swim."

Tasmae walked in, her bare feet silent against the mossy floor. Like Joshua and him, she was unclothed, but unlike them, she carried her towel loosely in one hand. Not even her long hair covered up her figure; her rich dark tresses were pulled up in an elaborate bun held together by the unusual hairpiece.

The words he intended to tease Joshua with caught in his throat. His awareness narrowed to just her.

He heard Joshua's yelp and a large splash.

"Josh!" Deryl moved to rescue his friend, but Joshua had already clawed his way to the surface and was struggling to the edge. Tasmae leaned down to offer her hand, but he waved them both off.

"I'm fine!" he sputtered, as he hooked one arm over the edge. He coughed and hacked water and kept his face averted.

Tasmae squatted beside him. "So you can swim?"

"Yes! No. Sort of. Not well. I sink like a stone." He paused to cough again, but nonetheless refused to look her way. "My throat is burning! What kind of stupid baths are these?"

Deryl felt Tasmae's confusion—what other kind of baths are there?—but to Joshua, she said. "It's not meant to be drunk. Did you swallow much?"

"Enough!" he croaked and hacked again.

"Then I'll get you something to soothe your throat, and meet you in the shallow end. Or there are smaller baths if you so prefer."

She stood to go. Deryl, too, did his best not to watch and instead concentrated on his still hacking friend. "You okay?"

"You could have told me the baths were co-ed!"

"I didn't know. She said they were empty for a while. I thought it'd be just us. Besides, what's it matter? You're in love with Sachiko."

Joshua gaped at him as if he'd said something incredibly clueless. "All the more reason for me to get out of this tub—and considering the suspicion people have for us right now, you should, too. To wash my hair—I just duck under?"

"Yeah. Shouldn't take long, with your hair so short."

Still holding the edge, Joshua took a breath and submerged, one hand clinging to the edge.

Deryl's arms had tired of treading water. He hung onto the side and waited until Joshua surfaced. "You know, they don't think like that here," he said. "I mean, a body is a body."

"Yeah, well, we're not from here, remember? I'm pretty certain that guy in brown at our table isn't going to forget that. Have you?"

Deryl started to protest, then thought about Leinad's glares—and his own reaction to seeing Tasmae. "I'd better get your towel," he said.

"Good. 'Cause I'm using yours."

Joshua waited until Deryl had dived under then checked to room to see if Tasmae was around, trying to keep his eyes at floor level. She'd apparently gone off to fetch him something for his throat. He didn't know where he could go without an escort, but he did not want to be in the same room with a naked woman. He had enough to confess as it was.

Seeing the area clear, he pulled himself up, snagged Deryl's towel and strode to the lockers. If nothing else, he could dress and wait there.

What if she's in the locker room? He shoved down his panic. *I'll just ask for privacy. Even if they don't understand lust, they have to have some concept of privacy, right?*

He stepped through the weird door to find two everyn circling the room. He froze at the threshold. *What? Co-species as well as co-ed?*

A young man in a colorful vest over a beige shirt and pants rose from where he lounged. "You are Joshua?" He spoke with Tasmae's accent—Deryl's accent.

"Yeah...?"

The stranger nodded, his eyes moving over Joshua. "She said you had the color of rich earth. I am Ocapo, Bondfriend to—" He made a piercing cry followed by a warble, so Joshua guessed he was talking about the tiny dragon over their heads. "but you may call him Spot."

He made a second sound. "—is not bonded, but serves with us. Tasmae has given me your language and asked us to befriend you."

"Okay," Joshua said slowly. "Uh, can I dress first?"

Deryl retrieved Joshua's towel, flinging the sopping thing onto the ground, then swam the length of the pool. He concentrated only on how his strokes cut through the water, trying to decide if the water really was more viscous than regular water or if it was just his imagination. He did not want to think about Leinad's distrust, Joshua's worry—or his reaction to seeing Tasmae.

But when he turned around to head back to the shallow end and saw Tasmae lounging there, he knew evading the problem wouldn't help. At least she was up to her neck in the dark water.

He swam underwater until his fingers brushed the bottom, then surfaced and walked the rest of the way. The edge was lined with seats, and he took one not far from hers.

"Joshua decided to go in," he told her.

She nodded in that odd way they had, but didn't open her eyes. She sent him the image of a young man with wild hair, a large grin, and an everyn on his shoulder, and he understood that Ocapo and the everyns had the juice to soothe Joshua's throat and would keep watch over him awhile.

Which left him alone with Tasmae.

He found his thoughts jumbled and his tongue—even his teleping tongue—tied. Fortunately, she had a topic of conversation in mind, and she did not intend to let him put her off as he had earlier. He'd seen his Joshua; he knew he was fine; now, Deryl would answer her questions.

He embraced her determination and the distraction it brought from...other things.

I'm here because you Called me, he told her. *I was in danger, and I was thinking about escape just as you Called me.*

Danger? You said you had been sick, had almost died—

That was my appendix. He shared with her what little the doctor explained about the surgery and his recovery.

"Wait a minute!" He set his hand on his side, found it smooth and whole. So the healers had taken care of him. He felt awful for doubting them.

They did not touch your mind, she assured him. *You are the Ydrel. But why has the oracle of God come to us now?* He felt her doubts. Was he, then, an imposter?

He impressed negation on her. He was no oracle, of God or anything else. But he was the Ydrel who had given the Miscria the information they'd sought.

What else could you be? Tasmae sat forward.

Once again, her unusual beauty struck him, and part of him answered that he was very much a man. He squashed that thought, and all the ones that wanted to follow, before Tasmae picked it up. Joshua was right: that line of thinking would only lead to trouble, and they were in enough trouble as it was.

Joshua has a better handle on the situation, and he's not even psychic. I should have focused more on Leinad and Salgoud. Tasmae trusts them. I have got to pay better attention. I need to be what these people expect from me...even if I'm not sure what that is.

On Earth, he could have read the person's mind and played into the persona. Here, he had the feeling such an intrusion would earn him a knife in the gut.

Tasmae still watched him intently. He tried to look at her face, but his eyes moved down.

Three parallel scars marred the front of her shoulder, just above the waterline.

She touched them. *From the times I have killed.* The she reached out and took his hand, turning it over to examine the jagged scar that ran the length of his wrist.

"From the time I refused to kill," he whispered.

"But you are the Ydrel." She replied in a whisper, but because of her touch, he felt her confusion, so strong it hurt: An oracle, an angel, she could understand. But a man, teaching her war and refusing to kill?

His stomach twisted with her suspicion.

I don't understand this any better than you! He jerked his hand away. His resolve crumbled in his need—her need—to make her understand. *Tasmae, I didn't know what I was doing. You asked questions, I gave answers. It wasn't until my birthday that—*

Madness Unbound ⊕ 89

You refused my questions. She finished his thought.

And I found out what you really were. I still don't know what all of this means. I swear, if I knew—if I had a hint—I'd share it with you.

He felt a clutch of fear and knew it was hers. *You do not know, but Gardianju does.*

Who?

Her surprise hit him like an electric shock, bringing with it a fury of information. *What are you?*

Images and emotions strobed into his mind, confusing him. He fought to think past them. *Deryl. The Ydrel. But I don't remember... Who is Guardianju? Another Miscria?*

She pulled away from him, psychically as well as physically. He gasped at the sudden emptiness.

I must experience her Remembrance. You may not see me for several days.

She released her hair from the clip and swam away, her long black tresses moving in sinuous waves. He leaned back against the wall of the pool, fighting to catch his breath as the knowledge she'd passed to him played in his mind.

Gardianju! Another Miscria—who had been in contact with him. Gardianju, the first Miscria.

Gardianju, who went insane and died over five thousand years ago.

Chapter Eight

Deryl rose from the pool and went to change, his head swimming with confusion and his stomach queasy. He noted with relief that Ocapo had taken Joshua somewhere, and that someone had left fresh clothes for him. He pulled the pants drawstring tight and slipped on the shirt, not bothering to tuck it in, and headed to one of the observation "nests," where he could pick apart the tangled ball of information that had wrapped itself around the name "Gardianju."

He didn't remember Gardianju. He didn't remember any of the Miscria besides Tasmae. In fact, he hadn't realized there were others until she'd told him. Their Callings had followed the same pattern: pull him from consciousness and instill in him a compulsion to learn something, transmit the information, and wait for the next Calling. Only after Joshua suggested he stand up to this mysterious Miscria, had he discovered "it" was Tasmae.

I should have known, though. He navigated the narrow hall to the open platform that overhung the compound. The view was stunning, and he wished he could distract himself with it. Elbows on the low wall, he buried his face in his hands and closed his eyes. *No one could have put all my suggestions in place in five years. The medics, the weaponry, the fortresses. But five thousand years?*

Yet after his operation when he'd forced her out of his mind, blocked her altogether, she had turned right around to Call him again. Hours for her, but over a week for him.

Time is relative and irrelevant. The Calls must come based on need.

He took a deep breath, making himself relax as the information unknotted in his mind. Gardianju, the first Miscria. Generations followed, but not all spoke to him. Most spent their talent holding the world together.

But what does that mean? He shook his head.

Most held the world together, but when Kanaan had great need, the Ydrel blessed the Miscria with its presence, gave it knowledge—to save lives, to protect the Kanaan, to fight the invaders.

The compulsion comes when Barin shows itself in the sky. When Barin outshines the moons, the Ydrel retreats and the Miscria...she...

The Miscria what? Tasmae, what? Deryl dug his fingers into his hair and pulled, trying to concentrate.

Pain. Madness. Raging at the invading planet. Drawing strength from others, like psychic vampirism.

No.

Plants, animals, people fall around them.

No, please, no!

One thought consumes.

Please! Stop it!

GO AWAY!

"Deryl, you all right?"

"No!" Deryl shouted and spun, pushing with his mind. His eyes flew open.

Joshua had staggered and grabbed the low wall to regain his balance. "Hey! Deryl, what is it? Are you all right?"

"I, I'm not sure." He fought to control his breath. "I—"

"Well, get it together," Joshua hissed and jerked his head toward the young man just coming through the door. "Someone wants to meet you."

"Right," he said, running his hands through his hair, brushing off the last of the visions. He had to be missing something. He took a breath, made sure his shields were in place, and greeted Ocapo with the same salute Tasmae had given him.

Ocapo rushed to him and enveloped him in a hug.

All the fearful memories of Gardianju and the other Miscrias were washed away in waves of gratitude, and new images filled his mind. Ocapo's people, the Bondfriends, alone, too few to defend themselves against the Barin, but doomed to be apart from the Kanaan. Until the Ydrel taught Tasmae how they could help.

Tasmae coming into his village, speaking to his chiefs. As she outlines her plans for the Bondfriends, the excitement grows, and others gather around the fire. A few, like Ocapo, are chosen to join the Kanaan in the fight against the invaders; in return, the Kanaan armies would defend the tribes. Trust grows between the two peoples.

Ydrel, you saved my people. You've returned us to our brothers. Ocapo squeezed him.

Deryl looked over Ocapo's shoulder at Joshua.

Joshua grinned. "Nice to know someone appreciates you, huh?"

Deryl found himself grinning back; still, the credit went to Tasmae, not him, and he told Ocapo so. Ocapo released him with an unembarrassed grin.

"Each Miscria learns something different from the Ydrel," the Bondfriend said aloud for Joshua's benefit. "If it had not been for you, Tasmae would not have thought to come to us."

"Okay." Deryl shrugged. He didn't know what else to say. He desperately wanted a few minutes alone with his own thoughts to get his bearings, but didn't think that would happen anytime soon. At least for the moment, he was with someone friendly to him—friendly and non-threatening.

Joshua moved over to the wall and looked out. He whistled. "That is some view. Ocapo, is that an actual, like active, volcano?" He pointed to a mountain that had a reddish glow.

Ocapo followed his gaze and nodded. "There are many in this area. This mountain is one."

"What?" both humans shouted together.

Ocapo laughed. "Tasmae has taken care of it. Its fires lie dormant, waiting for her command. We have more earthquakes now, but she takes care of those."

Joshua turned to face them, leaning on one elbow on the low wall. "Okay. Someone needs to explain this."

Deryl said, "That's the primary talent of the Miscrias. They control weather."

"Weather," Joshua repeated. "Like *earthquakes* and *volcanoes*?"

"Rain, too," Ocapo said. "When the Barins come, she will shroud the maze in fog."

"How?" Joshua started, then shook his head. "Never mind. I don't think you could explain it. But for the whole planet? I can't even imagine how much power that would take."

"What happened to 'faith the size of a mustard seed?'" Deryl quipped, but a horrible idea struck him. *Ocapo*, he teleped, *how do the Miscrias die? Do they ever give all their life energy to Kanaan?*

Ocapo responded with a psychic shrug. He only knew children's stories about Kanaan's Caretaker.

Joshua had taken his barb seriously. "Do you think it could be that easy? Hey!" He laughed as a green everyn with yellow streaks on its cheek crests landed on his shoulder. "There you are. Deryl, meet Cochise."

"Cochise, eh?" Deryl reached out to touch the creature, and tried to hide his surprise that it was settling itself comfortably on his friend.

"Yeah, he likes me. Probably because I gave him a cool name. Tasmae named Ocapo's 'Spot.'"

"SPOT?" Deryl asked, turning to the mottled dragon now perched on Ocapo.

"MM-hmm," Joshua said, scratching Cochise under the chin. "So Cochise is named for a warrior, while poor Spot is named—"

"SPOT: *Satellite Probatoire d'Observation de la Terre*," Deryl whispered. This was Tasmae's solution to his suggestion?

Joshua dropped his hand. "She named him after a French *satellite*?"

"Better than a lame dog's name like you were thinking. I must have told Tasmae about aerial observation..." He closed his eyes, remembering. He'd been reading about the history of air power. The Miscria hadn't asked him about it specifically, but so much modern warfare strategy depended on commanding the skies, and that had gotten him interested in satellites. But that was last Spring, and Ocapo said she had come to his people two years ago.

"We taught her, as well," Ocapo said. "The Barins do not understand about the Greater Beasts, so they consider the everyn and the...wolves?...mere animals. That means, they can wander around the battlefields or even the compounds, part of the scenery, and spy."

"That's brilliant," Deryl said.

"It has saved our tribes more than once. Sometimes, a group or commander will 'adopt' a Bondfriend as its mascot."

"So they think they've got a pet, when in fact, they've got a spy." Joshua snickered.

"Or a chaperone," Deryl said, with a pointed look at Cochise.

"Know what? If it makes people more comfortable, I'm cool with it." Joshua scratched the little dragon lizard behind the cheek crests. It turned its head into the caress and trilled.

Ocapo smiled, and Deryl felt relief emanate from him. "I am pleased to hear that, friend Joshua! So, my work is complete for now. I hope we shall meet again." He bowed and left.

Joshua watched him until the door folded shut behind him. "Okay, then! Speaking of purpose, you and Tasmae figure out why we're here?"

Deryl sighed as he joined him by the low wall. The maze Ocapo spoke of stretched to the horizon—forests, some glimmering, some a deep and lush green, flowery meadows, and a tangle of deep valleys. To the right, a mountain range, including Joshua's volcano, created a jagged line against the sky. How long had it been since he'd seen a view that didn't end in manicured trees "hiding" a stone wall and the threat of restraints should he try to scale it? Would anyone stop him if he took off across the compound now?

"I don't know. I'm not even sure we talked about it."

"What does that mean?"

He could run through the gate and out to the meadow. How far would he get? He couldn't remember what it felt like to run in something other than a circle.

"I don't know. Leinad thinks the answers might be in the Remembrance."

Run and run.

"What's that?"

Deryl pulled himself from his fantasy. He shifted to face Joshua, wondering how far he could push his friend's credulity.

"It's a plant, that, um, psychically stores memories."

As expected, Joshua crossed his arms and leaned back. Cochise gave a disgruntled chirrup and left his shoulders to perch on the wall. "You're kidding? So, what? She has to go ask this plant about its memories?"

"Actually, it stores the memories of another Kanaan. She'll psychically link with the plant and re-experience those memories." The answer came smoothly, though he hadn't realized he'd known it. It must have been in the tangle Tasmae had given him when they'd touched.

What had she taken from him, then? He suppressed a shiver.

Joshua gave a short, disbelieving laugh. "And the memories of some dead guy are going to help us how?"

"I don't know."

"Okay," Joshua rubbed his temples before speaking again. "She's obviously not going to relive someone's whole life. How long will this take?"

"I don't know!" However, more of the images were coming together, and his anxiety grew as they did.

"Well, what do you know?" Joshua snapped.

"She's scared!" Deryl snapped back. "Remembrances can be dangerous—and this one is the worst of all. And it's all my fault!"

"What?"

Deryl buried his head in his hands, grabbing his hair and pulling as the last thread of knowledge revealed itself to him. "Gardianju was the first Miscria. The first to contact me. And I drove her insane."

Joshua gripped his shoulders. "Are you sure?" he hissed.

"No, I'm not sure," Deryl moaned. "This is Tasmae's knowledge—what she shared with me—and I don't think she's thought about it this way."

"Which is my point about experiencing someone's memories, anyway! Listen: if you're not sure, then calm down before you freak someone out. Don't make assumptions, especially ones that will get us into more trouble. Let's just figure out what will satisfy them as to our 'purpose,' so we can get out of here. Okay? Deryl, look at me."

At Joshua's strong voice, Deryl let out a shaky sigh and met his friend's gaze. Joshua held it, his own breathing slow and relaxed, and emanating a confidence Deryl knew he didn't feel. Still, Deryl began to calm.

Joshua released him. "Better. So, you've been teaching Taz strategy, right? What if she's just totally missing something important? Something that could help them win the war? If you figure that out and set them straight, that could fulfill your purpose, right?"

Deryl shrugged. It made sense. "But what about you?"

Joshua rolled his eyes. "Who else is going to keep you on track? Shall we try?" Josh held out his hand.

Deryl shook it. Joshua was right—especially about his needing his friend to keep him focused. "So, I should go find Salgoud, offer my services? Want to come?"

Joshua grimaced. "I can't think of anything I'd rather do less, actually. Unless you need me, of course, but I'd be a fifth wheel. Is there a salle around here?"

"A salle?"

"Yeah. You know, a big empty room, where you can practice sword fighting? Usually has mirrors?"

"I know what a salle is." Deryl huffed. "What do you want one for?"

"Well," Joshua said as he stretched, "I'm totally keyed up, and regardless of what we just said, I have nothing to do but worry. I'm thinking a workout could distract me, and I'm assuming there's no weight room? Besides, whether you get me back right before my audition or right after we left, I promised Rique I'd have a routine ready. An empty salle would be a good place to practice."

"Oh. Right, okay." Once again, he envied his friend's ability to take control of a situation, even of his own fear. He pushed that thought aside and reached out with his senses. "There are two, and the small one doesn't get used much. Cochise can lead you, and I'll find Salgoud, if that's okay?"

Joshua looked at the everyn, who raised its head and stretched its wings with a large flap. "Sounds like a plan. Look, Deryl, we're going to be stuck here awhile. Lighten up and enjoy yourself. You've spent most of your life locked up with people telling you what to do and hardly anything under your control. But here, you're *the Ydrel*. Even if you don't want to buy the oracle routine, you've got skills, and you've got a fresh start. Enjoy it."

"Seriously?"

Joshua shrugged. "It can't hurt. Besides, it's pretty clear to me that if you keep spinning yourself up, you're going to send out a signal that you aren't the Great and Powerful Ydrel. That could get us both killed."

Chapter Nine

Deryl tried to find a comfortable seat on the log without looking like he was squirming. He hadn't thought his "fresh start" would include roughing it, but Salgoud had sent a warrior to his room with a uniform and instructions to meet him at the unicorn fields. The outfit fit like a wetsuit, but proved surprisingly comfortable while riding to where the warriors had set up for their next exercise. He'd spent the day observing their maneuvers until the sun had set, and the "kills" were racked up and a winner declared. Now, he sat around a campfire with Salgoud and his aides as they awaited his assessment.

He looked around at the circle of people who were focused on him.

Salgoud, the equivalent of commander-in-chief of the world's army, peeled a piece of fruit with his dagger. The firelight played off the scars on his face. Despite his fearsome appearance and Joshua's misgivings, Deryl felt most comfortable around him. He seemed confident in his ability, yet ready to listen to what Deryl had to say.

Ocapo eyed Deryl with barely restrained hero-worship. At first, he'd enjoyed it, but now it made him almost as nervous as the expectant, dubious looks of Salgoud's staff did.

Anything he said, anything important, they would relay, in perfect detail, to the rest of the warriors. Should he say anything stupid...

No pressure.

They watched and waited. Their expectation grew. He couldn't even stall by filling his mouth with food.

He shut his eyes and thought about the battle. They were definitely missing something, something obvious. He focused on the cliffs. Why weren't they utilizing these?

He heard a snort from one of the commanders. Apparently, some expressions were universal.

Fine. He had a better idea, too. He showed them his sight of the battlefield, all the people in red. He showed them from Spot's eyes—red and red among the green. Then he showed them Spot sitting in a tree, his mottled pattern blending. He concluded with the memories of a veteran who had spent time at SK-Mental, and how their battle dress uniforms with the mottled greens and browns let them blend into the scenery.

He felt that sense of expectation come crashing down: That *was the best the Ydrel, an oracle of God, could do? Fashion advice?*

Well, if it's so simple and obvious, why haven't you done it, then? Nervousness made him snarly. When he got no answer, just a sense of disappointment, nervousness morphed into anger. He welcomed the anger, wrapped it around himself like a shield, and let it feed his natural arrogance. *I don't know what miracles you expect from me, but understand this: I am the Ydrel, but my skills are limited. I didn't come here to win a war for you. For millennia, I've done one thing, and only one, for your people: Offer my wisdom and*

advice. Even that has its limit. God may be all know-
ing and all-powerful, but He has not passed that on to
me. Now, you want what I have to offer? Here it is. If
you don't, I can go.

He felt their surprise—how could one be so haughty
about his limitations? He didn't acknowledge their
feelings. All he had aside from his knowledge was his
arrogance. He had to bluff. Where would he go? He
didn't know how to get back to Earth, though he'd have
to figure it out for Joshua's sake. Still, they didn't know
that, and his shields were strong enough that they
couldn't have picked up on his thoughts if they'd tried.

He felt a second disappointment, from the liaison to
the healers. She had hoped the Ydrel had come to prevent the war.

I'd like nothing better than to find a way to keep
the Barins away from your world, he teleped. *But I*
don't know how. God has not told me how, any more
than He's told you. What I do know is how to help you
better defend yourselves, to try to minimize the loss of
life. That's what I've always tried to do. Whether or
not you accept my ideas, big or small, is up to you.

He held himself tight against their doubt. He didn't
want to argue, and he did not want to sit there, where
their doubt pressed upon him like the muggy heat back
home Joshua used to complain about.

Know what? I don't have to. I'm a free man here.
He stood up, gave a respectful bow, and left.

He headed through the campground, ignoring the
warriors gathered around their own fires as they
turned to look his way. If he paused now, they might
see his own self-doubt and consider it weakness. No.
First rule of engagement: maintain the high ground.

He reinforced his mental shields and kept a stern frown on his face, while he let his feet carry him through a dense but narrow wood and his mind bounced and brooded.

Was Joshua okay? Salgoud spirited me off without explaining his plans. Someone would have told him, right?

I should have snagged a memory from Joshua's mind and taken us both to Colorado. But no, Tasmae had to Call me at just the wrong time, and my stupid scared and drugged mind latched onto it.

Tasmae. Was she all right? Salgoud said no one, not even Leinad, thought she was ready to experience the Remembrance. My changing things between us forced her into this. What if he was right?

Salgoud said even the most skilled Miscrias would lose themselves in Gardianju's memories—sometimes, permanently.

He shivered. *Come back to us, Tasmae. We need you. I need you.*

That thought surprised him almost as much as the fact that he had left the woods and stood in a large meadow. A thick blanket of stars bathed the meadow in silvery light almost as bright as a full moon. How long he stood there, looking and not thinking, he didn't know. Then it occurred to him that if they were in their own galaxy, they had to be near the core. He turned in a slow circle, taking in the view, until he faced a small, bright disk.

Barin. Once, when he was at SK-Mental and Tasmae had called him away, she'd shown him the planet in the night sky and explained that when it grew to a certain size, the invaders would come in their ships and fight like demons to secure a foothold while the world waxed in the sky.

Each time the war grows longer, she'd told him. Each time, they succeed in killing more of her people, taking a bit more of land, but they could not hold it. Yet they kept coming back, and no one understood why.

This whole thing's whacked. He glared at the disk, as if he could will answers from its blue-bright form. *Why fight a pointless war? Are they that evil or that desperate?*

Deryl knew what the Kanaan thought. Tasmae may have used the proper name for the planet and its people, but the warriors had other "names." Contagion, Hell, Asylum.

An entire planet of criminally insane—generations of criminally insane? Deryl shook his head. *Maybe this is how they purge their world of the violent? Then why let the worst of the lot—the survivors—return?*

You don't make sense! he thought at the planet, and despite his shields, he felt a flare of anger that wasn't his own: Demon sun—bringing its evil to us!

No, this isn't me!

The anger grew, morphed into vision, and he was standing on a dry and thirsting Kanaan, staring into a sky with two suns.

Stop it! These are not my memories!

Anger and vision became heat and pain. Every cell in his body caught fire with the pain of the world. In the vision, he screamed.

NO! This isn't me! Get out of my mind!

Something "pinged" on his mental radar, throwing him out of the vision. Without thinking, he spun, one arm up to block a blow he didn't consciously realize was coming.

Salgoud's sword impacted against the telekinetic shield he'd projected.

Salgoud's eyes widened in surprise. Then he smiled.

Joshua did a cross step that led into a full turn and down into the splits. He held the pose a moment, looking at himself in the salle mirror and trying to imagine the positions and poses of the rest of his friends. He frowned in thought, then noticed Deryl's reflection. Deryl lounged in the doorway, wearing a grin and one of the tight red uniforms of the warriors. "Hey," Joshua called. "Come on in. I'm about done for now."

"That looked cool," Deryl said as he walked all the way in and took a seat on the bench. Cochise looked up from his nap to give a chirrup of greeting. Deryl scratched the top of the everyn's head. "How's the routine coming?"

"Not bad. Still too complex to teach the guys in a couple of hours, though, but I can tone it down. I'm not sure I'll remember all of it, anyway, but it was fun to make up. Did you know they haven't invented paper? Who doesn't need paper?"

"A psychic people with plants that record memories?"

Joshua held up his hands in defeat, then snagged a towel and rubbed the sweat off his face.

"You been doing this the whole time I was gone?" Deryl asked. His friend certainly seemed more relaxed, even like he was enjoying himself. Deryl wished he could say the same.

Joshua jerked his head to where Cochise perched on a weapon's stand. "For all that he's a winged lizard and my jailer, Cochise is a pretty perceptive guy and a good guide. He took me out to the unicorn fields, too. I didn't realize how much I missed my horse." His wistful smile turned to a smirk as he looked Deryl over. "So, snazzy outfit."

Deryl rolled his eyes. "Yeah. Salgoud's insistence. I felt kind of silly in it at first, but this stuff is tougher than Kevlar."

"Serious? You look kind of super-hero-ish. Just don't tell anyone I said so. Have a good time?"

Deryl grinned. "I think I know our purpose."

Joshua cocked an eyebrow.

Deryl held out his hand to the everyn. "Cochise, bite me."

"What?" Joshua yelped. Cochise cocked his head.

"Well, I know you won't hit me. Go ahead, boy. Give it your best shot."

With a humanlike shrug of his shoulders, the everyn snapped his teeth around Deryl's hand. They stopped with a click before hitting his skin.

Deryl laughed. "Remember when those monsters from the Netherworld were attacking me, and you told me to concentrate on defense—making a physical shield and wearing it like armor?"

"I thought you were delirious. I was just trying to keep you from trashing your room and hurting someone." Joshua rubbed his hair and set the towel around his neck.

"Yeah, well, your lesson worked, and yesterday, when Salgoud tried to ambush me—"

"He what?"

"He does that a lot, apparently. Keeps people on their toes. Anyway, without even thinking, I put up this shield and blocked him. I thought he was going to drop his sword, he was so surprised! They don't know how to do that. So we're going to teach them."

Cochise continued to gnaw on Deryl's shield, worrying at it like a bone. Deryl grinned at him and withdrew his hand.

"We?" Joshua sat down on the other side of Cochise. "I don't know how to do that. Anything I know about psychic powers—or magic, for that matter—I got from reading fantasy novels, and then I tossed in some basics from my Neuro Linguistic Programming training for you. You figured it out."

"Do you want to get out of here or not? I may have to teach them, but you're the one with the ideas. I'm the Ydrel, remember? I'm just a conduit for information."

"You are more than that." Tasmae startled them with her words.

Deryl spun on the bench and looked at her, aghast. At first, Joshua thought he was afraid because of what he'd just said, but instead, Deryl asked, "What are you doing here? The Remembrance—" He paused, then frowned with worry.

"I...was thrown out of it," Tasmae said, still lingering in the doorway. "It should not happen that way." She pinned Deryl with her stare, and Joshua had the idea that she was wondering if he had something to do with that. From the way Deryl squirmed under her gaze, Joshua thought his friend wondered the same.

If something happens to the Miscria and they decide it's our fault... "But you're okay, right? No harm done?" Joshua asked.

She gave a shrug that didn't reassure him in the least.

"Okay," Joshua said, though he didn't find anything okay about the situation. "So! Uh, Deryl has a great idea for you."

"That's right!" Deryl grinned. "Hit me—"

Before he could finish his sentence, Tasmae struck him with a roundhouse kick that knocked him off the bench. Cochise squawked and flew to a high shelf, where he crouched and gekkered.

Joshua looked at his prone friend and burst out laughing.

"Yuck it up," Deryl said as he rolled to a stand. He was grinning at Tasmae, who Joshua noticed, looked confused. "She didn't touch me."

"You mean you flinched? That hard?" Joshua chortled.

"It's a personal shield," Deryl explained as he approached Tasmae. "Telekinetic. I imagine it covering me like armor, but I control it. I can protect myself from anything, but, if I want to touch something—" He reached out and brushed back a strand of her hair. "I can," he finished, his voice softer than before.

Tasmae raised her arm to knock his away, but again encountered his shield. Slowly, she set her hand on his arm. It passed through his shield without problem.

He smiled.

Tasmae raked her nails across the back of his hand.

"Yeow!" Deryl jerked his hand away. He backed up fast when she followed up with a kick.

"Must you always concentrate on them?" she asked. Though she continued to advance on him, swinging and kicking, she didn't sound angry at all. Just calculating.

"Only to alter them," Deryl replied, puffing a little as he ducked and blocked her blows. She kept pushing him back to the far wall where practice weapons waited neatly in a rack.

"Do we teach this to children, then?" she demanded. "Or can you fight and keep the shield?"

"Oh, I can fight!" Deryl spun, snagged a sword in his left hand and lunged toward her, swinging the sword wide. When she stepped back, he returned to a more natural stance while swinging his blade in a back-handed figure eight.

"Nice," Joshua called from the other side of the room.

"Sachiko taught me that one," Deryl replied. He started to make a "come on" gesture at Tasmae, but she didn't give him a chance before grabbing her own blade and coming at him with a fierce attack.

"Sachiko has four black belts," he informed his friend. Even though he puffed a bit and continued to let Tasmae drive him back, he kept his voice level, as if this were nothing. "She's something to watch. You know she's got a temper. Sometimes, on really bad days at work, we'd sneak into the gym after hours and go at it with broomsticks."

Joshua settled more comfortably on the bench and watched the two spar. This was at least as interesting as the stuff he'd seen in the movies; perhaps more so, since the swords were real and the steps not choreographed. At first, he marveled at some of Deryl's moves—real, Jedi-style combat acrobatics, but without the help of wires. He wondered if his psychic friend was unconsciously using a little telekinesis, then his thoughts turned more personal as they headed back in his direction. Despite himself, he leaned back in his seat as they drew near. Then Deryl swatted Tasmae with the flat of his blade and skipped off in another direction, drawing Tasmae away from him.

"Why do you keep running away? I gave you that opening!" she snarled as she again drove him in Joshua's direction. "This is battle! You accomplish nothing treating this like a game!"

He laughed as he parried her attack. "*Au contraire*, I seem to be doing just fine keeping your attention."

She spun through her deflected thrust and swung toward Joshua.

With a yelp, Joshua threw himself backward behind the bench. His towel fell on the floor. Cochise shrieked and flew to protect him.

"Hey!" Deryl lunged to stop Tasmae. His foot hit the towel and he slipped, crashing into Tasmae and knocking her to the ground. Both their swords went flying. They rolled and he ended up on his back, with her knee in his gut and her dagger at his throat.

"You would both be dead!" she shouted. "I do not know how you make war on Earth, but when you fight on my world, you fight to win! If you have an opening, you follow through!"

"What?" his voice was hoarse with shock.

She leaned back and returned her dagger to her hairpiece. "I said you didn't follow through."

He shoved her off him and backed away, shaking his head. In fact, he shook everywhere. "I didn't come here to fight—not with you, not in a war. And if that's your plan for me, then you can go to hell!"

He turned and fled the room.

Tasmae shrieked in frustration. "What is it with you humans?" she shouted at the closing door, not sure why she was still speaking. "How will you defend yourselves when the invaders come?"

"Who said we're staying for your war?"

Tasmae spun at Joshua's hard, quiet voice and faced the tall dark man. He no longer cowered. In fact, she recognized his calm. Salgoud took on that same kind of calm just before calling her to task for something terrible and stupid she'd done.

Like she sometimes did with Salgoud, she stuck out her chin stubbornly. "You will remain until God's purpose for you here is fulfilled," she snarled.

"Really? Are you *really* sure that's what you believe? Or are you keeping us here until *your* purpose for us is fulfilled? Because you're afraid to deal with the next war alone?"

"How dare you!"

Joshua merely raised an eyebrow. "I think your people are a lot closer to God than mine. Maybe you should ask Him about it. And while you're at it, you might want to think about who it is you want by your side—the Ydrel or Deryl. I'm not sure that you can have both, anymore."

He bent down, picked up his towel, and pointed at her with it. "And the next time you want to make a point, don't do it with my life."

He strode away, whistling to Cochise, who settled down on his shoulders. The everyn sent one parting thought her way—not words, but anger and embarrassment at her actions.

She waited until the door folded shut behind them before letting out another, though more subdued, howl of frustration. Even the Beasts sided with the humans!

With a lifetime of habit, she picked up the swords and returned them to their places, but she shook inside. She'd hoped when she'd been thrown from the Remembrance that perhaps the mystery had been solved, the reason behind the Ydrel's appearance discovered. Instead, he revealed unimagined abilities, then spurned her—and his companion has the nerve to tell her she must choose—the oracle or the man.

The Ydrel, duty answered. Her people needed his wisdom. Yet he claimed to be just a conduit. And when they had touched...

The Remembrance. She clenched her fists in determination. *Gardianju had the answers. She must.*

Chapter Ten

Deryl took corridors at random until he found himself in an area he knew wasn't being used, and ducked into a room. Once the door closed behind him, he strengthened his shields—physical and mental—and pushed them outward until they surrounded him like a large bubble. Next, he "tied" that bubble to a ley line. Sure he wouldn't need to concentrate on keeping his thoughts away from others, he put his back against the wall, sank down, and gave in to his anguish.

"You didn't follow through." Why did she have to say that? Why those words? Could she be...?

A cold wave of panic swept over him and he fought to steady his trembling hands. *Stop it! She's not the Master. No one here is. I know that mind, and it's not anyone here.*

She's not satisfied with defense, part of him argued. *She'll press you to kill. First with swords, then with your mind. Isn't this how the Master worked?*

It was Spring Break, he suddenly remembered. He was home from boarding school. Aunt Kate had just had a miscarriage and was in bed, with Uncle Douglas tending her. Deryl had wandered around the house, lost and alone, until he stepped into the den and found his grandfather drunk and brooding. His eyes bored into Deryl with tangible hate.

"Devil's spawn!" he spat at him. "You've brought nothing but evil to this family since the day your father took my little girl. You think I don't know—I saw her change, you still in her. Ruined my lovely daughter— then you killed her. But for you, she'd be alive, successful... And now, you're the only progeny I get? Get away from me before I do what God should have done!"

Deryl had fled to his room and cried until he'd fallen into an exhausted sleep.

That was when the Master had come, offering to teach him to be strong, to take care of himself. He gave him a sword and taught him to use it. He spent hours talking to him, serious lessons he never heard in school. *The strong must rule the weak; it is their right and their responsibility. Strength lies in the body and the mind. Aggression is a tool, tempered by skill and cunning. You are chosen to walk a narrow path. Trust your skills. Trust my tutelage. Do not trust others. Do not trust technology. Trust yourself and me, but no one else.*

The Master was a stern teacher, but Deryl hadn't cared. He welcomed the distraction from his misery. In those dreamtime sessions, he was special. The Master gave him the attention he'd craved. As the Master became more demanding, Deryl became more determined to prove himself, to please him. Failure brought anger and shame, but success filled him with tangible joy.

Looking back now, Deryl could see how skillfully he had been manipulated. He hadn't been aware of it at the time, but the Master's dreamtime preaching had influenced his attitudes. At first, though, it had seemed to help: He went from broody and withdrawn to haughty, yet began to make friends. He threw himself into sports, quickly making up in skill and determination what he lacked in size. He developed a patronizing disdain for anyone who preached nonviolence. They were the weak; he'd take care of them.

He took fencing. His body retained the skills and reflexes that he had honed with the Master. His coach stepped him up to more aggressive freestyle lessons he normally reserved for seniors. He praised his competitiveness and even talked about the Olympics.

Deryl knew better now. The "competitiveness" he'd learned from the Master was predatory, a desire—a need—to draw blood. To wound. To kill.

Deryl ran his hands partway through his hair, clenched them into fists, and pulled.

You didn't know, he told himself. *You couldn't know. When it got out of control, you realized what had happened, and you stopped.* Nonetheless, he couldn't quite block the memory of his sparring partner with a long gash across his chest, blood staining his fencing tunic, nor of his own fierce joy at having done it. "Bloodlust" was a disturbingly accurate term.

You did stop yourself. You threw down your sword and never picked it up again.

Yet the Master did not leave him. Training had continued intermittently but with greater intensity. When his psychic powers started to manifest, the Master tried to train him to use them as another weapon. When he had refused, he'd been forced to fight monsters or take painful blows that resulted in real bruises he'd had to hide with long sleeves most of the year.

The pleasure the Master had forced upon him as rewards became equally intense, until Deryl had promised his obedience if only he'd not reward him so. Nonetheless, the feelings of wellbeing he pressed upon him instead had been equally addicting. The lectures, too, had continued until he couldn't even look at a television without falling into a seizure. The school doctor had called it epilepsy and added it to Deryl's growing list of mental problems.

Then, his fourth year at school, Deryl had lashed out at Perry, the senior who'd been tormenting him all year. When Perry gasped and collapsed, Deryl realized with horror that he had done more than wish him dead—he'd struck out with his Master-trained reflexes and stopped his heart. As the Master screamed at him to follow through, Deryl had started CPR—he hadn't known how to wish Perry alive—and when adults took over from him, had run upstairs and tried to kill himself.

Deryl pulled his hands from his hair and looked at his arms. He'd managed to slice both wrists properly, but he'd forgotten to lock the bathroom door. Again, he had not followed through.

So instead of dead, you ended up institutionalized. Maybe that was a good thing, after all. There were demons in his soul, hidden insanities that he could never let out. Maybe he didn't deserve freedom.

Deserved or not, you have it. So what are you going to do about it? demanded a voice that sounded annoyingly like Joshua's.

He could never let Tasmae convince him to fight.

Defense, he thought. *Teach them the shields for defense. She's right; children can learn this. Save lives; don't take them.*

And stop this war. The thought came unbidden, but he filed it away to think on later.

The memories behind him for the moment, his mind began to still. He used a trick Joshua had taught him and channeled his negative feelings out of his body and into the ground. His quaking eased. He took a cleansing breath, disconnected his shields from the ley line and pulled them back into himself. He stood, took another breath, and went in search of Joshua.

He found him in the healer's den, laughing as the healer they'd met before held his hands over his.

"That is so cool!" Joshua exclaimed.

"What's going on?" Deryl asked.

"Hey!" Joshua turned a big smile to him. "Come here! Terry—show him! This is way cool! Put your hands like this." He held them palms up.

Deryl complied, and Terry hovered his hands over Deryl's and concentrated.

"Feel that?"

Deryl shrugged. "Kind of a tingle."

His friend snorted. "Please! That's like comparing 'Twinkle Little Star' to Mozart!"

Terry laughed and backed away. "Psychic or not, Joshua has healing ability. I'm trying to teach him. Perhaps he has come to us to learn."

Deryl blinked. Neither he nor Joshua had thought of that; of course, he didn't really believe had a God-given 'purpose,' anyway. Still.

"About that. I'm sorry about earlier," he told Joshua.

"What? Storming out on Tasmae? I was right behind you, dude. She was out of line."

Terry motioned him to sit, and took a seat himself. "It could be the Remembrance. You aren't supposed to come out of it until it releases you. Her healer is worried. Right now, she is...tainted by the memories. And even when released, few recover from their experience of this particular Remembrance."

"No?" Joshua asked. "Why not?"

"Gardianju was..." Terry stopped to consider his words.

But Deryl knew. "Insane," he whispered.

Terry nodded. "I feel that means something different to your people. For us, insanity is not just a personal mental state. It can pass through mental contact."

"A contagion." Deryl resisted the urge to wrap his arms around himself. He stared at his hands clasped in his lap. Silence stretched.

Deryl could feel Joshua trying to not look his way.

"So, if it's a disease—an actual illness—to you, you can heal it, right?" Joshua asked.

Terry, too, looked at his hands, fingers moving as if over a wound. "It's too dangerous. We isolate the person; they survive—or not—according to God's will."

I did this. Deryl hugged himself and closed his eyes. "And Tasmae? Will she?"

Terry shrugged. "It is different with Remembrances, but it is said no Miscria survives the encounter unchanged."

Joshua set a hand on his shoulder. Deryl forced out a breath and unclenched his teeth.

"Slow down," Joshua said. "What do you mean unchanged? They're haunted by the memories but otherwise able to function? They end up gibbering in the corner? What?"

Terry watched Deryl with concern. "Ydrel, you do not know?"

Deryl shook his head.

Then he knew, knew as all Kanaan knew in a composite memory/warning. Barin, huge and heavy in the sky. The Miscria, unkempt and wild eyed, "screaming" at the planet while around her plants wilt, crops fail, people and animals falter and collapse around her.

Leave us! Go Away! Move! The more she screams, the further the blight spreads—

Deryl tore himself away. "Why is Leinad making her do this?" Deryl exploded.

"It's not his choice."

"What?" Joshua demanded.

"She goes insane and takes out half the planet." Deryl gasped and tried to catch his breath. *I caused this. I caused this.*

"*What?*"

"People, animals—even the grass! Then, then she..." He couldn't say it. He placed his hands over his nose and mouth and breathed slowly, trying to halt his hyperventilating.

Terry took up the tale, his voice soothing, as if to a scared child. "She dies, but afterwards, there is recovery and a long period of peace. For many years, Barin keeps itself aloof. Then, the cycle starts anew, the Miscria are chosen, and eventually one must sacrifice herself."

"Not this time!" Deryl stood up and looked at his friend, the psychiatric intern. "I know your purpose."

Chapter Eleven

Deryl stood on the slight outcropping of the cliff cave and looked over the scene with satisfaction. On the opposite side, archers worked in the caves, building natural blinds by transplanting the scraggly bushes that grew along the sides of the cliff. Ropes disguised as vines ran from the caves to the top of the mesa, some for climbing, some for hauling weapons down or injured up.

Beside him, Salgoud watched a vine that lowered a bush to one of the caves. He frowned, and Deryl knew he was worried that in battle, the motion of the vines would alert the Barins to the archers' locations.

Deryl projected an image of a quiver of arrows being lowered slowly, with frequent stops at varying moments. It would be noticed by someone with the leisure to watch, but in battle, could easily go unnoticed, especially if the quiver were camouflaged. He further added an image of the archers in camouflage uniforms and face paint, all but invisible, until they started shooting—and if they timed the shots right, the Barins would have a difficult time pin-pointing them.

He felt Salgoud's grudging approval, followed by his doubt about how effective these tactics would be in general. Not everywhere had such convenient cliffs.

Convenient. Deryl snorted. The forty-foot climb down to the tiny ledge had been one of the most harrowing experiences of his life—and he'd had plenty.

Once on the outcropping, he'd been relieved to find it bigger than it had looked from above, but it was still too narrow for his taste. He had a dizzying image of standing on the ledge of a skyscraper, looking thirty-three stories down, wind whipping his hair and threatening to sweep him off—

He leaned back, trying to ignore the lurch in his stomach. Those were not his memories, he reminded himself.

Salgoud glanced at him, but Deryl hid his feelings behind his shields. Instead, he replied that the ideas used here—camouflage, hide-and-ambush, attacks from angles the enemy didn't expect—could be applied anywhere. He never could get Tasmae to understand camouflage in the Netherworld. She kept insisting that the enemy would *know* they were there. Now, he understood the attitude: As psychics, Kanaan had the natural ability to *know* where something was.

But the Barins aren't psychic. They have to depend on their eyes. You know, Salgoud, when you practice, even the Barin team acts like Kanaan. They need to act like Barins—with the same limitations. Then you'll see for yourself that you have a natural advantage you should be using.

YOU HAVE A NATURAL ADVANTAGE OVER THOSE AROUND YOU. USE IT! The words of the Master came echoing back into Deryl's mind and he suppressed a shudder that he should be repeating that advice. *Just because he was an evil manipulating megalomaniac doesn't mean he was wrong.* He glanced at Salgoud, relieved to find him focused on relaying the Ydrel's ideas to his people, and not on him.

Get with the program, Ydrel. Concentrate! Deryl stepped forward out of the shadows to see how well he could spot the now-hidden archers hunkered down in the holes in the cliff walls—

—holes in the walls. Spiders crawling out of the holes in the walls. They're coming after me—

—They're after me. They want the secrets I know. I'll never give in, never! I'll die first. I'll kill—

—kill them all. Who do they think they are? Don't they know I am God? I'll make them bow down or they can die, the insignificant—

—Insignificant. That's what I am. No wonder no one wants me. Why didn't they just let me die? Why'd they stop me from jump—

—jump. I could, you know. It's okay. I can fly—

A hand on Deryl's shoulder jerked him back to reality, and he spun, causing Salgoud's grip to tighten lest he fall. He realized with a start that he'd been poised on the edge of the cliff. His heart thundered in his chest.

Voices. Images. Feelings. Vaguely familiar. Not his. And they'd struck without warning. That hadn't happened with such intensity since he'd first been committed, even before his transfer to SK-Mental. What was going on?

He searched Salgoud's face. Had he realized what had happened?

Fortunately, Salgoud had picked up on his fear, but not the thoughts behind it, and had come to his own conclusions. He peered over the edge and spoke in English. "It's not the fall that's so bad, but the sudden stop at the bottom."

Deryl laughed incredulously. "We have the same joke on Earth."

"So our people share something. Not all are comfortable with heights. Let us see the caves from the other side. If you wish, you may bind yourself to me." He made the offer matter-of-factly.

Although grateful for his concern, Deryl nonetheless shook his head. He'd come down halfway on his own. He could handle the rest solo, too. Better not to show weakness to the commander-in-chief of the world's defenses.

He took a firm grip on the rope and lowered himself over the edge, and all the thoughts about voices or the Master vanished in the need to get to the ground in one piece, avoiding any "sudden stops at the bottom."

With effort, Tasmae pulled herself away from the drooping fronds of the Remembrance, away from the anguish and confusion. She looked around for the person who she thought had set a hand on her shoulder; but finding no one, she sank back onto her heels, then fell to one side, curling up into a tight ball of misery. Images and emotions continued to overtake her: spiders and people who hated her, feelings of unnatural power and of falling into endless night.

Helpless against them, she was dimly aware of Leinad and the healer watching her, even more aware of how neither offered her aid or support. Loneliness and fear crashed down on her. Sobs escaped her throat.

I'm not ready for this! I don't know what to do—no one taught me how to handle this. Did my mentor know? Did it die with her? Why didn't you teach me?

Tasmae grabbed her hair, pulling at the crown, as if she could tear the experiences out with each yank. She remembered the agony of first experiencing the pain and motions of Kanaan. How nothing those were. *There's too much—too many emotions, too many insanities. Too much!*

Too much crowding her. The walls too close, cold and windowless, square and an unnatural pink. She wanted to run, and couldn't. Her arms wanted to wrap themselves around her waist. Lying on her side, she tried to rock.

She thought of the other Miscrias, screaming uncontrollably, falling unconscious for weeks, forever changed. *It's happening to me! No, worse. I'm half-trained, half-skilled, all alone. No one will help me.*

Stop it, she scolded herself. *I may be a half-trained Miscria, but I am a fully trained warrior. I will fight this! I am not alone. My people are here, and they need me. The Season of War approaches—there is no time for self-indulgences of pity.*

A wave of despair washed over her but she fought to its surface. *They need me. The Ydrel is here. Deryl. I must find out what it means.*

The panic died, leaving exhaustion. She reached for the Remembrance, but her hand trembled violently and she let it drop. Her tears had stopped; her eyes felt gritty and oh-so-tired. She closed them. She felt her responsibilities call to her, but she couldn't make herself move. Maybe if she just rested a moment...

She sensed a stern command to wake up and felt the toe of Salgoud's boot dig into her side. She rolled over on the hard ground, psychically muttering a plea for just a few more minutes. They'd marched half the night...taken shelter in this cave. It was so cold and close and the rosy color of the rocks frightened her for some reason. She hadn't been able to sleep before, but was unwilling to wake now. A rock pressed into her side.

Salgoud's urgings sharpened. She had a duty. She was the Miscria, and a warrior for her people. She had no time for self-indulgence.

Again, she protested, shifted away from the rock, which had dug into her painfully. Salgoud's boot found the same spot. Pain lanced through her, tearing her side, a ripping of the earth—

Tasmae's eyes snapped open. An earthquake! She reached out with her powers to heal the wounded land, but she was too drained from the Remembrance. The earth did not obey her command, refused to be gentled by her psychic touch. She sent out an alert, but the shielded room rebounded it upon her. She turned to Leinad and the healer, but they were as shielded as the room.

"Please!" she rasped. "An earthquake—in the sea— a tsunami—the villages on the coast must be warned!"

She watched them look at each other, surprised at her coherence, suspicious of her words.

"Listen to me!" she said desperately. "They have to be warned. They have to run!" She forced herself up. The room spun and her knees threatened to buckle, but she'd fight the two watchers and escape this room if she had to. "I have to tell them."

Tell me, the healer finally said. *I will relay the message.*

Tasmae leaped upon the offer, ignoring the healer's fear. She shared the location of the earthquake, the movement of the waves as they grew to deadly strength, the villages that lay in their paths. She watched, trembling, as the older woman relayed the information. After a moment, the older woman nodded. *It is done. The villages have been warned. It is evening there and the boats are in. All should be safe. Rest now, but you must continue.*

The healer returned to her seat against the wall and fell into a cleansing trance.

Tasmae staggered the few feet to her sleeping mat and lay upon it. She felt Leinad's worry. Something had gone wrong again. Twice now, she had ended the session prematurely and recovered enough to be coherent, even to perform her duty. That had never happened before that they knew of.

This has been thrust upon me out of time. I should do this in the Season of Calm, not now. She rebelled against the interference to her duty.

She felt the building tsunami as if it were of her own blood and turned her meager energies to her own cleansing, banishing the warnings now that they had been recognized and dealt with. Even as she did, she realized how close those warnings had come to being useless. She opened herself to the Divine, thanking God that the healer had agreed to send out the warnings, then reaching out for strength and wisdom for what lay ahead.

The disasters would only get worse. She knew that from her own experience and the experiences of the other Miscria. If the Remembrance's pull became stronger, would she be unable to sense them in time?

She looked around the room. Her eyes saw a regular sleeping room, large and airy with curved green-gray walls. Yet her mind kept insisting it was cold, sharply cornered, and pink. If she returned to the Remembrance, that would become her reality.

She shivered.

Deryl was climbing down the cliff when his vision blurred and he imagined himself back in the high intensity ward at SK-Mental. Then pain lanced his side.

He let go of the rope.

Too disoriented to remember his shields, he hit the ground hard, crying out in real pain as landed in a bush. His uniform kept the brambles from scratching him, but clambering out, he discovered it did not protect him from bruised ribs. He ended up on hands and knees—or rather, elbows and knees. His hands stung with tears and rope burns.

Someone grasped his shoulders and helped him sit. He tried to smile his thanks at the healer, but the grin turned to grimace as she laid hands on him. In a moment, he could breathe more easily. That's when he realized he was shaking.

Enough. You are not a warrior. Deryl felt her disdain, not for him, but for the way the warrior class expected everyone to have their prowess. She directed him to go to the baths to soak his bruises, and he felt her wishing for the same herself.

A stallion with a gentle demeanor carried him home, and he went straight to the baths, his mind focused on the strange visions. *First, the thoughts of fellow clients at SK-Mental's H-I ward, then the appendicitis? No, wrong side. What, then? And why now?*

Tasmae drowned in cold, heavy waters; bathed in fire; was torn from the inside. The whole time, images and emotions pounded up on her: anger and hate, despair and confusion, passion and ambition.

Make it stop! Make it stop! Makeitstop!

That's enough! her warrior self shouted into the maelstrom. *Gardianju! Tell me what this means. We don't have time for this.*

Too many signals, all in conflict. She hung by a thread over an abyss, but when she blinked, it turned into a padded pink box. She screamed and tried to climb.

The rope snapped.

She fell.

Tasmae was again flung from the Remembrance, this time full of adrenalin. Taking advantage of her guardians' surprise, she dashed from the room.

She ran through the empty compound thinking only that the walls were too close, the air too heavy, the shadows full of phantoms poised to ambush. She cried with delight to see the sun burning bright. She drank in its heat.

A unicorn waited at the door.

Despite muscles that felt bruised and hands that felt raw, she threw herself onto his back and let him carry her to an open field.

Once there, however, she panicked at being alone with the images left from the Remembrance. She couldn't make herself go back, either. Leinad would take her, by force, if necessary, and make her complete the Remembrance.

I can't let him, she'd thought wildly, *I can't.*

She couldn't be alone, and she couldn't seek out anyone Kanaan. Not like this. Contaminated with the insanities of Gardianju, she couldn't risk touching someone's mind now. *She* was barely handling it, and it was part of her talent. No healer would touch her, no friend offer comfort.

Her mind reeling, she slid from the unicorn's back and sat upon the ground, legs crossed, arms wrapped around her stomach, rocking slightly. She didn't know why she was doing it. She couldn't make herself stop. The unicorn nuzzled her gently, sending a cautious query, but she didn't respond. She was trapped. Alone.

Suddenly, an everyn dove out of the sky and landed beside her, wheedling its way onto her lap. *No, sister*, he told her. *You are never alone.*

Another everyn joined, then another and another, until she was surrounded by a dozen or more, until her lap and arms were full of small dragon-like creatures, their cheeks stroking her skin, wings enveloping her. Carefully, they teased the tortured memories of Gardianju from her, replacing them with affection and reassurance.

We are the first of the Greater Beasts and brothers to the animals; share the chaos with us. We can handle it. It is our God-sent talent, our avocation, and our joy. Take our aid, sister. Accept our love.

They guided her through a cleansing, led her gently to Divine Love. Words floated through her mind: *Mercifully guard my every thought and grant that I may always watch for Your light, and listen to Your voice, and follow Your gracious inspirations. I cling to You and give myself to You and ask You, by Your compassion to watch over me in my weakness...*

She blinked, suddenly aware of her surroundings. Not only everyn surrounded her now: Unicorns and some lesser beasts had joined the circle of love and support. A large wolf had shoved his way through enough to lay its shaggy head upon her lap, and she scratched its ears gratefully. Normally, they were solitary creatures, feral and sometimes dangerous. She thought she knew which images it had absorbed for her sake.

It tolerated one more scratch and took off with an explosion of motion that sent several everyn flying and squawking in protest. She found herself laughing, and thanked the beasts who had saved her from herself and helped her back to sanity. Then she closed her eyes again, gave her gratitude to God, and felt His love in reply.

The words came back to her. Sometimes, the Miscria were given words, like the recitation to Call the Ydrel. But these were not from the Remembrance, or from Deryl. Even the accent was different.

Joshua. Tasmae rose and asked the unicorn to take her to the human.

After half an hour, sweat ran down Deryl's face in rivulets and dampened his hair, and still he had no answers. However, he did feel physically better. He rose, took a quick dip in the pool—shockingly cool after the hot spring—and dressed. He grabbed some food, searched out Joshua in his mind, and headed for the unicorn fields. He might no longer be in a mental institution, but he could use the opinion of a psychologist right now, even if he was an intern.

Deryl found Joshua in the field, brushing the neck of a unicorn and the others crowded around, eager to have their turn. He was humming, and when one of the unicorns bumped him impatiently, he laughed as he told him to get in line with the rest.

"So this is where you hide?" Deryl called as he approached.

"Hey! You found me out," he called over his shoulder as he made a few short strokes around the horn. "Here." Joshua reached into the messenger bag slung over his shoulder and pulled out a second brush. He tossed it to Deryl. "There's a whole herd waiting to be groomed—again, mind you. Not that you could be any more beautiful, could you, girl?" he cooed at the mare he was tending.

The barrel-chested, broad-horned mare turned her head, careful of her horn, and nuzzled Joshua. He gave her a kiss on the nose, murmuring to her.

Deryl snorted as he gave the nearest unicorn a few disinterested swipes. "You flirt with horses like you flirt with nurses."

"You don't think this fine lady deserves it? Still, I think you've had enough for the day, huh, Glory, my baby? How about we go for a quiet ride?"

Deryl didn't feel that much better. He gave the unicorns a bow. "Actually, if you don't mind, can we sit and talk?"

Joshua shrugged and put the brushes in his satchel. The unicorns wandered off, some breaking into a run. Cochise gave a chirrup and flew after them. Joshua laughed. At least someone was enjoying himself.

They went to a shaded tree, and Deryl lowered himself carefully onto the mossy ground. The thick, spongy material gave like a pillow, and he sighed. It was a physical and a mental comfort. He recognized the moss from the shaded glen in the Netherworld where he and

Tasmae used to converse. She had designed the glen f from her own memories, but it still surprised him to find the moss in an area that should get a lot of sun.

"You all right?" Joshua sat down beside him.

"Yeah, just sore. I fell off one of the cliffs this morning."

"What? Are you sure you're okay?"

Deryl smiled at his friend's concern. Even if it wasn't true, it seemed a long time since anyone had been concerned about his wellbeing without having an ulterior motive. "Just aches and bruises," he reassured his friend. "I actually landed in a bush. The healer took pity on me and sent me back to soak out the kinks. Did you notice the hot spring in the bath?"

"Oh, yeah. Very nice," Joshua said with feeling. "Terry and I hung out there a while today."

"How's the healer training?" Deryl asked. Suddenly, that seemed more important than his petty problems.

Joshua sighed. "Deryl, I'm not psychic."

"But you can feel the healing energy, sense it like music! And when I was catatonic, you got into my mind and brought me out," he pressed.

"I don't know how I did that! That's never happened before—not to me, not to anyone in the whole recorded history of NLP. You may have done it."

"Still!" Deryl started, but Joshua cut him off.

"Even so, psychology—especially the kind I'm trained in—depends on understanding body language, especially eye movement. I don't know the Kanaan signals."

"Well, figure it out!"

"Fine!" Joshua threw his hands in the air. "Right away! Want to tell me how when I can't even tell if someone is thinking or talking to someone else or receiving a visual thought from someone? Want to tell me how to accomplish in a few days what took decades of research on Earth? Got any answers for me, O Great Ydrel?"

"We have to do something!" Deryl yelled, fighting the twist in his heart. "I'm not going to lose her!"

"You? Please, *please* tell me you're not falling in love with her." Joshua rubbed his forehead as if expelling a headache.

Deryl opened his mouth to protest, but nothing came out.

Joshua watched him with narrowed eyes. "Have you *done* anything about it?"

"What?" Deryl asked, even as he plucked the implication from Joshua's mind. "No! I, no…"

"Good. Because according to Terry, aliens carry their own kind of insanity. They've been making an exception for teleping with the Great Ydrel—"

"Stop calling me that!"

"—but *Deryl* might be a whole 'nuther story. Not to mention, we don't know anything about their idea of dating."

The shakes returned. Deryl leaned back against the tree and stared at the sky shimmering through the leaves. "I don't know what's happening to me."

He meant the visions, the confusion, the feeling of panic in his gut, but for once, his friend totally missed the signals.

Joshua smiled at him, and his tone gentled. "Look, just remember that we're out of here in a week—and there are plenty of beautiful Earth women."

And that pain in my side, like the tearing of the land. He latched onto the diversion. "Like Clarissa, you mean?" They'd met Clarissa when he was in the hospital recovering from his appendicitis. Maybe the pain was a transference?

But why would I compare it to the land? Forget it now. Think about Clarissa: sweet and blond, turned up nose that wrinkled when she laughed.

"There ya go! She was fine lady. Played a mean game of Uno."

"Not a half-bad kisser, either."

Joshua snorted. "How would you know that, chaperoned as you were all day?"

"No one thought I needed a babysitter at night."

Joshua groaned and smacked his forehead. "I was responsible for you. I'd have been so fired if anyone had found out!"

"That's why I didn't mention it. Anyway, it wasn't that big a deal. She'd sneak across the hall to talk around midnight, and the night before she was released, we made out."

"And?"

Suddenly he felt uncomfortable for whole new reasons. "And can we change the subject?"

Joshua raised his brows at him, but leaned back on one arm. "Yeah, sure. How far did you drop, anyway?"

"Twelve, maybe fifteen feet."

"No way! You're lucky all you got were bruises. How come you didn't just levitate?"

Deryl burst out laughing.

"No, really. You can move objects. Why not use telekinesis on yourself?"

Deryl fell silent, thinking. Could he? How? Maybe...

Pushing away from the earth, but not hard; just a gentle nudge, like pushing on a pillow. The body floating, riding on that push.

"Whoa! That is so cool! How are you doing that?"

The moment Joshua exclaimed, Deryl lost control. He flung his arms back to catch himself, landing on his elbows and behind. He yelped and rolled onto his stomach. "It takes a lot of concentration!" he chided, rubbing his abused tailbone.

"Sorry."

Deryl sighed as he sat back up. "I probably wouldn't have been able to catch myself from falling, anyway."

"Why did you fall?"

"Slipped."

"Yeah," Joshua said in response to Deryl's terse reply. "And the rest of the story?"

Before Deryl could explain, Tasmae thundered up to them on a unicorn.

Chapter Twelve

When she saw Deryl with Joshua, she felt her heart leap, and a funny yearning well up in her. She pushed it aside. Just one more thing she didn't understand.

She could not, however, avoid his concern.

"You're not done, are you?" he asked.

She shook her head. The Beasts had helped calm her, and she didn't want to think about returning to the Remembrance yet. Besides, she had a new mystery to unravel.

"Explain this to me, Joshua," she said and repeated the words she had been given.

Joshua crossed his arms, and his brows knitted with confusion. "The Novena to the Holy Spirit. But how'd you know it?"

"That's what I'd like to know."

Joshua gave Deryl an accusing glare, but he just shrugged. His emotions, though gentle, played upon her strained senses. Concern, confusion…. She understood those. However, he also felt pressure—specifically, about something Deryl wanted from him. Something that involved her.

Deryl, on the other hand, had closed himself off. Nonetheless, she got the impression of the eye of a hurricane: fully calm, fully still. Potentially dangerous.

But whatever Deryl expected, Joshua knew it, and she could sense that he didn't think he'd have much choice but to comply.

She huffed in frustration and started running her fingers through her tangled hair, yanking when she got to the tangles.

"Take it easy. Here." Joshua reached into his pack, pulled out a wide-toothed comb, brushed it off against his pants, and handed it to her. "How come you didn't put it up before you left?"

She didn't want to explain her hasty escape.

"'Kay," he said after the silence stretched. "Never mind. You're here now, and this is a safe place."

Both she and Deryl snorted.

Joshua gave them both a stern glance. "It's dangerous for you to telep with other Kanaan right now, right? That's why they isolate you until you finish the Remembrance?"

Tasmae blinked, surprised. "Yes. How did you know?"

Joshua nodded. "Terry told me as much. But that's obviously not working for you. Maybe Gardianju's Remembrance is too much to handle alone? But there's never been anyone to share it with, to, you know, talk it out? Help make sense of it?"

She thought of the Beasts. They'd relieved the pressure, but offered no insight. Joshua was right; the Miscria had no one to help them.

"Until now," Deryl breathed. He grinned at his friend, and Tasmae felt through his armor a hint of happiness, and smugness.

"Until now," Joshua confirmed. He did not share Deryl's happiness, but she felt his determination. He took the comb from her hands. "So, come on. Let us help you."

Joshua had no idea how to enter uptime and get in sync with Tasmae's thought processes, so he decided to try an old tactic he used on Rique's sister, and started to work at her tangled hair with quick, deft strokes. Rique had teased him about being Sabrina's hairdresser, but he'd gotten her through a lot of high school angst that way—and they'd had a pretty nice summer romance when she turned sixteen.

Exactly why he wasn't sharing this duty with Deryl.

Tasmae didn't say anything for a long while, and even Deryl seemed distracted, his eyes focused on an indefinite nothingness, so finally, Joshua said, "You've got a lot of hair. It must take forever to brush."

"Miscria do not cut their hair."

"Really? Why not?" He finished one long plait, and ran his fingers through the rest to separate another. It felt soft and warm, but body-temperature warm rather than sunlight-heated warm.

"It is of Kanaan now. It gives me strength."

"Like Sampson?" Joshua regarded her tresses with new respect.

"Sampson?" Tasmae repeated.

"From our sacred Scriptures. Sampson's hair made him strong until Delilah convinced him to cut it off. That reminds me, though. 'Kanaan' sounds a lot like Canaan, which is a very special place in the Old Testament. So who named your planet and why?"

"We use words only for your benefit, Joshua. It's quite noisy when you're around."

Joshua picked up her teasing tone and chuckled. "But that didn't come from me, and while I did give Terry his name, I'd have never thought of Salgoud."

"That is Barin. Salgoud is a kind of fighting devil?" She paused, brow knitted and shrugged at Deryl.

Deryl frowned, but this time in concentration. "It doesn't translate well. —ud means leader, salg is the name they use for Kanaans, but it's kind of insulting, like demon or subhuman or abomination. And the 'o' denotes a certain amount of viciousness."

"So, 'leader of vicious subhumans'?" Joshua said.

"More like 'vicious leader of the demon-spawned subhuman abominations,'" Deryl deadpanned.

Joshua blanched. "And he's *okay* with that?"

"Of course," Tasmae replied. "To us, it is a mere arrangement of sounds without real meaning."

Joshua nodded. It was like when someone called him "nigger." He blew it off because the word said little about him personally but spoke volumes about the other person's attitudes. "Oreo" bothered him more, because it suggested that who he was on the inside was somehow wrong because of his race. "Incompetent," however; that one really bugged him.

Tasmae was saying that Salgoud's name was tactically useful. "The Barins fear it. Our warriors have learned when they can secure a retreat by merely chanting his name."

"That is cool! All right, so why isn't your planet called Salgan? Where'd Kanaan come from?"

"That would be my doing," Deryl grinned sheepishly. "I think the Miscria must have pulled other things from my mind somehow."

"Many things have their names from the Ydrel," Tasmae chimed in. "Spot. Everyn. Even Miscria."

"Really," Joshua said slowly. "Kanaan I get, then. 'Bondfriend,' makes sense, kind of descriptive. Even 'everyn,' since they're not wyvern-sized, though if you'd read Anne McCaffery, you might have called them fire lizards. But where'd 'Miscria' come from?"

"Something my mother told me."

Deryl turned away then, again unreadable, and Tasmae turned her head just enough to look at him.

Joshua suppressed a moan. Bad enough Deryl had feelings for her, but if she returned them? He set his hands on either side of her head and turned it forward again, hoping she'd think it was so he could brush it more easily. Regardless, she crossed her arms and let Joshua play with her hair, and he felt her try to relax into his soothing ministrations.

Tasmae's attention brushed feather-soft against Deryl's shields, but caught in the memories of his mother, he didn't notice.

"I told you my mom was psychic, right? Well, she told me that one day, a spirit would contact me—the Miscria. I was supposed to obey it. She thought it might be my guardian angel; what a joke."

Deryl laughed, a bitter sound even to his own ears. Tasmae reached out to touch his arm. He tensed against the urge to flinch away and redoubled his shields against her.

"What happened to your mother?"

Deryl looked across the field, where a colt played under the watchful eye of its mother. "She was protecting me from a...a boarder we'd taken in. He got angry and killed her."

Deryl didn't look their way and tried hard to keep his tone matter-of-fact, but he still felt Joshua's sudden pity. The unicorns ran off, and he followed them with his gaze, forcing himself to see them rather than his mother crashing against the table edge and slithered to the ground. Where was his guardian angel then?

Tasmae spoke softly. "My parents were killed protecting our training ground. I'd just come into my Miscria talent. I was not allowed to fight."

"I didn't even know how, then. If I could go back..." He heaved a shaky sigh, releasing his emotions, and added in a more natural voice. "So that's where Miscria came from. 'Ydrel' was something my mom called me now and then. I never knew why; I figured it came from my father. I don't know about 'Tasmae,' however."

"Another Barin word, given to me in the last war. A tasmae is a small but fierce animal on their planet that's hard to catch and wreaks great damage."

"Told you," Joshua deadpanned.

Deryl burst out laughing. It felt good.

"On Earth, we have an animal called the Tasmanian devil," Joshua started, "and there's a cartoon—"

"No! Let me! I loved Looney Tunes when I was a kid." Stifling giggles, he teleped an image to her.

Tasmae gaped in astonishment. "And I gave you this impression?"

"Well..." Deryl started teasingly.

Joshua smacked him with the comb. "It's a pun, a play on words. Tasmae. Tasmanian devil. Tasmanian she-devil. Humans have lots of fun with words and sounds. Puns. Word games. Poetry. Songs—words put to music." Seeing Tamae's curiosity, he started singing one of Chipotle's songs.

Tasmae frowned. "So it's not another of your languages? It's not to communicate information?"

"Oh, sure," Joshua answered, and when Deryl looked dubious, sang, "A B C D E F G. Or, if you want to get more technical..." He sang another ditty, this one a rather technical one about C-sections.

"You made that up?" Deryl asked, impressed.

Joshua gave Tasmae's hair one last pass with the comb, then ran his hands over it, settling it into place. "Yup, for Sachiko when she was taking that Procedures for the Reproductive Systems class. But I do it all the time. Humans sing for lots of reasons, Tasmae. To memorize information, to entertain, to commemorate an event—" He sang a verse from "Battle of New Orleans." "—to express an emotion—"

Something pulled at Deryl, something he couldn't quite focus on. It made him lightheaded and closed his eyes against the dizziness. "To alter reality," he murmured, though he didn't realize he was speaking. "To bend the world to your will."

Then, the feeling was gone. He blinked as if waking up from a dream.

Joshua was giving him an odd look.

"What?" he asked his friend.

Before Joshua could reply, Tasmae asked, "Why did you sing while confined?"

Joshua gave him a long look before answering Tasmae's question. "Comfort. I was scared, worried, lonely; after a while, bored. I sang whatever came into my mind at the time. Lots of them were religious songs, prayers—asking for help and comfort, mostly, but there are a lot for praise, too." He sang the chorus from "Sing to the Mountains" to illustrate his point. "And there are love songs—for God, for others, wanting to be loved, having loved and lost—"

"But it is not a language," Tasmae pursued. She twisted to face Joshua, her brows knit in concentration.

Deryl couldn't help but smile. Many times, he'd been put under the same interrogation. It was nice to watch her apply it to someone else for a change.

And just to watch her. Her hair, detangled and sleek, settled itself on her shoulder with an alluring curve before draping down her back. His hands curled into fists against the desire to reach out and touch it. Her dark eyes shone with interest, her lips pursed slightly, her whole self so keenly directed on Josh that Deryl found himself mesmerized. It wasn't beauty, per se; it was too intense, too focused. Yet it drew him.

"Yes and no," Joshua was saying. "The language—I mean, the words themselves—are separate. There are hundreds, maybe thousands of languages on Earth, and each can be put to music. However, the music can change the language—songwriters bend some rules, like grammar, in favor of the rules of rhythm and meter. Music can also alter the emotional element. Change the tone and tempo of a song and you can change the meaning without altering the words."

To demonstrate, Joshua sang the slow, jazzy version of "Blue Moon," then the rock-and-roll Beach Boys' version of the same song.

"How do you humans keep track of it all?" Tasmae finally demanded in frustration. Joshua laughed, and Deryl, broken from her spell, joined him. "How do you can understand each other?"

"We don't," Deryl told her, "not all of us, and not always. There are a lot of wars on our planet."

Deryl and Tasmae both fell into a broody silence.

Chapter Thirteen

Joshua cleared his throat. "Hey, language—communication—has also prevented a lot of wars, you know. And it's fun to play with words—and with music. It boggles my mind that you don't have music."

"No, we do," Tasmae corrected. "The Bondfriends have something similar, but not as complex. I think it is more language than your music, but music, our real music, is so different from yours. I'm not sure I could explain."

Again, she took on that look of fierce concentration, but this time it pointed inside as she tried to find the right alien words. "It is...spiritual? But not as your hymns. It is of our spirits. The song is always sung; how we sing depends on what we are doing, our talents, our mood. It is sometimes audible, usually psychic... I'm not explaining well. Your words are hard!"

"Why don't you demonstrate? Sing something."

She hesitated, suddenly reluctant, even ready to bolt. Joshua leaned back, giving her some physical space, but Deryl took her hands.

"It's all right. We're not Kanaan. Sing for us, please?"

She gazed into Deryl's eyes, and Joshua bit back the urge to groan. Had anyone else noticed? Maybe that was the real reason she was being occupied with the Remembrances.

He wanted to snatch their wrists and pull them apart, but he remembered how Rique's trying to separate him and LaTisha just drove him to her all the more. Deryl was even more willful and stubborn than he was. *Just keep it together, Josh. A few more days and we're out of here. You can help him control himself for a few days.*

Her hands still in Deryl's, Tasmae closed her eyes. A slight grin lightened her expression. Around them, the wind rustled in the trees, and birds broke into song. Then Tasmae joined them, her voice mimicking them, then moving into some kind of harmony, low notes, almost coyote or whale-like. Deryl relaxed, and Joshua noticed how lightly his hands clasped Tasmae's. *Maybe this music has a touch component, then?*

It was different, kind of interesting, but not what Joshua would call music. What he knew as music had patterns: time scales, beat and rhythm, sections that repeated. Even the healing power, which he likened to music, had pattern. Tasmae's song more resembled the wind in the trees, or a field overrun with wildflowers and weeds—lovely, even beautiful in some places, but without clear logic. His mind struggled to find an underlying melody, then gave up. If there was one, it was too big for him to grasp.

He looked at Deryl. The young man swayed, thoroughly caught up in Tasmae's "song," his mouth open and smiling slightly. His pupils had contracted so that they were mere dots in a sea of blue.

So there is a heavy psychic element. Suppressing a sigh, Joshua leaned back against a tree and shut his eyes, trying to release his preconceptions about music and enjoy what he could hear. The wind seemed to have picked up slightly and with his eyes closed, he could almost imagine that its light touch against his skin was part of the song.

Abruptly, Tasmae stopped singing. The wind died down. Even the birds went silent. Joshua opened his eyes in surprise at the sudden stillness.

Deryl, too, broke from his half-trance, delight shining in his eyes. "That was magical," he whispered, and Tasmae smiled. He turned to Joshua, a faint smile on his face, and Tasmae also turned to him expectantly.

Joshua shrugged. "It was...interesting. Really. I guess it loses something without the telepathic element."

Tasmae nodded, but Deryl cried in disappointment, "You didn't get any of it?"

"It was just sounds to me," Joshua half-apologized. "Don't worry about it."

Deryl continued to scowl. "It's not fair. It was so—it was just—amazing! What if I translated?"

Joshua sat up. "Tell me."

"I mean, what if I could help you, um, experience the song like, well, like I did?"

"You can't make me telepathic."

Or could he? Joshua suppressed a shudder at the thought. Even as a kid, he'd never thought telepathy would be cool, and after having worked with Deryl and all the problems his telepathy had caused him, he liked the idea even less.

"No, of course not, but I can get into your mind and give you the experiences. I did it with Isaac all the time, didn't I?"

"Yeah, well, that was a pretty special case..." Isaac had been an Alzheimer's patient at SK-Mental—a rotten place for him to be, in the opinion of Joshua and most of the staff, but his grandson was on the board of directors, and they hadn't been able to turn him down. Isaac had survived Auschwitz, and Deryl had "protected" Isaac from reliving those horrors (and himself from sharing them) by impressing upon him the illusion that he had been rescued by the underground. In the end, had Isaac known which memories were real?

"I'm not going to mess with your head. You'll know what's going on all the time. You'll just be able to understand the telepathic part, that's all. I promise."

"Why is this so important to you?"

"Because!" Deryl almost shouted. "Come on, Josh, I dragged you halfway across the universe; and I know I didn't intend to, but here you are, and you're stuck until I figure out how to get you back, and you've been so great about it for the most part. This is probably the most incredible, alien, thing we've come across so far and it's music, which you love. I just—I want to share it with you!"

Joshua's resistance weakened under his earnest gaze. "That great, huh?"

"Better!"

"All right—but I want to be able to stop if it gets too weird."

"Absolutely!" Deryl promised and clamped a hand on his wrist. On cue Tasmae began to sing. Joshua felt the wind pick up—

—And he was caught up in the wind, lifted and tossed gently like a fall leaf in a soft breeze. There was joy in the movement, and the joy was given to God as praise.

—He was a budding plant, opening itself to the nourishing sun, uncoiling blossom and leaves. There was beauty in the simple act of converting light into food and the beauty was a song of praise.

—A field of flowers, the wind playing over them. He was the flower and the wind and the grass and earth and song. The pattern was there, deep and complex. His human mind could never grasp it but his soul gloried in it and it was the Glory of the Lord.

—He was the wind, swirling

—Spinning

—Rotating around an axis as he described a near-circular ellipse around a brilliantly burning star. As he turned, he felt the heat of the sun and the cold of space wash over him. Around he danced, others circling him in his path. Friendly partners, the attraction between them strong, but comfortable. He felt their pulls upon him like gentle caresses. It was part of the dance, more of the song. It was good.

But another approached their path, tried to interfere with the dance. It pulled upon them. It brought discord, shattered the pattern, broke the verse. It yanked upon him. Something inside tore—

"Whoa! Stop!" Joshua snapped back into reality. He opened his eyes and saw Deryl and Tasmae watching him expectantly.

"What was that?" He demanded. The incredible joy had been destroyed by the final images, and with it, the peace he'd been feeling all day. His ribs ached with the memory of phantom pain, and he rubbed his side.

"A simple song of morning," Tasmae said, though her eyes darkened as she understood his expression.

"Simple?" Now that he was out of it, the pattern was again too complex for him to comprehend, though he felt he could just catch the verse of the wind if he listened hard enough. He'd never be able to listen to the wind in the same way again. "Simple?" He repeated, still slightly breathless. "What does being a planet have to do with morning?"

Tasmae looked at him with alarm. "What do you mean?"

He felt a little alarmed himself. "I'm telling you, I felt like I was a planet—literally. I was circling a sun, *I had moons*, and I felt like my ribs were pulling apart." He realized he sounded ridiculous. "It hurt!"

"That was not the song," Tasmae whispered, her face pale. "That was Kanaan."

Both she and Joshua turned to Deryl in askance.

He squirmed, but didn't say anything—to Joshua, at least. He kept throwing glances at Tasmae.

Joshua's temper flared. Something bizarre had just happened, had just happened to *him*, and he was not going to sit idly while they discussed it telepathically. "*Excuse* me! You want to tell me what's going on? In English? And don't you start rocking—I'm not doing therapy on you!"

Deryl had wrapped his arms around himself, straitjacket style, and had begun to move back and forth. With effort, he stopped, though his arms remained wrapped around his waist. "I'm sorry," he said quietly. "I didn't realize I'd..." He shut his eyes, shook his head.

Tasmae took up the explanation, though she was no more enlightening than he was. "There was an earthquake this morning."

"So?" he demanded, then something clicked. "Wait a minute—you mean that pain was *the earthquake*?"

She shook her head. "You must have sensed the aftershock from just a few minutes ago."

"Oh, come *on*! That doesn't make sense. You said you were singing about the morning. It's mid-afternoon."

"It is not part of the song."

"Then why did I feel it?"

Again, they looked to Deryl, who shook his head, bewildered.

She looked from him to Joshua, her eyes wild and frightened. "This was a bad idea."

She stood up and ran down the field.

"Taz!" Joshua called, not sure what he planned to say next. It didn't matter: A unicorn galloped up to her and in an easy motion, she swung onto his back and rode off.

Joshua rounded on Deryl. "Very smooth," he snarled. "How is she supposed to trust us now?"

But Deryl just stared after her.

Chapter Fourteen

Deryl whirled in circles through a star-strewn sky. Although he knew he was moving thousands of miles an hour, he did not feel the speed. It was a natural movement, a dance that brought coolness and warmth, darkness and light, night and day to those that made their home on him. It was good.

A grand menagerie of creatures called his body home. Sometimes, he felt the effects of their actions, mere tickles upon his skin. one, however, knew his needs and kept balance between them and the needs of those upon him. He knew her as Miscria. And it was also good.

But there were others, from the Intruder, the one who would pull him out of his perfect dance. They had killed their world—or had it already been dead? He did not know. He did know that they now sought him, like a virus seeks a new host. It was not good.

His Miscria and her kind fought to stop them. He felt their struggles, experienced the changes, mostly through his Miscria. His Miscria changed, too, though he did not understand why. It mattered not. As long as they kept the contagion at bay, he could concentrate on the dance, and on the ones that danced with him. Together they moved about the source of light. The interplay of distance and attraction between them flowed over him like a lover's caress. It was very good.

—Deryl danced with Tasmae, his hand on the small of her back, moving in slow circles. The attraction between them tingled through every nerve of his body. There was distance between them, too. The barriers that protected him from the minds of others, even from the memories of the lunatic ravings that had often invaded his mind while at the asylum, also kept Tasmae at bay. It was comfortable and safe, yet the attraction between them was strong and, at the moment, it was more exciting than frightening.

He pulled her closer. To his body. To his mind. Like a ghostly spirit, she flowed through his barriers.

In his sleep he hummed with pleasure.

Then the voices came.

Ten or twelve, he couldn't tell for certain. More than voices. Memories. Fantasies. Each lost in its own pain and delusion, unaware of him. Oh, but he was aware of them! They pulled at him, tearing him away from Tasmae, dragging him away from sanity. He felt Tasmae pull away, lurch closer, then get swept away by the confusion.

—The Intruder comes too near. It pulls at Kanaan and the moons. The moons jerk away, lurch closer, wobble in their paths. Balance is lost. Where once there was comfort and caress, now came pain. He feels himself tearing from the inside. Miscria!

—Tasmae! He searched for Tasmae as the fears, desires, and needs of a legion pressed upon him. Then one thought sliced through them all, like a powerful spotlight in the murky dark. It caught Deryl, pinning him in its painful light.

DERYL. YOU DID NOT FOLLOW THROUGH.

The Master! He froze, transfixed with fear. Out of the corner of his eye, he saw Tasmae caught in a similar beam. He wanted to scream for her to run, but his throat constricted, and all he could manage was a breathy whine.

WHY DO YOU FEAR ME, DERYL? I AM YOUR TEACHER. YOU ONCE TRUSTED ME.

Deryl couldn't move. Where could he run? Outside the light, the insanities of others waited to devour him and Tasmae.

—Kanaan Is pulled out of its path, struggled to regain balance. Deep beneath the ocean, its skin rips.

—WHY ARE YOU IN SUCH FEAR, DERYL? DID I NOT TEACH YOU HOW TO DEAL WITH THESE CREATURES? WHY DO YOU HIDE BEHIND BARRIERS WHEN THE PERMANENT SOLUTION IS SO SIMPLE?

The insanities hissed at his mind, formed a new barrier between Tasmae and him. A sword lay at his feet, but he didn't need it. He could cut a path to her with the power of his mind. With his thoughts, he could remove their threat permanently. Never again have anything, anyone, come between him and Tasmae, between him and anything he wanted.

A high breathy laugh escaped his lips. If only.

IT CAN BE, the Master hissed. LISTEN TO MY TEACHINGS. FOLLOW THROUGH. WIPE THEM OUT. HIDE NO LONGER. THEY ARE INSIGNIFICANT, AND THEY ARE BETWEEN YOU AND WHAT YOU WANT.

He focused. He knew them, knew each one's weakness. The Master was right.

No!

—Kanaan resists the Intruder's pull.

—THEY ARE NOTHING, DERYL. THEY ARE THE MONSTERS. REMEMBER THE MONSTERS, DERYL?

Fighting in the Netherworld, hideous creatures coming at him, tearing at him. They hurt him again and again. He had to fight. He reached out with his mind.

The voices surged toward him.

No! I won't do it!

—The Intruder tears at Kanaan. Brilliant flashes dot its surface. The contagion comes.

—STOP THEM, DERYL. STOP THEM ALL. FOLLOW THROUGH.

Follow through.

Follow through.

—He was thirteen. He stood in the hallway outside the counselor's office, betrayed, humiliated. Perry's friends laughed at him while the high school senior spoke in reasonable tones.

"You didn't think I'd let you get away with telling the counselor all those things, did you, Deryl? I had to defend myself."

All Deryl wanted was for the teasing and the hurtful practical jokes to stop. How could Perry tell all those lies? How could the counselor believe him?

How? Why not? Perry was the charismatic senior, the good student, the leader. Deryl was the one with "psychosocial issues."

The boys snickered. They'd keep at him. It'd be even worse now. His last chance for help had failed. The Master's voice rang in his head, disparaging.

YOU NEED NO HELP. DEFEND YOURSELF. THEY ARE THE MONSTERS. THEY ARE DEMONS. THEY ARE NOTHING.

He glared at Perry through tears of anger. It would be easy...

DO IT. KILL.

Perry's face, wide with shock, gasping, clutching at his chest, falling.

—A brilliant flash. Barin explodes into a million parts, falls.

—The voices and insanities between him and Tasmae are suddenly blown away by the force of his thoughts.

YES. FOLLOW THROUGH.

—A thousand meteors bombarde Kanaan as the remains of Barin strike it.

—"Perry! Omigod! Is he dead?"

—Tasmae blown away with the demons.

no

NO!

NOOOO!

"No!"

Deryl bolted upright in his bed, his scream still tearing from his throat. The suddenness of his awakening had chased the dream away; it lay hidden from his conscious mind, though he still felt its effects. His heart hammered in his chest, and he trembled with fright and excess adrenalin. He flopped back against the pillow, fighting to control his breathing while frantically trying to remember what had terrified him so. It was important!

He sat up, rested his head against his knees and willed himself to concentrate, despite the dread that coursed through him and made even his skin tremble. Something about Tasmae—and planets—and the voices—more than voices...

People out of control of their own minds. He could feel them, the pressure of a dozen personalities, some real and pleasing; others, imagined and desperate for dominance. Over themselves. Over him. They'd closed in and he hadn't been able to fight—

When he came back to himself, he was backed into the corner of his room. He remembered cowering this same way in the padded room of the high-intensity treatment ward at SK-Mental. With a cry of anguish, he stood and paced the room. Although large and sparsely furnished, he felt crowded and trapped.

He ran to the window, shoved it open, and scrambled through it into the night.

He crossed the compound and had gotten halfway to the gate before he caught hold of his panic and slowed to a stop. The dry, churned-up soil of the practice yard felt rough under his bare feet. He had on only loose sleeping pants, and the air cooled his panic-fevered skin. He inhaled deeply, the strange scents of alien night flowers tickling his nose. A musky odor permeated the scent, as if the ground still held the sweat of the warriors who had spent so many hours in practice there. The stars were again brilliant, yet Barin outshone them all. He heard the warbling call of some creature he did not recognize. Psychically, everything was quiet. The very differentness of it all comforted him.

I'm not trapped, he reassured himself. *I'm free. I can go anywhere I please. Do whatever I want. No one thinks I'm crazy, and no one has to know I was.*

Madness Unbound ✤ 157

Funny how the thought came so easily. It was immediately followed by the thought of how someone would react to seeing him walking around in his pajamas. Maybe they'd think he was nuts after all.

I ought to change clothes. He made no effort to move. He couldn't return to that room. Not yet. *Besides, they're not much different from sweats, and it's not like anyone's around to see me. Salgoud has all the warriors sleeping in the cliffs for practice.* The night was warm enough, and he was wide awake. He turned in a slow circle, trying to decide where to go.

He was equally distant from the perimeter wall as from the main building, but he hesitated to wander outside the gates. He didn't want to interfere with any nighttime exercises Salgoud might have planned, nor did he want to check. Even a psychic "peek" at the cliff area might alert Salgoud to him, and the general might invite him to join them.

Nonetheless, staying in the compound with the walls in front of him and the building behind didn't appeal, either. Despite the differences, the closed-in courtyard reminded him of the one just outside his room at SK-Mental. Even now, he couldn't shake off the feeling of being imprisoned against the world.

For a moment, he saw the familiar courtyard of the asylum, with its manicured lawns, resort-style umbrella'd tables and lawn chairs, and rows of trees and tall hedges that didn't quite hide the wall beyond. He remembered the building itself, two-story and brick, with five single-story wings radiating from the main building like splayed fingers.

He'd met Joshua in one of those wings, at that depressing birthday party his aunt had thrown for him: a banner with his name misspelled (Aunt Kate, at his grandfather's urging, insisted it be spelled the conventional way), the disgusting chocolate cake that he'd choked down because "normal" people like chocolate.

Poor Isaac with him because he couldn't stand leaving the old man alone to his terrifying memories and had caught him up in another fantasy of rescue and safety, his aunt and uncle watching him nervously as he played the part of freedom fighter and Isaac's protector and thinking that he was just as crazy as Dr. Malachai had been telling them...

No wonder I was so hostile Joshua Lawson, Star Intern. He'd circled him then, insulted him, sneered that Dr. Sellars had hired him to be Deryl's Summer Buddy as a birthday present, and tried to intimidate him. With one remark, Joshua had put him in his place. Then he'd helped him deal with his psychic problems, coached him on ways to show the others that he wasn't crazy, even told him that normal people could hate chocolate and put syrup in every hole of their waffle without being considered odd or obsessive.

He's turned out to be a genuine friend. And what kind of friend have I been? I read his mind, snatched him away to a world where they don't build their homes so much as weave them out of living trees, and expect him to cure an alien!

And he tried! Tried to talk to her, build a rapport— but I had to get too deep into her mind and ruin everything.

He wandered over to where the building branched out to a lookout tower. "Branch" being literal in this case: a long, thick branch did stick out almost to the fence. Despite the low walls from which crouching archers could fire their arrows, it would feel more open than the large but high-walled courtyard. But how to get up? He couldn't bring himself to go inside the building even to get to the lookout.

Could I levitate, maybe? He concentrated, thinking of his feet pushing away from the ground.

His feet slipped from under him and he fell hard on his behind. He rubbed it, hissing. It was still sore from the earlier insults of the day.

A vine dropped down in front of him.

Thanks, he teleped to the branch as he climbed up. He clambered over the wall, then stretched himself out on the floor, looking at the incredible majesty of the night sky.

I wonder if Joshua has seen the stars? I should bring him, but not tonight, he told himself. Even if the thought of going inside didn't give him the creeps, he had no desire to talk to his friend after the "counseling" he'd given him just before they'd gone to bed.

"If I were you, I'd be doing some serious apologizing to Tasmae for this afternoon," he'd told him. "You knew how the thought of teleping scared her—knew it better than me—but you got into her mind big time."

I didn't consciously do it, he thought. *I was just caught up in the music, in the dance...*

Bits of his dream returned: dancing with Tasmae, wanting her, longing to pull her closer.

Joshua was right. I am in love.

The Intruder nears, bringing its contagion. His mind nears Tasmae's, infecting her psyche... Would he hurt her? What would happen to Kanaan then?

"We have to get home," he whispered to the starlight.

But then what? Where could he go? The moment he'd disappeared with Joshua, Malachai must have reported him as criminally insane. If he returned, would they arrest him or commit him? Would he end up back at SK-Mental or a prison institution? He shuddered at the kinds of personalities he'd be exposed to there.

So, don't get caught. Find someplace safe, away from SK-Mental, to drop off Joshua, then run. Teleport away.

He couldn't see it happening. He needed to be able to imagine the place in his mind to get here, or so he thought. He didn't want to try otherwise—no telling where they'd end up. Maybe (if Joshua would let him get into his head again), he could try for Colorado. He grinned, imagining the intern trying to explain his presence halfway across the country, especially if they managed to time-travel and got back the day they'd left. They'd have to come up with a good cover story.

And find out what airports were nearby, Deryl thought to himself. Before he'd left, he'd gotten control of the remainder of his inheritance, thanks to a fellow client who at one time had been an embezzler for the Mafia. He had money enough to set himself up just about anywhere. Everything he needed was in the stuffing of his bear.

Maybe he could go to South America. If Terry could pick up both English and Spanish from Joshua, he should be able to pick up Spanish—or maybe Portuguese. Spend his money on a little hacienda on the beach and lots of paints, just an American recluse. *So maybe, if I can get Descartes...*

Could he do it? Could he have a normal life? Joshua had helped him learn how to shield himself against the thoughts and emotions of others, and he could do it pretty well, provided he had time alone to "recharge" his psychic reserves.

But what if he couldn't? What if he got stuck near someone who projected too strongly? He still felt the horror of the weekend when Dr. Malachai had forced him to stay in a room next to a bipolar patient. He'd driven himself catatonic rather than let loose the violence the man projected upon him. There would be no Joshua to bail him out if something like that happened again.

What if he got sick? He'd managed to keep most of the pain of the hospital patients around him at bay, but toward the end, especially when he was feverish from a post-op infection, he was pretty sure he'd said some things in his delirium. Fortunately, the orderly assigned to guard him was wrapped up in her novel. But there had been a man, just before they'd sedated him... He'd felt him dying...

And he hadn't said anything. He hadn't wanted to ruin his one chance at a normal life. No one there would have believed him, and Joshua was not there to listen. The man had died. He knew it. He'd felt it.

He sat up and pulled his knees to his chest and rested his head against them, his arms wrapped around his legs in a tight ball of misery.

The authorities would go after him. Malachai had convinced nearly everyone that he was incurable and dangerous. His aunt and uncle feared him more than ever. He'd kidnapped his best friend in front of his fiancée, his only other friend.

Could he go back?

He lost track of time. His thoughts became dis-jointed and tangled, until he stopped thinking. Then he felt a presence behind him that forced him back into thought, and he had just enough time to get himself to-gether before Tasmae sat down next to him. Even so, he didn't feel ready to face her, though she had seated herself so that she faced his profile. Instead, he made sure his shields were up and tight and said, as casually as he could, "Lovely night."

She reached out, cupped his cheek in one hand, and turned his face toward her. He clenched his jaw as she studied the tracks of the tears he hadn't quite scrubbed off. She traced one with her thumb. He trembled slightly, torn between the desire to kiss her and the de-sire to lay his head on her shoulder and cry.

"I'm, I'm fine," he managed to lie. He knew she didn't believe him, so he tried something a little closer to the truth. "But I am so sorry."

She dropped her hand and turned away from him, ducking her head. Her hair was in a loose bun, so that a great curve of it obscured her face. "I am the one who is sorry," she whispered.

Her vulnerability struck him, and he had to fight a new desire, this one to throw his arms around her and protect her. Yet another part of him remembered the time she'd nearly overwhelmed him with her grief and fear, and he drew back from her instead.

"It's not your fault—" he stammered, but she cut him off.

"Yes. It is. All of it. I never should have sought you out today. I never should have opened myself to you as I did, even if only for a song. I was *supposed* to be ex-periencing the Remembrance. I shouldn't have had contact with anyone until I've completed it and been through a cleansing. A complete one, I mean. I thought that, because you were human—"

He knew she needed him to understand, but between her words and his own conflicting desires, he felt very confused.

"Taz, what happened was an accident—" he started, but she shook her head violently. The movement made her hair capture and absorb the starlight in sensual waves. For a moment the need to reach out and stroke it threatened to overcome his restraint.

Instead, he ran his hands into his own hair, gripping and pulling at the crown. For some reason, it always helped him concentrate.

"You do that?" she asked.

"It's a bad habit," he said, continuing through his hair, brushing it back from his face.

"It is Gardianju's habit, I think. It is becoming mine since the Remembrance. What is your connection to the Remembrance?"

He couldn't meet her eyes, but again, she touched his face and drew his gaze to hers. The attraction between them was so strong. He leaned a little closer. He could feel Kanaan move beneath him, caught in its own dance of attractions.

Attraction was good. Distance, necessary. Kanaan stays in balance with the moons, and all is well. Kanaan stays in balance with the sun and all is life. Destroy the balance—

"Deryl?"

He heard her voice, felt her concern, but mostly he was aware of the dark velvet of her hair, the starlight illuminating her face. Her eyes were darker than deepest night, yet he thought he saw a single light in them. A planet illuminated by the sun.

The balance tips.

Destroy the balance and life is destroyed. The Intruder comes. Its inhabitants want Kanaan.

DON'T LET ANYTHING STAND IN THE WAY OF WHAT YOU WANT.

Desire overcomes balance. He felt himself falling.

A brilliant flash. Destruction falls upon Kanaan.

With a gasp, Deryl jerked back from Tasmae, reflexively turning his eyes to Barin, breaking the spell. It shone bright and stable in the distance, but he knew that that stability was just an illusion.

Tasmae followed his gaze. "It was in your dream," she said with certainty. "I *have* tainted you."

"*You* tainted *me*?" He wasn't thinking clearly and couldn't tear his gaze from Barin.

"The Remembrances leave impressions. Like with healers, how they can be impressed with bits of a person's personality. I have explained this to you."

"I remember." He forced his focus away from the sky, fixed it on a point in front of his feet. He took slow, deep breaths. "Are you saying *you're* tainted? And you think I picked up and transmitted something during your song?"

"And the Remembrance of Gardianju is the worst of all. She had a mind illness as had never been known. I'm sorry, Deryl. I was proud. I thought I could handle it, and when I couldn't, I refused to admit it. I've put you and Joshua in danger—"

At the mention of Gardianju's insanity, a cold wave washed over Deryl. If she was insane, he knew how she got that way.

Madness Unbound ⬧ 165

"I don't remember her. What knowledge did Gardianju want from me?" he asked in a small voice.

"I don't know. So much of it doesn't make sense, even to me. The Age of the Sister Suns was a terrible, violent time for Kanaan and for our people. It is thought even time itself became somehow confused. Gardianju, as Miscria, was caught in the thick of it. That is why her mind shattered into disorientation, but she never tainted anyone. God shielded her specially. But the Remembrance is not so shielded. I thought I had controlled her contagion, but Joshua's experience, your nightmare—"

"No, hey, don't worry about us." He grasped her shoulders. Now that he was reassured about Gardianju, he could look at Tasmae, offer her reassurance himself. "Humans are a pretty adaptable species. Joshua's fine, and I'm sure my nightmare was just my mind's way of releasing some stress. It's not easy to be an oracle come to life, you know."

He smiled at her. He was glad to see a slight smile tease her lips.

"I am glad you've come," she said.

"Me, too." The attraction was there again, but its pull not nearly as strong. Ironically, that made it easier for Deryl to lean toward her and kiss her.

"Do me a favor and don't tell Joshua about this," he murmured.

"Or Leinad," she agreed and kissed him in return.

Chapter Fifteen

Joshua awoke from yet another nightmare of being stuck on Kanaan while Sachiko went on to marry Malachai, of all people. He sat up and rubbed his face, trying to dispel the image, but it didn't ease the heavy ache inside. He cut himself shaving and went to breakfast in a bad mood.

On the way there, he passed Leinad with a tall woman in green blouse and skirt. He couldn't read the cool expression she wore when she glanced his way, but the look Leinad gave him as they passed made Joshua's heart thunder and his feet quicken their pace to the cafeteria.

As he neared, he heard laughter. He paused at the doorway, listening. Deryl sounded relaxed, happy...and flirtatious.

Please, let me be wrong. Joshua took a breath and composed his features before entering.

His friend and Tasmae sat alone in the large room. They'd pushed their breakfast plates aside, and were talking in low, warm tones. They weren't touching, but they didn't need to. The look on Deryl's face said enough.

Anyone else—back on Earth—and Joshua would have cheered him on. Here, now, with her—

Joshua shoved the implications into the back of his mind, but he skipped the buffet and went straight to their table.

"Well, this looks cozy." He tried to keep the venom out of his voice. *Please, let me be wrong.*

The two smiled up at him. Deryl leaned away from Tasmae, just slightly, but enough.

Stay calm. Right now, you need to salvage the situation. He sat down. "So, saw Leinad on the way here. He didn't look happy."

Tasmae shrugged. "He does not like my decision."

"Oh?"

Deryl, either oblivious, shielded against Josh's feelings, or too love-struck to care, started, "Tasmae and I were talking last night—"

"Talking? Really?"

"—and we think we might have figured out what's going on with the Remembrance. Tasmae may only be half-trained as a Miscria, but she completed her primary warrior training."

"I received my Miscria talent late," she explained. "I would have been perhaps fifteen by your years."

"And we're getting close to the Season of War, so there's a lot for a warrior to do, plus their own Talents rev up naturally about this time, anyway. But the Remembrance can't take that into account—it's pure Miscria."

Joshua shrugged. "So?"

Deryl rolled his eyes. "Tasmae's warrior Talents are fighting it. That's why she keeps getting thrown out."

Joshua felt the grip on his heart ease. "So it's not us! That's some relief, anyway. But why's Leinad pissed?"

Tasmae shrugged. "I will rejoin the warriors today. Salgoud wants to show me their innovations, anyway. I will exercise my warrior talent; tonight, I will use my Miscria talent to try to predict and perhaps prevent any natural disasters from occurring. Tomorrow, I will enter the Remembrance, but only for the day."

"Can you do that?"

Again she shrugged, this time with uncertainty. "They have a limited intelligence; usually they know better than to demand attention in this season. This one is behaving badly."

Deryl snickered at her words, but Joshua didn't find anything funny about it. "Maybe there's a reason?"

"That is what Leinad believes, yet I am thrown out, without control over the timing. I gain nothing but confused impressions. No understanding, no insight. I learn nothing. Perhaps this way, I can influence the Remembrance to show me the order in chaos."

"And I thought if we taught her how to create a control room..."

Joshua nodded. The control room was a simple NLP concept: work with your subconscious to create a command center where it could watch out for certain situations and create and test solutions. Joshua had taught Deryl to make one for his telepathic shields. "Well, it's worth a try. You're not teleping?"

"No. I am afraid to." But she and Deryl exchanged glances.

"Uh, huh. Well, I'll talk you through it when you come back."

Tasmae nodded, then stood. "We should go. It's a long ride."

Joshua stood with them, but caught Deryl's sleeve and held it until she was ahead of them.

He leaned toward this friend's ear. "You want to play with dynamite, you wait until you've gotten me home."

Deryl rolled his eyes. "Relax. I've got it under control."

Joshua released him, but he couldn't help the sinking pit in his stomach.

He'd told Rique the same thing about his relationship with LaTisha.

They rode at top speed to the high cliffs, stopping only once to share a kiss where no one was around. They might not be able to telep, but Deryl could feel her emotions strong against his shields. He could sense her, the whole of her, and he knew if he gave into his desires, they'd share more than just their bodies.

He pulled away first. He had to keep his promise to Joshua.

They found Salgoud and a small team waiting at the observation point on one of the lower cliffs. Salgoud nodded to them and sent a telepathic query Tasmae's way. He nodded with satisfaction as it bounced off the shields Deryl had taught her to create last night. He'd also taught Salgoud; and Salgoud in turn taught the warriors playing the Barin side. Today, they would fight using only their five mundane senses, and Deryl had coached the team leader how to do that.

I never did get any sleep after that nightmare, he suddenly realized. Didn't matter; the excitement of being with Tasmae buoyed him, as did the energy of the warriors. Without realizing it, he drank it in, and as the exercise drew on, he felt the adrenalin of battle surging through him.

Back off, he told himself when he found his hands clenching into the grass against the urge to jump in and join the fray. *That's not you. Perspective. You're here to observe.*

Nonetheless, when he heard a yelp and saw a Barin-dressed warrior grab Tasmae by the hair, something in him snapped and he stood, roaring.

Joshua ate alone, grateful for the chance to get a hold of his temper. He still didn't feel much better, however, and when he went back to the salle, he couldn't focus on the routine. It was getting harder and harder to believe he would return in time for Chipotle's audition. He missed his friends, his woman, even his keyboard.

He tripped over a combination he'd had perfect before. He stopped, panting, resisting the urge to shout in frustration. As he stared at his reflection in the mirror, a small case caught his eye, and he went to it.

It held daggers of varying lengths. He stood, building his nerve, then grabbed one and headed back to the bench, where he spent the next hour etching out a keyboard onto its surface. When it was done, he ran his fingers over it. The grooves were rough, the proportions not quite right, and he had to hollow out the black keys, but it was close enough. He'd have to rely on his imagination for the rest.

Something soft and heavy fell on his head, and he blinked as the pillow tumbled onto his lap. He looked up in time to catch the second one that fell from Cochise's claws.

"Thanks, buddy! It won't sound nearly as good, but I'll sing the notes for you while I play, okay?"

He arranged the pillows into a comfortable seat while Cochise settled where he could watch Joshua's hands, and Joshua hummed the scales for him as his fingers moved over the makeshift keyboard.

He'd progressed beyond scales and was describing more complex fingerings to the everyn when a warrior ran into the room. Both man and everyn looked up in surprise. Joshua recognized her as the woman who'd had her leg healed the day he'd met Terry. Her eyes followed his arms down to the vandalized bench.

"Oh! Uh, I was..." He clamped his lips shut. He had no idea how to explain to her that he'd *needed* to play a piano, and any reasonable substitute would do; besides, a stubborn part of him said, it was none of her business, anyway.

"Something I can help you with?" he asked instead. "Can you understand me? Or have you been sent to fetch me to some appointment no one told me about?"

She paused, her head tilted as if listening. "I understand some." She finally answered. "Walls help."

"Really?" *So the walls have ears, too? Funny how no one's mentioned that. Wonder if Deryl knows?*

The warrior was haltingly saying something about Deryl. "Pardon?"

"The Miscria wants you, now," she repeated. "The Ydrel has done something—" She paused, and Joshua got the impression she was asking someone—maybe even the walls—for the right word. "Something bizarre," she concluded.

An hour later, Joshua found Deryl sulking under the same tree where yesterday they'd been laughing and sharing songs. The young man's back was to him, and he had his legs bent with his arms tight around them, but at least he wasn't rocking.

That's something, anyway. Joshua got off Glory, and kissed her nose. After all she'd been through today, she still brought him here. She bumped against him affectionately, then wandered off to graze. He walked the rest of the way to the tree and sat down beside his friend.

"*She* send you?" Deryl asked.

"Uh-huh."

Deryl didn't answer, just reached out and picked a daisy-like flower. He began to pull of the petals, one by one.

She loves me, she loves me not? Other mangled flowers lay scattered around him. He sat next to his friend, and plucked at the grass.

"She tell you?" Deryl asked after a minute.

"She showed me." The warrior had taken Joshua to the spot where they had apparently been watching the battle. There, he'd found Tasmae waiting for him in the middle of what Joshua could only think of as "aftermath."

To one side, healers worked on several injured warriors. Two supported Glory in a standing position while they worked. He could feel a symphony of healing energy. Salgoud sat leaning against a large tree, a healer beside him with her hands hovering over his head. *Concussion*, Joshua had thought, though he didn't know how he'd known that.

A sword was buried six inches into the tree. A good distance away in several directions, swords were stuck in the ground to the hilt. Near the cliffs, arrows fanned out in a half-circle, pointing in multiple directions. Tasmae looked a lot like she had the first time he'd seen her—wisps of hair coming out of a tight braid, clothes dirty and torn, and sweat and dirt on her face. Then, she had been grim and confused; this time, she was seriously pissed.

"What is he hiding from me?" was all she had asked.

"So, you want to tell me about it?" Joshua asked Deryl.

"She tricked me!" Deryl exclaimed, tossing the flower away as if it had dared to disagree with him. "We were up on the mesa, watching. Things were getting pretty serious; I mean, I could feel it, it was— I was leaning close to the edge, trying to see how the archers were faring, when Tasmae shouted. I turned around and there were three soldiers after her, and she's wailing away, but there were so many and others were coming. I, I thought they'd gone crazy! I thought they were Barin! I yelled at them to stop, but they didn't, and— What was I supposed to do? I just wanted them to get away from her!

"Next thing I know, they're scattered everywhere, and there's a unicorn on its side and it's screaming and, and Tasmae... She just looks at me. No 'Thanks for saving me,' no 'My God, what did you do?' She *teleps* for me to *teach* her. I trashed the meadow, threw *her people* like rag dolls, and she wanted me to teach her!

"She tricked me!" he repeated. "I can't believe I trusted her, thought she wanted me for me. She planned this whole thing, put herself in the middle so I'd fight!"

"Wanted me for me"? Oh, great. "Salgoud planned the attack on the two of you," Joshua cut across Deryl's rant. "He'd had it planned for a day. He told me when I was at the meadow."

"Great! So he's also trying to—"

"Come off it, Deryl!" Joshua's patience snapped. "Not everything revolves around you and your precious psychic abilities. Tasmae's a warrior, right?"

"She's the Miscria."

"She's both, and didn't the enemy try to kill her in the last war? Isn't she a prime target?" Joshua demanded, eying Deryl expectantly.

Deryl met his gaze, but dropped his eyes as he thought it through. "Salgoud sent some folks to surprise attack her to keep her on her toes. But she didn't even try to tell me what was going on, just let me jump to conclusions!"

"It was an exercise, Deryl."

"Those swords were real!"

Joshua rolled his eyes and threw up his hands. "She's in armor. So are you, for that matter."

"Whose side are you on?"

"Yours, believe it or not! I agree, the whole set-up was whacked, okay? I just want you to think things through. Consider it from her side. All she wants is to protect her people, and if that means better fighting, so be it. I don't really think she enjoys killing, do you? Okay, then. So here's the Great Ydrel, font of all knowledge military, yet he won't take her seriously when he's sparring with her—*her point of view, not yours*—then when they get attacked, he lets loose with these amazing telekinetics he's never told her about, and people go flying, swords embed themselves in trees and in the ground, arrows bounce off him like rubber balls—"

"What arrows?"

"You kidding? When you went postal, they tried to shoot you. The arrows ricocheted. You had some heavy-duty shields up."

"I didn't know. I wasn't thinking, I just—" He put his arms around himself, shivering.

"Did I hurt anyone?" he asked in a small voice.

No use denying it. "They're all going to be fine. The unicorn—Glory—even brought me here. Tasmae said they'd seen worse."

"But we were so near the cliff. I didn't, well, toss anyone...?"

"Yeah, you did," Joshua told him gently. "But you also apparently stopped her before she hit the ground. She was more scared than anything. Still, you might expect folks to look at you a little differently after word gets around. That was some pretty powerful defense." He smiled, but Deryl, focused on the horizon with haunted eyes, did not answer.

"There's so much more power on this planet," he finally said. "It's like having a feast whereas before I was surviving on crusts of bread and thimbles of water. I don't know why I felt like it was a real attack, I just did, and I drew on that power and reacted. Afterwards, it was like I woke up from a nightmare, and I saw all the wreckage and knew I'd done it. Then she demanded I teach her how!"

"So you need to work on your control," Joshua concluded.

"Control?" Deryl blanched. "You can't be suggesting I actually do that again?"

"Trash the place? Fling people around? No. But you've got to admit, being able to deflect arrows is pretty cool stuff." He grinned and shrugged, inviting him to see the brighter side.

"Oh. Well, yeah, I guess..."

"And as for repelling things, imagine if you flung their supplies into the next county? Or redirected their ships to where *you* wanted them to land? I don't know—do you have enough power to just send their ships back to Barin? There's a lot you could do without ever hurting anyone. You just need to use your imagination."

"We could end this war," Deryl whispered. He turned pleading eyes on Joshua. "Help us?"

Joshua sighed in exasperation. "What do you think I'm trying to do?"

"No, I mean help us—help me—stop this war." He shifted position so he was on his knees, sitting on his heels and facing him. "There're still a few months before the war—if we practice and work together—

"Months? I don't think so!"

"I don't understand," Deryl stammered.

Joshua found himself gaping. He closed his mouth, gritted his teeth, and forced himself to speak slowly and clearly. "Listen, I don't know about you, but I don't want to be here when a war starts. Frankly, I don't want to be here *today*. I will help you and Tasmae figure this out. I'll give you what ideas I can. But not for months. *No way*. I am not a military advisor. I didn't want to come here. I don't belong here. I belong on Earth—with Sachiko, and my parents, and my own ambitions of making it as a musician. I want to go home—the sooner the better."

"I told you I'd get you home before the audition."

Again, he forced himself to keep a level voice. "How? Have you even thought about it? *How* to get us home, not what you plan to do afterwards or where you'll drop me off or whatever—*how*?"

Deryl blinked. "I will, I promise."

"So you haven't." Joshua's nightmares returned to make a tight knot in his stomach.

He stood up and whistled. Glory picked up her head and came to him. He mounted.

"Tell you what. You want my help? Fine. I'll brainstorm. But I'm not telling you anything until you tell me—no, you *show* me—that you can get me home." He started to ask Glory to go, then thought better of it.

"Want a ride back?" he asked, just managing to keep the grudging tone out of his voice.

Deryl hesitated, then nodded and stood. Joshua gave him a hand to help pull him onto Glory's back. They rode in silence to the field where the unicorns hung out, but when they got there and dismounted, Deryl caught Joshua by the shoulder.

"I'll talk to Tasmae about getting you home. Today. I promise. Even if there still are storms, like she said, every storm has lulls. Maybe she can predict them. I'll get you home. And you don't have to give me anything in return."

Joshua smiled. "What, and give up the chance to save the world?" he replied lightly. "I may not be in the superhero suit, but that doesn't mean I won't help if I can."

Then, Deryl's words caught up to his brain. "You're not staying on Earth once you get me back, are you?"

"I don't know," he whispered. "I'm not sure I could. I'm a fugitive."

"You can teleport, and the world's a big place. You could find somewhere."

"Yeah, I suppose."

"Or, you could stay, and we could work it out. I'd vouch for you, and if you could return us within a few minutes of when we'd left, what are they going to do? For that matter, how's Malachai going to explain you kidnapping me right from under his nose? Especially if Sachiko and I are on your side? I'd talk to your aunt and uncle. My dad has a lot of contacts on the East coast—we'd find you a better psychiatrist until you can convince them you don't need help anymore. Then, go to college. Find Clarissa and hook up with her. Have a life. That is, if you want a life on Earth."

A laugh escaped his throat. "Oh, man, do you know how ridiculous that sounds? You've got to be the only person who's ever really had a choice between two worlds."

Deryl kicked at the rocks in the worn path. "Problem is, I don't know if I'm welcome on either one. Not unless I'm ready to do their bidding."

"Oh, come off it, Deryl. Everybody has to do the bidding of somebody, and it isn't always fun. You think I enjoy getting up at 6:30 every morning to do Malachai's bidding for twelve hours a day? Case studies, and sitting in on group therapies, and being told to keep my mouth shut 'cause I'm just a lowly intern—"

"Playing best friend to a sulky client?"

"Exactly!" He moved his hand in a seemingly casual wave. In fact, it was a feel-good anchor he'd established with Deryl when he'd first started working with him, a kind of subtle motion-based mnemonic to instill hopeful, positive feelings. He'd been slipping thanks to the stress of the past couple of days and hadn't thought to use it lately, but it worked, nonetheless. Josh smiled, and the former "sulky client" smiled back.

"The point is, I'm willing to do it, because it's getting me things I want: money for tuition next year, work experience, and I'm learning a lot, too."

Deryl grinned at his friend. "You didn't always do what Malachai wanted."

"And I got called on the carpet for it, too. Even by Edith."

"That was Malachai's doing," Deryl told him.

Joshua grunted doubtfully. "I don't think he told her to threaten to personally send me back to Colorado and get me a job at Carl's Jr. for the rest of the summer."

"No way!"

"Way. I was this far from using my psychiatric skills to convince people to biggie size their order. At any rate, what I'm trying to say is that no matter where you go or what you do, there's got to be some give-and-take. Still, if you're not comfortable with what Taz and her people want with you, you have a choice: go back to Earth, or stay here and forge a new role for the Ydrel."

"You're right, Joshua. Thanks." Deryl turned off the trail.

"Hey, where you going?"

"Tasmae's this way. May as well do this now. I'll see you later."

Deryl headed to a small grove not far from the paddocks. The trees stood tall and heavy with leaves, though no fruit. In places, he had to twist sideways to make his way between them, but suddenly, the trees opened up to a small clearing. They encircled an area of thick moss about twenty feet in diameter, but the branches intertwined above so that very little sunlight came though, giving the area a dappled, twilight effect not too different from that of the bathing grotto.

Deryl smiled as he recognized it. It looked much like the clearing Tasmae had imagined for him the first time he'd actually spoken to her in the Netherworld, and when later, she had "changed" the location so that they could see the sky, she had kept the same springy moss that grew with almost mattress-like thickness.

Tasmae was barefoot in the middle of the mossy clearing now, her sword in her hand, moving through a form that mixed the techniques he'd taught her people with moves they'd developed over centuries of fighting. He lingered by the forest edge, watching and admiring her grace and strength. She moved with lethal precision. Her face was grim as she concentrated.

This is life and death for her, and I treated it as a game. I know she's a warrior. Maybe it's time I accept it.

Sighing, he reached out with his mind and took hold of her sword.

She jerked slightly as it froze in midair, resisting her motion. She gave it one experimental tug before releasing it, letting it hang in the air, and turned toward him. She crossed her arms over her chest and waited. He watched her from where he stood against the tree. Silence, both psychic and verbal, stretched.

Then they teleped, both at the same time, waves of reassurance and understanding washing over them both. He hadn't been holding out on her; she knew. She hadn't tricked him; he knew. Both were sorry.

Madness Unbound   ❦

Remorse, then relief, then affection, and Deryl closed the gap between them and pulled her into his arms. As he kissed her, he knew he didn't want to leave. He had to find a way to make this work. Then, there was only her, and their kiss.

He lost his concentration on the sword. It fell with a dull thump, drawing them back to reality. Tasmae chuckled.

"Perhaps we should talk instead," Deryl said, pulling back without leaving her embrace. He felt a little dizzy, pleasantly so, but he'd promised Joshua...

"Will you teach me?" she asked.

He was too aware of her arms around him. "I'll try. I don't really know how I do it. Malachai—" Had he ever mentioned Dr. Malachai to her? "I mean, I tried for years, but I just sort of got it in the past few weeks. I'd want something; it'd come to me. I don't think I can explain it."

She turned her face from his, thinking. Her hair brushed against his lips. He fought the urge to bury his face in it. He tried not to breathe in her scent.

"Try something," she suggested. "Let me in your mind, then try something."

"In my mind?" Why did that thought make his heart race with such fear and desire?

"Like when I Call you," she said, leaning back to look into his eyes. "Move something. I'll draw out how you did it."

He touched her hair, and he remembered how jealous he'd felt about Joshua brushing it. Without really thinking, he used his mind to pull her punch dagger hairpiece from her bun. As her hair fell about her shoulders, he used his telekinesis to gather it, separating it into three sections and braiding it. All the time, he felt her Call, but this time teasing rather than forcing the information from him. The sensation echoed across his skin.

Nonetheless, she shook her head. "You're right: You want something to happen and it happens. But I don't understand how."

"I'm sorry." But he wasn't sure that he was. If she couldn't figure out how his telekinetic skills worked, he wouldn't have to teach them. He'd never have to worry about their forcing him to teach them to use the ability offensively.

"You've shielded yourself from me."

"Those shields are keeping us both safe."

Images flashed into his mind: civilians forcing back attackers with the strength of their will; children flinging objects to impede a Barin's pursuit or to construct a safe hiding place. Healers working in safety in the middle of a battle as another created a shield that deflected incoming arrows. He realized how much he'd underestimated her imagination.

Let me join your mind. Then I will know as you know.

The thought tempted and terrified. If he gave in, he wouldn't hold back. She'd know everything. His nightmares. His fear of the Master. His insanities. Even now, voices from the past pulled at him, and he didn't know why. He could ignore them, mostly, but if he gave in to her, let her into his thoughts...

He shook his head. She could never *know* as he did. "I can't. We can't."

He looked at her, saw the light of Barin reflected in her eyes. Her desires pushed at his shields.

She had to have time to teach the world. If she could teach her people in time, no one had to die.

His mind flickered on Joshua's idea. They could force the ships back even before reaching Kanaan.

The power of her need pressed upon him.

"I need you," she whispered. "We need you."

To be needed by an entire world...

A flaw appeared in his shields, became a buckle, then a tear. It was small, but enough. Her psyche flowed through like water and filled his consciousness. He gasped with pleasure.

It felt like a caress upon his soul when she directed him to lift the sword, and he moved to kiss her as he started to obey.

A cacophony of voices exploded in his mind.

Chapter Sixteen

Deryl screamed and lashed out at the thoughts that bore relentlessly on him. The sword he'd been levitating flung sideways and buried itself into a tree.

Deryl. Tasmae cried, her call dim and distant in the tornado of thoughts tearing at their minds.

Get out! Get out of my mind! With a psychic and physical shove, he threw her from him. She slammed into a tree, jarring her into awareness while jarring her teeth, and her legs bucked under her before she could react. Her head spun with confusion. The world blurred.

When her vision cleared, she saw Deryl curled up on the ground, gripping his hair as if to tear it out by the roots. He breathed in fast, shrieking gasps.

"Deryl!" Tasmae reached out to him. A maelstrom of bizarre and conflicting images took hold of her before he shoved her away again. She gasped.

The Remembrance!

She scrambled backward, crablike, until she again bumped a tree, then turned and fled the grove. She had to find the healer. She'd infected him with the memories of Gardianju!

Halfway through the grove, a unicorn met her in answer to her summons. She jumped upon his back, and he raced through the twisting path and ran full-out to the compound, even ducking his head to enter the building itself. At Leinad's door, she slid off and pounded upon it. When Leinad opened the door, the light of the setting sun from behind shrouded him in shadow.

"It's Deryl!" she cried. "I thought—I didn't think— Please! Send the healer!"

In a moment, the healer came running down the hall to them. She gave Tasmae one quick check to see that she was all right, then mounted the waiting unicorn and headed to the clearing.

Leinad glared at her. "Do you understand now?"

She nodded, gulping back tears of shame, and let him lead her to the Remembrance.

You are not me! You are not my memories. I reject you. Get out of my mind!

Deryl beat back the invading thoughts and regained his mind. He managed to uncurl himself and lay spread-eagled on the mossy ground. He looked at the tree-obscured sky dully. Minutes or hours? He didn't think the shadows had changed much. It didn't seem important at the moment. He supposed he should feel some satisfaction at coming back to himself, but couldn't make himself care. Without moving much, he glanced around the area. Tasmae was gone. He couldn't care about that, either. Being alone was good. He felt drained. He closed his eyes, seeking comfort in the numbness.

The sound of hoof beats jerked him out of his malaise. Was someone looking for him? He couldn't let anyone find him like this! He jumped up and headed into a dense part of the trees. Once out of sight, he crouched behind a large trunk and concentrated on making himself psychically as well as physically invisible.

He felt someone's concern, and a little surprise at not finding him. Not Tasmae. Had she sent someone for him? Why hadn't she stayed, or returned, or... He squashed his thoughts as he felt attention move like a beam in his direction.

He chanced forcing a thought at the person: *He must be okay. Perhaps Tasmae read too much into this.*

He felt a flicker of doubt, then resignation. A moment later, he heard the hoof beats retreat down the other side of the grove.

Once he could hear them no longer, he released the breath he was holding and sank his head onto his knees. His body ached as clenched muscles relaxed. Even his scalp hurt. None of that, however, compared to the battered feeling inside his mind.

What were those voices? They were the same as his nightmares, from his time at the asylum. Yet they felt like they'd come from outside his shields. How could that happen? And what happened to his shields? After he'd fled the aftermath of the battle, he'd built them up as tightly as he could, pinning all the power of Kanaan behind them. They should have been impenetrable. Yet Tasmae's will sliced through them like a hot knife through butter.

That's not quite true, he told himself, remembering how much he'd wanted to let her though his shields, the sudden rush of pleasure when he felt her mind moving within his. Even the memory of it overwhelmed his senses and made his pain and fear seem momentarily insignificant.

He'd battle a hundred minds if only to share Tasmae's again.

Like that'll ever happen again. I'm the Kanaan equivalent of a leper. With that bleak thought, his battered mind fell silent and he stayed there absorbed in his own misery until it occurred to him that if he lingered past sunset, he wouldn't be able to see well enough to leave the grove until morning. Even so, it took all of his will to force himself up to make the long walk to the compound.

The walking helped draw him from his stupor, but he was still loath to meet anyone. Fortunately, the warriors were still out on the cliffs.

He snuck into the dining hall, snatched the leftovers still on the serving table for late-night snackers, and headed to his room. He needed to think.

Nonetheless, after he'd gotten to the room, spread out his cache on the table, and settled down in one of the soft bag-like chairs, he found himself drained of thought, and he sat there, knees up under his chin, enshrouded by his misery, for hours. Occasionally, he roused himself enough to ask, "What am I going to do?"

His thoughts had come to nothing when the first earthquake hit.

Joshua stood on the plateau of one of those high, narrow, lonely mesas in the middle of Utah, the kind they used in SUV commercials. The altitude and a slight breeze cut the heat some, but it was still dusty, dry, and barren, and as he looked around at the bizarre desolate landscape, he wondered how he'd gotten there—and how he'd get down.

"Joshua!"

"Sachiko!" Joshua turned at the sound of his fiancée's voice and started to run to her. No sooner did he take his first step, however, than the mesa shook violently, knocking them both off their feet. Joshua fell hard, but his need for her drove him up again, only to be tossed up and thrown to the ground by another forceful tremor. A ripping sound, then a roar like he'd never heard before, like a Niagara Falls of dirt and stone, and the stretch of mesa between him and Sachiko disappeared.

Sachiko, still on hands and knees, looked to Joshua in horror.

Joshua judged at the rift, decided he could jump it, and ran.

A third tremor knocked him backward. Sachiko screamed. The ground crumbled in his direction and he scrambled back. The wind picked up, as if the air rushed to fill the gaping hole between them.

"I'm okay!" He had to shout to be heard. His heart pounded almost as loudly as the splitting rock. When the tremors finally stopped, he crawled his way to the crevice and gawked at the gap filled with blackness and stars.

He looked up and across to Sachiko's despairing face.

"I'll find a way!" he shouted.

"I believe you! I love you!"

"I love you! Wait for me!"

"Forever!"

When Joshua awoke, he knew why tears dampened his face, but he couldn't figure out what he was doing on the floor. Then, the room shook and swayed.

Earthquake! He froze, unsure of what to do. All he knew about earthquakes was from disaster movies or the news. Should he go outside? Stay indoors? People got buried in the rubble, but wasn't it more dangerous outside? Could a plant-building collapse?

Tasmae collapsed one, but Deryl made it sound like she talked it into doing so.

The room shuddered.

"What do I do?" he demanded out loud, though he didn't know why.

The leaf door to his room opened. He hastily threw on pants and dashed into the corridor. He'd find someone and ask or follow them. People here knew what to do, right? As he neared the main hall, he heard hoof beats and broke into a run.

He rounded the intersection and saw a unicorn carrying an unconscious warrior who was bleeding slightly at the temple. *The warriors were spending the night at the cliffs. Didn't Tasmae warn them?* He hurried to the unicorn.

"Are there more?" he asked, hoping the stallion understood. Joshua didn't recognize him.

The unicorn jerked his head in the horsy equivalent of a nod. Joshua noted although blood stained his gray hide, it didn't seem to be his own.

Gently, Joshua pulled the woman off the unicorn's back. "I'll get her to the healers," he said, glad that he'd finally memorized that route. "Go see who else you can help."

Again the nod, and the unicorn spun in a turn that should have been impossible for so large a beast in so narrow a hallway. As he headed back outside, Joshua hastened to the healer's den, doing his best not to jostle the injured woman.

He got to the healer's area just as another tremor hit, and he braced himself against the wall until it stopped. It was milder than the one that had tossed him from his bed, and he wondered if that was a good sign. A healer wordlessly took the warrior from his arms and carried her to a low bed to be examined. He took no notice of Joshua; no one did.

Now what? Head back the way I'd come and hope to run into another unicorn? Joshua looked around the room. Anyone who wasn't a healer was scurrying about on seemingly urgent tasks; no one was going to take time to give him directions. He started out the door, but another tremor made him hold back.

What if my route isn't the safest? It's not the most direct, I'm sure. Maybe I should wait until someone else comes and follow them. He saw Terry, bent over another injured warrior, his expression serene yet deep in concentration. For a moment, Joshua thought of a saint in prayer. The room itself remained eerily quiet, except for the muffled footsteps and the occasional moans of the wounded. No machine sounds, no spoken directions, no swearing.

There was, however, the healing energy, calling to him, teasing. He felt like he should know it.

A half-dozen others came in, two of whom carried a third that was unable to walk. As a healer rushed to them, Joshua stepped out of the way, sidling toward Terry as he did. No one took heed of him, and he hesitated to offer his help, for fear of jarring Terry out of whatever trance he was in. By the time he'd looked back to the people at the door, they were gone.

Well, there's always one thing I can do. He closed his eyes a moment and opened his heart to prayer.

With a rush, the healing power moved into him, filling him with light and music and a sweet taste.

Terry's patient began to convulse.

Without thinking, Joshua hurried forward to help hold him down. No sooner had he set his hands on the man's shoulders, than the power began to course through him and into the wounded warrior. He started to jerk away in surprise, but Terry slapped his hands over Joshua's, pinning them down. He had no choice but to let the power rush through him and try not to lose himself in the flood.

The music crescendoed and faded, and the flow of power slowed. Terry released him, and Joshua sat down hard on the floor, huffing. He felt dazed and giddy. He blinked several times, then looked at Terry and the patient. The warrior, though unconscious, breathed normally.

Terry smiled at Joshua. "And you said you were not a healer."

"I'm not. I—" Joshua shook his head, trying to focus. He couldn't catch his breath. He felt the melody of power around him, both comforting and pulling at him. *There are more*, it crooned.

He shook his head again, looked back at Terry. "What just happened?"

Terry took hold of his shoulders. "You are untrained, but you can channel power. There are others who need our help."

There are more. The music whispered, luring him.

"I, I don't know what to do. This didn't happen when we were practicing."

"*No es importante.* I will guide you. Just call the power as you did before. Can you do that?"

He licked lips gone dry. "I suppose..."

There are more. Sing with me. Make healing music.

The initial confusion faded, leaving him with the kind of natural high he felt after Chipotle gave a great performance. He grinned and held out his hand for Terry to pull him up. "Let's do it!"

Terry guided Joshua through healing the next patient, having him call the power then directing it himself to where healing was needed. He let the music/light/taste/caress overwhelm him so that he barely noticed moving on the next patient, then the next, then from healer to healer. He was suspended in a kind of rapture, until at last the melody faltered, the rainbow faded. He stumbled; still, power flowed through him, and healers wordlessly passed him among themselves, and he could not break free of the flood to voice a protest.

When at last the song released him, he crawled into a vacant cot and gave himself to sleep.

The power called out to Joshua, singing his name. "C'mon," he protested weakly. "Let up. I'm so tired. I'm only human."

Rest, human, the power sang. *Rest and know you have done well. Your purpose reaches fulfillment. You will be home soon, soon...*

Half-asleep, Joshua stirred uneasily in the muggy heat. Sweat made his shirt and shorts cling to his body. The mechanical roar of his window fans invaded his slumber, but barely made a breeze.

Fans?

Joshua opened his eyes and stared at the ceiling fan of his Rhode Island flat in mute disbelief. Was he really back home?

He sat up, saw his laptop on the end table, his synthesizer in its spot between the two windows. He turned his head toward the door.

"*'Ko!*"

Sachiko, bent over her backpack, stood up with a yelp of surprise. "Jeez! You scared the life out of me!"

He bounded over the coffee table and wrapped his arms around her, kissing her with a week's worth of pent up passion.

"What was that all about?" she asked when he'd finally stopped kissing her mouth to press his lips against her neck and ear.

"I've missed you so much!" he whispered.

She laughed. "That's what you get for sleeping the day away."

He backed away from her. "What?"

She held up the motorcycle helmet she'd been pulling out of her backpack. "I stuck around because I was worried, but you were sleeping normally, and I need to stop falling asleep at your place. Engaged or not, your landlady's going to get some funny ideas, and I wouldn't put it past her to call your parents about us, ya know what I mean? But seriously, you've got to get up for work in a couple of hours. I mean, if you're up to it. Edith said—Joshua, hon, what is it?"

He'd sat down hard on the coffee table. It felt real enough. "What day is it?"

"Tuesday, about 2 a.m." She sat down next to him. "Why?"

"This is going to sound stupid, but which Tuesday? Did Deryl do anything...odd?"

Sachiko set her hand on his arm. "Deryl...took you somewhere. We don't know how. Then, half an hour later, you showed up in an empty conference room. You were pretty dazed, so I brought you home. You said you wanted to sleep for a week. I thought maybe the concussion—"

"Yes!" Joshua jumped up, cheering. He pulled Sachiko into his arms again and kissed her. "Have I got a story for you!"

"Well, that's good, because Malachai and the police—"

"Uh-uh. As far as they're concerned, I have no memory of what happened between Deryl and me disappearing and me reappearing half an hour later. This is for your ears only."

"Now, I'm intrigued." She settled herself on the couch, helmet at her feet.

He sat down next to her, cross-legged and facing her. He couldn't keep back a grin. "It may have only been less than an hour here, but it was nearly a week we were gone. Remember Tasmae, the Miscria? She and her world are as real as Deryl's abilities, and he took us there."

She leaned back on one hand and cocked an eyebrow at him. His heart skipped as he gazed into her eyes, exotic like her Japanese mother's, and the smirk that was all-too-much her father's. Her blouse, damp with humidity, clung to her body. Just enough buttons were undone that he could see the curve of her breasts. Below her skort, her legs were shapely and tan. One of them pressed lightly against his.

He forgot all about the adventure. "I didn't think I was ever going to see you again," he whispered.

"Know what I think? I think you'll say anything to get me to stay the night."

"Do I really have to say anything?" He leaned toward her, and soon they were settled against the pillows of the couch he forced himself not to think of as a bed. Their kisses grew more passionate, their caresses more eager, until he found himself wishing it was a dream so he could follow through on his desires.

As if summoned by his silent wish, someone grabbed him by the shoulders and shook him roughly. "Hey! Wake up!"

Startled, Joshua pulled back and had one last look at Sachiko smile with irony before the scene around him faded.

"No!"

"Wake up!"

"No," Joshua moaned and pulled the light sheet over his head, desperately trying to find his way back to his dream.

Someone ripped the sheet off him. "Quit goofing around and wake up!" Deryl yelled.

White-hot anger shot through him, and he threw himself into a sitting position and whirled on his friend. "What? What could possibly be so frickin' important that it couldn't wait another half-hour?"

Deryl flinched, but he set his jaw and demanded. "Tell me your name."

"What? Are you out of your mind?"

"No, but you may be. Now tell me your name. Your full name."

Joshua opened his mouth to say, "What?" again, realized that would be redundant, closed his mouth, and
looked around. Deryl still wore the clothes he'd had on
yesterday, and his long blond hair pulled back from his
face in a tangled mess, as if he'd tried to tear it out
again. His eyes searched Joshua's face. At the foot of
the bed, Terry, too, was watching him expectantly.
Four of the five other healers crowded around the bed
and even the fifth watched curiously from where she
sat beside a patient.

He was still on Kanaan. "No fair!"

"Well?" Deryl demanded.

The tremor in his voice melted some of Joshua's anger, but he still answered with poor grace. "It's Joshua
Abraham Lawson, named after my great-great grandfather. Good enough?"

Without answering, Deryl looked at Terry, who
nodded.

"Joshua," he said grimly, "the Barins have attacked
early. They are at the gates now."

"What!" Joshua yelped. "What do we do?"

To his amazement, everyone grinned.

Deryl sighed. "Never mind. Relax. I lied."

Terry added, "I'm sorry, but we had to test your response."

"My...response?" The sudden change from anger to
panic to confusion left him weak. He leaned against the
wall and tried to sigh instead of whimper. "Would
someone please tell me what's going on?"

"You healed twenty-seven people in a row—did you
know that?" Deryl accused. For some reason, he was
still inexplicably angry.

"I wasn't counting. Besides, I didn't heal them, really. I was more like a—I don't know—maybe a conduit for the healing power. They did the healing." He waved his arms at the healers around him.

Terry smiled at his modesty. "Perhaps so, but we were able to heal better and faster with your aid. In several cases, that saved a life."

"Really? Cool. But I wasn't really doing anything—you guys—"

"*If* the mutual appreciation society is over," Deryl snapped sarcastically, "the fact remains that you healed twenty-seven people—*aliens*—in a row."

"So?" Joshua felt himself grinning like he had after the first time he'd kissed Sachiko. Could he have really done something so incredible? He knew later he would probably be struck dumb with awe—this was something *saints* did!—but right now, he felt like laughing and cheering.

Deryl, however, growled. "*So?* Didn't you listen to anything Terry's said about healing—or what Tasmae's said for that matter?" His voice rose in volume.

Terry stopped him with a touch and took up the explanation more calmly. "When a Kanaan healer does his work, he has to share the person's essence—his spirit, personality, memories, what makes him individual. Even when the healing is done, the healer may still retain some of that person's essence."

"I remember," Joshua said with a dirty look at Deryl. "Holding on to too many or too strong an essence can make you go crazy. So you have to expel them or 'cleanse yourself' periodically."

"Except," Deryl interrupted heatedly, "no one saw fit to remind you about it today, when you're doing real healing work. No, and when one dropped out to take care of his own psyche, they just passed you on to someone else, never mind what danger they put yours in!"

"It is second nature to a healer to know his limits," Terry explained, embarrassed, nonetheless. "Each of us assumed you would know yours."

Deryl snorted. "Not you, though. You just kept going until you passed out."

"Okay. First off, I didn't 'pass out.' I 'sacked out.' There's a difference. In the second place, I'm not a healer. I was a conduit. I was no more involved in someone's psyche than a power cord is in a computer's program, okay? Third, I am neither Kanaan nor psychic. Could someone's essence get tangled up in mine? I don't think so. As far as I can tell, my turning into a warrior from bumping minds with one is as likely as my turning white from bumping into you."

But Deryl wasn't ready to concede. "What's 'frickin' mean?"

Joshua made an impatient sound with his teeth. "It's a nicer way of saying something else. Frick-in. Think about it."

"It's not a Barin swearword?"

"How would I know? It's a British evil genius swear word." Then he changed to a nasal English accent and quoted, "'You know, I have one simple request. And that is to have sharks with frickin' laser beams attached to their heads!' *Austin Powers*. No one's ever quoted that around you? You can't be that out of touch!"

As he'd hoped, the tease made Deryl relax slightly. "Now that's the Joshua I know."

Joshua's stomach gave a great growl. "Well, the Joshua you know is starving."

"Come on then." Deryl headed for the door without waiting for Joshua. Cochise flew in and landed on Joshua's bed.

Joshua huffed and rolled his eyes, but as soon as the door folded shut behind Deryl, Terry helped him to his feet, keeping hold of him until a moment of dizziness passed. Then he handed him what looked like a couple of tortilla wraps.

"Something has happened between him and the Miscria," he said. "We found him in his room, shielded against everything. No one has seen Tasmae."

"What now?" Joshua groaned, and taking the everyn onto his shoulder, set out after his friend.

"Took you long enough," Deryl snapped at him as he entered the empty room. He glared at Cochise. With an indignant squawk, the everyn left.

Joshua had no intention of getting goaded into a fight; at least, not until he knew what they were fighting about. He held up his sandwich as he perched himself on the table. "I hate to eat and run, so I walked. You camping out here awhile?" he asked as he eyed the pile of food dumped on the table. He helped himself to one of the "coconut" drinks.

"This isn't the time to be funny! I need you to help me, to do your, your NLP stuff."

"My NLP stuff?" Joshua rubbed his forehead wearily. His nap had only taken the edge off his exhaustion, and his nerves were fried both from the events of the day and the dreams of Sachiko. "Look, Deryl, it's been a long day. I've been through earthquakes, a wild experience with the healers, and some pretty intense

200 ✦ Karina Fabian

dreams. So if you want my help, you're going to have to be a little more specific than my 'NLP stuff.'"

"Dammit, Joshua, you have to help me!"

"Then chill. Sit down, look at me, and start at the beginning." He waited to look up until he heard Deryl stop pacing and flop into a bean-bag type chair. Then he rid himself of all thoughts and concentrated on Deryl.

Neuro Linguistic Programming worked around the simple principle of studying your patients, discovering their thinking process, then using their own tools to help them find their own cures. Much of it involved learning to track someone's thought processes through the motion of their eyes as well as other visual and verbal cues.

Naturally observant, Joshua had quickly mastered the art. It was part of the reason he'd gotten the job at SK-Mental—and why he didn't get on well with the chief psychiatrist there. Dr. Malachai did not approve of his "NLP tricks;" whether because he truly didn't feel they were sound psychiatry or simply because Joshua had applied his "tricks" successfully, especially with Deryl.

Even now, looking at his friend's distressed face, and the way his eyes were twitching and pinning, he had a fair idea what was going on.

"There are these voices in my head, not just voices. Images and feelings and—"

"Deryl, check your shields."

"There's nothing wrong with my shields! Besides, these 'voices,' they're familiar to me. I've know them from before, from when I..." He choked off whatever else he planned to say. "Please, Josh, help me! I can't lose control now. There's too much at stake."

"Then check your shields," he repeated calmly.

"There's nothing wrong with my shields. My shields are fine! They're tighter than they've ever been, *and* we're in a shielded room. So think of something else! Or is that the best you can do?"

"Look," Joshua said, matching his response to Deryl's visual-tactile way of thinking, "I know you're feeling pretty desperate right now, but I think that in your anxiety, you're not seeing what's there. I have been observing you closely over the last few weeks, and I know how you look when you're under a psychic 'attack.' Something is getting through, around, or under your shields."

"It's not coming from outside!" Deryl howled. "I know these thoughts! These were clients at SK-Mental. Can't you understand that?"

"I know—it seems impossible. But from where I'm sitting, I can see that something is getting through your shields."

"What? I'm receiving the thoughts of a dozen human lunatics light years away?" Deryl snarled sarcastically.

"Well, how should I know? Tasmae could Call you from light years away. Where is she, anyway? Why didn't she warn anyone about the earthquake?"

Suddenly, Deryl was very still. The pupils of his eyes shrank to mere pinpoints, and the blood drained from his face. "Oh, my God."

"What?"

"Tasmae!" He dashed out of the room.

Chapter Seventeen

"Deryl!" Swearing under his breath, Joshua tore off after his friend.

Even running, Joshua could barely keep up with him. Deryl would have bowled over anyone in his way, leaving Joshua to trip over their bodies. Joshua followed blindly, though he had a vague sense that they raced upward and into the mountain itself.

"Deryl, wait up!"

He rounded a corner in time to see his friend stagger against a wall, groaning and grabbing his head. Joshua caught up to him, and Deryl clutched him for support. His irises were a sea of blue. He didn't know pupils could contract so tightly.

"Deryl!" he poured all the command into his voice he could. "Shields!"

"Taz," he gasped. "Help her. Please." He managed to point to the single door on the left before his knees gave out and he curled up on the floor. A muffled shriek escaped his lips.

It was echoed by a louder shriek from within the room.

Joshua cast a look at his shaking friend. *The best way to help Deryl is to help her.*

He left him and headed to the room.

His training with his father at the Colorado State Mental Health Institute made him pause with the doorway open only a crack and assess the situation. The bare, dome-shaped room held no objects but a simple mat and a flower pot. The Remembrance? The pot was cast upon its side, dirt spilling, as if dropped. Leinad and a healer he'd seen earlier were in the room, sitting and watching Tasmae, who, like Deryl, lay curled up in agony. Why didn't they do something?

She was half-lying, half-sitting against the wall, not far from the discarded plant. Her clothes were wrinkled and twisted, her hair wild and standing up oddly as if she had been trying to tear it out by the roots. In fact, she did have one hand gripping her forelocks tightly, as he'd seen Deryl do many times. She writhed slightly, sobbing and babbling in several languages. Joshua heard English, Spanish and something oriental, not Japanese. He caught some of the words: in English, things like danger and someone being after her, spiders; in Spanish, feeling worthless, no one understanding.

It didn't make sense. Joshua knew Deryl didn't speak Spanish, and didn't think he knew any other language either. Besides, he'd never heard Deryl say anything about arachnophobia. And the Spanish thoughts weren't his own, that was certain. LaTisha's abortion and their subsequent break-up may have left him depressed, but he'd never felt worthless, and he always knew his parents would understand, if he'd just get past his shame to tell them about it.

Okay, he pulled himself away from those dark thoughts, *so she's not getting this from me or from Deryl, not directly, anyway. What is it? She's acting like she's got multiple personalities—all of them bad. And what's with those two?* Leinad and the healer looked worried, as far as he could tell, yet not inclined to do anything.

Tasmae switched back to English, but to another mood and a new delusion. Then, she buried her face in her hands, hissing and gasping with effort. Down the hall, he could hear Deryl chanting, "PleaseStopPleaseStopPleaseStop—"

He was on his own. Joshua glanced once more at his friend, took a deep breath and stepped through the doorway.

"Tasmae?" he called gently. "Taz, can you hear me?"

She looked up at him, slowly, though narrowed eyes. Her voice rasped. "Human."

Leinad and the healer gave a start, and Leinad stepped toward him, but at Tasmae's venomous hiss, he returned back to his spot at the far side of the room with a shrug. Joshua didn't need psychic powers to know he was saying that Josh should not have interfered, but now he was on his own.

"Human." Tasmae didn't so much rise as uncoil and stalked her way to him, her shoulders hunched and her eyes hooded. Even without weapons or her lethal hairpiece, Joshua had no doubt she could do him serious damage. He stepped back.

She continued to close on him, stealthy, predatory, herding him away from the door. "You did this," she snarled.

"What do you think I did, Tasmae?" Joshua asked, keeping his voice as calm as he could despite the fact that he was quivering inside. He found himself desperately wishing for a couple of big orderlies—Sachiko, even—a straitjacket, and some Haldol.

Or maybe an animal tranquilizer. Why don't Leinad and the healer do *something?*

"Tasmae, I'm willing to listen, so why don't you just tell me what—"

"Shut up! Don't play stupid with me. I know what you planned to do. Human!" She spat the word. Even though she stood only inches away from him, her eyes were so dark that even if he knew the process of her thinking, he could not have seen it. He didn't have enough information, and he knew with all his being that any wrong move would get him killed.

He used his only tool, his words. "Tasmae. I'm your friend. I know right now, you've got a lot of confusing tho—ungh!"

She hit him. Hard.

As he folded over, she caught him in the throat with her forearm and pinned him against the wall. She was tall enough that she could glare into his eyes with only a slight tilt of her head. "You thought I wouldn't find out? You thought bringing the Ydrel here would make me trust you? That you could sing your pretty songs and make me forget my duty to my people? To the Remembrance?" She gave a maniacal laugh. "I know now. The Barins are a minor threat compared to humans! Humans, with their wild emotions and too many thoughts. Too many riddles. Riddles within riddles, thoughts within thoughts, feelings-within-feelings-within—" She shook her head, and when she looked up her eyes were shiny with tears. "You are contagion!"

She shoved her arm against his throat, and Joshua gagged. He clutched at her forearm, but he didn't know how to break her hold. He couldn't get a breath to answer her, couldn't get a breath.

Light and dark flashes dazzled his eyes.

"Taz, stop!" Deryl shouted from the doorway as he staggered into the room. He fought to hold himself together until he could draw her away from his friend. "Tasmae, please! It's not Joshua's fault."

"Deryl." As Tasmae turned to him her demeanor changed. First, it softened; gently, almost distractedly, she released Joshua. He collapsed onto hands and knees, taking in great gulps of air.

"Ydrel," she spoke again, and this time, her voice was low and seductive and she sauntered her way to him. He blinked in confusion.

"Taz, don't," Deryl whispered, but she didn't seem to hear him. Did she even see him? His eyes flicked to Joshua, but he was still on one knee, a hand braced against the ground, fighting for breath and consciousness. Leinad and the healer watched, though his muddled mind couldn't tell if they were fascinated or horrified.

"Ydrel mentor, Ydrel guide," she breathed as she moved in close, too close. He backed up until he was against a wall, a mere foot away from the plant, which seemed to turn its blossoms toward them like a plant turns toward the sun. He tensed and trembled as she leaned into him, her face barely an inch from his. He could feel her mind flowing against his shields, and he knew if she got through, they were both lost.

"Please, Tasmae, don't."

"Shhh," she breathed into his ear. "I understand now, I do. You tried to warn us. You showed Gardianju the humans. The dangers. She didn't understand. But I understand. No one will hurt you now."

Her hair was in his face and he could feel its softness, breath in its scent. It made him dizzy; he couldn't think. Dimly, he heard Joshua gasp at Leinad to do something.

Tasmae was placing feather-light kisses on his ear and neck. Warm shivers moved over his body. The smell of her hair—

It's just pheromones, he thought wildly, but it didn't help. Her body was too close. Her mind was too close. His shields sang.

He would give himself to her. Give himself to the insanities. And for a moment, it would be so sweet. He whimpered, but he didn't know if it was fear or need.

"It's all right," she breathed. "We'll protect you."

"We?" he squeaked. *Run! Hide!* part of him screamed.

"Josh!" he managed to whimper.

Joshua looked up, saw his friend was in trouble and forced himself to act.

"Tasmae!" He stood and faced her, ready to run if necessary. "Stop it, now! The only one hurting Deryl is you."

"Shut up!" Tasmae whirled away from Deryl, who sagged against the wall and started to rock, his arms wrapped around his waist.

"Deryl, snap out of it! I need your help!" Joshua called.

"Stay away from him!" Tasmae snarled as she advanced. Joshua retreated, but she didn't pursue. Instead, she stepped back toward Deryl, protecting him like an animal protects its young.

Work with that, Joshua's training told him. He held up empty hands. "I want to help Deryl, too. He's my friend—"

"Liar! You don't think I know the things you humans have done to him? Would do to us? Gardianju didn't understand. The other Miscrias didn't understand. But I do. Human riddles within riddles—I am the Queen of Riddles. I am the Mistress of Riddles!" She threw her arms over her head and spun.

Her foot bumped the plant. She stopped, looked at it and laughed, breathy and excited. She knelt beside it, cradling the blossoms and cooing.

Joshua took the moment of her distraction and moved quickly but quietly to Deryl's side. Still keeping an eye on Tasmae, he gripped his shoulder, willing him silently to focus.

Slowly, Deryl stopped rocking, though he continued to shudder as if feverish. With effort, he turned his face toward first Joshua, then Tasmae.

"It's all here," Tasmae sing-songed in one language, then another. The blossoms opened further. "The Barins are not the real threat. Humans. They get in your mind, overwhelm your thoughts. Humans. Contagion. Gardianju didn't know, but I know. Mistress of Riddles, I know. The Remembrance tells me all." And she plunged her face into the fullest bloom.

Deryl screamed, "Taz, no!"

The plant fell as her hands flew to her head, nails pressing into her skin. She collapsed and lay on her side, curled in agony.

"Get them out!" she screamed, suddenly sounding like herself. "Make them go away! Deryl, please! Help me. Someone! Please!"

No one moved. Leinad and the healer continued their silent vigil. Deryl reached out, but he touched the flower and moaned. Even Joshua found himself frozen, his mind blank.

Then her sob turned to a hiss then a shriek of rage. "Their fault! The humans did this. We have to drive them out. We have to kill them!" She lunged toward Joshua, her hands outstretched.

"Miscria! STOP!"

At Deryl's shout, she froze. Joshua watched her struggle against invisible bonds. She turned her eyes and snarl at Deryl, and Joshua followed her glare.

He swayed, obviously fighting several battles to keep his focus on stilling her. He held the Remembrance in a shaky grip. His spoke haltingly through clenched teeth, but his voice was strong and commanding. "Miscria. You *don't* understand. You...don't... know...everything."

"I am the Queen of Riddles!"

"I am the Ydrel. Ydrel...Mentor..."

"Ydrel Guide." Her face softened into confusion.

He took a slow, agonizing step toward her, then another. "None of the Miscrias understood."

He gasped, winced against whatever attack he felt, then continued. "They couldn't. I wasn't there to guide them." He reached out to her with a hand that shook like an aspen branch.

Freed from his telekinetic bonds, she took it.

Deryl convulsed slightly. "Can't run. Can't hide." Several times, his body jerked as if trying to rock. Sweat beaded his face. Still, he held Tasmae's gaze.

He's not going to last much longer. Please God, help him. Lend him your strength, Joshua prayed.

"The only way out...is through," Deryl gasped. "Let me...guide...you through."

Now she was twitching and trembling as hard as Deryl. Nonetheless, she nodded. She stepped toward him and again lowered her face into one of the blossoms.

With an inhale that was half-sob, Deryl plunged his face down next to hers.

This time, there were no screams. The two crumbled lifelessly to the ground.

"Deryl!" Joshua ran to his friend. "Oh, please don't be dead. Oh, God, please don't let him be dead!" Anxiously, he felt for a pulse. It was too light and too slow, but steady. "Oh, God, thank you. Thank you."

At last the healer moved, but she only did as cursory a check on Tasmae as Joshua had on Deryl. Then she set the plant upright between them. Both Deryl's and Tasmae's hands remained on the fronds as if attached, their other hands still clasped together.

The healer stepped back and sat down again beside Leinad.

"That's it?" Joshua raged. He stormed over to the two and flung his arm toward the unconscious pair. "That's all you're going to do? Dammit, answer me! What's going on? What do we do now?"

Leinad regarded him with barely controlled anger, but his words were emotionless. "We wait."

"Wait? I don't think so! It may be perfectly normal for your people to freak out then go catatonic, but it's not for mine, and if you won't help them, I will!" He spun back toward Deryl and Tasmae.

Two warriors with crossed swords blocked his path. He'd never seen them enter the room. Where were they when Tasmae was all but breaking his windpipe?

He closed his eyes, as if in pain. "Tell me this isn't happening."

"Joshua!" Terry rushed into the room, breathless. He gave Deryl and Tasmae the merest glance, then grabbed Joshua's arm and pulled. "Come with me, Joshua. Let's go to your room. I'll explain everything."

Joshua gaped at him. "Explain? In my room? Deryl and Tasmae are, are *comatose* and these two won't do anything, and you want me to go to my room?"

The warriors stepped forward.

Terry pulled on his arm. "*¡Por favor, Joshua!*"

He couldn't much help Deryl if incapacitated (or decapitated), and he had no doubt that the warriors would not have hesitated to do one or the other if he continued to resist. He marched between them in silence, saving his fury until he and Terry were alone in his room. Then, he related in detail what had happened, particularly the seemingly uncaring behavior of Leinad and the other healer.

"They didn't do anything, not even for Tasmae! They just sat there like it was some kind of, of show! What is up with that?" Joshua stopped his pacing to glare at Terry.

The Kanaan healer nodded sympathetically. "It is not something you or I could do. We are men of action. One who works with the Remembrances must have infinite patience. What's done is done. All we can do is pray and wait."

"How long?"

"Most Miscria have been weeks in the experience."

"Weeks?" Joshua's voice cracked.

Terry shrugged. "It may be less. It is unusual that the Remembrance, especially that one, should call upon the Miscria in this time. It has an intelligence; it knows the danger our world is in. Perhaps, too, it will be quicker since the Ydrel shares the experience with her."

"Or maybe not. He's not Kanaan. And the way they just...fell over. It was spooky. What if they can't get through it? Could they die?"

"The Remembrance healer will not let Tasmae die."

"What about Deryl?"

Terry didn't answer.

"Terry, what about Deryl? He's my friend and, and if he dies, how do I get home?" Joshua felt like a heel for thinking that now, but he couldn't help it. He had to get home!

Suddenly, homesickness gripped Joshua so tightly, he couldn't see; he almost couldn't breathe. His neck throbbed from Tasmae's choking, and his head with it. He felt Terry's touch on his shoulder, sending healing warmth through him. His pain eased, though his misery remained a tight knot in his stomach. He sank onto the bed and looked at the floor.

"Am I a prisoner again?" He jerked his head toward where the warriors had posted themselves outside his door.

"Leinad will not let you interfere. No one has done what Deryl has, and he is afraid of what else may happen."

"So they are in danger." He closed his eyes.

"Trust, Joshua. God brought you here, to this place and this time, for a purpose. Now, here." He pressed a

Madness Unbound ✸ 213

cup of something warm and fragrant into Joshua's hands. Joshua looked up just in time to see someone leave his room as silently as he'd entered.

"What's this?" he asked suspiciously.

"It will help you sleep. Make the waiting easier. Drink it all."

Joshua started to protest that he had an alien physiology and strong reactions to medications, anyway, but a moment later decided that at this point he didn't much care. He gulped the liquid down too quickly to taste and handed back the glass to Terry as a tingly warmth spread over his body. Almost immediately, he felt his muscles relax and his head get woozy. "Whoa!"

Terry chuckled as he helped him lie down. "Now, you sleep."

Joshua only half-heard the words. Already, his pains had faded and his eyelids drooped. Idly, he wondered if Haldol felt like this, and if the potion would have an amnesiac effect. He didn't want to forget...

He must have spoken his thought, for Terry said gently, "You won't forget anything, Joshua. And I'll stay to watch over you awhile."

"Like a guardian angel," Joshua murmured, his speech slurred and his eyes half-shut. A thought struck him and he opened them to look at Terry. "Hey, guardian angel. Do you think?"

"What?" Terry tucked the covers around him.

His thought fluttered away on angel's wings. The bed felt so wonderfully comfortable.

"Hmmm? Terry, will I dream?"

"No, Joshua, not this time."

"Good," he slurred as darkness took him. "Because I can't bear to lose Sachiko, not even in a dream."

For Deryl, there were no dreams, either. Only nightmares.

In the waking world, his body lay frozen, his mind shorted out, overloaded by the pandemonium of images assailing his mind. In the world of the Remembrance, he struggled and thrashed and could not stop screaming.

He felt himself being torn apart from the inside. Fire blazed across his back and legs. His blood pooled, threatening to burst his veins and his skin. He tumbled helplessly through a hurricane of pain, in too much torment to notice his fall until he smacked hard against something like water or quicksand—and like water or quicksand, it pulled him under.

Mental anguish replaced the physical torture as the "sea" morphed into a mass of lost psyches. They bumped and swirled against him, tried to press themselves upon him, into him. Snatches of memories, most of them painful, flooded his mind. They pulled him down. He fought them psychically as he fought physically to reach the surface. He'd rather face the agony of the surface than the insanity of the sea.

He was losing. Thoughts tangled around him, too many, too strong. He was going to die there, drowning in a strange sea that was half-psyche, buried by the painful experiences of others. His thrashing grew more violent, but he knew he couldn't fight them.

Then stop fighting, a memory of Joshua called faintly. *Defense! Get your shields in close and strong!*

Desperately, Deryl tried to imagine his ragged shields pulling in, knitting themselves close and tight, strong as armor. The psyches faded only slightly, but it was enough. The sea became water again.

He broke the surface, gasping and trembling, tread water, and forced his mind to think coherently as he sought his bearings.

The world reflected the turmoil he felt. Above, the sky glowed red shot through with black. Cruel-looking blue lightning arched from cloud to cloud, though he could not hear the thunder over the blaring wind. The sea churned around him, and the rain fell in cold sheets. Two large stars fought to shine through the darkness, yet oddly, the planet between them flared, clearly visible. Barin.

A wave forced water into his mouth and nose. He sputtered, felt the world gray. Pain wracked him.

Where was Tasmae? What was this—a kind of memory? Could Gardianju have really experienced *this*? No wonder Tasmae—

"Tasmae!" he called, his words immediately ripped away by the wind. His telepathic call fared better; he could almost feel the psyches below him pounce upon it like sharks feeding. Buffeted among them was a dark shape, nearly a psychic null point.

"Taz!" All his fear and pain suddenly vanished in the need to get to her, and he plunged in again to pull her from the depths.

The depths were not so eager to release her, and they had had longer to ensnare her. Tendrils of thought, like seaweed, clung to her body, but unlike seaweed, these thoughts had weight and a kind of intelligence. They dragged her down and him with them. No matter how he struggled, he could not pull her to the surface.

Even if he could, what then? They were trapped. There was no way out of Gardianju's memories.

No way out but through.

Swallowing his fear, he stopped struggling and allowed himself to be pulled down, and as he did, the memories of Gardianju the Miscria insinuated themselves into him until he could no longer tell the difference between her, Tasmae, or himself.

Chapter Eighteen

Despite Terry's reassurances, Joshua awoke from a nightmare about arguing with LaTisha.

The sun shone brightly through his window. He sat up, filled with awful but undefined feelings he couldn't find a reason for. A quick glance told him Terry had left. He schlumped over to the clothes chest and pulled out a fresh outfit, trying hard to remember his dream. He considered shaving, decided it wasn't worth the effort, and tried the door. It refused to open, and he flopped back onto the bed, feeling his bad mood justified. He was contemplating his next move when Terry came in with a tray of food.

"I thought you would be hungry," he offered.

"I'm still under house arrest?" he asked as he grabbed some kind of fruit. At the moment, he didn't much care what it tasted like.

Terry, too, grabbed a piece of fruit, but twisted it in his hands. "I will speak with Leinad. I think I can convince him to let you move about the compound again, if you promise not to interfere with the workings of the Remembrance."

"Terry, that's whacked! I have to help Deryl. You saw him. He's catatonic or something!"

"He is caught in the Remembrance with Tasmae. Right now, that's all that's keeping him alive."

Joshua dropped the fruit into his lap. "What?"

Terry held up his hands, making little erasing motions. "*¡Espérate!* That's not what I meant, exactly. He is not dying. He is in danger, as you are. Tasmae has declared you 'contagion.'"

Joshua felt his stomach sink. Terry had told him that the Barins were contagion; and because of that, the warriors killed any Barins left behind when their armies retreated. He swallowed against a suddenly dry throat and tried to keep the desperation out of his voice. "Terry, Tasmae was delirious. She's not thinking clearly."

Terry set a hand on his wrist, but his words didn't comfort. "She is caught in the Remembrance. Leinad has from the beginning felt that it awoke out of season to deliver a dire warning. He is close to her, as a father, and he has doubted the changing actions of the Ydrel. Now, he feels his fears verified."

I taught Deryl how to talk to her. Joshua pressed his fist against his mouth. He felt panic making his breath shorten and forced himself to inhale and exhale deeply. It came out shaky and he clenched his teeth to keep them from chattering. *I taught Deryl how to talk to her, and that's what changed their relationship and brought us here, and now they want to kill us!*

He forced his mind away from that thought.

"Leinad is the ultimate authority when a Remembrance is concerned, but he can do nothing to interrupt the workings of a Remembrance. Deryl should not have been able to enter into it with her, but while he is there, Leinad cannot risk doing anything that will interfere."

"So he's safe for now? What about me?"

"You have allies here. We healers know you are not contagion. You could not have helped us heal as you did, otherwise. But you are something different, and we do not understand. Leinad fears what he does not know. The warriors find threat in the unknown. But others of us desire answers."

Joshua leaned back against the wall and shut his eyes, fighting the urge to be sick. "Answers to what?"

"Explain to me the human mind, Joshua."

He barked out a laugh. "Explain the human mind? Terry, people spend their entire lives trying to understand the human mind! I've got a year left on my bachelor's in psychology and you want me to explain the human mind?"

Terry shook his arm. "You have to try, Joshua. If I can explain that you are not a threat—"

"We're dead," he muttered. "Terry, if I understood the human mind, I wouldn't be here! Heck, I wouldn't have been in Rhode Island!"

"¿Qué?"

"Listen, the only reason I was in Rhode Island, where I met Deryl, was to get away from a really bad relationship."

"Relationship?"

Joshua sat up and glared at the healer. "Yes! Relationship—a really heavy one I should never have gotten into. If I understood the human mind, Terry, I'd have never gotten involved with LaTisha, much less... Can we get back to the subject?"

"This is the subject," Terry asserted. "LaTisha is your mate?"

"No!" Joshua sputtered. "Sachiko is my soul-mate. Lattie was a mistake."

"But you had a 'heavy relationship' with her? Why?"

Joshua flung his hands. "Because she was hot and I was stupid. Is this really such a big deal?" Then something clicked, and the blood drained from his face. "This is a big deal, isn't it?"

Terry nodded. "Kanaan mate for life."

Joshua hadn't thought he could feel any sicker. *Please let me have been wrong about Deryl and Taz!* "Mate? Okay—no dating? Romance? Stolen kiss between the young and foolish?"

Terry shrugged. "One soul-mate. One romance. No stolen kisses."

"Great," Joshua muttered, and before Terry could guess at his new source of anxiety, he said, "So! I guess we'll start with Freud."

Lost deep within the Remembrance, Deryl and Tasmae could not think, only share the torturous experiences of Gardianju as she tumbled through what she thought was an endless sea of demon-specters: alien thought and alien emotions so strong and chaotic they tore her away from the physical agony she shared with Kanaan as the planet itself struggled to keep from being torn apart. She screamed, and Deryl and Tasmae screamed with her, *as* her, and in the real world, their bodies convulsed then lay still once again.

As suddenly as it had come upon her, the sea of demon-specters retreated, leaving Gardianju alone in a dark fog. She immediately fell onto hands and knees and vomited, then pushed herself away from the mess and rolled onto her back, sighing with relief.

She didn't understand what was happening, neither here nor on her world. Her people had seen the star growing in the night sky, had seen it for hundreds of years, yet it was in her generation, her lifetime, that it had become a sister to their own sun. It was in her lifetime, too, that the earthquakes, volcanoes and storms of Kanaan had become unbearably violent.

She was the Miscria, bonded with Kanaan, feeling its changes as her own. She was the God-sent one tasked to bring healing to her world. But she couldn't! She'd tried and she couldn't! It was too much, the changes too hard and too fast; she could not keep up with them. She could not stop Kanaan's pain, nor protect her people from its violence, and her failure seared itself upon her senses. So she had fled her Calling and her mind and been caught in the demon-spawned seas.

At least it's over now, she comforted herself. She shut her eyes. It was wonderfully cool and calm here. The fog folded itself around her like the softest blanket. She dozed and dreamed of Kanaan, with its two suns. There was another planet, and she feared it, though she couldn't understand why. How could it bring greater torment than she'd already felt? Yet in her mind it flashed with a thousand tiny sparks and she knew each spark brought death to her people.

But the sparks were nothing. The planet itself crumbled, then exploded, and rained destruction over half her world.

She awoke with a start and sighed gratefully to find herself still safe in this misty Netherworld. She sat up and stretched, feeling comfortable for the first time in longer than she could remember, when she heard a small voice:

"Hoosthehr?"

She turned toward the sound and was amazed to find a boy. His size and the soft curves of his face suggested he was younger than her, just starting the transition to manhood, yet the hooded and wary expression made him seem older and somehow deformed. He sat curled up against a corner she could not see. His short blond hair hung lank and filthy about his face. His head was tilted and twitched spasmodically. Otherwise he did not move, but regarded her with suspicious yet dull eyes and a jaw at once set and slack. The air around him seemed thicker, and the gray fog had an odd pinkish tint.

Slowly, tentatively, she made her way to him. He watched her but made no attempt to approach her or to run. She wasn't sure he could move. As she got nearer, she could see that part of his "deformity" came from the play of the gray lights on his bruises.

Suddenly, he focused beyond her. His head snapped up.

He began to scream.

Without thinking, she threw herself over him to shield him as the demon-specters attacked.

Before, the specters had swirled over and around her, bumping her, tossing her about. It had been painful, yes, but somehow impersonal. Not so now. For whatever reason, the demons were targeting this boy and she could not protect him completely. He cowered under her, keening like an animal, struggling when one got through. He fought her and made bizarre sounds she did not understand. Then the demon would leave— perhaps he forced it out—and he'd cling to her again and resume his high-pitched wails until another took its place. She couldn't protect him.

But she also couldn't leave him to suffer alone.

Hugging him close, she used her talent, her ability to bond with her world and join in its sufferings, to bond with this boy and take some of his agony onto herself.

She thought she had known madness.

She was wrong.

Gardianju had never felt such fear as she did huddled in the dark mists of the Netherworld, anticipating the next attack. The demons had left them again, and she didn't know why or where they had gone. She didn't know when—or if—they'd come back. *No*, she corrected herself, *they'll come back*. She looked down at the boy who slept, shivering, his head in her lap. They were drawn to him, and somehow she knew that as long as a shred of his identity, his self, was left, they would return to savage it.

Why?

How long had he been here, alone? There was no time in the Netherworld, so she couldn't know if the attacks had lasted hours or days. Subjectively, it had lasted both an eternity and an instant, with so many thoughts, feelings, and sensations coming upon her at once that she hadn't been able to identify them, much less defend against them. Even now, in this brief and eternal respite, her mind lay flayed beyond the ability to think or feel.

The boy stirred slightly, opened his eyes. Although battered worse than she, he looked at her and made sounds, like some of the Greater Beasts did when communicating with each other.

"Miscria? Momma said you'd come. It's me, Deryl." He pointed to himself, murmured something that sounded like "iddryl." His eyelids fluttered, and he focused with difficulty. "Please. Help me. I'll do anything. Don't leave me, my guardian angel." He slurred over the last words and his head lolled as he again lost consciousness.

Through her shock, she registered his plea. She felt the strength of his Naming and of the bond between them. "Gardianju," she repeated, mimicking the sounds as best she could. She pulled him a little closer. Her mind touched his, enveloped it while being absorbed by it. She curled herself around him and shared his dreams.

"So," Terry summarized as he leaned against the bathroom door, "the ego balances the base desires of the id with the moral desires of the superego."

"That's about it—'what I want to do' vs. 'what I should do.'" Joshua paused to flatten his cheek as he ran the blade over it. Terry had told him they were going to Ocapo's camp, and he didn't know when he'd have a chance to shave in front of a mirror again. He rinsed the blade. "And remember, this is an oversimplification."

Terry shook his head. "It sounds like a Bonding between Kanaan and Beast. Perhaps humans have more in common with Ocapo's people. We know so little about them. If we can reassure Leinad..."

"Are you sure we should leave Deryl alone with him?" Joshua asked as he rinsed then dried the razor. "I am not comfortable hightailing it outta Dodge knowing he's stuck in that Remembrance with Tasmae."

Terry took his razor and stuffed it into his pack. "When they return from the experience and he sees that Tasmae is all right, he will understand there is nothing to fear—especially if Tasmae is all right. Meanwhile, the only reason the warriors are on the other side of the door is because the door will not open for them."

"You mean the—" Joshua indicated the keep with a wave of his hand. "—won't let them in? If that's so, why'd it let Deryl and me into Tasmae's room?"

Terry shrugged. "It shouldn't have admitted anyone while Tasmae was under the influence of the Remembrance. In fact, it shouldn't have let her out, either. That's part of what keeps Leinad from acting. It is possible the Remembrance has influenced the keep to bring Deryl to Tasmae. Perhaps with the Ydrel to guard and guide, Tasmae will unravel Gardianju's mysteries."

Guard and Guide. "Salgoud, where did her name come from?"

"Tasmae or Gardianju? Tasmae is a Barin word. Gardianju, it is thought, came from the Ydrel, though none know for certain."

"Hmm," Joshua shut his eyes, morphing her name with slurring. Gardianju. Gar-di-ahn- jool. Gardiangel.

Guardian Angel.

How many personalities did he see Tasmae manifest? At least four, and all of them very human. Deryl may not have known the languages, but then again, he'd seen him speak fluent Yiddish to Isaac, and Joshua suspected he didn't learn that language through any conventional means. Tasmae screaming about humans being contagion. The fits and visions and prophecies Gardianju supposedly had. Were they all because she'd somehow contacted Deryl when his abilities had first manifested and he'd been fighting against losing his sanity to the psychic influences of the patients around him?

That was five years ago, but time's irrelevant, Deryl said. Still, five years' experience of dealing with outside thoughts—can he teach Tasmae, guide her through the experience? Or will he think he's relapsing?

They heard the door fold open. Joshua's heart hammered in his chest, but rather than an armed warrior, the healers crowded into the room. They formed a half-circle and waited.

"Our escort," Terry said.

Joshua shouldered his pack and moved to the center of the circle. On the way through the corridors, he tried not to think about the wary looks of the warriors they passed.

Silently, he recited the Guardian Angel Prayer for Deryl and Tasmae, and Gardianju.

Gardianju awoke with a start and glanced around, her heart pounding. The mists seemed to have thickened around them, but in a way that felt protective rather than sinister. She couldn't see any shadows moving in the still grayish-white. She released the breath she had been holding.

The boy, the Ydrel, slept beside her, a relaxed, natural sleep. Her lap pillowed his head, and she caressed his hair and marveled at all the things she'd learned from her contact with his mind.

The demon attack had left her shaken and terrified, yet this boy had been enduring attacks of varying size and intensity for over a year. Despite that, he had only recently come to this place, driven here by forces he could not control. Mere weeks into her role as Miscria, the agony and the feelings of failure had made her flee her mind. Yet her experiences couldn't compare to the horror he'd experienced.

He doesn't know what's happening. He's had no defenses. And no one will believe him, much less train him, except— She shivered. There had been an influence, a dark one, more sinister and more fearful than the demons. And he'd chosen—*chosen*—this rather than that evil one's help. Tears of shame trickled down her cheeks, and she wiped them away lest they fall upon his face and wake him. He was depending on her. He'd named her, sworn his aid in return for hers. Now, they were joined. Neither would be alone.

So much help he could give her! She thought again of what she had learned through their bond. In his mind, she had found the answers to so many questions of Kanaan's odd behavior and pain. She hadn't even known her own questions, yet the answers were there: how earthquakes start and how they may be calmed; the mechanics of volcanic eruptions; the crazy—no, the *chaos*—theory behind storms. So much information, and with it, ideas. Direction. She could help Kanaan. She could help her people. The Ydrel had shown her how. She would return to her people, use his knowledge to help them.

She would help him as well. There were methods, ways of deflecting or dismissing the throes of Kanaan, that all Miscria knew. She had passed that knowledge to him through their bond. He could fight his way back to his world and rejoin his reality. There, he would gain even more knowledge for her.

The Ydrel stirred, lifted his head, and sat up. He weaved slightly, and she clasped his shoulders to steady him. He blinked at her, not quite seeing. "Guardi-angel?" he murmured.

"I'm here."

He focused on her with eyes shiny and wet. "Help me die," he whispered.

With a sad smile, she shook her head.

"I want to die!"

He cried like a child, like one who had lost everything, even hope, yet without the wild hysterics of before. Again, she marveled at his strength. She had to remind him of it, bring him back to it. He could no longer afford to be a child.

Neither of them could.

She clasped him to her a moment, letting him cry the worst out, then pushed him back. "Look at me," she instructed in this strange spoken language she had picked up from their bond. She did her best to ignore the fact that the demons had used it, too. He used it; the rest was coincidental and unimportant.

"Look at me," she repeated, emanating determination in her voice and expression, and through their bond. "You cannot die here. You will not die here. You are the Ydrel. Ydrel Mentor, Ydrel Guide."

"No, no." He shook his head, rejecting her words and the will behind them. "Please guardian angel, I can't. I can't."

"You can. You will. You have fought the demons before—these and others. Yes, I know this, my bonded. You are not like him, the one you call Master. You have given my people a chance at life with your wisdom and knowledge. But I must have more. I have shared with you my skill. Use it to find your way back, beloved, but don't fear. I will always be with you. When the demons come, I will be with you. I am the Miscria. I am your Gardianju. Trust me."

"I'm scared."

Her eyes filled with tears. "Me, too."

They held each other.

Chapter Nineteen

Deryl was forced out of the Remembrance.

He lay on the floor where he'd fallen, blinking slowly. Stunned and disoriented, he glanced around the darkened room, saw one of his hands was next to the Remembrance. Idly, he noted the blossom nearest him had closed. His other hand brushed lightly against Tasmae's. Her blossom was still open, and she did not move.

"Tasmae," he tried to call, but his voice was gone. He wondered if he'd screamed himself hoarse. He forced himself to focus and sighed with relief when he saw the rise and fall of her chest.

Run, Deryl! Get out! An urgency spiked into him with such force, he unconsciously threw up shields.

Something ricocheted against them.

He didn't even bother to check what had hit him. He forced his lethargic and protesting body up and half-ran, half-staggered from the room, blindly taking turns as some *thing* compelled him.

He saw no one until he reached an exit and stood blinking in the daylight. A unicorn offered its flank to him.

Hurry! The unicorn urged.

"No," he murmured, "Tasmae."

You cannot help her if they kill you. Now mount!

He didn't understand. His head swam with images, feelings, memories. Some his, some...

"Gardianju," he whispered. "I forgot her. She loved me. She saved me, and I forgot her. And Tasmae...."

He clambered on. His hands tightened in the unicorn's mane as he took off at a full gallop. Then he could only concentrate on staying seated. The unicorn rode in a direction he'd never gone before. He caught sight of cliff faces, forests, green meadows instead of the purple-flowered ones. It didn't mean anything to him. It hardly seemed real compared to the confusion in his mind.

Perhaps an hour later—just enough time for his body to protest the ride—the unicorn stopped in another isolated glen with a small, clear pool. Deryl slipped off more than dismounted. He clung to the mane to stay upright as the beast led him to the water. He splashed his face, drank, gradually came back to himself.

The unicorn stood patiently beside him.

I didn't know you could speak, he told him.

You never asked, the beast replied.

"There were two suns," he whispered. Somehow verbalizing it helped. "It was tearing Kanaan apart. Gardianju didn't know what to do. She fled, to me. How did she find me?"

The unicorn's hide shook in an equine equivalent of a shrug.

He rubbed the scars on his wrist, remembering the terrifying weeks after he'd almost killed Perry. He'd gone to the hospital, and when he couldn't defend himself against the thoughts around him, the institution. So many minds. So much pain. And then, Gardianju.

"She found me in the Netherworld. She protected me. She joined minds with me and took some of the worst of the attacks onto herself. She held me. She reminded me I wasn't alone." He stopped and again rubbed his wrists. "I guess she learned about weather and geology and such from me. I loved that stuff; wanted to be a climatologist. I wanted to die, but she wouldn't let me. She said she needed me. Her people needed me. She gave me some of her Miscria skills, to use against the 'demons' of the Netherworld, and to protect myself in the real world. That must be how I managed until Joshua came and taught me better—and I thought it was Malachai that had helped me.

"It's me. The whole Remembrance is about me."

You think too highly of yourself. There is more.

"Where's the other sun?" He was so tired. Things blurred and focused, blurred and focused. He scooted back from the water's edge so he didn't pass out in it.

Gardianju made it go away.

He couldn't sit up any longer. He blinked up at the specter of Barin just topping the trees. *She didn't do it right. Something went wrong. She didn't know enough. I didn't know enough. And the Miscrias don't understand. They don't know what to ask.*

He saw a model of the solar system in his mind, all the planets aligned and stable. He felt the dance of Kanaan, the Intruder breaking the path, and tried to trace the lines of its movements.

"Orbital mechanics," he murmured before exhaustion finally took him and he fell into a dream-filled sleep.

Once mounted, Joshua, Terry, and Ocapo hurried away, the unicorns making great awkward leaps up steep embankments. Joshua couldn't shake the feeling of arrows pointed at his back, and he with no psychic shielding, so once they reached a long flat stretch, he let Glory have her head until there was nothing but the wind in his face and the thunder of hoof beats under his seat. When Glory slowed down of her own accord, he looked back and saw Ocapo and Terry, two small figures hurrying toward them. He laughed with relief.

"Wish I could take you home, baby," he said as he patted her neck. She snorted.

She came to a stop at the edge of the mesa. He gasped as he looked out across miles of mesas with long flat valleys in between.

"Whoa! It really is a maze," he whispered. His mouth worked silently for a moment, then he burst out, "God had a lot more fun on your planet than mine!"

Ocapo laughed as he pulled up beside him. "God did not create this. Tasmae did."

"Tasmae?"

"It is both protection and trap. After the last war, Tasmae knows she will be a prime target. She intends to lead the bulk of the Barins into the maze and defeat them here. That's why Salgoud focused on the Ydrel's idea of using the caves. In fact, one of the things I must do tonight is recruit more Bondfriends to search the maze for caves, or places where Tasmae can coax caves from the stone."

"Are we in the middle?" he asked as he tried to gage the length of the maze. *Five, ten miles on this side*, he thought.

"What good would that be? The Barins have devices that can see from the air—another reason Tasmae thought of recruiting the everyn. You see that the mesas are narrow? They cannot land their ships here, either. Also, Tasmae will shroud the area in fog. We don't doubt that they might still find their way around, but we can make them pay for every step. There are decoys, hidden tunnels and traps throughout the maze. The keep itself is actually to one side, and one of several. The bulk of the maze is behind us, on the other side of the mesa."

"Really." Joshua whistled. He struggled to take all of it in. Colossal was too small a word to describe it. His head filled with so many questions that he hardly knew where to start. Ocapo's casual acceptance didn't help. "Um, so how long did it take to build this?"

Ocapo looked out over the winding valleys and huge land formations arranged like hedgerows with pride but no particular awe. "I'm not certain. They say she got the idea in the Season of Recovery, but of course, the first thing she had to do was pray. When I say God didn't build it, I meant that it was not His direct design, but obviously, she could not have done this without His help."

"Obviously," Joshua agreed dryly. *Talk about faith the size of a mustard seed.*

"So once she had a plan that was acceptable to God, He led her to this place. It was fairly empty, but with lots of volcanic activity. It was also a very unstable area, and she was able to use that to bend Kanaan to her will. I'm told it took the better part of the Season of Recovery and the Season of Calm, and even into the Season of Preparation. For all her natural talent, she never completed her training, after all."

"Oh, sure." He tried to keep his voice casual, even though he felt rocked to his toes. What could a fully trained Miscria do? "Can I ask you something? If she can do this by herself, why can't she stomp the Barins single-handedly? Just fling a few mountains at their spaceships or something?"

"When the War comes, Tasmae will be useless as a warrior. She will spend all her talent just keeping Kanaan from destroying itself. It is always so in the Season of War. It was early in the last war when her mentor was killed. Can you imagine trying to care for Kanaan while being sent from hideaway to hideaway? No wonder she wanted a safe haven. Look!"

He pointed to the right, to where two small dots dove and swirled in the distance. "A mating dance! We have even more reason to celebrate tonight! Come. We will follow the edge of the canyon awhile, and then fly down to an open area where my people have set up camp."

He started off, but Glory, sensing Joshua's mood, lingered a little longer while Joshua tried to take in what he'd just learned about Tasmae, who could, for all intents and purposes, single-handedly alter the face of a planet, control volcanoes and earthquakes with her mind, had the charge of literally holding a planet together, and was essentially Ground Zero for an upcoming war.

And she thought that Deryl had even more power and importance than her?

Deryl thrashed in his sleep, powerless against his dreams.

Across a field, Tasmae stood, face tilted to the sky, screaming words of furious command. Behind her, stretched in time, the other Miscrias mirrored her posture and mood. And they were wrong—all of them wrong.

He was Kanaan, content in its dance until the Intruder forced it from its steps.

He danced with Tasmae, and they laughed at her pregnant belly between them. Something grabbed her, pulled her. Her hands slipped from his.

"Tasmae!"

Leinad sat in the corner of the Remembrance room, watching Tasmae, so still, and tears traced lines down his cheeks because he was watching the end of their world.

Deryl yelled across the field, "Tasmae! You have to stop! They are wrong! All the other Miscrias were wrong!"

Help me! Her command echoed across creation. He felt her pull with all her will. At her feet, the grass wilted.

"No! Tasmae!"

The circle expanded, and with it, death. Animals and birds entered the circle and fell motionless.

"Stop it! It's wrong!"

One by one, the Miscrias sank to the ground and faded away.

Tasmae began to shake with the power she could barely contain. Deryl felt as much as heard the roar growing within her.

Kanaan's energy turned from the dance to the Intruder.

Intruder! Leave us!

Tasmae! Listen to me. Deryl ran toward her. He stepped into the circle and felt himself weaken. He threw up shields, but they drained as he ran. *Please, beloved! You don't know how.*

GO AWAY! Tasmae shoved with all her might.

Wait!

Kanaan pushed the Intruder.

Stop!

The force of Tasmae's will, fueled by the power of her world, slammed into Barin.

Deryl sank to his knees. "No!"

Her will was too hard, too focused. The Intruder did not leave the dance; rather, Barin exploded.

Deryl saw the sky falling and with the last of his strength, threw shields up to protect himself and Tasmae.

It didn't matter. When he crawled to her, he found her dead, their child with her.

"Lie?" Terry asked as though he wasn't sure what the word meant. A few moments later, he said, "To deliberately tell an untruth? Can your people really do that?"

"Deryl did when he told me the Barins were attacking, remember? What, can't yours?" Joshua asked, then realized it made sense. When your communication was all mental, the only way to lie convincingly would be to believe it yourself, and such self-delusion would probably count as a mental illness that the healers would pick up on. He wondered what it'd be like to know that whatever someone told you was true.

"No. We can withhold information, but not fabricate it."

"Okay. What about fiction? Storytelling?"

"They are not different for your people?" Ocapo asked, amazed.

"Usually." Joshua hedged.

Ocapo, however, laughed. "How confused your people must be! Cochise and Spot tell me as a Kanaan, I could never understand. In some ways, I think you humans have more in common with the Greater Beasts."

"Oh, thanks loads. Ocapo, maybe you shouldn't try to help."

They had ridden to the end of the narrow mesa and flown back into the canyon and were on the way to a rest area Ocapo knew about. Meanwhile, Terry had been questioning them both, testing a theory that humans might be similar to the Bondfriends.

"But I think it's so!" Ocapo insisted. "Multiple desires. Multiple emotions. Multiple talents. *And* you can manage many of them at the same time. No wonder so many Kanaan are afraid of you." Ocapo smiled indulgently at Joshua and reached over to slap him on the shoulder. "Do not worry! Not so long ago, they feared the Bondfriends. In our bonding to the beasts, we too are exposed to chaotic minds. "

With a shriek, Spot dove in front of them and let loose with his opinion. Ocapo's unicorn skipped to the side to avoid stepping in it.

Ocapo continued, thoughtful and oblivious to the ire of his friend. "You will be safe with us. We owe that much to the Ydrel."

"What's the Ydrel have to do with anything?" he asked.

"You understand that there are hierarchies of being?"

"Not really."

"I shall try to explain. There are Kanaan, made in God's image. There are the Greater Beasts, companions to the Kanaan, their peers in intelligence and reasoning, yet different in their thoughts and passions. Then there are the Lesser Beasts—animals—who have some intelligence but not the ability to—telep is your word?—yes, telep with the Kanaan or the Greater Beasts. Some of these have been domesticated, some remain forever feral. Then of course, there are the animals. All of this was determined by when and how they ate from the Trees."

"What trees?"

Ocapo looked at him in askance. Terry, too, gaped. "Did God not give your kind the Trees?"

Something impossible clicked in Joshua's head. "Wait a minute—you're not saying the Tree of Life and the Tree of Knowledge? Like in the Bible—Adam and Eve in Eden...?"

Glory bobbed her head as if in affirmation, but Terry said, "Tree of Knowledge, yes. But Tree of Life—I'm not sure that is the right name. Perhaps, if you mean the kind of Life you share with your soul-mate. It is different, but similar. It is the life-relationship with God."

"I don't think the Bible ever really specified," Joshua muttered. Things were getting a little surreal. Did every planet have a Garden of Eden? "So, what? The Kanaan ate first and—"

Ocapo sputtered, and even the unicorns seemed to laugh.

Terry explained. "No, of course not. No species was to eat until it had reached the fullness of its time—potential, I suppose would be the word. The animals, of course, never ate of the trees; the fruits were not pleasing to them. The Lesser Beasts ate next, and stripped the trees bare. It was many seasons before the trees were ready again, and the Greater beasts each took their turn. Again, all the fruit were eaten and it was many seasons before it was ready again. Finally, God invited the Kanaan. And our minds were opened so that we could understand each other and the Greater Beasts; and our hearts were opened so that we could love each other in...*agape*?" He looked at Joshua.

"Uh-huh. *Agape*: universal, brotherly love. Go on."

"And our souls were opened to communion with God. Did God do something different on your world, then?"

"I'm not sure you'd say God did... According to the Bible, Adam and Eve, the first humans, were already in communion with God, and he told them *not* to eat from the Tree of Life and the Tree of the Knowledge of Good and Evil, but they did, anyway. Satan took the form of a serpent— a long slithery animal? You know, I haven't seen any around here. I haven't seen many animals in general, except Greater Beasts and a few birds."

Ocapo nodded. "The Miscria warned them away for the exercises. Most may stay away until after the Season of War. This will be a major battlefield if all goes according to Tasmae's plan. We shall run into more soon. None of these serpents, though."

"Lucky you. Anyway, the serpent tricked the woman, Eve, into eating the fruit of the Tree of Knowledge, and she got Adam to do the same."

"Women seem to have much influence on men in your world," Terry observed.

Joshua waved a dismissal. "It goes the other way, too. Trust me. Anyway, that was the original sin, and it separated us from God." He stopped there, embarrassed and unsure he could go on.

Ocapo, however, begged like a child needing to hear just one more chapter of a bedtime story. "But God didn't abandon you. He didn't let Adam and Eve die? He's still with your people?"

"Sure, God's still with us. We keep failing Him, and He keeps forgiving us and we try again. Two thousand of our years ago, he sent us his Son, born of a virgin, living as a human and as Divine until he sacrificed himself for the forgiveness of our sins. At least, that's the Christian belief." Even though Ocapo said nothing, Joshua could tell he'd simply confused him.

In for a penny. "There are a couple of dozen major world religions and a bunch of, well, sub-religions, I guess you'd call them, like Lutheran, Baptist or Catholic faiths are subsets of Christianity in general, if you define 'Christianity' as the belief that Jesus was God and Man who sacrificed himself for the forgiveness of our sins. For example, I'm Catholic, but my parents are just generally Christian; I have stricter beliefs in how my relationship with God works." His voice trailed off. "This isn't making any sense to you, is it?"

Ocapo shook his head. Even his unicorn gave Joshua the fish-eye.

Terry asked. "All this because your Adam and Eve couldn't wait to eat?"

Despite himself, Joshua laughed, especially since his stomach chose that moment to give a complaining rumble. "Moses called the Jews a 'stiff-necked people,' but I think that applies to humans in general. We're impatient, too. And, yeah, always hungry in some way or another. Speaking of, when's dinner?"

"The earthquakes have stirred up the Lesser Beasts, and a couple of the more dangerous ones wandered into a populated area. My people sent out a hunting party. We will feast tonight!"

"Like...steaks?" He couldn't believe the longing in his voice. He could feel himself salivating. He cleared his throat. "I thought you were vegan."

Ocapo shrugged. "Kanaan are. Not Bondfriends. Would make it hard to be bonded to a carnivore, wouldn't it? We've another of your hours, I think. Several tribes are coming, and there will be feasting and games and music. I'm told you like music."

"I love music," Joshua hedged.

Ocapo caught his hesitant tone. "Bondfriend music is different."

They stopped near a large pond of clear water. They dismounted, and despite all the riding Joshua had been doing the past few days, his legs welcomed the chance to stretch. He went to the pool where Glory was drinking, her face bent over the water so that her horn dragged along the surface. Tentatively, Joshua scooped some water in his hands and sipped. It tasted sweet and pure as the water from his parents' reverse-osmosis filter back home.

"Do unicorn horns purify water?" he asked Ocapo.

"What an interesting notion."

"It's a myth back home. Not nearly as interesting as being able to share your mind with an animal," Joshua replied.

"I didn't explain that, did I?" Ocapo said with some surprise. "We got distracted with the story of the Trees. But they play into it as well.

"It is said that there was one more harvest of the tree, and that God invited the Kanaan to wait for it if they wished. Those that waited until the fruit was fully ripe joined in perfect communion with God and are no longer of this world. However, there were some who wished to wait, but grew impatient—like your people, Joshua—and ate the fruit before it was ready.

"They found themselves trapped in this world but not fully of this world. They were both blessed and cursed with serenity. Even though they had intelligence and the power of communication, they had lost the basic desires for survival—food, drink, companionship. God took pity on them and directed that some of the beasts would bond with these Kanaan. In that way, we would share our intelligence and our desires.

"In every generation, a few of us are born. Some to other Bondfriends, though the trait does not always breed true, and some to Kanaan. It's difficult for those of us born to Kanaan. We start out normal enough, but gradually ordinary life grows confusing, then unimportant. Even pain becomes immaterial: We recognize it, but don't understand what it means. If the child is lucky enough to be in the vicinity of the bonding beasts, one finds him. When that does not happen and the trait is recognized, usually the parents will seek out a Bondfriend camp. Sometimes, such children...fade away. Bonding beasts who do not find a bonding child will slowly revert to a feral state and an animal intelligence. Cochise, of course, is very young, so he is still— not tame? No, wait—not sentient. He will seek a

Bondfriend in the next couple of seasons, however, and if he does not find one, he will fly away and join his animal brothers in the wilds. A child who does not find a Bondfriend...fades away until they die."

Spot flew down and settled onto Ocapo's lap.

"You?" Joshua asked.

The Bondfriend nodded, swallowed hard, and continued. "My family's village is very remote. They seldom contacted anyone beyond, and no one like me had been born there. They did not know what to do. They were afraid. I do not blame them. By then I'd gone beyond caring to eat or to communicate. It was all so immaterial. It didn't even matter when they left me in the middle of an open field on top of the highest hill around. They trusted God to help me, and of course, He sent Spot, who was also on the edge of losing himself."

Ocapo rubbed him along the neck and smiled. "There was a wild storm. It threw Spot off his course. I was standing, oblivious to the rain and wind, and he slammed into me and we both went tumbling. By the time we'd rolled to a stop, I had the revelation that I was wet and cold and didn't like it! We ran for cover. The next day, we made the trek back to his village."

"You didn't return to your parents? Why not?"

Ocapo shrugged. "I had been reborn as a Bondfriend. Bondfriends are apart from Kanaan. We do not think the same way. It's not always easy to communicate. Have you no equivalent in your world?"

"Well, we have different languages and cultures."

"So Terry mentioned. It's more than that." He paused, a frown of thought on his face. "Right now, from Spot, I feel conflicted between the desire to hunt and the loathing of leaving a comfortable lap and neck scratching. I also feel excitement at seeing my people. That's three emotions, two of which are not my own. What are you feeling right now?"

"Okay, well, I'm enjoying this conversation, though I'm still confused, which annoys me, and a little freaked out about all the parallels. I'm kind of relieved to be out of the compound, though I feel guilty about leaving Deryl behind. I'm also a little worried, too, that something might happen to him, and I'm scared about getting stuck here. Even though I'm actually kind of relaxed and excited to meet your people—and looking forward to something besides rabbit food—I'm seriously homesick. I miss my family, and Sachiko. She's my fiancée—my soul-mate."

"But not the one you've mated with?"

"No," Joshua groaned. "So let's add shame to that list, shall we?"

"This is my point, though. You've described a dozen different emotions that you're feeling at the same time."

Terry spoke up. "But this is normal for you?"

"Why not?"

Terry shook his head. "Do you know how many emotions a Kanaan—not a Bondfriend, but a Kanaan like me—feels? One."

"One? What's so unusual—?"

"Only one, Joshua. We do not balance multiple emotions. One will replace the other, but two can never compete or conflict. Yet you say humans can feel conflicting emotion?"

"Oh, yeah." He thought about last year with LaTisha. "We don't always enjoy it, though."

"Most Kanaan would not even be able to handle two agreeing emotions, and conflicting ones could harm them beyond recovery. We healers can handle multiple impressions, but only during the healing. It's why we perform a cleansing."

"Is that why Leinad's so afraid of us?"

Ocapo and Terry exchanged looks. Joshua checked his impatience.

"We still have a long ride." Ocapo stood, dumping Spot off his lap, and headed to the unicorns. Terry followed.

Joshua chased after him and grabbed his arm. "Come clean, Terry. What's got him so afraid?"

"Leinad, too, has the ability to handle conflicting impressions for a limited time so that he can work with the Remembrances. He holds some knowledge of all of them, but not all of each."

Joshua forced back the urge to yell. "Jack of all trades. Right. So what does this have to do with Deryl and me?"

"You know that not all Miscria contact the Ydrel—only a handful?"

"Hadn't thought of it, but yeah. So?"

"All who do eventually succumb to insanity and die. No one understood why—"

"And now they do." Joshua moaned. Glory moved beside him, offering him support. He leaned back against her flank. "Terry, he didn't know. He didn't even realize the Miscria were people until Tasmae. Maybe this time will be different."

"It already is," Terry replied. "The Miscria who contact the Ydrel all died early in the Season of Calm, and from their sacrifice, Kanaan was spared war for generations. We are almost at the Season of War."

"He thinks Deryl's going to kill Tasmae?"

"Not intentionally, perhaps."

"That's ridiculous!"

Ocapo rode up beside them. "Of course it is!"

Terry nodded. "Many of us believe he is here to save her—enough to stay Leinad's hand for now. But when he entered the Remembrance, he became part of Leinad's domain."

Tasmae stirred slightly, still caught in Gardianju's life. The memories passed more quickly, so that she tumbled helplessly in the swift current and was only fully aware of snatches of time.

Twin suns loomed in Kanaan's sky, so that there was no night, no comforting starshine and shadow, only glaring light and heat and the drying of her world. Gardianju stood on the cracked dirt of a dry lakebed and gazed dully at the heat-seared sky. Kanaan's throes had worn past her defenses, beyond her training, and manifested themselves upon her. She rubbed her hand against her arm, so dry that the skin came off in chunks rather than flakes, and raised bloody hands to the burning sky. The Ydrel was there, and was not there, still caught in his own battle against the demons. She longed to help him, to cure him, but knew she could not. In her state, she would only bring him more pain, so she stayed away. Nonetheless, if she'd had moisture for tears, she would have wept for him.

The suns faded, and with them the heat. The people sighed with relief. Soon, however, the sighs turned to moans as the temperature continued to plummet. She had an apprentice now, and they spent much of their energy on keeping Kanaan and its people warm. It left little for themselves, and they lay listlessly under blankets near the hot springs where her village had retreated. All around her, she felt the despair of her people, and the loss of hope worried her most of all.

She escaped her mind and found herself with the Ydrel. He was better now, able to understand and to answer her questions.

Winter, he told her, and shared an image of a small blue world moving along an elliptical path around a star, tilted on its axis so that the sun's rays shone more brightly on some areas than on others. Then he showed her even more alien visions: thick cold white ash falling from the sky, covering the land in the softest of ice. Children oddly hampered in thick clothing that covered even their faces, ran about, molding the ash—no, the *snow*—into balls and shapes, throwing them at each other and laughing.

She didn't understand the images, but they comforted her, as did the gentle trust of his mind. It was the only real warmth she felt.

"Ydrel. Deryl," Tasmae whispered as the scene changed and she was again caught in the rushing current of the Remembrance.

Chapter Twenty

"Oh, man, do you smell that?" Joshua moaned in ecstasy as they broke through the trees and the aroma of cooking meat reached them.

Ocapo inhaled and hummed in pleasure. "Not much longer. We can stop and walk from here."

"I have so missed meat! The only thing that could make this better is a Diet Coke and about 400 milligrams of ibuprofen."

"Are you in pain?" Terry asked as they dismounted. He pulled the pack off his unicorn then hurried to Joshua, who moved more slowly.

Nonetheless, he waved his friend off. "Just stiff from all the riding. I haven't ridden this much in years. I'll be fine—though tomorrow might be a different story."

He pulled the pack off Glory and set it on the ground. "Hold on, baby, let me see if there's a brush in here—"

Glory tossed her head and took off.

"Hey!" he called after her.

Ocapo closed his bag and handed it to him. "There is a waterfall in a cove down the trail. They are going to bathe. She said she will return for her brushing later."

"Great. Wet horse. You know, a shower doesn't sound half-bad."

Ocapo clapped his shoulder and led him down the path, Terry just behind. "Later we will go together. You should not wander off the trails alone. Remember what I said about traps? The plants may not recognize you as a friend."

Joshua cast a suspicious look at the trees beside him. That creeped-out feeling started crawling along his spine, when a heavy beat with a flying melody distracted him. "Music!"

Ocapo laughed. "I told you."

"Do you have dancing?" He could not think of a better way to work out his kinks or his anxieties.

Ocapo nodded and quickened his pace. "I, myself, am not very good."

"I'll teach you—but I want to learn your dances, too." He saw Terry lagging behind and reached back to include him. "Come on, Terry! I declare a hiatus on any heavy topics. Tonight, we party."

Gardianju fell to her knees in the middle of the marketplace and concentrated all her strength on keeping two of Kanaan's tectonic plates from shearing each other apart.

Help me, she commanded, and her apprentice, then some villagers, knelt beside her and offered her their strength. She took it, pulled, and gradually, Kanaan's struggles ceased. She focused the last of their energy on the mountain near the site of the quake. It shook, then crumbled, pouring tons of trees, rock and debris into the gap that had opened.

She and twenty others had to be carried to the healers, but Kanaan would survive another day.

A season of calm came, though it held no calm for her. The torments of the Ydrel had increased as the torments of Kanaan lessened, and she devoted her talent to healing his mind, working with synapses and neurons as she would earth and flora, and sharing in his sufferings as she had shared in her world's. She sat in the corner of her room, arms crossed over her stomach, rocking, and her walls seemed unnaturally pink.

Another progression of the seasons had come, and again, they were in a season of calm. Even the Ydrel seemed to have calmed, though she did not know whether the demon attacks had lessened or if he could better defend against them. It did not matter; if he had been in torment, she could not have helped him this time. The events of the last Progression had left her unable to think, barely able to care for the world—or herself. She lay on the ground in an open field, staring up at a blue sky in which the smaller sun was catching up to its sister. She saw them but did not see them, for visions filled her mind. Kanaan caught in a deadly dance with another world. Bright flashes on an alien planet. Wrong. Bringing the demons. Bringing insanity. Insanity all around her. All around the Ydrel. Ydrel comes, but not to her. To another. A Miscria. Tasmae.

A surge of jealousy, then the visions reassert themselves.

The Ydrel comes to Kanaan, bringing change—and peril. Too much change. Too much peril. The other world explodes. Its pieces rain on Kanaan. Ydrel reaches out, clasps the demon planet. It is whole. It survives. The aliens survive. Kanaan changes. The dance, so perfect, so comfortable, changes. Snow falls from the sky.

She didn't try to interpret or even understand the visions, merely let them play in her weary mind until they became one with her dreams.

More seasons of pain and confusion, torment and visions. Then, a sudden clarity, like awakening from a deep sleep. She looked at her hands, shocked to see the wrinkles, stared in amazement at the gray in her hair. Had it been so long? *The Ydrel*, she thought. *The Ydrel is still a child.* A moment later, she wondered why she thought that. No child could know what he knew. No child could have battled as he had. Ydrel Mentor, Ydrel Guide. Not Ydrel Child.

She pushed the thoughts aside. God had given her this clarity for a reason. She had duties. She summoned the Keeper of Remembrances, and closed her eyes to rest until he arrived and presented her with a seedling. She caressed its tender shoots, opened her mind, and imprinted it with her memories, experiences, and visions. It burst into bloom, then one by one, the blossoms closed into buds. Only at the proper times would they open again to reveal their secrets.

Next, she summoned her protégés, one of whom had been newly discovered during her time of visions and was being trained by her own apprentice, now nearly her equal in caring for Kanaan. Nonetheless, he had not had contact with the Ydrel. That must change. She would help him forge the link.

But when they touched the Ydrel's mind, her protégé fell to the ground screaming and did not stop until God took him two days later.

When he breathed his last, Gardianju whispered heartfelt thanks that his suffering had ended, then turned to her newest student, who knelt beside her, terrified.

This will not happen again, she vowed. *To commune with the Ydrel is too dangerous.* Yet they needed his information; she knew that, too. Her visions had shown her that.

Once she had fled her mind to a Netherworld, where she had found the Ydrel hunted by demons. Now, she would find a way to pull him from his own mind to a place of her choosing. Somewhere neutral. Somewhere safe. Somewhere where there was only the Will of the Miscria and the Answers of the Ydrel. Her own Netherworld.

She would never allow another Miscria to die as her apprentice had.

In the hidden grove, with a unicorn keeping watch, Deryl whispered in his sleep. "I'm sorry. I'm so sorry. Don't worry, Gardianju. I won't hurt Tasmae. I swear, I won't. I'll make it right."

The sun was setting on the mesas, but with the clear sky and incredible density of stars, everything was still visible, if a little washed out. Nonetheless, Joshua got hints of the variety of patterns and colors whenever someone's costume caught the light of the several bonfires in the center of the camp. The Bondfriends—and maybe regular Kanaan for all he knew—loved color and pattern. He looked forward to the morning when he could see everyone's outfits in detail.

As with any large but close-knit community party Joshua had known, small groups had formed up, with people of all ages moving from group to group, the kids often at a full run. For the most part, they avoided Ocapo, Terry and Joshua, content to cast glances their way. Even the children observed the rule, which impressed and touched him. He smiled and winked at one little girl who hovered near a tree just on the edge of what she'd apparently been told was the boundary, but before she could take that as an invitation to cross that boundary—and start a flood of curious kids, no doubt— he looked away toward the bonfires in the center of the campground. Over one roasted a huge animal with way too many limbs.

He shouldered Ocapo and pointed to it. "So, everybody gets a drumstick?"

As if in answer, the same child he'd smiled at appeared before him, bringing him a roasted leg that would put any turkey to shame. He chuckled—it felt so good to laugh—and took a bite. His eyes closed in pleasure as he chewed.

Ocapo nudged him and he opened his eyes to see a young lady skipping out of the way of a young man. Laughing, she dashed past, with him in pursuit.

"Oh-ho," Joshua commented.

Ocapo gave him a knowing smile. "You know the everyn who are doing the mating dance? Those are their Bondfriends."

"Really?" He watched as the man caught his mate. They spun a moment, nuzzled, then she squirmed loose, and the chase was on again. A few people looked up with tolerant amusement. "They haven't been doing that the whole afternoon, have they? I'd be too exhausted to—uh—you know," Joshua finished lamely.

"Everyn do have greater stamina than Bondfriends, though Spot thinks Cawa drags things on. Krrrass doesn't seem to mind, though. For that matter, neither do they." He watched the flirting pair, wistfully.

"You have a soul-mate?" Joshua asked.

"Not yet. Do you miss yours?"

"More than words can say." Joshua breathed through pursed lips, letting go of his sorrow before it could overtake him, and stood. "But this is a party, and I'm not going to think about that now. Come on. If I've got to meet anybody, let's meet them, then let's get the groove on, Kanaan-style."

But Ocapo wasn't listening—not to Joshua, anyway. Rather, he was stock still and focused, his head turned toward a path in the maze. Joshua looked at Terry, found the healer mimicking his own confused expression.

Soon, everyone had turned toward the edge of the clearing. The music faltered and died. The dancers stilled. Everyn landed on the trees or sat up from where they were resting on the ground. Even the children stopped their wild games to turn and focus. Joshua couldn't see what they were looking at, yet he hesitated to ask or even move lest he disturb something important. Instead, he followed Ocapo's stare.

The camp was near one of the openings of the maze, and Ocapo had told him while they ate that Tasmae had created the woods beyond it to hide the entrance while at the same time corralling the Barins into it. Around the only clear path, thick woods discouraged straying, except for a few clearings, where plants like the ones that made up the walls and keep waited to attack any non-Kanaan. He thought he saw some of the trees swaying, though whether of their own volition or because something was moving through them, he couldn't tell.

Suddenly, the everyn began to keen, and the Bondfriends joined them, adult and child alike, in a one-note chorus that echoed throughout the mesas.

Joshua clapped his hands over his ears, but the sound still reverberated in his head. He glanced at Terry and saw the healer wincing as well.

Then it was over; and just as if nothing had happened, everyone went back to what they were doing, though Joshua noticed that most of the children ran to edge of the clearing.

"What was that all about?" he asked Ocapo.

"Come on. I'll show you. You'll find it interesting."

As they made their way to the far end of the camp, Ocapo explained. "A new pride has arrived, and they bring with them a child who has entered the Serenity. Remember what I'd told you happened to me before Spot found me? Her time has come. They are hoping an unbonded everyn here will choose to join her. What you heard was us alerting any everyn in the area."

They stopped behind the crowd of children who stood a respectful distance away yet stared with curiosity as some adults settled a young girl by the fire. A woman placed a cloak around her shoulders—her mother, Joshua guessed from the tender way she stroked her hair before sitting down next to her. The child didn't look older than eight, and a frail eight at that. Her mousy brown hair hung limply around a too-pale face, which combined with her deeply shadowed eyes, gave her an ethereal appearance. Her eyes glowed with otherworldly joy and her dry, cracked lips parted in an unearthly smile. She was beautiful, in a spooky sort of way, like an El Greco painting.

"Is she all right?" Joshua whispered. "She looks like she ought to be lying down, preferably in the healer's den." In fact, the healer had just knelt down in front of her and was hovering his hands over her head and neck. He was older than anyone Joshua had seen, and his hands trembled as if with palsy, but he still had a keen light in his eyes. Terry went to join him.

"There is nothing they can do," Ocapo whispered back. "She has entered the Serenity. But she has not eaten in days. If she does not find a Bondfriend soon, she will starve to death."

"She'll die of dehydration first," Joshua muttered. She reminded him of paintings he'd seen of saints caught in ecstasy. If she had been human, he would not have been surprised to see the stigmata, the wounds of Christ, manifesting on her hands and feet. "On Earth, we'd put her on fluids with an IV. Anyone tried to force feed her?"

"She won't swallow. They have been traveling for many weeks. If a Bondfriend is not found here, she will die." Ocapo regarded Joshua shrewdly. "Is there anything in your talents that can help her?"

Despite himself, Joshua had been wondering just that. Ecstasy and alien origin aside, the psychologist part of him would have diagnosed her with catatonia—and that was something he'd worked with before. "I don't know," he said, thinking aloud. "I might be able to get her to eat, but I can't guarantee anything. I mean, I'd be using alien techniques. I have no idea if they'd work. But if it's okay, I'd try."

Suddenly, Joshua found himself grabbed and pulled through the crowd of children to stand in front of the girl and her mother, and Joshua realized Ocapo had been translating the whole time. Nonetheless, he emphasized, "Tell them I don't know if this will work. I could make things worse."

"They trust you as I do," Ocapo reassured. "If you can get her to eat, it would buy her some time for the right everyn to find her."

Still Joshua hesitated. What if he messed up something that caused the everyn to not want to bond with her? His mother had taught him never to touch a baby wild animal because the human scent would make the mother reject it. What if he put some kind of psychic taint on her?

The aging healer looked up from the girl and met his eyes. Even though he wasn't psychic, Joshua could feel his reassurance.

"Okay," he said, letting out a breath he hadn't realized he'd been holding. "I need two cups, one with something the healers think she can tolerate—broth or whatever—and one for me. Water's fine in that one. Then, just don't disturb us for a while. I don't know how long it'll take."

Ocapo clapped his shoulder and left to get the drinks. Joshua knelt down beside the girl. He observed her for a minute, taking in her posture, her breathing, anything he could use to reach her.

"I don't suppose you'd make this easy on us, would you, baby?" he asked her. "Your mom's awfully worried about you."

Ocapo brought the two cups, and experimentally, Joshua set one against her hands, waved the fragrant broth under her nose. Her nostrils didn't even twitch in reaction.

"That won't work," Ocapo commented.

"Didn't think it would. Just curious is all. What's she looking at, do you think?"

Ocapo sighed such a wistful sigh that Joshua turned to look at him. His expression was a near match to the girl's. "Your language doesn't have words for it," he said, then nodded and went to sit near the parents.

Joshua turned back to the girl. "Well, whatever it is, we'll see if we can make a dinner show of it, okay, honey?"

He shook himself to release his tensions and doubt and, despite his earlier objections to Deryl, tried to practice Neuro Linguistic Programming on an alien.

The first time he heard the story about using NLP techniques to bring back a catatonic patient, he'd been fascinated. He'd bugged his father for weeks to try it out on someone—or better yet, let him try it out—until his father had finally scolded, "This is not a game, Joshua. NLP is a tool. If I think the conditions are right, I may attempt it, but only if I'm comfortable. As for you: Give yourself time. I have no doubt that when you're older and more experienced, opportunities will present themselves."

His father had been right. So far, Joshua had used this particular method on an autistic child he babysat for a client of his father; as a case study with his father in Colorado; and on Deryl. Now, he'd try it with an alien.

He set the cups in identical positions by his knee and hers, settled himself into a complimentary posture, and readied himself to enter "uptime," match the girl's rhythms, and get into her world.

Maybe it was because she was psychic. Maybe it had to do with the training Terry had given him, or something about the world itself. Whatever the reason, he found his awareness almost immediately swept away.

Something similar had happened with Deryl, but it had taken hours, and he'd found himself in a cloudy and gray world. Her world dazzled his mind's eye like being inside a ray of sunlight. As he saw with her, he, too, focused on its source, and it was everything beautiful, holy, and right.

"Oh, God," he whispered, and it was a prayer. In his vision, he sank to his knees beside the girl. Of course she was content to sit there, gazing and longing, yet patient. That rapture, heaven, was hers, too. She just had to wait to be invited in.

He would wait with her.

No, came a knowing, gentle and amused, in Joshua's mind. He was loved, he was cherished, but he was not invited in now, nor was it his place to sit and wait. There were things he must do, beginning with this child beside him.

He became aware again of his own body and of the girl sitting entranced before him. Automatically, he checked to make sure he was still in sync with her, and reached for the cup, raised it to his lips, and swallowed.

She mimicked his moves.

He heard the gasps of amazement from the people around him, but filed them away along with the amazing rapture he'd felt. Right now, his only focus was on going through the motions of drinking. When the cup was empty, someone refilled it and he took her through the motions a second time. When no one refilled it again, he let her return to her position of waiting while he decided what to do next. He could try to bring her out of it entirely, but he wasn't sure he should, or that he wanted to. She rested in a place of near perfection—

what would happen if he took her away from it with nothing to offer in return?

Better let the everyn do it if it's meant to be. Dying didn't seem like such a fearful thing, after all. Still keeping his breathing in sync with hers, he leaned forward and grasped her hand. "Be patient a little longer, sweetheart. Heaven will always be there, but right now, I think you're meant to stay with us awhile longer."

For just a moment, she focused on him, and smiled a more natural, childlike smile. Then the unfocused rapture returned.

He sat back on his heels. "That's the best I'm gonna do," he said to Ocapo, then laughed as the girl's parents threw their arms around him.

"Tell them they're welcome," he said to his friend as he returned their hugs.

The healer knelt down beside the girl, his trembling fingers moving over her face, turned to Joshua, then Ocapo, then Joshua again. This time, his eyes were wide and amazed.

"He wanted you to do a cleansing," Ocapo said, "and I told him human healers didn't need to, and that at the keep, you'd healed dozens of injured Kanaan without break."

Joshua shook his head. "Tell him I didn't do the healing. I was a conduit, more like glorified jumper cables or something."

Terry smirked at his analogy. "Perhaps so, but no healer could have done this."

Joshua felt himself blushing and just a little giddy. He snagged Ocapo by the arm. "Tell you what, though. I do have some excess energy I'd like to work off. What say we go find the dancing? We can teach each other some moves."

Summer again. Too hot. Too bright. Anguish returned for Kanaan and Gardianju. For the Ydrel, too, and this time, his agonies insinuated themselves into her mind, so that sometimes she could not tell their realities apart.

She sat in the middle of an open field under the blazing sun, yet couldn't escape the feeling that she was trapped within padded walls and the light was wrongly bluish and cool upon her skin. She felt confined, bound, and her arms kept crossing themselves across her stomach. Things in her head skittered and bustled: whispers of thought, passing streaks of emotion, mists of attitude, and they crowded her as well. Her mind struggled to sort them out, and she reeled in confusion until:

One feeling loomed over all else: Pressure.

One thought shouted over the others: This is Wrong!

One emotion overrode the rest: Anger.

One target became her focus: The twin suns.

You are not sisters! She snarled at the smaller of the two stars. Fury burned inside her more hotly than the heat that stripped her world of its moisture. *You are an intruder!* She saw it so clearly now: two suns—one villain, one hostage. Caught in a struggle of domination vs. freedom. Kanaan caught in the middle. Kanaan being ripped apart in the battle. She being torn with it.

No! Intruder! She stood, shaking, glaring at the suns. They seared her retinas. She didn't care. They could take her vision, but they would not take her world.

Leave us! She seethed. *Go away!*

Hardly aware of what she was doing, she reached deep into her fury, deep into the heart of Kanaan, drawing all the power into herself. It filled her, coursed through her. She no longer saw, no longer felt, no longer heard. There was nothing now, not even her anger: just power and one single focus.

Leave!

She felt the power race from her like a beam, sharp, focused, violent. She felt it impact against the star, felt the star knocked off its route. But it wasn't enough.

She reached out, found lines of power in the atmosphere, in life. Across her world, people and beasts fell unconscious where they stood, and flowers wilted as if in a sudden freeze.

LEAVE!

She reached to the Ydrel, grabbed the power of his mind and pulled. She felt his strength move though her, until she no longer felt him, just power.

GO! With an animal scream of fury, she threw her power at the star. She held the scream, held the power, held her fury, until she felt the star grudgingly release its ties to her sun and again move on its way.

Then she collapsed among the dying flowers, blood streaming from her ears and nose, the power gone, her life spent, her mission complete.

But as she let out her last breath, she saw the planet faint in the sky and knew she hadn't completely succeeded. Too late. There would be others. And the Ydrel... Tasmae...

Tasmae suddenly spasmed and it was all the healer and Leinad could do to steady her against the seizures. They were absorbed in holding her down when the earthquake hit.

Deryl was in the high intensity ward again. He didn't remember why—so much had confused him then. Anger he couldn't control burned through him—anger at the voices, at the staff, at the cold lights that nonetheless seared his eyes whether they were open or closed.

He was standing in the padded room, screaming for everything to leave him alone, when he felt...something, someone...reach into his very soul and drain him. He collapsed into a catatonic state. Only when a lovesick nurse, Sachiko, was somewhat mischievously whispering the secret of her affair with the chief psychiatrist did he open his eyes and turn to her, nearly scaring her out of her wits. She screamed.

Tasmae screamed as the shock of Gardianju's dying shook her system. Deryl felt her convulse as her body fought against the compulsion to follow the first Miscria into death. Her abilities went wild; her control of Kanaan slipped; the world reflected her throes.

Deryl reached out with his mind to steady her; to embrace her.

The ground beneath him shook.

"Nothing personal," Joshua apologized to the tree as he buttoned his pants. He'd been a little hesitant when Ocapo had pointed him down the path and essentially told him "Go down a hundred yards or so and pick a tree," but so far, nothing had reached out to grab him.

He did say I was safe as long as I stayed out of the clearings, Joshua reminded himself as he passed a spot where the trail branched off into one. The starlight reflected off a small pool of water to one side and frosted the grasses and leaves with silver. Under the willow-like trees grew the heavy moss that he knew felt softer than the most expensive carpet back home. It looked very inviting, and he wondered if that were part of the trap, and that once a weary Barin had settled himself to rest, the graceful, low branches would coil themselves around him.

Joshua heard a loud rustle and froze, still facing the clearing, ears straining to determine where the sound came from. He couldn't help thinking of the strange creatures roasting on spits in the camp. Were there other dangerous creatures nearby?

The rustling grew nearer.

Then he heard a playful, feminine shriek, and the two lovers who had been flirting and chasing each other at the camp came crashing into the clearing. The woman dashed into the pond, paused to splash water at her mate, then started off again. He lunged to reach her and when he caught her, she didn't resist, but moved in close, cooing and giggling. She nuzzled his neck, breathing in his scent, and he followed suit, caressing her hair and bringing it up to his face. Her coos turned low and sonorous.

Joshua realized he was staring.

As quietly as he could, he backed up and headed to camp, face burning and missing Sachiko anew. He decided he'd ask Ocapo where their tent was and call it a night.

As he neared the camp, he heard the everyn kreeling again, and wondered if that had anything to do with the mating dance coming to an end. When he got to the campground, however, he found everything in a controlled fury. Parents dashed about, gathering children, herding them to the large dancing area and making them sit. Others threw dirt and water on the fires without worrying if they got any on the still-roasting meat. Joshua started to call out to ask what was going on, when the ground shook violently enough to knock him off his feet.

Everything happened at once. Children screamed. Adults were knocked to the ground, one just missing the fire. Joshua heard a screech and Cochise came flying at him, claws extended. As he rolled to get out of his way, he heard a loud *CRACK!* A tree as large around as he was fell just where he'd been laying. He gaped at it a minute, then rolled back and huddled against it. There was no way to get up; the ground trembled—*like a hurt, living thing*, came the snatch of verse. He shook, too.

Then came a sound like out of his nightmare, a huge groaning, ripping noise, and he saw the ground tear into two. The rip snaked its way into the camp—right toward the young unbonded girl he'd met earlier.

"No!" Joshua yelled. He tried to crawl toward her.

The crack grew two, three feet wide. Steam rose from it. It sped right beside her. Under her. She tipped and fell.

Her mother screamed.

An animal cry joined her scream, and a large everyn dove into the rift. He rose, wings laboring, the girl in his claws. He skimmed the ground to a safe spot, lowered her, and curled protectively around her.

The shaking stopped.

The noise silenced.

Everyone remained still, but when the ground showed no sign of resuming its wild dance, people rose. Some ran to others, embracing and reassuring those who were all right. The Bondfriend healer and Terry hurried to those who were injured, directing some of the men to carefully move them to a safer part of the camp. Others cleaned up the damage, and rekindled the fires. To one side, the entranced girl was awake, aware, and hugging her new everyn Bondfriend, while her family surrounded them, rejoicing.

Shakily, Joshua got to his feet. Cochise landed on his shoulder. "Thanks, buddy. You can be my jailer anytime," he said and rubbed his neck.

Ocapo came running up to him. "Are you all right?"

He still felt himself quaking inside. "Uh, yeah, thanks to Cochise. But down the trail—in one of the clearings—the soul-mates—"

Ocapo nodded. His eyes unfocused for a moment, then he grinned. "They're all right. Their everyn checked on them—they didn't even notice!"

Despite himself, Joshua laughed.

Chapter Twenty-One

Deryl woke up weary and achy and not quite sure what he was doing in the middle of a strange glen. He sat up and started to run his fingers through his hair, but pulled them back with a grimace. His hair felt greasy and gross.

And you smell pretty bad, even for a human, the unicorn said.

Deryl blinked at him. *You can telep?*

He shook its skin in an equine expression of annoyance. *We already established that.*

Deryl rubbed his temples. He didn't remember.

It will come to you. Bathe and clean your clothes while it does.

Obediently, but without much energy, he waded into the pool until he was knee-deep, then knelt until the water reached his shoulders. The cool water woke him up some. He pulled off his shirt and swished it around in the water. An everyn dove from a tree and took the wet garment from him.

Thanks, he teleped. He started to untie his pants but realized he still had on his socks and shoes. He backed up to where it was shallow enough to sit, removed them and his pants. Again, the everyn relieved him of his garments and draped them over a stout branch.

As he ducked and rinsed and rubbed the dirt and sweat off his body, snatches of the past few days came back, sluggish and distant. The Remembrance. Gardianju.

She loved me, he thought, his heart clutched with grief and guilt. *She loved me and tried to help me. She even joined minds with me. And I didn't remember her! I didn't even know she was there!*

Are you certain? the unicorn asked. *Think carefully. See the past with new eyes.*

Then again, maybe he did. As he sorted through the chaos of memories from that first year at SK-Mental, he recognized times when he'd felt cared for, watched over, even loved. *Like I had a guardian angel.* He'd never said anything to anyone about it; sometimes, he'd thought it was the spirit of his dead mother, and there was no *way* he was going to say something so, well, crazy, to any of the psychiatric staff there. Neither had he admitted, even to himself, the feelings of loneliness when he didn't sense her presence.

Was that when Kanaan was taking all her concentration? he wondered. It hardly mattered; more important was that after her, his relationship with the Miscrias changed, so that when they Called him, they felt distant and impersonal. They demanded and he supplied, and none gave him the nurturing he'd gotten from her. Maybe he'd forced himself to forget because of that?

He walked onto the shore and found an everyn waiting for him, a bag of food at its feet. He unwrapped the contents: a gourd with juice, several of the fruits and vegetables he'd become familiar with—and a turkey leg?

From the Bondfriend feast, it explained. *Joshua enjoyed them. We thought you would, too.*

Joshua!

Is Joshua all right? he asked as he bit into the meat. Even cold, it tasted wonderful.

He is with the Bondfriends. He is safe.

Why would he be in danger? Deryl asked, then a rush of memory returned: Tasmae, wild-eyed and out of control, trying to choke Joshua while Leinad looked on, approving. Falling to her knees, begging for him to stop the voices in her head. Caught in the Remembrance. Fighting the death throes of Gardianju—

It was his fault, all his fault.

The drumstick fell from his fingers.

He felt the unicorn bump him with his horn, and looked up to meet his large green eyes. *Tasmae will be all right,* he told him.

How can you know? Deryl teleped back. He didn't want blind reassurance. Too many times in his life, he'd been told things would be all right. Nothing ever was.

This will be, the unicorn affirmed. *We Beasts understand more than the Kanaan—or you humans. We know the Prophesies of Gardianju, and we know what is to come, far better than any of you.*

Then tell me! he urged, but he felt a gentle refusal. *Fine! Tell me what to do.*

Tasmae is strong, and you, together, are part of what is to transpire. Trust in her strength, Deryl, and turn your thoughts to protecting our future.

He couldn't think about the future. He had to protect Tasmae—and there was only one way to do that. Deryl stood and with his mind, called to him his still damp clothes. *Take me to Joshua,* he demanded as he dressed.

The unicorn cocked his head back. *That is not a good idea. You are weak, vulnerable; you need to listen to Tasmae.*

He didn't care. He had to find Joshua, get as far away from Tasmae as he could. He'd contact her in the Netherworld, where she was safe. *Please?*

The unicorn looked at him, then with a huff of resignation, allowed him to clamber onto his back. As they rode, Deryl fought back his fear as more of the Remembrance sorted itself out in his mind.

No Miscria after Gardianju had ever dared communicate with him, just asked their specific questions and accepted his specific answers. They couldn't, lest they risk losing their sanity. None even tried—until Tasmae.

I made her communicate with me. I made her go deeper into the Remembrance than she probably ever could have otherwise. And I, I let her touch my mind.

She was going to die, just like Guardianju.

And that would be his fault, too.

Tasmae returned to herself.

For a moment, she simply lay still, letting herself grow aware of the pressure of the matt against her side, the dampness of her hair, the bittersweet sadness that lingered in her soul. She opened her eyes and glanced up at the Remembrance. It had closed its buds tightly and its fronds drooped as if exhausted by the experience, too. Exhausted, yet satisfied. At last, it had completed its purpose.

She understood. She had shared the life of Gardianju, and she understood it as no other Miscria could.

She smiled. *I am the Queen of Riddles—and Ydrel, the biggest riddle of them all. Of course, he was a mystery to the others. They knew him as Gardianju did, even less than she did. All knew Ydrel—but not Deryl.*

"Deryl?" She leaned up on her elbows and looked around. Where was he? She'd felt him there, at the end, holding Gardianju, holding her, reassuring them. Loving them. *Deryl?*

Leinad knelt beside her. *Do you understand now? Have you learned the danger he is?*

She reached up, touched his cheek, felt his fear. Poor Leinad, dear Leinad. Like the Miscria before her, he didn't have all the information. He could not know the truth.

I will explain all later, she promised him. *First, I must find Deryl.* She stood, pleased to find she could do so without assistance.

The healer moved to block her way. *First, you will do the cleansing.*

Yes. It would reassure Leinad and the others that she had recovered well. Besides, she should not be with Deryl like this. She nodded and meekly followed the healer to the baths where she could purify her body and psyche.

Then, she would find Deryl and complete her purpose. Their purpose.

She shivered in anticipation.

Deryl looked at the unicorn field, frowning in doubt. Off to the far side, he saw a few unicorns grazing, but no people; the stable looked empty, though shadows hid some of it. *Are you sure Joshua is here? I don't see him.*

Joshua will arrive soon. We will wait here.

The unicorn walked to the stables, but stopped outside them. Deryl dismounted, his muscles grateful for the rest, but his mind racing to remember how he had teleported without actually teleporting now. He leaned for a moment against his ride. One thing was certain; he needed some food or he'd never have the energy to make the journey.

Where would you go, Beloved?

"Tasmae!" Deryl spun and for a moment, stared at her in disbelief. It was her: a little tired, a little wan perhaps, but otherwise healthy and whole, and looking a bit smug. She was all right?

Her expression vanished as she sensed his desperation. *Deryl, what is it?*

"You lied to me!" He turned to snarl at the unicorn, but he had moved off to join the others. Deryl twisted back to Tasmae. Every muscle in his body ached with the need to run to her, to pull her close, to press his lips against her hair. His mind yearned to touch hers.

He stepped back. "Please! You have to stay away from me. We have to go back to the way it was, meeting in the Netherworld. You asking me questions. I can give you better answers now, and it's safer." He stopped, and his misery morphed into surprise then anger when she tossed her head and rolled her eyes. "Don't you understand? I don't have a choice! I love you, and I won't do to you what I did to her!"

So, you do not understand, either?

He shook his head. He moaned. "Please. I can't hurt you. I promised."

Tasmae spoke slowly, stepping forward with each word: "I am not just any Miscria."

"Gardianju..."

"She loved you."

"I know."

You loved her.

His mind filled with remembered warmth, the pockets of hope in the midst of hell.

"She was my angel." He felt a tear trace its path down his cheek. "And I hurt her. I can't...not you."

"You were a child. She protected you as a child and you protected her. Protected us. But you were a child— and you are a child no longer."

"No. But..."

"I am not Gardianju." She removed the punch dagger from her hair and let it drop to the ground. She pulled out the pins that held the sheath in place, and her hair tumbled about her shoulders. Deryl shivered and his gaze flickered over her, marveling how it caught and held the light, drinking it in, rather than reflecting it. Despite himself, he breathed in deeply, and he felt his blood coursing hot through his body.

"I am stronger than Gardianju," she whispered, moving closer.

"I know," he whispered back. He swayed slightly. He felt himself falling into her eyes. She was so close, but he couldn't back away.

"And you are stronger." She murmured into his ear.

He could hear her slow intake of breath as she caught his scent, feel her gentle exhale warm against his neck.

"You have conquered the demons," she whispered.

"Yes. No. Maybe," he sputtered. He was having a hard time thinking. He wasn't sure what he was protesting. "Taz, there are things Gardianju didn't know."

Nonetheless, he murmured his warning against her ear. He reached up and caressed her hair.

I know you, Deryl Stephens. I know you as Gardianju knew you and I know you as you are now. She teleped the thoughts in sensuous waves as she teased his lips with her kisses. He felt his mental shields buckling even as his lips responded to hers and his hands hovered over her hips.

She was so close. Too close. Not close enough. He could feel her mind flowing over his shields, making them pulse in time with his blood. He felt his desire growing into need. *Taz*, he pleaded, though he wasn't sure what for.

She moved her hands over his chest, played her will over his shields. *I have solved the riddle of her life,* she offered. *Together you were strong enough to defeat death and madness. Together, we will be strong enough to bring joy and life.*

"Yes!" he whispered and pulled her closer to him: body, mind, and soul.

<hr/>

"You're sure this is safe?" Joshua asked as they emerged from the woods to the unicorn fields. "I mean, I know the beasts are on our side and all, but if Leinad—"

"Joshua, after what you did for the child, no one can consider you anything less than a friend. You are a mind healer!" Ocapo insisted.

Terry nodded distractedly. He had focused toward the stables, where two figures stood embracing.

"Let's not get carried away! That was probably a one-in-a-million..." Joshua's voice faded as he followed Terry's gaze and saw the two. "What? Is this the season?" he started to joke, then that mirth, too, faded as he recognized the guy's shoulder-length blond hair and the long black hair of the woman. "Oh, no. No, no, nonono—"

"Joshua, stay calm," Terry urged.

"This is *not* happening!" Joshua exclaimed and without even having to dig his heels into Glory's flanks, set her off at a full gallop.

He was not alone. Spot called out from above, and Ocapo pointed to a unicorn thundering in from the other direction. Leinad.

"This will not be good!" Terry moaned as he, too, took off at a gallop toward the oblivious pair.

There were too many barriers between them. Too many clothes. Too many shields. His hands fumbled at the ties on her shirt while hers slowly but more surely worked the fastenings on his.

Her mind worked the same way upon his shields, teasing them until one by one they fell with a rush of pleasure and a need for more. Already their minds had joined enough that he had a sense of tactile double vision. The nerves of his fingertips echoed every sensation of her touch, and he felt his every caress play upon his own skin as it had on hers, and when he at last undid the tie of her shirt and pulled one side of it away, he gasped with the intensity of her pleasure.

He heard a distant thundering, but he couldn't tell if it was the galloping of hooves or the galloping of their hearts.

Then she slid his shirt over his shoulders and he was too lost in the sensation to worry about it.

Madness Unbound ✸ 277

Joshua saw Leinad approaching, and his own anger vanished into panic. He dug his heels into Glory's flanks, but she didn't complain, just put on even more speed. Leinad was clearly furious—and he was closer.

Their passion flowed over Deryl, making the last of his shields sing. He moaned, half-ecstasy, half-anguish. Still, a part of his mind protested, *There are things you don't know—the Master—*

Then show me! her will commanded. *There is nothing we cannot handle together.*

Her confidence flooded into him, drowning his protests. The last of his shields trembled against her desire and he knew he wouldn't stop them from falling before her.

Leinad howled with fear. He concentrated that fear into a tightly focused command and threw it at Deryl.

Joshua watched in horror as Deryl was flung backward and knocked to the ground, his arms covering his head, convulsing with pain, yet terrifyingly silent, as if the pain were so intense he couldn't even shriek.

Leinad, meanwhile, grabbed Tasmae by the shoulder and spun her around to face him. She slapped his hand away and screeched more like an animal than a person. The two stood glaring at each other, and it was obvious even to a non-psychic that a battle raged between them.

Glory reared to a stop, nearly unseating Joshua. He leaped from the saddle and knelt over his friend. "Deryl!"

AWAY FROM HER!

A red-hot ball of terror hit Deryl like a missile, blasting away the last of his shields and leaving him vulnerable and open to every psychic impression around him.

He'd thought his shields had been all but useless when he'd first arrived on Kanaan. Now he realized just how much he'd blocked. Every person on Kanaan, every beast, every animal—he could feel them all, hear their thoughts. He could even sense the grass growing, the flowers opening themselves to the sunrise on the other side of the world, the movements of Kanaan's continental plates miles below him. They all pressed upon him, seeking his attention, demanding his recognition. His mind instinctively struggled to block them out, but every shield had been shattered by the intense emotions of those nearest him:

Joshua, his fear like a lance.

Leinad, his fear now anger as he confronted his rebellious student and leader. How dare she put herself—their world—in such danger!

Tasmae, her fury like a volcano, like the heart of a star. It caught him up in it, burned away every defense, seared his mind—

"Taz!" he tried to gasp, tried to telep, but his words were lost in his fight to breathe, and his psychic scream drowned in the avalanche of impressions crashing upon him.

"Stop it!" Joshua jumped between Tasmae and Leinad, shoving each for good measure. "Stop it! You're going to kill him!"

Madness Unbound ❄ 279

Jolted out of their rage, the two blinked at Joshua in surprise.

In that moment of release, Deryl's shields snapped back into place and he gave himself to blessed oblivion. His last impression was of Joshua's fear, strong, but distant.

"Deryl, don't you do this to me! Come, on, man. Don't do this."

Oblivion felt so good. He couldn't muster the strength to apologize as he let himself get swallowed by its tender nothingness.

Chapter Twenty-Two

Deryl's first impression upon waking was that someone had flayed his mind.

Every synapse burned, and every nerve in his body echoed their agony. He rolled onto his side, moaning. His stomach heaved.

Someone pushed a bowl under his face just in time and he gratefully threw up into it. Then he fell back onto the unfamiliar sleeping mats and fought to catch his breath.

"You ought to be thanking God you're even alive."

The quiet voice nonetheless hammered itself into his head. He wanted to protest, to beg for quiet, but he couldn't remember how to make himself speak. He started to shiver, felt a warm heavy blanket being pulled up over him. He forced his eyes open, saw Joshua. He wanted to say something, to ask what happened, but he couldn't find the words. He felt like half of himself had been stolen away. It was a struggle to think, to remember who he was.

"Deryl, come on, say something," Joshua urged.

"Tasmae?" The name sent a flood of yearning through him, and he forced himself into a sitting position. Dizziness swept over him and he fought the urge to vomit again.

"She's all right. Better than you, I'm told. Now lie down—"

He shook his head, despite the lances of pain. "Tasmae. Need..."

"Uh-uh. You don't need anything to do with her right now." Joshua tried to ease him back down.

"Yes, I do!" His sudden desperation gave him strength to shove his friend away and to push back the pain. Words returned in its wake. "Where is she? What did you and Leinad do?"

"Me? Listen, you selfish little pain in the ass! I saved your sorry life. You, on the other hand, were the one who decided to get busy with the caretaker of an entire world, the most powerful and the most valuable person on this planet! Did you know that these people believe if anything happens to her, their whole *world* is doomed?"

Joshua's anger seared into him like salt on an open wound. "Josh," Deryl protested weakly.

"Don't even try to excuse this! You *knew* Leinad doesn't trust us! I *told* you to stay away from her. Yet you decide to get it on with her in the middle of a frickin' meadow? What the hell were you thinking?"

Deryl couldn't think. It was getting hard to keep track of who he was again. Something was missing. Someone... "Where's Tasmae? I need—"

"Let me tell you what you need!" Joshua grabbed him by the front of his shirt and pulled him up. "You *need* to get better. Then you *need* to talk to someone *else* about teleporting. I've asked around and guess what? There are plenty of people *right here* who know how to do it. Then, you *need* to get me home, preferably in one piece and within twenty-four hours of after we'd left. Anything you *want* to do after that is your own damn business, but I am not going to be around to bail you out. Do you understand?"

Joshua's anger—Joshua's fear—scraped upon his raw nerves. Desperately, Deryl nodded. "Yes, yes. I'm sorry."

"I'll accept your apology when you're ready to get me home." Joshua released him and left the tent.

Deryl leaned toward the bowl and threw up again, then fell back against the covers shaking with fever and with the need to find Tasmae. Only remotely did he wonder where he was.

Joshua hesitated outside the tent flap when he heard Deryl vomiting a second time. He even turned around to go back in when he stopped himself. *Don't do it. You'll just end up yelling at him again, and that's not going to help anybody.*

Instead, he turned to Cochise, who had been waiting for him outside, sprawled out like a cat basking in the sun. "Cochise, tell Terry that Deryl's awake finally. I'm taking a walk." The everyn gave a chirrup of assent, then stretched and yawned before curling up again. Apparently, he had no intention of moving. Joshua watched him a moment, assumed he'd teleped the information to Terry, and headed out toward the woods, his own stomach churning with the combination of anger and shame.

How could I have done that? Deryl was barely coherent, and I grab him by the collar and scream at him? What the hell was I thinking?

He reached the end of the camp and headed out onto the path in the woods, wandering blindly, focused on his thoughts.

He knew what he was thinking. He was thinking how close he'd come to being stranded on an alien planet umpteen billion light-years from home. When he'd stopped Tasmae's and Leinad's psychic argument, Deryl had stopped twitching, all right. He'd also stopped breathing. Terry had looked at him with such terror that Joshua had known there was no way the healer would help him. Fortunately, just as Joshua was about to start rescue breathing, Tasmae had shoved away from Leinad, who'd been trying again to restrain her, knelt beside Deryl, and placed her hands on his temples.

"Return to me," she'd whispered, then fallen beside him unconscious as her almost-lover—*thank you God, that it was almost*— started to breathe in huge aching gasps. He was alive, but if Leinad's look said anything, any more wrong moves, by whatever Leinad termed was "wrong," and he'd make sure Deryl stopped breathing permanently. Leinad had carried the unconscious Tasmae to a waiting unicorn and headed back to the keep, but Joshua, Ocapo, and Terry decided it was best if they took Deryl back to the Bondfriend compound.

"Can he make that long a trip?" Joshua asked, though he really didn't have an alternative.

"I will take him through the Void," Terry said grimly.

And that's when Joshua found out that at least half the people around him had known all along how to teleport.

Joshua's strides grew longer and faster as his anger resurfaced.

So all the time, we were surrounded by people who could have taught Deryl how to get us home, and nobody said a word, not even Leinad, and he wanted us out of here more than anybody!

The path forked, and he blindly took the path toward a clearing.

And to make things even better, these "storms" Tasmae and Deryl talked about are short and with breaks in between. We could have left days ago. And no one mentioned a thing! Probably Tasmae and her "will of God" jazz—

Cochise flew at his face shrieking.

"Yeaghhh!" Joshua jumped back, startled out of his reverie and probably a year or two of his life. "What was that all about?" He stopped as he realized he'd almost blundered right into one of the clearings he'd been told to stay away from. In fact, he *was* in the clearing by a few steps, and the trees swayed in his direction. One snagged his foot and Cochise snapped at it, ripping it with his sharp teeth and freeing him. He turned and ran, and kept running until he was about halfway back toward the camp and the pain in his chest made him stop and cling to a tree for support. He tried to breathe and found he couldn't catch his breath.

Oh, great! his panicked mind blithered. *I escape from the enchanted trees just to die of a heart attack on an alien world billions of light-years from everyone I love—* Then he couldn't think in his struggle to breathe.

Relax, the clinical part of his mind instructed. *You're hyperventilating. Heart attacks don't run in your family. An anxiety attack, though? That makes sense.*

He sat down on the trail, covering his mouth and one nostril with his hands, forcing himself to take deep easy breaths.

His breathing had started to normalize and the tightness in his chest to ease when he heard footsteps racing in his direction. He'd lowered his hands and was taking normal, if shaky breaths when Ocapo and the Bondfriend healer got to him. They knelt beside him.

"Joshua?" Ocapo asked tentatively.

Joshua wanted to brush him off, tell him he was fine, but instead he found himself saying miserably, "I gotta go home, Ocapo." Before this summer, he'd never even left Colorado, never been more than an hour's drive from his parents, never, never been so alone. He squeezed his eyes shut and shook his head.

Just like his grandfather would have, the healer moved beside him and pulled his head against his shoulder. Joshua leaned against him, letting someone else be strong for just a little while.

After several minutes of silence, Ocapo spoke. "You will get home, Joshua. I promise. If Deryl is unable to take you, and if the Kanaan are unwilling, then we Bondfriends will find a way. I know it is hard for you to trust right now, but trust us on that."

Joshua nodded. After all, what choice did he have?

Terry had come into Deryl's tent not long after Joshua had left. Deryl struggled to sit up and confront him. "Tasmae?" he demanded weakly, and cursed his weakness. He had to get to her, he had to!

Terry reassured him even as he restrained him. He spoke in English, as if he guessed at how raw the state of Deryl's psyche was and didn't want to aggravate it more by teleping. "You will go to her, Deryl, soon. But we must figure out how to do this. Leinad—"

"He stopped us! He took her!" He heard himself raving. He thought he was. He felt so hot. Feverish Incomplete. He had to get to her. "Leinad—"

"He did what he thought was best for Tasmae, and for us all. Tasmae underestimates his understanding of the Remembrances and of the Prophesies, and that has caused trouble. For better or for worse, however, you have started something that must be completed. You will be with her again, Deryl. But you must give me time to convince Leinad. In the meantime, lie still. Gain your strength."

"Can't!" Why didn't Terry understand? He needed Tasmae! How could he have ever thought of leaving her? "Taz—"

"You will hurt Tasmae if you go to her as you are now," Terry said sternly. "Is that what you want?"

He shook his head. He fought the urge to sob.

Terry nodded, satisfied. "I didn't think so. And you will hurt yourself. Why do you think I'm using your English? Your mind is weak and injured, and the only thing that can help you is time. And rest. Now try to sleep, or I will have to drug you, and neither of us wants to do that."

"No," Deryl agreed, and Terry stood.

"Rest, Deryl," he said gently. "Rest and heal. I'll be outside if you need anything." Without waiting for an answer, he left.

But Deryl hadn't heard him. At that moment, he'd felt a familiar tickling at the base of his brain, and he'd joyfully given himself to the Miscria's Call.

He found himself in the small glen Tasmae had imagined for them the first time they'd actually "spoken" together in the Netherworld. The canopy of branches and leaves shrouded them in privacy. It cut off the view of the sky, yet somehow, he saw everything clearly. It didn't matter; Deryl only cared about seeing one thing.

"Tasmae!"

She ran to him, and they embraced. Then he pulled away.

"Terry said I'd hurt you—"

She touched her fingers to his lips, and he understood that Terry didn't know everything, and that the only pain she felt was at their separation.

Then she flooded into his mind, and where she touched, waves of cool healing washed over his psychic wounds. He sighed with relief, and actually swayed a little. She caught him, and he wrapped his arms around her, first for support, then for something far more intimate. This time, they would be alone.

A familiar voice, a voice from nightmare, interrupted them. I WOULDN'T BE SO CERTAIN ABOUT THAT.

As one, they turned toward the intruder and blanched.

"Alugiac?"

"Master!"

They gaped at each other. They both knew him?

The Master, once known on Kanaan as Alugiac, laughed. A triumphant satisfaction flowed from him like the thick fog that slowly rolled from where he stood at the glen's edge.

AT LAST I RETURN TO YOU, DERYL—AND LOOK AT THE GIFT YOU'VE BROUGHT ME!

"Tasmae, run!" Deryl shouted. A sword appeared in his hand, but though he held it at the ready, he was shaking so hard the blade quivered.

The mist had surrounded them now. The trees, moss, even the rocks had eroded at its touch. Colors fled, leaving them in a gray and black world, with only an indeterminate ground and low fog as landscape.

"Run, Beloved!"

Tasmae felt the tangle of Deryl's emotions—fear, anguish, guilt, hatred toward himself and toward the one he called Master.

"No." She pulled the punch dagger from her hair. She did not know what hold Alugiac had on Deryl, but they would end it together.

Alugiac laughed, an ugly sound. LITTLE TASMAE. ALL GROWN UP. IT WAS ALMOST WORTH IT, FAILING TO TAKE YOU IN THE LAST WAR, JUST TO SEE YOU AS YOU ARE NOW.

He leered at her, and she felt her heart break again. She had adored him before the madness had scrambled his mind. She forced back the tears. She could not cure him. The greatest mercy was to be quick.

She sprang.

"No!" Deryl cried as Alugiac flung his hand in her direction, laughing.

Tasmae slammed into a wall of hideous half-formed beings. Their viscous, grayish skin, darker than the fog, oozed over and around her as they bound her to their gluey bodies. Her dagger was more sucked out of her hand than taken. She screamed and struggled, but all her blows were absorbed, like hitting liquid rubber. Their toothless mouths latched leech-like onto her. She

Madness Unbound ✸

flung her head violently to keep them from covering her mouth and nose.

"No! Stop it, Master, please!" Deryl begged.

I CAN DO NOTHING OF THE SORT, DERYL. YOU KNOW WHAT YOU MUST DO.

"I won't kill!"

THEN SHE IS MINE.

Two of the creatures' lobes caught her head, held it. A mouth opened before her, a gaping void moving toward her face. She looked straight into oblivion.

No! Tasmae, get out of my mind!

She felt something grab her, not just her body but her mind, her soul, her very self. Grab, and pull. She jerked backward, though quicksand, through space, through consciousness. She heard Alugiac howl with fury.

She sat up screaming, back in her own room.

Deryl! Suddenly, little clues she'd picked up from his mind and from his behavior came together in blinding clarity. The Master, the one he feared so—he was Alugiac!

And Deryl was caught in the Netherworld with him.

She would not leave him alone with a madman! She reached with her mind, found herself cut off from her beloved. She needed help, and she knew just where to find it.

By the time Leinad and the healer had reached her room in response to her screams, Tasmae was gone.

Deryl sagged onto hands and knees, weak from the effort of forcing Tasmae out of the Netherworld. The torn, half-finished feeling threatened to overtake him again, but he fought it down. There was only one way out of this and back to Tasmae, and that was through. He forced himself to rise and glare defiantly at the Master, though he didn't take up the sword. "Now what?" he demanded. "More monsters? Is that the best you can do?"

FUNNY YOU SHOULD ASK THAT.

The attack he threw at Deryl was not of monsters or weapons, but of madness itself.

Chapter Twenty-Three

Joshua sat in front of Deryl's tent with one of the musicians, trying to play a simple scale on a wooden flute. Although roughly the size and shape of a recorder, it was subtly different, not in the least because it required some psychic ability to alter the shape of the flute itself to reach some notes. Joshua tried to replace the psychic pressure with physical pressure. Ocapo laughed when an indignant squawk came from the instrument.

"It sounds like Spot when someone steps on his tail!" he said gleefully. He'd made similar comments all afternoon.

"Give me a break! I'd just started learning to play reed instruments at home. The sax uses totally different lip action." But Joshua chuckled, too. Deryl was sleeping; Terry had checked him and said he was fine; Ocapo had spoken to some of the pride leaders about finding a way to get Joshua home; and the challenge of learning a new instrument had helped him relax.

Then, with a soft BAMPH! of displaced air, Tasmae appeared in the compound and staggered to him.

"Oh, no!" Joshua moaned as he set the instrument aside and ran to her. He caught her by the shoulders. "What are you doing here?" he demanded angrily, causing some of the nearby Bondfriends to gape at his effrontery.

She grabbed his arms. Her eyes were wild with relief. "Joshua! Where's Deryl?"

"Asleep. We checked on him a few minutes ago."

She shook her head. "Not asleep." She tried to push past him, but he held her fast.

"Does Leinad know you're here?"

"Let me go, Joshua! Deryl's in trouble!"

Joshua almost started to say that they would be in even worse trouble if Leinad found her here, but her urgency stopped him. She pushed past him, and he followed her into the tent.

"See?" he said as she sat down beside him. "He's asleep, just like I said."

"Not asleep," Tasmae whispered. "Alugiac has him."

"What?"

"Alugiac—the one he calls Master—has him trapped in the Netherworld." Tremblingly, she brushed back a strand of Deryl's hair, then squared her shoulders and faced Joshua. "You will help me get him back."

Joshua sat down on the other side of his sleeping friend and took his wrist, counting his pulse. It was shallow and steady, but wrong for sleep. The number of beats tickled a memory.

"Oh, don't do this to me," Joshua murmured as he sat his unconscious friend up.

Just like one of Sabrina's baby dolls, Deryl's eyes snapped open, unseeing and unreacting, as soon as he sat upright. He wasn't rocking this time, though Joshua didn't know if that was a good sign or a bad one.

"Would it help me to know how he got this way, or would it just make me madder?" he asked Tasmae.

"Alugiac has him," Tasmae said, then looked at Joshua questioningly. "Deryl called him Master."

Madness Unbound ✦ 293

Joshua swiped a hand over his face, and raised his eyes heavenward, seeking strength. "The Master was this entity—kind of like you, really—that used to call him from consciousness. Only the Master was trying to train him to be a killer. Deryl has been resisting him for years." He pulled up his catatonic friend's sleeves and checked under his shirt. "Usually, whatever wounds the Master inflicted on him in the Netherworld show up on his body, but I don't see any new bruises or anything."

"He's doing something else this time," Tasmae whispered. "I felt Deryl's terror, then...madness. And now I can't sense anything. He's trapped, Joshua, and you have to help me bring him back. I know you can reach him. You've done it before."

Joshua sighed. "What do I do?"

"Go to him as you have before. I will follow. Together, we can find a way to help him."

"If I ever get back home, I'm changing my major," Joshua muttered as he prepared to enter "uptime" and get inside the head of his once-again catatonic friend.

Deryl tumbled in a sea of chaos; the thoughts, emotions, and memories of thousands forcing themselves upon him, searing themselves into his mind, re-opening the psychic wounds Tasmae had just healed. Once again he was flayed, his shields destroyed, his psyche laid bare and raw to the conscious and unconscious whims of others. A vortex opened before him and he swirled down into it—

His eyes snapped open. Everything was quiet and still, padded and tinted pink. His arms were bound in a straitjacket.

He was in the high-intensity care ward of South Kingston Mental Wellness Center.

This isn't real! something inside him screamed, but confusion left him off-balance and unable to process the thought. With difficulty, he sat up and turned toward where he knew the surveillance camera was hidden. "Hello!"

He heard a click of the intercom activating, and a woman's voice said, "Good afternoon, Deryl. Good to see you awake. How are you feeling?"

Idly, he wondered how many patients had freaked out at a disembodied voice talking to them from thin air. Again a part of him nagged that this wasn't right, but he pushed the thought aside. He needed more information. "I want to talk to Joshua Lawson."

There was a long silence. He forced himself not to fidget, repeat his request, or give into the thoughts that none of this was real. He had to stay calm, act sane.

Finally, the voice answered. "That would be up to Dr. Malachai. I've contacted him, and he'll be up momentarily."

"I don't want to talk to Malachai! I want to talk to Joshua—or Sachiko. I'll talk to Sachiko Luchese. Could you at least ask *her*?" But the nurse or orderly had turned off the intercom, and he forced himself to settle back against one padded wall and wait patiently. He wouldn't help himself by getting angry now.

If this is even real, that part of him persisted, and he bit his tongue to keep from snarling that, yes, he realized that. Even if it weren't real, he had no idea how to break the illusion. *There's no way out but through.*

He heard the subtle click of the lock, and the door opened. Dr. Malachai stepped in, calm, well dressed as always, the bruise and split lip Deryl had given him still healing, though looking better than he'd remembered. Two orderlies entered behind him. One turned away only long enough to ensure the door closed securely.

"So what day is it supposed to be, then?" Deryl asked in as level a voice as he could.

"Friday. I'm pleased to see you taking things so calmly, Deryl, considering what happened Monday. I also find it interesting that you want to talk to Joshua— or believe that Joshua would speak with you. Do you remember what happened?"

Deryl didn't answer. He wasn't going to let Malachai lead him into a trap.

The chief psychiatrist sighed. "As it happens, this is his last day with us—"

"You fired him?"

"In fact, it was decided by his family and yours, as well as the Board, that it was in everyone's best interest if he returned home and we put this whole unpleasantness behind us. He's receiving his full salary for the summer—he deserves that much—as well as a sizable settlement from your family. Small compensation for what he's been through, of course, but at least he can pay for college, which was his financial goal."

"What are you talking about?" Despite himself, Deryl let himself be lured in. He leaned forward.

By way of answer, Dr. Malachai signaled to an orderly, who knocked on the door. It opened, and he slid through. Deryl heard Malachai say to someone that he had only a few minutes, then Joshua stepped in.

Deryl gaped at what he saw.

His friend wore dress slacks, but a polo shirt took the place of his usual shirt and tie. The collar loosely surrounded a bandage that covered his throat. He gave Deryl a wan grin and a wave, then pulled out pencil and paper and wrote a note. The orderly passed it to Deryl.

Got out of the hospital yesterday. Docs say if I take it easy, my vocal cords should heal well enough to talk by the end of the summer.

Deryl stared at the note, looked again at Joshua, then laughed.

"Okay, Alugiac!" he called. "Now I know this isn't real. You think you're going to play on my guilt, but I'm not buying it!" Through his peripheral vision, he saw Joshua lean against the wall, shaking his head sadly. It made him angry.

He stood up, and shouted. "This isn't real! Come out here and fight me. I'm tired of playing your games."

An orderly hustled Joshua out of the room. A nurse came in bearing a syringe. "Deryl, you have to calm down, or I'll need to sedate you. Dr. Malachai's orders."

"Malachai-Schmalalachai! This isn't real, and I know it! Now, come on!" He turned in a circle, seeking a break in the illusion. The orderly took the opportunity to grab him. He felt a prick on his neck. "This isn't real!" he screamed, struggling, nonetheless. "I don't believe this! No!"

Deryl sat up in bed, a shout catching in his throat, stealing his breath. He leaned forward, wiped his sweaty brow in a sheet that smelled like fabric softener.

"Honey, what is it?" came a sleepy voice beside him. Someone switched on a bedside lamp.

He turned and gaped. "Clarissa?"

Chapter Twenty-Four

I must be getting good at this, Joshua thought as his awareness returned and he found himself in a spooky, dim, and foggy world. He spun in a slow circle, scanning the abyss, but Deryl was nowhere to be seen.

That hadn't happened before.

"C'mon, Tasmae," he muttered through clenched teeth. He didn't know what he'd do if she didn't show. *Find Deryl and hope Taz can fend for herself, I guess—though I have no idea where I am, how to find him, or what I'm supposed to be doing here. Come on, Taz!*

A shimmer caught his eye. The fog swirled, and Tasmae appeared.

"Am I glad to see you!" Joshua said fervently. "So where's Deryl?"

She, too, made a slow circle. "They're not here." She sounded surprised by the fact.

Joshua felt his heart sink. "That's bad, isn't it?" It was more statement than question.

Tasmae nodded. "I don't know how to find them. The Netherworld is not a place. There're no real space or time. It's mental, it's..."

"Great. It's the *Twilight Zone*." Joshua started to whistle the show's familiar theme song.

Suddenly a voice, controlled and moderate yet a little creepy, echoed across the foggy vastness: *There is a fifth dimension beyond that which is known to man. It is a dimension as vast as space and as timeless as in-finity...*

"No way," Joshua whispered with awe.

Tasmae moved closer to him. She held her dagger before her. "What is that? What did you do?"

"Shhh!" Joshua hushed her, then muttered. "Come on, signpost, signpost."

...the dimension of imagination. It is an area which we call the Twilight Zone.

Joshua swore. "Season one. Why couldn't we get season two?"

"What are you talking about? What did you do?"

Joshua shushed her as the voice took up again.

Suspended in time and space for a moment, your introduction to Mister Joshua Lawson, a nineteen-year-old psychiatric intern whose primary ambition was to hit it big in the music industry until he be-friended a patient whose psychic delusions turned out to be real. Joined by an alien woman with the power to change worlds, Mr. Lawson will be challenged to use all his talents as he attempts to rescue his friends—and himself—from the depths of madness as his in-ternship makes an unexpected turn—into the Twilight Zone.

"If we get out of here alive, that will have been so cool," Joshua said.

Tasmae grabbed Joshua by the shoulder and spun him around. "What is going on? What was that?"

"Rod Serling. *The Twilight Zone.* It's a television show—used to watch it all the time with my mom. The real question is, what was he doing here?"

"Nothing happens in the Netherworld without a purpose," Tasmae snarled at him as if he were purposely being stupid. "This Serling person was right. This is the dimension of imagination. We control what happens here by our wills."

"So why can't you 'will' Deryl to us?" Joshua snapped.

"We tried to will ourselves to him!" Tasmae flared back.

"Okay! Listen, let's just both calm down. We won't get anywhere if we're fighting."

Tasmae nodded.

Joshua took a deep cleansing breath. "Good. All right. For whatever reason, we're not where Deryl is. Why would that happen? Could Alugiac have taken him somewhere else?"

"There is no 'somewhere else.'" Tasmae rolled her eyes impatiently, but kept her temper contained. She was holding onto her anger, however, and from the way she shook, Joshua guessed it was the only thing that was keeping her from collapsing completely.

He tried to take on a soothing tone. One of them had to stay cool. "Metaphorically speaking, Taz. Could Alugiac have hidden him in another illusion, or maybe Deryl has fled?"

"Maybe we weren't meant to confront him directly. If we find Deryl, we will find Alugiac, and I could not defeat him the last time. I'm not used to *doing* things in the Netherworld. It's supposed to be for communicating with the Ydrel."

"I think if this is the same place—dimension, whatever—that Deryl got dragged into by the Master, it can be more. But tell me what you know about this pla— about the Netherworld. What's happened to you here?"

"Before Alugiac, not much. I would Call Deryl to me through it, to receive his information. Then he refused me. He said he wanted to talk and to see me. He complained the place was dark and boring, so I imagined for us the grove where I had gone to pray and Call. Then today, I Called him, and Alugiac was there. Deryl knew him, called him Master—"

She closed her eyes, her face screwed tight with anguish.

He grasped her shoulders. "We'll find him. Just tell me the rest. Who's Alugiac?"

"My—he was once a great healer until contact with the Barins infected his mind. He joined them. He led them to kill my mentor. To kill me. And he was here! Then Deryl had a sword and was telling me to run. I attacked Alugiac, but these...creatures...blocked me. They would have killed me had Deryl not stopped them."

"How?"

"I don't know. One minute they were about to overwhelm me; the next, I was back in my own body."

"Deryl talked about being forced to battle creatures for the Master; obviously, both of them have more experience in this place than we do. I don't think Deryl knew they were the same place," he quickly reassured Tasmae. "And trust me—he may call him 'Master,' but Deryl was no willing apprentice. He was absolutely terrified by him, yet trying to break away. I'm sure he's fighting him as best he can now. We just have to figure out how to get to him and how to help him."

Tasmae nodded and took a long deep breath. When she spoke again, she sounded more like her controlled, warrior-trained self. "Perhaps that's why we did not get to him immediately. If they know how to manipulate this...dimension...then perhaps we're meant to learn how before we can confront Alugiac."

"Or how to avoid Alugiac altogether. Frankly, after what you and Deryl have told me, this is one dude I do not want to meet, especially in this creeped-out version of a dark alley." He shuddered then, and Tasmae grabbed him by the arm.

"Don't think about it," Tasmae warned. "You might alert him to our presence. So how do we learn to manipulate this world?"

"You sure you can't just Call Deryl?"

"I think it would bring Alugiac as well."

"Last resort then. So how did you manipulate the Netherworld?"

"I've only changed the setting."

Joshua snapped his fingers. "'Change worlds.' That's what Rod Sterling said. You have the power to change worlds. He was helping us. And he said I had to use my talent to get us all out of here safely."

"Which one, Joshua? You have so many."

Joshua laughed. "Not by the Earth sense of the word. Besides, he called me a psychiatric intern with ambitions in music. And he showed up when I whistled his show's theme song. It's got to be music. The question is, how do I use it?" He paused, thinking, then smiled and started to whistle a lead in, then began to sing.

"What are you doing?"

He ignored her as he sang the first verse and chorus of Geno Vanelli's "Black Cars Look Better in the Shade." Then he paused, waiting to see what would happen.

"You forgot 'sitting pretty in her dim lit covers,' and it's my favorite verse," a husky mezzo voice pouted from the distance. A tall, lithe woman in tight jeans and a halter top sauntered toward them.

"Lattie!" Joshua exclaimed. "What are *you* doing here?"

She gave a half-laugh, half-huff. "What are you asking me for? I was in the middle of a perfectly good dream when I heard you singing and here I am. So what'd you want *me* for?"

Now Joshua huffed, though without amusement. "I just need a car."

She smirked, tilted her head. "That song's not about a car and you know it."

Joshua was spared a reply when Tasmae stepped between them. "Where's Deryl?" she demanded.

"Who's Deryl? For that matter, who are you?" She eyed Tasmae up and down, appraisingly, the tip of her tongue playing over one side of her lip. She looked over Tasmae's shoulder to Joshua. "Aren't you going to introduce me to your friend? She looks like she likes the rough stuff. Maybe we find her friend and—"

"Dammit, Lattie, just lend me your car!"

With a victorious grin on her face, she sidled around Tasmae, who circled her warily, and held out her keys to Joshua. Just as he reached for them, however, she snapped them back. "Why *my* car? Why not yours?"

"I didn't want *your* car. I just need *a* car."

"Yet you didn't sing '409?' 'Pink Cadillac?' 'Big Black Car?'"

"It was the first song I thought of," Joshua growled. She just grinned wider. He kicked himself. She was goading him, he knew it, and he'd let her make him react.

"And you didn't even change the words. Sure there isn't some Freudian ulterior motive going on?"

"Not a chance."

"Uh huh," she said disbelievingly. She gave him one of her long slow looks, lingering around his belt line. "Maybe a change of costume?"

"Joshua, we're wasting time," Tasmae warned.

But suddenly, LaTisha was in the outfit, the one from Joshua's daydreams, the one that had never failed to get his blood boiling and him into her bed no matter what his previous resolutions. She twisted a little, posing. "Do I cut a perfect silhouette?" she purred.

This time, however, he found nothing alluring about her. She just looked cheap and annoying. "LaTisha, are you going to help us or not?"

"Maybe I should drive?" She stuck her key in her mouth.

What did I see in you? Joshua pursed his lips, thought a moment, then pitched his voice up. *"American Woman—"*

She chuckled. "Cute."

"Get away from me-ee—"

She again wore her street clothes, and her expression grew serious. "You're never coming back to me, are you?"

"After what you did?" He shook his head, biting back everything he really wanted to say to her. Tasmae was right; they were wasting time. "Right now, I really, really need to find our friend, and if you can't help, then just go on back to your dream, okay?" He tried to sound stern, but found his voice shaking.

She looked down, played with the keys in her hand. "Yeah, sure. Would it help if I said I was sorry?"

Joshua studied his feet, wondering what he should say. What he wanted to say. He'd so seldom seen her vulnerable like that. He wondered how sorry she was and exactly what she was sorry for.

"Joshua!" Tasmae hissed.

He sighed. "Maybe in the real world, the waking world, it might mean something. But I can't talk about it right now."

"Sure. I understand. I'm going to make it up to you, somehow. Someday."

"But not now?"

She shrugged. "Would a dream be enough? Good luck finding your friend." She turned and walked into the mist. Soon she was gone.

Joshua released the breath he hadn't even realized he was holding. He could feel himself shaking inside. He desperately wanted to sit down, but the fog was over his knees. He shut his eyes and forced himself to take a couple of long slow breaths. Why her? Why now?

She hadn't left them her car keys, either.

Tasmae struck him on the shoulder, making him open his eyes and look at her. "What was that all about?" she demanded.

"I don't know."

"Deryl is being held prisoner by the most dangerous madman in our world and you're wasting time talking to—" She flung her arm toward the mist, evidently unsure what to call LaTisha. "What were you doing?"

"I said, I don't know!" Joshua shouted. "I screwed up, all right? I just wanted to get us a car, a way to travel around this muck!"

"This isn't a place! There's no 'traveling!' Why can't your human mind comprehend that?"

"Fine! *You're* the brilliant military mind. You wanted to come here! *You* tell me what to do!"

Tasmae stopped, breathing heavy in her anger, but looking a little lost herself. "You're a mind healer," she said softly. "I thought you'd know."

Joshua bit down on his lips and pinched his brows with one hand as he took hold of his temper. "I'm sorry, Taz. We're in this together. But you've got to understand that this is totally new to me—even more than it is to you. I don't know what I'm doing."

She looked at him, and he saw the disappointment in her eyes. He tried not to feel resentment. How many times would he have to bail out his friend? Why was this all on him?

Perhaps she sensed his frustration, for she shut her eyes. He imagined her abandoning him there, but instead, the scene changed to a small but well-lit cave with a few large cushions.

"Thanks," he muttered as he sank into one.

"This was one of my hiding places in the last war," Tasmae explained as she sat in front of him. "Alugiac shouldn't be able to sense us here. You're right about one thing. We need to plan. And we need more information. But I don't know how to get it."

"Let's start with what we know." Joshua leaned back against the wall and gazed at the ceiling while he thought out loud. "Serling said you have the power to change the world—obviously, he's right there. What else can you do?"

In answer, Tasmae got up and again pulled her dagger from her hair and moved through a few steps of some martial arts form. She attempted a complex high kick, but fell among the cushions. "Anything I can physically do in the waking world, but nothing more," she said as she stood up, rubbing her elbows.

She concentrated on the wall opposite them, concentrated, and it dissolved then resolved into the weapons wall of the salle. She picked out a sword and a dagger that she strapped to her calf. "And now I'm armed."

"Sweet. That's a comfort, though I think we're better off avoiding a physical fight. I'm betting for every minion you bring down, monster or otherwise, Alugiac will think up three more. Can you Call in the cavalry if you need to?"

She frowned. "Again, I think that would not be the best plan. I don't know if I can, or if there was something special about the Ydrel and Miscria. I have never heard of another Kanaan in the Netherworld. Except Alugiac." She shivered.

"Try Salgoud. You know him pretty well, right?"

She sat down, moving the sheathed sword aside with a practiced gesture. "He is like a father to me. And he is our greatest war leader. If we could defeat Alugiac here, now, it would give us a great advantage in the upcoming war." She closed her eyes and concentrated.

After a few minutes, she shook her head. "It appears we are on our own."

"Not quite. I brought LaTisha, or whatever passes for LaTisha in this world, here."

"Yes. Why did you do that? What help was she? She is not your soul-mate—what hold does she have on you?"

Joshua squirmed uncomfortably under her gaze. "None! Like I said, I didn't plan for her to appear—I was just singing a song to get us a car."

"But she said that song wasn't about a car, and she seemed to think you'd sung it on purpose to bring her here."

"No, she said I had some Freudian alternative motive," he contradicted, then sighed. "Maybe she's right. Maybe I need to be aware of any subconscious messages or associations I have with a song."

He tapped his fingers on his lips, rehashing their conversation, then gave a surprised laugh. "You know what else she said? She asked me why I didn't change the words. She always did have a way of seeing the obvious when others didn't. Maybe she helped more than we thought." He shook his head ruefully.

"She also tried to distract you," Tasmae warned.

"Right, right. She definitely had her own agenda—which is something else to keep in mind. We're not dealing with automatons..."

"So you can summon people—or perhaps a psychic specter of real people." She shuddered.

"What?"

"The Remembrance. Gardianju was in the Netherworld with Deryl. They were attacked by...she called them demon specters. I think they were minds that Deryl could not block. Perhaps it's a human talent?"

"Maybe, but let's neither of us think about demons or anything if we can help it."

Tasmae shifted, restless. "Agreed. What else?"

"I don't know. We didn't get a car, but that was my fault. Lattie did offer her keys."

"Do we need a car? There is no 'to' and 'from' here."

"'The only reason for time is so that everything doesn't happen at once,'" Joshua quoted. "So the reason for space is so everything doesn't happen in the same spot. Regardless of what you're telling me, my mind insists there is a 'here' and 'there,' and Deryl is 'there.' We have to figure out how to get to him. We need somebody we can ask, somebody I can associate with a song."

He fell silent again, running songs through his mind. He couldn't believe how hard it was to come up with a song when he knew so many. Meanwhile, Tasmae fidgeted, toyed with her hair, got up and looked over the weapons, sat back down, got up again—

"I'm trying to concentrate," he muttered through his teeth.

"Deryl's falling away from us. I can feel it." She looked younger and more scared than he'd ever seen her.

"Can you telep to him?"

She shook her head. "I get a kind of angry static. It is Alugiac's doing. It must be! I may be able to push through it, but then may he find us before we are ready for him. We don't have a lot of time," Tasmae pressed. "He is playing games with Deryl's mind."

"Games! That's it." Despite himself, Joshua broke into a grin. "I have an idea, but it's going to sound weird."

Chapter Twenty-Five

Deryl stared, askance, at the lovely blond woman in bed beside him. She was looking at him, not in surprise, but with concern, like his being there wasn't unusual, but his behavior was.

"Hon, what is it?" she asked again.

He licked his lips, tried to quell his confusion and panic, and asked, "I know this is a weird question, but how did I get here?"

"Oh, God." Suddenly, she was up on hands and knees and leaning toward him. "What's the last thing you remember?"

"I was at SK-Mental, but it was an illusion. Alugiac—"

"The last *real* thing, Deryl! The last thing you remember that doesn't involve aliens or time travel."

He wanted to protest that the aliens and time travel were real, but couldn't make himself do it. He couldn't bear to see the fear in her eyes. He dropped his gaze, caught a clear view down her chemise, and quickly turned his head and focused on the dressers in their room. He shook his head—why did he think this was *their* room?

"All right, then," he said, playing the game and buying himself some time. "'Real world...' SK-Mental. I'd figured out how to teleport—that is real, Clarissa—"

"I know."

"All right. Good. Malachai drugged me. I took Joshua hostage. I was desperate. I just wanted a couple of minutes alone." Holding broken glass against his best friend's throat...

Anxiety clutched his stomach. He had to make her understand, to not be afraid. "Clari, I never meant to hurt him!"

"Shhh." With her right hand, she set her fingers lightly over his lips, and he stilled at her touch. "I know. And you didn't. Now, we're not going to panic, got it? Dr. Acker said if this happened again, just to start from when you last remember and help you remember back to the present."

Her face closed with pain and her hand trembled against his mouth.

This isn't real! Don't play this game! His mind screamed protests, and there was an odd ache at the base of his neck, but he found himself filled with the need to reassure her. He gripped her hand in his and spoke gently. "Come on. We'll work this out together. Why don't you tell me about Dr. Acker. He's my new doctor, right?"

She sniffled and tried to laugh. It came out shallow and breathy, but she seemed to be calming down. Her fingers closed around his thumb as she nodded and explained. "After the fiasco at SK, your aunt and uncle found Dr. Acker. He's a psychiatrist and a neurosurgeon. He believed you, and did some real tests—MRIs and all that—and found there was a certain spot in your brain that was overactive. Any of this ringing a bell?"

"I, I don't know." The pain at the base of his skull made it hard to think. He released her hand and rubbed at the back of his head, stopping as his fingers moved

Madness Unbound ❁ 311

over a long, slightly upraised scar under his hair. "He operated on me?"

She smiled and nodded encouragingly. "Yes! Yes, he did a partial lobotomy. He disconnected the part of your brain that was making you 'psychic.' I never did understand all the details. He could tell you better.

"The important thing is, it worked. No more voices in your head, no more accidentally breaking things or doing things to people with your mind. You could finally have a normal life."

A normal life. The words whispered seductively in his mind, more compelling to him than the lovely woman smiling hesitantly at his side. Could it be real? The pain receded momentarily as he absorbed these new thoughts. He slipped out from under the covers, heedless of the fact that he wore only boxers, and wandered the room, seeking something familiar. He paused at the 8 X 10 photo in an etched glass frame. He looked at himself, clad in a tuxedo, his hair short and his eyes behind glasses, smiling, with his arm around Clarissa. Her old-fashioned bridal gown had a heavily sequined bodice and a six-foot train that curved over their feet. "And twenty-five buttons in the back," he murmured.

"You *would* remember that," Clarissa said warmly.

He didn't know how he knew it, or even why he'd imagine it. He resisted the urge to ask the obvious questions about their wedding, and turned instead to a photo of them with Joshua and Sachiko. They were in ski gear, someplace snowy with tall, rugged mountains rising gray in the background.

"Colorado?" he guessed.

"Uh huh. Last year. We went skiing in Vail. Joshua promised Sachiko that he'd go sailing with her if she'd do the black slopes with him. He hates the water."

Despite himself, Deryl nodded. "Especially after his bachelor's party," he said, though he didn't know why.

But again, it was the right thing to say. "Yes! That's right! You saved his life when he fell off the boat during that stupid prank 'Ko's cousins set up. Pictures are helping, then?" Without waiting for an answer, she got out of bed and headed to a bookshelf. Her chemise was short, and Deryl couldn't help staring as she bent over to pull out a scrapbook.

"Are you checking me out?" she cut across his musings.

"No!" He averted his eyes guiltily.

She laughed, but let him off the hook. "Well, check this out instead." She sat on the edge of the bed, and he sat next to her, close so that the book fell open on both their laps. The first pages were of buildings, nondescript and academic-looking with their brick and ivy and large stone signs with subjects and sometimes who the building was named for.

"I went to college?"

"Of course you did, silly. How else would we have met again?" She bumped her shoulder against his and smiled playfully. She had a great smile.

Suddenly he saw her smiling at him, but in a different place—smaller, crowded with books and stuffed animals—and the emotions were different—happy, excited, nervous. He gasped against the intensity of it.

"What do you remember?" she asked breathlessly.

"I, I don't know," he stammered. "You smiled at me, and then, I saw you smiling like that, only your hair was shorter, spiky, and you had painted a mask on your face, and whiskers. And you had on this black leotard with orange stripes and a tail."

She turned to face him, her smile brilliant and joyful. "The Halloween party. Our first date."

"I wanted you that night." The words were out of his mouth before he'd realized he was speaking. The feelings were still strong in his mind, amplifying the attraction he was feeling now. He leaned toward her.

Stop it! This isn't real! Think of Tasmae!

A fierce pain lanced the back of his head. He buckled over with a cry. The scrapbook slipped from their laps.

"Did you take your medicine today?"

"What medicine?" he choked out.

"Your medicine!" she repeated.

His head throbbed as the bed moved when she got up. He was dimly aware of her walking out, a second light coming on, and her rummaging through a cabinet. Slowly, each step bringing a new agony, he rose and followed her. He found her in the bathroom, a bottle of pills open and spilled onto the counter. She counted them as she put them back into the bottle. As she spoke numbers under her breath, he forced himself to lift his head and look into the mirror.

It was his face, but he was wearing glasses. When did he get glasses? He remembered them on the dresser, but didn't remember putting them on. He didn't recognize his hair, so short and layered. His face was fuller; his chest, too. He was both himself and a stranger. How old was he?

"You took it. You took it," Clarissa muttered. "They're just not working as well. Here. Dr. Acker said if it got worse, you could take one extra."

Deryl looked at the green pill in her hand. "What are they?"

"Realitin. A neuro-suppressor. After the surgery, you were fine for a while, then you started having delusions, remember? Nightmares, at first, like tonight. Dreams of being on another planet. Some of your abilities came back, but you couldn't control them. It turned out that in the absence of whatever he cut out, your mind was going overtime trying to make up for it, or re-forge a link or something."

She'd managed to explain that much calmly, but something in Deryl's look must have unnerved her, for her tone started to grow frantic. "Yeah, I know, I'm not explaining well. I never understood this stuff, Deryl, you know that. The point is, you've been taking these every day for the past three years and you've been all right. Then last week, you started having nightmares about someplace called Canan and people named Leanad and Tasmay and some evil overlord named Al Lou Jiak. I thought maybe you'd forgotten to take your pills, but Dr. Acker thinks you might be developing a resistance. So please, take this now, and call him tomorrow?"

He wanted to protest that he didn't even remember Dr. Acker, much less his phone number, but she looked so scared again that he forced a smile and swallowed the pill. If it wasn't real, it couldn't hurt him, anyway, right?

"It worked pretty fast last time," she told him, though she also seemed to be reassuring herself. "It'll help your headache, too. Shall we look at some more pictures?"

They settled down on the bed again with the scrapbook. Already, Deryl's headache was receding, though he wasn't sure that comforted him much. He concentrated on the photos. One, of a modern building, drew him, as did the large stone and brick sign that declared "Computer Science Building" in the front.

"That's where we met, remember?" Clarissa asked. "I was walking by with some friends and you were hanging out by the sign, and you called out, 'Hey, Clarissa, kissed any crazy psychics lately?'"

"I planned that line for a week," he told her. Again, words he didn't know where his came from his mouth, and memories he didn't remember poured into his mind. Other things shifted into place and it was his turn to dash out of the room. Instead of a left to the bathroom, however, he took a right, passed through their living room and went into the study. His study.

Breathing fast, he approached the first desk and the computer there. It was large and powerful, top of the line. Beside it waited a stack of paper with computer code. On the opposite wall was another desk with a blue, stylized computer with a glowing red alien face in the front.

"One for work and one for your games," Clarissa commented from the doorway.

"But I can't look at a computer—or television, for that matter. I get seizures."

"Not since the surgery. The glasses help, too, I'm told. Something about the way they're ground. They're hideously expensive, I know that."

He flipped through the pages on the desk. "I program computers."

"You're brilliant at it, too," Clarissa said as she wrapped her arms around him and leaned against his back. "At least according to Mom and Dad. You're the reason they got that NASA contract. I think they were as happy for their business as for me when we got married."

She sighed happily as she snuggled in closer.

It felt very natural to have her lean against him like that, but his mind was on the papers before him. He shuffled through a few more slowly, saw something, and grabbed a pencil. He felt the silk of her nightgown caress his back as she shifted to peer past him.

"New subroutine?" she asked.

"No. I screwed this part up. I need to bone up on orbital mechanics." How did he know that?

Her arms tightened around him. "Don't tinker with it too much. You're already late enough that Mom and Dad have come to me about it. It's all coming back, now, isn't it? Oh, thank God. Are you feeling better?"

"Some," he said uncertainly. "The headache's fading, but I feel...confused."

"Maybe we should go to bed."

He took her hand and let her guide him back to their bed. He even kissed her softly goodnight. But when she turned the lights out, he rolled with his back to her and stared out at their dark apartment until his eyes would stay open no longer.

When Deryl woke up, he felt a moment of panic when he didn't know where he was. Then, things snapped back into place and he rolled over and caressed the side of the bed where Clarissa had slept. There was only a note on the pillow now.

He grabbed the note with one hand, then pulled the pillow to his face with the other. He breathed deeply, smelling her perfume. For a moment, he saw her in his mind's eye, spraying the air before her then walking into the mist with her head thrown back. He loved watching her put on perfume. Somehow, just lying there with her pillow against his face helped ease the odd, empty feeling that had welled up inside him.

He leaned back, happier now, and read the note. *Honey, didn't want to wake you after last night. Tried to get the day off, but I've got pre-school gym plus swim, and Regionals are coming up, so there was no way. I'll be home by 5, promise! In the meantime, relax, take you pill, and Please! Call Dr. Acker. I love you!*

Laughing, he slid out of bed and headed to the bathroom. He showered, dressed, shaved—yes, he needed to shave, even used a straight-razor like Joshua—and ran a comb through his hair. His glasses were dirty, and as he reached into the medicine cabinet for cleaner, he saw the small prescription bottle of Realitin. He started to open it when something made his hand stop.

Don't do it! Tasmae's coming, and she can't reach you if you take those. Don't buy into this reality. It's not real! Remember Tasmae!

The feeling of incompleteness rushed over him, and he dropped the unopened bottle and staggered back, hitting the shower doors and sliding down. What was he doing? Alugiac was out there, manipulating his mind the way he had as a child; only this time, he was using elements of Deryl's memories to weave a complex trap.

Clarissa's antique perfume aerator caught his eye, but a different hand held it, and the woman who walked into the mist wore a wedding dress and hairstyle more suited to the 1940s.

Not his memories alone—the memories of all the minds that had touched his! Deryl started to shake.

Tasmae! He teleped with all his might. *Tasmae!*

He felt nothing in reply and fought back a sob. Without consciously realizing it, his arms folded themselves over his middle and he began to rock. The world around him grayed.

"You know, it's a good thing I work out, or I'd be in so much pain by now."

"Joshua?" Deryl blinked and saw his friend sitting beside him, rocking in time with him. In his surprise, he stopped moving and Joshua sighed with relief.

"Thank you. Now let's get out of here. Don't know what you've experienced, but this is Land of the Nasty Exes as far as I'm concerned."

"I, um, saw Clarissa. She was okay."

Joshua looked at him searchingly and Deryl felt himself blush. "Maybe you'd better not say too much about that to Tasmae," his friend advised.

"Tasmae! She's here?"

As if in answer, they heard her cry for help. The two stood and ran, kicking up the fog as they went.

They found her in a meadow like the one where he'd watched the battle from what seemed ages ago—and like on that day, she was under attack. Three warriors battled against her at once, pushing her back against a tree. Others were on their way.

"Deryl, you gotta do something!" Joshua yelled.

"What?" Deryl pointed, confused. "That's Salgoud."

"What are you talking about? Those are like, orcs or something! Deryl, use your telekinesis—kill them before they kill her! Quick!"

"Orcs?" Deryl turned back to the scene.

One of the soldiers had knocked Tasmae's dagger from her hand, which bled freely. She was in obvious pain, yet brought her sword up again and again to counter the blows.

But they were her people. At least, he saw them as her people.

Kanaan or orcs, he had to stop them. He focused his energy on pushing them away.

Nothing happened.

"Deryl!" Tasmae yelled. "Point blows! Kill them!"

KILL THEM. The words echoed in his mind, bearing down on him. He shook his head.

"Deryl, what's wro—" Joshua's question ended in a strangled gasp, and Deryl turned to see that another warrior had run him through.

"Josh!"

Then the Kanaan's form changed. The sword became thick and claw-like, ripping Joshua's flesh as it grew and fused into the creature's arm. It pulled back its claw, and Joshua dropped to the ground. It lost its humanoid form, but not its triumphant smile.

"No!"

Behind him, Tasmae gave a last scream as the monsters ran her through. As she fell, she looked at him. Her eyes accused: Why did you hesitate?

"No-no-no-NOOOO!"

The world around him went red then black. The creatures changed again, surrounding him like a wall, bearing down on him like an avalanche. His ears filled with laughter that quickly grew into a high-pitched mechanical whine—

Deryl screamed and clawed at the inside of the MRI apparatus. He dimly heard people calling instructions, and he was pulled out. For a moment, he struggled against the nurses, but when they didn't change into some hideous form, he grabbed one by the shoulders and demanded to know the only thing of importance: "Are you real?"

Ten minutes later, he sat in an uncomfortable upholstered chair in Dr. Acker's hospital office, waiting for the results of the MRI. Clarissa occupied the chair beside him, but after he'd shrugged off her attempts to comfort him, had contented herself with laying one hand lightly on his shoulder. He didn't look at her, but stared at the floor and the large brass plaque that read Dr. Alouicious Grant Acker, MD, PhD, and answered her questions in monosyllables if at all. They both looked up with a start when Dr. Acker came in.

Dr. Acker's sweet round face crinkled in a sympathetic smile, but it didn't hide the worry in his eyes. He didn't speak until he'd settled his portly body into his desk chair and slid the CD into its slot. "Sorry to have kept you waiting. What we found was most...startling. Deryl, did you take your medication today?"

"No." He shook his head. Things were starting to come back. "I was going to. I'd gotten out of the shower. I had the bottle in my hands. Then." He shrugged.

"Go on."

He glanced uncertainly at Clarissa. He didn't want to scare her further. He considered asking her to leave, but a stab of fear echoed the stab of pain in the back of his skull, and he quickly discarded the idea. She was all that was keeping him together at the moment. She swallowed hard, nodding encouragingly.

He answered, keeping his tone as bland and factual as he could, though with each word, his head hurt more, and his anxiety increased. "I was in the Netherworld, like another dimension. Joshua was there. He said he'd pulled me out of the illusion I was in—this world—and then Tasmae was attacked, and they wanted me to use my telekinesis to kill the attackers, but they looked like friends to me. Then they—the attackers—they turned into monsters. They killed Joshua and Tasmae. They were going to bury me alive. Then, I was in the MRI room." He knew his explanation was disjointed and confused, but he prayed they wouldn't press him for details.

Mercifully, Dr. Acker asked, "How long did it feel?"

"Ten, fifteen minutes. How long have I been here?"

Dr. Acker nodded to Clarissa.

She swallowed hard before answering. "I came home at five-thirty and found you in the bathroom, just rocking and, and whimpering, so I called nine-one-one. We've been here about two hours."

His heart ached to see the tears welling in her eyes. "Sweetheart, I'm so sorry!"

He pulled her in close.

Chapter Twenty-Six

"How is playing this game going to help us find Deryl?" Tasmae demanded impatiently, as she stared at a huge stone lion with a man's face.

"*Survival of the Sphinx* is a new reality TV-game show on Earth. We get a mission—saving Deryl, right? Then the Sphinx gives us riddles that will help us complete the mission. If we can interpret the riddle before the buzzer goes off, we get things that can help us: time, more clues, sometimes stuff. And if we don't, we don't get the prize, but we at least have the clue. Come on. I thought you liked riddles."

"I don't like wasting time."

"Me, either. Listen. This is a half-hour show, half of which is eaten up with completing the mission. Take out commercials, and the quiz part is like ten minutes. It's time better spent gathering information than running about at random or brainstorming in a vacuum."

"Are you prepared?" the Sphinx asked.

Tasmae nodded.

"We're ready."

"When Roland and Fender get busy together, this is their issue, but its shape and soul are created by you."

Roland? Fender? The words made no sense to Tasmae, though she had the feeling they had to create something. She turned to Joshua, who was repeating the riddle in a whisper. Then, his face cleared into an expression of joy.

"Sweet! It's a keytar!" When nothing happened but the continued clicking of the timer, Joshua hesitated.

"Its shape and soul are determined by you," Tamae pressed.

"Right! Um, built in amplifier and power system with enough juice to last our mission, sturdy but lightweight, Yamaha SHS-10 body, special effect sound keys on the handle, silver, with a strap?"

A flash, and Tasmae's weapons cabinet transformed into a curtain, partly opened to reveal the oddest instrument she had ever seen.

"Yes!" Joshua pumped the air with his fist and snatched up the keytar. He caressed it lovingly before sliding into the strap and slinging it on his back. "Told you!" he said excitedly.

"Shh!" she hissed.

The Sphinx was speaking again: "Russian dolls. Celtic scrollwork. Gordian knots."

Joshua's triumphant smile faded.

"Are you saying the trap Alugiac has set for Deryl is like these other things?" Tasmae demanded.

The Sphinx merely repeated himself.

"Arrgh!" Tasmae ran her fingers through her hair. "He is worse than the Ydrel! Joshua, tell me what these things are!"

"Russian dolls fit inside each other; Celtic scrollwork—" Joshua drew one in the air with his finger. "—complex design, no discernible beginning or end. Gordian knot, ancient legend, too complex to untie; Alexander the Great cut it with a sword."

"You're describing Deryl's trap," Tasmae said with authority. "Illusion within illusion, each getting more tangled and complex, until he can't get out by going through."

"Correct. Here is your reward. Listen well.

"The Gordian's knot could not be untied, though luck and skill had many who tried. Alexander cut it to keep his word. Deryl's survival, and yours, rely on the absurd."

"What?" Tasmae started to argue, but Joshua gripped her hand.

"We'll figure that one out later," he hissed. The Sphinx was speaking again.

"The Master asks this of him, but it is not his Call. Ask this of him, and you endanger all. His spirit is strong, but not for this task. His purpose is set; beware what you ask."

Joshua looked at Tasmae. "Deryl told me the Master wanted to make him into a weapon. Sphinx, is it that we can't ask Deryl to hurt anyone?"

"To kill," Tasmae said, suddenly regretting what had happened at the salle and the field. "We must never ask him to kill."

When Clarissa got home from work, Deryl had the house clean, the candles lit and romantic music playing on the stereo, and was reclining on the couch, chuckling over *The Hitchhiker's Guide to the Galaxy*.

"What's so funny?" she asked as she set her purse on the side table and went to him. She set her hands on his shoulders and kissed the top of his head.

He realized he couldn't' remember anything from the novel except the "Mostly Harmless" joke. He held the book so she could see the cover. "Joshua sent it to me years ago, but I'd never gotten around to reading it. Found it this afternoon when I was cleaning up."

"Yeah, I noticed. The place looks great."

"Thanks." He set the book down and got up to put his arms around her. He kissed her lightly. "I cleaned the whole place, including that closet we never dare to open. And I hauled a bunch of junk to the Goodwill bin, took a long swim—"

"Did you do any work on that program?" she demanded.

He smiled proudly. "Worked, finished, compiled, and delivered. And I've made your favorite Chinese dinner."

She blinked at him with exaggerated awe. "Did you sprain your finger dialing?"

He did his best to look affronted. "I ordered on-line, madam! Speaking of... Joshua e-mailed. He has a break in his touring schedule in June and Sachiko's taking time off, so they're coming up to visit for a few days."

She sighed and hugged him closer. "I could get used to this. We should have put you on that extra medication a long time ago."

"I certainly have more energy," he replied, as he rested his cheek on her and started to shift his weight from one foot to the other, easing her into a slow dance. He really didn't want to talk about it.

It had been a week since Dr. Acker had shown them the MRI, which blazed with color and activity in the area that should have been dark and null, and had said that somehow, impossibly, his mind was rebuilding connections. They'd left with two new prescriptions and the warning that if these "seizures" continued, they might have to completely remove that part of his brain.

Since then, the days had been strange and full of holes. He didn't remember finishing the program, only sitting at the computer with the intention of working on it. When he returned to himself, he was pressing "Send" to deliver the finished product to her parents.

Even more, some of those blackouts resembled the "Callings" he'd had as a teen. The ones of Tasmae were hazy and shadowed, however; he could hear her, almost feel her, but not see her, and the feelings of incompleteness ate away at his soul. The Callings of the Master, equally distant and subtle, played a darker accompaniment: whispers of how Deryl was so much better, so much *more* than mere humans, gentle suggestions that he could get back his power, have anything—everything—he wanted, if only he would use that ability, succumb to the Master's training, and follow through.

The resurgence of his abilities frightened him more. Twice he'd picked up the phone before it rang, knowing who was on the other side, and when he'd opened the Closet of Doom and its contents had spilled out, everything had fallen around him, leaving him in a small clear circle.

Through it all, a small, but persistent voice insisted that none of this was real. The only time he felt truly normal was with Clarissa, and he had to fight his panic each time she left him for the fitness club where she worked as an instructor.

After the second day, he'd forced himself to call Dr. Acker about it, though he told him only about the blackouts. The psychiatrist had told him that it would take time for the medications to build up in his system and that as long as the "seizures" didn't last too long or become too intense, he should stay calm and busy and be patient. He'd hung up, only slightly reassured. He vowed not to mention anything to Clarissa. Thankfully, nothing happened when she was with him. He'd buried himself in activities he only half-remembered and tried to concentrate only on the present. It was helping, some.

"You're awfully quiet all of a sudden," she murmured.

He rubbed her back, reaching under her T-shirt. "Why are you talking?" he countered.

She pulled back with a smile that made his heart skip. "Maybe I should change clothes? Walk into a little perfume?"

"Only if I get to watch."

One of Joshua's CDs started playing as hand in hand, they wandered into the bedroom.

Joshua smiled at Tasmae as he sat on the cushions, running his hands over the keys of the guitar-style keyboard, playing with the function keys. The game was over, and the Sphinx gone, and though they had not been able to make out all the riddles, they did well enough that Joshua felt rather pleased with himself. "I told you this was a good idea. Now, I've got this, and we also have a lot more information to make plans with."

"Do we?" she paused in her pacing to snap. "We still don't know 'where' Deryl is or how to get to him. You have that thing, but do you know why? If the information is accurate, there's supposed to be no way we can defeat Alugiac!"

Joshua set his keytar aside and stood to lay a steadying hand on Tasmae. He could feel her quaking. "Calm down, Taz. You're not going to be able to help Deryl if you get this upset. Think with me. The Sphinx never said we can't *defeat* Alugiac. We just can't *kill* Alugiac, and we can't ask Deryl to kill him. Deryl is trapped, somehow, in the illusions Alugiac has set for him, and while we might be able to help him, only he can break himself out. Us, too, because we'll be in his 'world' once we find him. When we do find him, our talents will be at odds with Alugiac's, so we can't expect to do anything major. Am I right so far? What else?"

He waited encouragingly as she took a deep breath and released it.

"We need allies to help us find him—but I can't Call anyone!"

He flopped onto the cushions and picked up the keytar.

"*I* can."

Her eyes widened with realization. "Yes, you can!"

She knelt beside him. "Try, Joshua! Use your music to bring Deryl to us."

On the CD, Joshua was singing about returning to his True Love, and Deryl found himself humming the melody. That awful sense of unreality threatened to sweep over him, but he drowned himself in Clarissa's kisses.

ENJOYING YOURSELF, DERYL?

Go away! Deryl commanded the voice in his mind. *You aren't real!*

I AM THE ONLY REALITY, DERYL.

The world around him dissolved and became dark fog, then sharpened again until he was back in the padded room at South Kingston Mental Wellness Center.

He groaned. This time, he stood up and shouted, "Alugiac! Come out and fight me!"

"Shh!" Joshua hushed from behind him. "That is about the last thing we need right now!"

"Joshua?" Deryl whirled, and saw his friend was dressed in the loose tunic and pants of Tasmae's world. Then he saw her.

"Taz!" He ran to her, but stopped before he got too close. "Are you real?" he demanded.

"Is this real?" she asked, and flung herself into his arms, kissing him enthusiastically. He felt her mind flowing into his, filling him with wholeness. He responded with equal ardor.

Beside them, Joshua cleared his throat loudly. "Can we save that until after we're out of here?"

"How?" Deryl replied.

"Actually, it's easier than you think." Joshua grinned. "Turns out the Netherworld is all about teleportation. You just need the right key—and mine happens to be B Flat." He hummed a note, then sang, "Be it ever so humble / There's no place like home" as he pushed open the door.

Beyond lay a landscape of rough plains, with low grass and small scrubby trees Deryl had only seen in books. Past them were tall mountains, green moving to blue-gray in the distance. The sky was a fantastically deep blue with white puffy clouds. A few cattle grazed under the hot summer sun.

"Westcliffe," Joshua said fondly. "Mom and Dad's ranchland, in fact. I'll have some explaining to do about how I got there, but at this point, I don't really care." He turned back to Deryl and Tasmae and asked wryly, "You're not coming back with me, are you?"

Deryl stayed in Tasmae's embrace. "No."

Joshua shrugged. "Well, good luck. Taz? Tell everyone I said thanks."

He stepped through the door and was gone.

Deryl watched the scene fade before him, then looked back at his love. "So what do we do?"

"I Called you into the world. I simply need to Call you back." She whispered in his ear, "Return to me."

A moment of blackness, then he was lying on a mattress on the ground in a dark tent. He sat up.

"Tasmae?" he started to call, but she silenced him by placing her mouth over his. Soon, she had joined him under the blankets and the next time he called her name, it was with a moan of pleasure.

"What did you call me?" Clarissa's soft high voice demanded.

"What?" Deryl blinked and found himself back in their apartment, in bed, leaning over Clarissa. He pulled back from her hastily.

Her softly worried look just as quickly turned into one of alarm. "Oh, no. No. Did you take your pills today?"

"What?" He wasn't sure whether he should wonder why he was here or why he should find that wrong. He ran his hand through his hair and rubbed the scar at the base of his skull. The headache was back, along with the fear.

Clarissa didn't answer, just threw on a robe and ran to the bathroom. After a few moments, he pulled on some pants and followed her. As he expected, he found her pouring out his pills and counting them into her hand.

"You took them. You took them," she said tremblingly as she poured them into the bottle. A couple spilled onto the floor. Calmly, he picked them up and put them carefully back into the bottle, then took her hands in his. She looked him, her eyes glassy with tears. "You took them," she whispered, "so why is this happening?"

She looked so scared. He didn't want to hurt her. "Dr. Acker said it was going to take time."

"It's been a week!"

"He said it could take months. We have to be patient. Shhh. It's going to be all right." He tried to embrace her, but she resisted.

"Were you with her?" she demanded.

"No," he lied, and he pulled her close.

This time, she buried her face into his chest, shaking as she fought to contain her sobs. "I can't lose you."

"You won't lose me," he whispered automatically. "I promise, you're not going to lose me."

He kissed her hair, her forehead, traced her hairline with his lips to her ear. After a moment, she began to respond, her lips playing over his chest and neck. Soon, their kissing grew more urgent and they pulled at their clothing as they moved as one back to the bedroom.

Chapter Twenty-Seven

"It didn't work!" Tasmae paced the small cave, her fists clenched. She rounded on Joshua. "Why didn't it work?"

"I don't know!" He'd been singing almost nonstop for the past half-hour. His fingers were sore from the activity after so many days without practice, and he could feel the tightness in his throat.

He took a deep breath, forced himself to relax. "Maybe it can't be that easy."

"Does Deryl know we're here?"

"I tried to get him that message. Making up stuff on the fly isn't as easy as it sounds."

She stalked to where the weapons cabinet had once stood, turned and stalked back. He wished she would stop. He felt like he was watching a panther, with no protective glass to protect him if she decided to pounce. His neck reminded him of her strength.

"Does Alugiac know we're here?" she demanded.

"I don't know." He closed his eyes trying to banish the fear that thought brought. "We need allies."

"How? So far, you have called up imaginary creatures and disembodied voices."

"And Lattie."

"Who tried to distract us from saving Deryl!"

"Okay!" he jumped up to snap in her face. She froze in surprise, and despite her weapons and her status, she suddenly seemed incredibly young and vulnerable.

He backed away from her and brought the keytar in front of him. "Okay. I don't think we can come at Deryl directly—maybe that's good if that will put us in Alugiac's sights. And I can call people—I just have to be more careful."

"You should have a weapon," she said. Her voice trembled just a bit.

He held up the keytar. "I have a weapon. I just need to use it better. This helps because there's a lot of music on Earth that doesn't have words, but has specific associations—like the *Twilight Zone* theme. Certain sounds, too; things I can't recreate with my voice but can with the keytar. It also helps me when I'm changing words. Staying with the melody and rhythm adds to the power of the song, but I can play the melody first while I check the scanning without influencing anything—I think."

"You think?"

He nodded, his fingers playing scales, making adjustments. Just feeling the plastic of the keys reassured him. "I think I know what to do. We need an ally, and it has to be someone Deryl can trust, too. If he's really trapped in illusions made from his memories, like we think the riddle said, there's only one person I know who can help us." He closed his eyes, pictured his fiancée clearly in his mind, and played the chorus of the song he'd written to propose to her not a week ago:

I trust your heart
I believe your words
I really need your help now girl
We need to save Deryl, please do your part
So I can believe your words
And trust your heart.

"Joshua?" came a voice from the narrow entrance of the cave.

"In here!" he called, warning himself to stay cool. *She's no more real than Lattie was*, he told himself firmly.

Still, when he saw her at the entrance, his heart leaped. "Hey, beautiful!"

But instead of smiling in return, her eyes narrowed. "Joshua, is that you?"

His smile faded into confusion. "What's wrong, 'Ko, baby?"

"Where are your bandages?" she asked as walked straight to him, running her hands searchingly over his throat. He could feel the tension in her fingers and in her shoulders as he set his hands over them. Illusion or not, it felt so good to touch her.

"What're you talking about, 'Ko?"

"Where are your bandages? Where are your scars? He slit your throat; I saw him do it. I thought you were going to die, and the doctors said you'd never sing—"

She stopped, suddenly noticing the cave room with its pillows and abundance of plants. "Oh, buh! This is a dream!" She relaxed, though her smile was sad. "Will you sing for me again?"

"He what? No, babe, he..." A horrible idea occurred to Joshua. He'd somehow summoned the Sachiko from Deryl's illusions.

He placed his hands over his fiancée's and drew them from his neck, fighting back the feeling of loss. He guided her to sit next to him. "It's not a dream, babe. What I'm going to tell you is pretty unbelievable, but I swear to you, it's true, and it's real. And if we're going to help Deryl, I need you to believe me."

Madness Unbound   335

He explained everything, starting with Tasmae and ending with Sachiko's arrival in the cave.

Her lips curled into a half-smile. "So this is the *Twilight Zone*? Funny. It's more colorful than I'd expected."

Joshua chuckled with relief. Illusion or not, this Sachiko had a lot in common with the real one, including her quirky humor and ability to stay calm and focused no matter what the situation. He knew he'd made the right choice summoning her. They could trust her.

That same calm, however, made Tasmae suspicious. "You're taking this very well, considering that means you are also an illusion."

She shrugged. "It explains a lot. I can only remember specific—and none too fun, mind you—snatches of time, all at SK-Mental and all involving Deryl. All pretty horrific. I'm actually glad to know the real me's alive and fine in another dimension. Besides, if I'm an illusion, then that means my Joshua is, too."

She ran her hands over the smoothness of his neck again. "I'd rather you were the real one," she whispered, then her voice strengthened. "But if the real Deryl's caught in that illusion, then he's in big trouble. He's in the maximum intensity ward, he alternates between rocking and chanting that nothing is real, sobbing over what he's done to you, and raving at someone named Alugiac—and they've brought in some doctor—Alouicious Acker—who wants to lobotomize him."

Tasmae's eyes rolled into the back of her head and she swooned.

The two eased her onto the cushions. Almost immediately, she struggled to sit up.

"Just relax a minute," Joshua urged. "You can make plans lying down just as easily as sitting up, you know."

"I'm sorry. I didn't mean to shock you," Sachiko said.

"It wasn't that," Tasmae said. "Deryl. Something's happened." Suddenly, tears flooded her eyes. "Alugiac's winning. Deryl's starting to believe whatever illusion Alugiac has set up for him. I'm losing Deryl, I can feel it!"

"Deryl, look! How sad." Clarissa stopped and pointed at a father trying to console a little girl of about six.

Joshua and Sachiko were in town for their visit, and they'd decided to go to the street carnival. They were passing by the arcade area when they saw the father trying unsuccessfully to comfort the sobbing child. Clarissa, already feeling the mothering instinct, ran up to them to ask what was wrong. It turned out the father had been trying to win one of the large animals at the ball toss, and had finally had to call it quits.

"The game's gotta be rigged," he said to Deryl and Joshua as the ladies tried to comfort the girl. "I know it was probably the wrong thing to do, but her mom and I split up and I don't get to see her much now, and she loves white Bengal tigers, and I just—you know—wanted to be a big shot for her. I played varsity, you know? Now we have to go home early."

"No you don't," Joshua said as he quietly pressed some twenties into the man's hand. "Go ride the rides. Eat too much cotton candy. Have fun."

Deryl, meanwhile, was looking at the stand the father had pointed to, and his eyes narrowed as he watched the bored yet smug look on the carnie's face as he counted out his earnings.

"First, you're going to win your daughter a tiger."

"I told you, it's gotta be rigged."

Deryl crouched down in front of the sniffling girl. "Know what I think?" he told her softly. "I think your Daddy just needs one more shot—and maybe a kiss for luck. What do you think?"

"We don't have any more money," she sniffed.

"Sure you do." He reached up behind her ear and pretended to pull a five dollar bill from it. "I'll bet it's lucky."

The father clearly thought it was a bad idea, but his daughter looked at him with such hopeful eyes that he took the money and went back to the stand. Deryl and the others followed. The man behind it smiled and his eyes shone greedily.

"Back again! This is your lucky day, I can feel it! Your daddy loves you very much, little girl!" He almost shouted the words with plastic enthusiasm.

Deryl looked at the five baskets sitting at angles. "Which one should he aim for?" he asked the little girl.

She pointed. "That one, Daddy! It's lucky!"

"Sweetie, there're no guarantees," the man warned.

"You'll do it!" she said, and kissed his cheek for luck.

He sighed, took the ball and aimed at the basket. They all watched intently.

He threw.

Deryl concentrated.

The ball sailed in, landed and stayed.

"A winner!" the carnie said disbelievingly, then spoke with more enthusiasm as he heard the girl's screams of joy and the cheers of the others. "That's right, ladies and gentlemen! A winner, right here! Congratulations, little lady," he said with a false smile as he passed the tiger to her. He puzzled over the baskets while the father and child gave the couples enthusiastic hugs and heartfelt thanks and went on their way.

"Isn't that bear cute?" Clarissa asked, and Deryl laughed.

"Still a ball left," he said and threw it into a basket without bothering to aim...physically, anyway.

"We have another winner!" the carnie shouted enthusiastically, though his eyes didn't hide his surprise.

Clarissa squealed and clapped as he passed over a squishy four-foot velour bear.

"Where are we going to put that?" Deryl teased.

"We'll find a place," Clarissa replied smoothly as she hugged the bear. Then she bumped her shoulder against him. "Besides, if you didn't want it in our apartment, why'd you win it for me?"

"I figured it was another one of those craving-things."

Clarissa jabbed her elbow into him. She still wasn't showing and hadn't had much morning sickness or cravings, but that didn't stop him from making jokes. "Seriously, I just wanted to wipe that smug smile off that guy's face.

"Hey, let's go ride some rides," Sachiko said.

They got to the Round Up first, and the person running the ride wouldn't let them take the bear on, so Deryl volunteered to stay with it. Joshua elected to wait with him, and the girls gave the man their tickets and

Madness Unbound ❀ 339

got on. Soon the ride was whirling in a circle and tilting and they could hear their wives' laughter among the shouts and screams of the other riders. Deryl set the bear in front of him and leaned his elbows on the temporary fence. Joshua mimicked his posture.

"So how long have you been able to do that again?" he asked casually.

"Do what?" Deryl bluffed.

"You're not fooling me, buddy. There are going to be quite a few more winners at that game now, aren't there?"

Joshua looked at him directly, but Deryl couldn't meet his eyes. He stared at the whirling bodies in the spinning circular cage. "I just evened the odds," he murmured.

"That's not what I'm talking about, and you know it. Clarissa calls 'Ko a lot. She's worried about you. You are taking your medication?"

"Ask her. She counts my pills every night." He meant to say it lightly, but it sounded bitter even to him.

"I'm asking you."

"Fine." Deryl turned to confront his friend. "Tell me straight up: Are you real?"

Now it was Joshua's turn to drop his eyes. He swore softly. "Deryl, what do you think?"

"I'm asking you."

"How am I supposed to prove to you this is real?"

"Because..." Deryl started then stopped. How could he explain? Sometimes, he heard snatches of Joshua's songs—on the radio, in the elevator—and the world around him would seem so fake, so wrong. "Because I trust you. Just be straight with me."

Joshua sighed. "Seriously, I don't know how to prove it. The philosophers have been trying to do that for thousands of years. It's the whole 'brain in a vat' conundrum."

Or psyche in the Netherworld, Deryl's mind whispered. He tried to hide his disappointment and his frustration.

It had been over two months, and he still continued to experience blackouts and holes in his memory. Still, he had encounters with Tasmae, where he'd meet her, love her, lose her, often by her being killed in some kind of battle that he'd refused to take part in. Still, he felt the Master's whisperings, trying to lure him back to his training.

Now, he was having odd visions of two planets crashing, of the inhabitants falling into a trance, of power surging through him as he reached out, becoming large as a solar system. Through it all, that voice in his head, usually accompanied by pain, insisted none of this was real.

Yet somehow, he managed to get everything done he needed to, whether he remembered doing it or not, and no one had noticed anything unusual in his behavior. Except, it seemed, Clarissa. He'd hoped his friend, who had guided him through so much in the past, would be able to advise him now.

"You know, you were more help at SK-Mental," he groused.

Joshua snorted. "Dr. Acker helped you. You wouldn't be here, alive, sane, married, and about to be a father, if it weren't for him. All I did was give you a Band-Aid until he came along. Dr. Malachai was right about that much. Why do you think I chose music?"

"You were a terrific psychologist," he told him earnestly. "You still could be."

But Joshua shook his head. "I'm a musician. Want me to sing you sane?"

He felt a sudden urge to tell him yes. He rubbed at the base of his skull. "That's not funny. You left because of me."

Joshua snorted. "Don't flatter yourself, dude. Psychology was always my backup plan. But if you need a second opinion, I can ask my dad."

Deryl turned back to the ride. It had started to slow down. "No, I'm handling it. I am taking my medication. It just doesn't work as well as we'd hoped. But I'm not ready to have someone cut out half my brain."

"It's not half; it's just a small area that's causing you problems. And you were fine for the first three years after it was essentially disconnected. It's natural to be afraid—I'd be—but you've got to think about the consequences. Do you love Clarissa?"

Deryl closed his eyes and nodded. The only time he felt whole was with her. Reality didn't matter. She did.

"Then think about what's best for her—and the baby, *capice*? Say, did you take care of that phone caller?"

About a month ago, someone had started calling their house. When Clarissa answered, he made obscene suggestions, and she'd hung up furious and upset.

Then one evening Deryl answered, and the caller warned that he'd better protect her because he was coming. He'd felt cold terror wash over him because the voice sounded like the Master's.

He'd mentioned to call to Joshua, but not the voice, even though he craved reassurance. If it really was the

Master's voice, then this wasn't real, was it? Or was his twisted mind making an already sinister call even more insidious?

The ride had ended and everyone was exiting. He didn't have time to get into this now.

"They couldn't trace the call, so there wasn't much the police could do. We changed the number, and I walk her to and from the gym. Don't tell Clarissa he called me—she's worried enough as it is, and I don't want her risking the baby."

"Clarissa isn't like your aunt, Deryl. She's strong and healthy. She'll be all right."

"I'm not taking any chances." In fact, he hadn't wanted to come to the carnival at all, and Clarissa had finally called her doctor to have her reassure him that it was all right for her to ride some rides. Now, as she and Sachiko hurried over to them, he couldn't help but give her an anxious smile.

"Have fun?" he asked, though he really wanted to ask if she was okay.

She knew him too well. "Yes, and I'm fine! You're such a big worrywart. Besides, I had an OB right next to me the whole time, right Doctor Sach?"

"Absolutely!" Sachiko laughed. "Let's find something we can do together."

"Like the carousel—that's more Deryl's speed!"

"I've got a better idea," Deryl told his wife as he slipped an arm around her waist. "Let's go do the Tunnel of Love."

Chapter Twenty-Eight

As the last chords of Joshua's song faded, Tasmae sat up, took a long breath, and released it. "Thank you. I do feel better."

"You look a lot better," Joshua commented. After her fearful proclamation, Tasmae had fallen back upon the pillows, laboring to breathe and too weak even to sit up. In desperation, Joshua had tried singing to her, choosing a version of Psalm Twenty-Eight he had written some music for.

"That's a pretty versatile talent," Sachiko said.

"Yeah, but it won't do any of us any good if we can't figure out how to get to Deryl."

Sachiko cocked her head. "Can't you call him with your music—like you did me?"

He shook his head. "Didn't work. I might have made things worse." He glanced at Tasmae and bit his lip.

Sachiko rubbed his shoulders, and he leaned back against her, grateful for her strength, even if she was an illusion.

"All right, then," Sachiko said, thinking out loud. "Can I take you to him? Why can't I just talk to the guards, tell them you're in town visiting me and want to say 'hi' to some folks? All your info is still in the computers; you should be able to get a visitor's pass easily enough."

"What about Taz? She doesn't have any ID or records—and if we let anyone know about her, Alugiac will know as well."

"Don't take this wrong, but does she have to come?"

"Yeah, the game was pretty clear about that."

"All right, we sneak in. I'm going to be so fired," she sighed in exaggerated resignation, but when he glanced back at her, he saw the twinkle in her eye.

He couldn't help it; he grinned in return. "Blaze of glory, babe. So how do we do it?"

They turned to Tasmae.

She shook her head. "I don't know the area. The only part of SK-Mental I saw was a pink padded room."

"That's the place."

"—But I only know it from Gardianju. I would most likely send us back into that time, maybe even literally, rather than into Deryl's illusion."

"She's right," Sachiko affirmed. "They renovated a couple of years back. Put in new security equipment, changed the shade of the walls—still pink, but a less imposing shade. They even changed the layout some, added a couple more rooms by shrinking the existing ones. It's not the same. It's up to you, love."

"Great," Joshua pursed his lips and let his fingers play idly over the keytar keys. "SK-Mental have a theme song I don't know about?"

"What about that silly song you sang for Deryl and me?" Tasmae asked.

Joshua grimaced. "'Cure the Guy?' We'd probably end up in Randall's office—and I don't think he'd be happy to see us."

"So change the words," Tasmae responded impatiently. "This is taking too much time. We need to hurry—something's happening to Deryl."

"Don't rush me!" Joshua snapped back. "Remember the last time I sang the first thing off the top of my head? I didn't do my stint in High-intensity yet. I don't know it well enough to parody."

"Pick something else," Sachiko urged. "How about the grounds? Can you imagine them at night?"

He smiled, remembering one evening he'd stayed late and on her 8:00 break, had found her in the grounds, leaning against the glass of the wall, the moon illuminating her face and bringing out the blue in her black hair. He'd gone to stand beside her, also leaning on the glass, and while they talked, had looked out at the manicured grass and the evergreens that lined the wall because if he'd looked at her then, he'd have kissed her.

She caught the intention behind his smile. "Don't make it a romantic song," she warned.

"Right." He searched his mind and played a tune he and Rique had made up but didn't have the words for as his mind thought up some verses.

When Deryl came to himself again, he was standing alone in the elevator in damp swim trunks, a towel around his neck.

What time is it? he wondered. The elevator reached the eighth floor, and the doors opened. He stepped out, saw the darkened window at the end of the hall, and dashed to their apartment. Clarissa was closing that night, and he had to pick her up!

When he ran into the apartment, he saw the message light blinking and pushed it as he hurried into dry clothes.

"Hi, honey! I hope this means you're on your way! I was going to ask you to call us a taxi—I'm bushed—but I guess I'll wait until you're here. And don't worry! Jacob is staying with me, so I'll be fine. See you soon!"

Despite her reassuring message, he couldn't help feeling something was terribly wrong. He raced down the stairs and hailed a cab by jumping in front of it.

"What are you, crazy?" the Korean driver shouted at him as he threw himself in. Despite his heavy accent, he had plenty of rude American words for the idiot paying his fare. Still, he shut up once Deryl passed him a twenty, and he made a left at the next intersection, heading toward the gym.

"Go faster," Deryl urged tensely.

"I get ticket, I get deported. You want go faster? Get out and run."

Nonetheless, they arrived quickly, and Deryl dashed out, handing the man another ten and telling him to wait. He pulled at the door, but it was locked. He looked in and saw Jacob sprawled in one corner. Deryl didn't need psychic powers to know he was dead. He pounded on the door. "Clarissa!"

He was answered with a scream.

"Call the police!" Deryl shouted to the taxi driver, then shoved at the door. When it refused to budge, he gave it a psychic push and the lock sheared off. Ignoring it, he ran inside.

He heard a second scream, followed it, and found Clarissa, pinned down by large barbells while a man tore at her sweats. She struggled and screamed, and he punched her, first in the face, then in the belly. He laughed at her whimpers.

"Get away from her!" Deryl focused his power.

The man was thrown across the room and crashed into a rack of free weights. It toppled onto him.

IS THAT THE BEST YOU CAN DO?

For a moment, Deryl froze. He stared with horror as the man, the Master, rose out of the rubble. Bruises swelled and blackened his face and he spit out some teeth, but laughter bubbled out of his bloody lips.

"I told you to protect her," he now said with a human voice. "You didn't believe me. You thought I couldn't get to you. Fool."

I TRAINED YOU BETTER THAN THAT.

Deryl shook his head and stepped back. "Stay away from her," he snarled, but he could hear the tight, desperate edge in his voice. The Master laughed and ignored him, moving again to Clarissa.

Again using his telekinesis, he lifted the barbell with its 200 pounds of weight off Clarissa's neck and flung it at the advancing man. It struck him in the face. It had to have shattered his jaw, but the man continued to laugh, to talk, to advance.

"You'll have to do better than that. You'll never end this. I'll keep after you. I'll have her. Only death can stop me." KILL, DERYL. KILL ME TO PROTECT YOUR WIFE. KILL ME TO SAVE YOUR BABY.

Clarissa had managed to scoot herself back against a corner and was cowering. "Deryl?' she whimpered.

"Stay away from her, or I'll kill you!"

"You don't have the guts."

DO NOT THREATEN. ACT.

Deryl rushed him, knocking him back into a wall, pummeling him with fists and feet and mind. Things swirled wildly around them, sometimes hitting him as well as his enemy, but he didn't care. It was only when he heard Clarissa's screams and the police shouts to freeze did he pull away. They grabbed and handcuffed him despite Clarissa's weak protests that he was her husband and protecting her, but he hardly noticed as he focused on was the villain before him.

Despite his beating, Clarissa's attacker grinned, even laughed weakly as the police checked him and called for an ambulance. His eyes bore on Deryl, at once triumphant and accusatory, and Deryl knew exactly what he was thinking.

YOU DIDN'T FINISH, DERYL. YOU DIDN'T FOLLOW THROUGH.

"That's amazing," Sachiko said as she looked around. They'd arrived in the empty courtyard, which was dark except for a few motion-sensitive security lights that switched on in response to their arrival. "And the song was pretty good, too."

"Thanks," Joshua said as he slung the keytar on his back. He tapped Tasmae, who had scanned the area as if for potential attackers and was now staring aghast at the dark sky with its paltry scattering of stars. She nodded that she was all right. "What time is it, do you think?" he asked Sachiko.

"After nine. That's when we try to clear everyone out." She tried the door, but it wouldn't open. "That's funny. It's not supposed to be locked." She reached in her pockets for her keys, found them empty, and shrugged at Joshua. "What now?"

Tasmae tore her gaze from the sky and strode to the glass, unsheathing her sword.

"No!" Joshua grabbed her arm. "You'll set off the security system. They'll know we're here."

"Besides, that's impact resistant glass," Sachiko added. "You won't be able to break it."

"Anyway, I've got an idea. Close your eyes." Joshua took hold of their hands, then stepped forward slowly, pulling them with him as he sang, "We'll play cloak and dagger / Standing strong and tall / We'll walk without a cut / Through this plate-glass wall."

And they were inside.

Sachiko turned and looked at the tall picture window behind them. "You're good."

"That one was easy. I love the imagery in that song." He basked in her admiring gaze.

"It's one of my favorites."

"Mine, too." He could lose himself in her smile.

"If we could get our minds back to the mission?" Tasmae urged, her exasperated tone almost a perfect imitation of Deryl's.

He cleared his throat and stepped back, breaking the spell. "What now?"

Tasmae answered. "We stay together and move quickly. Sachiko, you'll go first into any intersections or around corners. Greet anyone you meet loudly enough for us to hear. Joshua, keep your instrument ready. We hide until they pass if we can; otherwise, we run toward Deryl if possible, you alter the situation with song, or we fight, in that order. Let's go."

They moved quickly down the corridor, taking the turns as Tasmae instructed. They met no one. Tasmae murmured nervously that it was what she would have done if she'd wanted to lead them into a trap, but Sachiko and Joshua both assured her it was normal for the time of night.

"We can't avoid meeting someone when we get to the high-intensity ward, though," Sachiko said as they paused in an unused office to consider their next step. "We've got about half an hour before shift change, so it may only be Danny—Kim usually makes the last check of the shift around now. If we wait too long, though, the next shift will arrive, and there'll be the usual half-hour of shift change briefing and shooting the breeze. I know Kim—he's a talker. So, got an invisibility song?"

"If I did, I'd have used it already. Besides, I'm not sure that would work. Would I get our clothes, too? What if it didn't apply to our stuff?" He and Sachiko grinned at each other at the thought of a disembodied keytar floating around the complex.

"Josh Lawson's ghost is haunting Max Security," Sachiko sang, and they giggled.

Tasmae gave them both a deadly look.

"Sorry. Stress."

"Shall we do this the old fashioned way? One of us distracts Danny while the other bonks him on the head?" Sachiko suggested.

Tasmae nodded, but Joshua blanched at his fiancée's casual suggestion.

She shrugged. "This place isn't real, remember? Besides, he's a big braggart. Thinks he's so hot because he 'earned' a black belt in two years. I keep offering to teach him some sparring moves—mostly, so I can show him up—but he thinks I'm flirting and cute." She sneered with distaste. "Might do him some good to find out a belt doesn't mean a thing in a real fight unless you've got the moves to back it up."

"There will be no fight," Tasmae said. "I will get behind him and incapacitate him with one blow. Joshua, stay out of the way and keep an eye on the corridor."

"I'm hanging out with a couple of Amazons," Joshua muttered, but agreed.

They got to the nurses' station without incident and paused at the junction just before it. Sachiko peeked around the corner.

"Just Danny," she said to the others. She looked over her outfit, shrugged, and undid a button on her top. "Hope this was supposed to be my day off. No getting jealous," she said as she readjusted her bra and pulled off her engagement ring. "This is just distracterfactor. Can you sing me a drink?"

Puzzled, Joshua sang "Margaritaville," until a large, umbrella'd drink appeared in Sachiko's hand. She drank it down in long steady gulps, spilling a few drops on her chest for good measure.

Joshua gaped.

"Are you this conniving in real life?" he asked.

She smiled, flipped her hair, and sauntered over to the station, letting her hips sway with enough exaggeration to suggest she'd been drinking more than she'd just had. Danny looked up when she greeted him with a warm yet kind of sad, "Hey there."

Soon she had him absorbed in conversation about how her no-good, immature excuse for a fiancé had gotten cold feet once he got back to Colorado, and how what she needed was a good fight and maybe a little fun. Tasmae waited until Danny was completely focused on her and silently sidled around behind him.

Joshua hovered by the corridor entrance, marveling at Sachiko's acting ability. What else didn't he know about her yet?

"What is going on here?" a stern, familiar voice said from behind him. Joshua whirled to face Dr. Malachai. "Mr. Lawson, what are you doing back?" he demanded. He looked past the still-gaping intern. "Who is that?"

Danny had looked up at the sound of the chief psychiatrist's voice—he had everyone well-trained that way—and noticed Tasmae sneaking up behind him. He spun with an exaggerated "HEE-Yah!" and sent a flying round kick in her direction. She swung her arm, but instead of blocking, caught his leg on the outside and used his own momentum to make him turn his back to her. A chop to the base of the skull and he was down.

By then, however, Malachai had Joshua in an iron-firm grip and several orderlies and a couple of guards were pounding up the hallway behind him. "Don't you think you've caused enough bad press for this institution?" he scolded.

"Matter of fact, no!" He couldn't play with Malachai holding one arm, but he sang, "Wanna make your living off the evening news / Well I got something, something you can use / I want Malachai to lose / Come get his dirty laundry!"

"What are you doing?" Malachai asked calmly, but his grip tightened.

"Could have been a singer but in the end / Gotta use my singing to rescue my friend / So come and shout out in his ear / He's got the dirty laundry!"

Suddenly, twenty reporters, photographers, and cameramen surrounded them. They thrust their mikes into Dr. Malachai's face, calling out questions, and he was forced to let go of Joshua.

He backed away, smiling as he watched the chief psychiatrist struggle to figure out what was happening even as he put on a professional face and replied calmly to their accusations.

"What about the allegations of Deryl Stephens' family that your inept handling of him has rendered him incurably insane?"

"Is it true that you have a real psychic here?"

"Are you holding a teen hostage?"

Must have gotten the grocery store gossip rag reporters. Sachiko and Tasmae had opened the door and were gesturing for him to hurry when a reporter asked Malachai, "And what about the rumors concerning you and Sachiko Luchese?"

What about Sachiko? Joshua paused, wanting to hear more, but Sachiko pulled him away. "Let me handle this. You have to save Deryl, remember? He's seventh to the left."

"What about you and Randall?" Without thinking, he used the chief psychiatrist's first name. Somehow he had the feeling the rumors were personal in nature.

"Go! Rescue Deryl!" She shoved him toward Tasmae, and he ran. He glanced back to see her button her shirt, replace her ring, and turn to the reporters.

Then the scene dissolved until only gray fog was at the end of the hall.

"'Ko?"

"Joshua! Here!" Tasmae shouted.

He turned and ran to Tasmae, the fog swelling up slowly behind him. He stopped next to her at Deryl's door. "Are you doing that?" he demanded, jerking a thumb behind him.

"We must be entering Deryl's reality. He's in here. I can feel it. How do we open the door?"

"Remotely, or with a key—both of which..." His voice trailed off and he indicated the now vanished nurses' station.

The fog moved inexorably closer.

Tasmae shut her eyes in concentration. She shook her head. "I can't reach him. I can't get through to him. His world, his perceptions, are behind this door. I can feel that much. We have to get through that door."

"No kidding." Somehow, he knew that if they were here when the fog reached them, they'd vanish with everything else. His heart pounded. He couldn't tear his eyes off the haze.

"Joshua!" Tasmae snapped, but he couldn't think of anything. His brain moved too fast to concentrate.

She slammed her fist against the keytar, and a heavy rap beat began to play. "Sing!"

"Okay! Um... Right! All right, world, you hearken to me / 'Cause I've got the words to change reality / Hold back the fog an' it be bogging 'cause the verses ain't a slogging / Don't see why we should need no key / You open up with Aladin's sesame!" He stopped, breathing heavily, praying.

The fog boiled upward, but no longer advanced.

The door opened with a quiet snick.

Despite himself, Joshua grinned and crossed his arms over his chest, rapper style. "Word."

Tasmae gave him a confused look, then pulled the door open.

They rushed in.

Madness Unbound ⊕

Chapter Twenty-Nine

"I don't understand!" Clarissa spat at the policeman who stood in their apartment, his hands nervously playing with his walkie-talkie. "He could barely move! How could he have escaped?"

The policeman grimaced, and Deryl fought to keep his own mouth from mimicking the gesture. He could feel everything the officer felt: embarrassment for his force, anger and a little fear that a man who had been beaten so thoroughly was still able to get up and walk out of a hospital, and sadness at having to bring such terrible news to a woman who had to be at least seven months along. "Ma'am. It happens. Not often, but—"

"I don't care!"

He winced a little at her vehemence, and Deryl felt a new emotion from him—annoyance that the poor lady's husband didn't do something besides stare at the floor. Deryl forced himself to put an arm around Clarissa and pull her against his shoulder, kissing her head softly. Her emotions seared into him, but at least the officer was satisfied.

He squatted down in front of them. "We'll increase the patrols around your house and work."

"For how long?" she sniffled hopelessly. "All you're going to do is make him wait."

"If we keep him waiting long enough, he'll make a mistake," Deryl spoke the officer's thought for him, though he knew it wouldn't happen. He looked at the policeman, tried to smile. He felt desperate to have him leave. He gave Clarissa a quick squeeze, then rose to open the door. "Thank you, officer. Anything you can do, we appreciate."

The officer set a card on the entryway table and left. No sooner had the door shut than Clarissa burst into full sobs. "It's not fair!"

"I know," he said dully as he sat beside her. The police had arrested him along with Clarissa's attacker. He was released on bail only on the condition that he see a psychiatrist. After everything he'd done that night, there was no hiding anything from Clarissa—or Dr. Acker. The lobectomy was scheduled for next week.

You can't let them do it, that part of his mind screamed again, drowning out Clarissa's muffled words as she sobbed into a Kleenex. *If you do this, there'll be no escaping. He'll have a hold on you forever. You have to remember what's real. You have to think!*

He sat beside Clarissa but couldn't touch her. When he touched her, there was only her, and the baby, and keeping them both happy and safe. When she was away, there were too many holes, too many doubts. He'd looked at his medicine yesterday, and it had seemed evil somehow. He'd flushed it down the toilet and done the same today.

Now he wasn't sure that had been such a good idea. The headaches had returned, increasing and fading, it seemed, with how involved he was with the world around him. Just like when he was a kid, the thoughts and emotions and even attitudes of others pressed themselves on him. He could feel the Master working on him, but in a new way, playing upon recent events so that he found himself regarding everyone as a potential threat until he was afraid to leave the apartment. Only his greater desperation to be alone enabled him to let Clarissa go to work that morning. He'd stood on the balcony that afternoon and looked longingly at the pool below, but couldn't overcome his fear even to go downstairs for a swim.

He'd felt Tasmae's pull, too, almost as if she were calling from behind his locked door. He couldn't let her in. Whether she was real or not, somehow he knew it was dangerous to bring her to him.

He'd had visions, too, all playing on a theme: things—balls, cars, worlds—colliding, him stopping them with a thought; people falling before him like autumn leaves as he grew in strength and power. He didn't know what they meant, but they *felt* so important! In the end, he'd reclined on the couch, a book in his hands as his cover story, and given himself to the visions until Clarissa came home, griping about being stuck working the office and telling him she craved Chinese. She had pulled him out of the visions and back to himself.

He looked at her now, his heart breaking to see her so distraught. He loved her. Or was it an illusion? He couldn't think when she was near. And now this.

You have to get her away, something in him urged, and he wondered if it was for her safety or his sanity.

"I want you to go to Sachiko's and Josh's for a while," he found himself saying.

"And leave you alone to have major brain surgery? I don't think so!"

"Listen to me!" He spoke urgently, but didn't touch her. He couldn't, not now. "I need you to go. I need to know...that you're safe."

He wanted to say, "what's real." He was torn between the desire to comfort her and the need to push her away.

"You hit him with a hundred pound weight and he *laughed* at you!" she croaked. "He *walked* out of the Intensive Care Unit! He said he'd never stop. He killed Jacob. He wants to kill me—and our baby! What makes you think going to Colorado will stop him?"

She paced the room. He wanted to make her stop, to reassure her, to remind her what her doctor had said about stress and the baby. He couldn't make himself do anything. He sank onto the couch.

She got to the Closet of Doom and spun to face him. "Why didn't you finish him off?"

"What?"

"You could have done it. You wouldn't even have had to hit him. You could have stopped his heart, and no one would have known!" She looked at him with red-rimmed eyes, her hair wild, her cheeks stained with tears, her lips curled into a snarl of anguish, and she suddenly seemed horrific and surreal. His mind felt scalded, his nerves shattered, and his dinner ready to come back up.

"You know what? I hope he comes back. Soon! This week, and I want you to kill him. Kill him so we can put this whole damn thing behind us and have our baby and be happy." She dissolved into tears.

"You don't mean that," he whispered.

"Yes! Yes, I do! Kill him for me, Deryl. Please!"

A stabbing pain through the back of his skull made him buckle over, gasping.

She looked up from her tissue. "Deryl? Deryl what is it?"

Something alive in his brain tried to claw itself out. For a moment, he felt his mind ripping; then everything resolved itself in a blinding flash. He still felt the pressure, but he had shields again, and he pushed it back. He looked up at Clarissa, saw the concern in her eyes, and felt nothing but a low-key horror. "This isn't real," he said, not realizing he spoke aloud. "How long have I been stuck here?"

"Oh, God! Deryl, no! Don't do this to me! Deryl, did you take your pills? Deryl!" She clutched his arm. For a moment, he felt a stab of tenderness. He swayed, but then stood, pulling himself out of her grasp.

"It won't work this time, Alugiac!" He looked around the apartment and laughed in amazement. Did he really have this vivid an imagination?

Disbelieve it all, his mind warned. *None of it is real!*

He picked a direction at random and started walking. He passed right through the coffee table.

Clarissa jumped in front of him, clung to his chest. "Come on, honey, please. I'm sorry. I was upset and the hormones and— Please, let's just both calm down, and you take your medication—"

He didn't even glance at Clarissa as he walked right through her, but couldn't help looking back when he heard her yelp. She was on the floor, as if pushed. She looked at him with shock and fear.

For a moment, his steps faltered.

She trembled, but stood slowly. "I'm going to call Dr. Acker."

Dr. Alouicious Grant Acker. Al Lou G. Acker. Alugiac. Again he laughed. How could he have been so blind? He turned from her and headed to the balcony.

Don't believe anything. Don't believe—

But again her scream brought him back to her reality and he found himself teetering on the balcony's ledge, eight stories from the ground. He looked down. The swimming pool seemed small and far away.

"Deryl, please, please come back in and let's talk about this! Deryl! Don't do this to me! I can't lose you!"

Yes, you can. Because you're not real. Without thinking about what he was doing, he stepped off.

She screamed.

He fell, and kept falling until his body smacked painfully against a surface.

And still he fell, deep into a nightmare. Gardianju's nightmare. Demon-specters flailed at him, pulling him down, ripping him apart. A sword appeared in his hand, and he knew one swing would destroy them. He forced his hand to open and the sword fell from his grip. *It's not real. It's not real!*

He fell out of nightmare and into a pink room. This time, when he hit the floor, he didn't continue through, but lay there, groaning and disoriented. When he at last had enough wits to look around, he found himself in the high-intensity ward at SK-Mental, his arms bound in a straitjacket.

Tasmae and Joshua were staring at him in open-mouthed shock.

Tasmae gave a cry of joy and relief as she stepped toward Deryl, but that step faltered when he didn't reply. He'd sat himself up and had scooted away until his back pressed against the wall, but otherwise showed no sign of being aware of his surroundings.

"Deryl?" Joshua approached him slowly. "Deryl, bud? We need to get out of here."

Deryl spoke in a dead voice. "Nice try, Alugiac. I'm not buying it, not any more. I'm tired of being your puppet."

"Deryl, what are you talking about?" Tasmae knelt in front of him. He glanced at her just long enough to dismiss her.

The Sphinx had warned them about this. Still in the background, Joshua brought his keytar around and softly started playing. "You can talk to me / Come, talk to me." He played the song through, changing the lyrics as necessary, pouring sincerity and love into each verse. He finished the song and was segueing back into the chorus when Deryl looked him in the eye.

"Singing me sane, Joshua? Fine. You want me to believe you're real? Prove it."

"All right," Joshua said softly, reasonably. "Remember how you told me I had to be real because you'd never have imagined me with five o'clock shadow? Ever seen a keytar before?" He was betting that five years in the institution and even longer without watching television, the answer would be no.

He watched doubt soften Deryl's features, then disappear. "Not good enough."

"Deryl," Tasmae said, and his eyes flicked his way. "Could Alugiac have really faked me? Could he have faked this?"

She gazed lovingly at Deryl, and Joshua saw his pupils pinpoint just before Deryl closed his eyes. Tasmae touched Deryl on the cheek, and he pressed against her palm, trembling. But when she leaned toward him, he jerked his head away with a sob.

Joshua swore. "What did he do to you?"

Deryl didn't answer, but neither could he look at Tasmae. He tried to hug himself tighter beneath the straight jacket.

Tasmae stood. "When we find Alugiac, I will kill him."

"Shut up, Taz," Joshua hissed. "The last thing we need is to go spoiling for a fight. We do *not* want to bring that maniac to us."

He knelt down beside his confused and grieving friend. "Deryl, listen to me. Tasmae and I came to help you, but once we came through that door, we entered this world. Your world. Now we're trapped, too, and no one can get us out of here except you. You've got to believe in us, Deryl, and disbelieve this world."

Deryl wouldn't look at him. Instead, he dropped his head, and rocked. "You'll die. You'll die, you'll die..." Tears trickled down his cheeks.

Joshua watched as Deryl slipped away from them. Tasmae again sat at an angle to him, her face a mirror of his misery. Her body started to rock slightly in time to his, and Joshua knew with horror that he could lose them both and end up trapped here forever. He sat down cross-legged, his keytar on his lap, and let his hands play randomly over the keys while he prayed.

Dear Father in Heaven, I could really use your help right now. St. Jude, patron of lost causes, show me the way through this. St. Cecilia, patron saint of music, inspire me. Help me get us home!

Suspended in time, the trio sat there, each caught in their own thoughts. Even Joshua began to rock slightly.

His fingers moved over the keys, filling the room with snatches of song—oldies, top 40, a chorus or two of Chipotle's, and hymns. Finally, his hands settled on one hymn in particular and he began to sing: "Brother let me be your servant / Let me show the Truth to you / Pray that I may have the grace / To let you be my servant, too."

As he moved through the second verse, he felt Tasmae's hand on his shoulder and she joined him in the third verse. He let her take the fourth on her own: "I will weep when you are weeping / When you laugh, I'll laugh with you / Let us share both hope and danger / 'Till we've seen this journey through."

Deryl turned and met their gazes. "You'll die," he said in a small voice. "That's how it works here. He'll make it so I have to kill something—someone—or you die. And I can't kill. If I do—" His voice cracked on the last word.

"What?" Joshua prodded as he continued to play.

Deryl's face scrunched with misery, but he shook his head. When he spoke, his voice was tight and small. "I don't know."

Tasmae answered, her voice hushed with understanding. "Something dies in the waking world. Something of Alugiac's choosing."

"Someone. Get out of my mind, please Tasmae. I don't want you to die!"

"No one's dying." The music ended in an abrupt musical squawk as Joshua smashed his fist on the keyboard. "And no one's killing. We're changing the rules. Look, I'll make you a deal. Alugiac's using information from your own mind to make you believe in this world, right? Trust in us for now, and I'll come up with something so, so stupidly ridiculous that there's no *way* you could have thought it up, okay?"

"Joshua!" Tasmae pointed at the far wall.

The pink padded wall of the containment room had turned into a wall of molten rock. It inched towards them.

Joshua didn't even waste time swearing. "All right, Deryl, this is it!"

Deryl gaped at the advancing lava and struggled to stand. "Help me get this straitjacket off!"

Joshua was already pushing at the door. "It's not real, you idiot!"

"Oh! Right!" The jacket disappeared. Deryl gave a short laugh of surprise.

"Joshua, sing something!" Tasmae shouted. She, too, shoved her weight against the door. Deryl stood, but otherwise did nothing.

The room was starting to swelter from the heat. The lava roared.

Joshua shouted at his friend, "Deryl, disbelieve us out of here!"

"I don't know how!"

"Then disbelieve the frickin' door!"

"All right!"

Suddenly, there was empty space where the door had been. Joshua and Tasmae spilled out, landing in a tangled heap on the floor, Deryl tripping over them as he rushed out of the room. Joshua shoved himself up. His heart skipped a beat and he reached behind him for the keytar. He gasped more than sighed with relief to find it intact. "Good. Good start."

"We're still in the asylum," Tasmae accused as Deryl pulled her to her feet.

"I'm trying!" Deryl cried, but when he saw the orderlies at the end of the hall, he nonetheless took off in the other direction.

"Deryl! They aren't real!" Joshua shouted at his retreating back.

"They are as long as he believes they are!" Tasmae replied as she ran after him.

Joshua groaned and followed.

Soon, they were running down hallways that had nothing to do with reality and more resembled a climax scene from the *Twilight Zone*. In one hall, a teenage boy was being worked on by paramedics while his friends blabbered, "He just looked at him! He looked at him, and he fell over!" Out of one doorway, Isaac, Deryl's elderly Jewish friend, stood in concentration camp uniform, while across the hall, another elderly gentleman shouted that Deryl was Satan's child and should have been destroyed in the womb. With each encounter, Deryl shouted a negation, yet continued running. Tasmae and Joshua ran with him.

Joshua slowed, however, when they passed Randall Malachai with his arms around Sachiko. The chief psychiatrist was kissing her neck, and she hummed as if enjoying it.

"What the..?"

She opened her eyes, saw Joshua and mouthed, "Run!"

He saw a scalpel in Malachai's hand.

She's not real! he told himself as he took off again, but that didn't stop his stomach from churning.

When he rounded the corner into a common room and skidded to a halt, even that was forgotten as he looked at the monster that blocked their path.

The horrifyingly malformed body sported too many eyes and teeth too large. Gore dripped off its huge, twisted body. It roared incoherently and made odd bog-like squelching sounds as it moved. It was hideous.

It was like some kind of monster from a B-rated horror movie—one with cheap special effects.

"You've got to be kidding!" Joshua yelled over the noise.

Yet Deryl and Tasmae stood frozen before it. It advanced, and they stepped back.

Tasmae held Deryl's hand and was quietly instructing him to not believe, yet she had pulled the punch dagger out of her hair. Her sword stuck out of what would be the monster's thigh, if it had had proper legs. Deryl shook and whimpered.

"Oh, please!" Joshua whipped around the keytar, played fifteen notes, a rising chord, and three computerized "PEW!" sounds.

Three streaks of colored light zoomed down the hall and resolved themselves into caricatures of little girls with pod-like hands, and eyes and heads too large for their squarish bodies.

"What's the emergency, Joshua?" the pink one asked.

Despite himself, Joshua smiled. "Think you ladies could handle that for us?" With a casual flip of his hand, he indicated the monster bearing down on his friends.

"Ewww!" the blue one squealed.

"All right!" cheered the green one.

"No problem at all," the pink one said cheerfully, and the girls swooped into action, zipping right between Deryl and Tasmae.

Madness Unbound ✱ 367

Deryl made a strangled gasp of surprise.

Tasmae dropped her dagger.

"Come on," Joshua grabbed them both by the arms and pulled them out of the way. Illusion or not, he knew very well what happened to the things around them when the girls fought evil monsters.

"My dagger," Tasmae protested as he shoved them under a table.

"Forget it! I've got a dozen superhero theme songs. Now look, Deryl. Look hard. Then you tell me you could have thought that up!"

Deryl watched as the streaks of pink, blue, and green zoomed around the monster, kicking, punching, shooting lasers out of their eyes, and bantering the entire time. The tension and fear on his face vanished, and he smiled, bemused.

"Nope. That's pretty unbelievable."

A horrible howl filled the room, rising to such painful volume and intensity that they covered their ears and curled up in agony. The world began to swirl around them as if it had become a tornado.

"Couldn't you disbelieve more quietly?" Joshua shouted as the table they were huddled under was caught in the twister and vanished into oblivion.

"This isn't my doing!"

The world faded and stilled.

Chapter Thirty

Once again, they found themselves in a featureless land of gray fog and dark horizons.

"Deryl!" Joshua groaned with annoyance.

"No. We are in the Netherworld," Tasmae said. "The true Netherworld."

"Well, good, then. How do we get back?"

YOU DON'T.

The mist before them swirled, and from it stepped Alugiac.

Joshua gaped. He was a short but large man, though Joshua guessed his muscle was starting to go to fat. He wore heavily brocaded, priestly robes that dazzled even in the dim flat light of the Netherworld. His hair was graying but full, and he had a goatee. He regarded them all with superior sneer.

He was every cliché of a supervillain Joshua could think of. He even spoke in all caps—his voice echoing and sinister, yet somehow toneless. All he needed was a white Persian cat and a garish pinky ring.

"You can't be for real!"

He turned his sneer directly to Joshua, gestured laconically, and Joshua found out just how real he could be.

Blue-white barbs of electricity flashed from his hands and struck Joshua, throwing him back. He shrieked and arched in uncontrollable pain.

"No!" Deryl lashed out with his mind. A mirrored shield interposed itself between Alugiac and his friend. The lightning ricocheted off it and struck Alugiac, knocking him back. He staggered, then laughed.

Deryl glanced fearfully at Joshua and almost sobbed with relief to see him roll weakly onto his back and shrug off the keytar, which had absorbed the brunt of the attack and was a smoking ruin. Joshua shoved it away and fell back panting.

GOOD. CONTINUE, Alugiac encouraged, but Deryl had already lowered the shield.

"No."

THEN THEY DIE, JUST AS THEY HAVE BEFORE. JUST AS THEY WILL AGAIN. OVER AND OVER. AND YOU WILL NEVER KNOW WHICH TIME WAS THE REAL TIME—OR EVEN WHO IS REAL.

"Deryl! Help me!"

"Clarissa?"

She was there, just to the right of Tasmae: pregnant, terrified, and being held by the attacker that had escaped the police. He pressed a huge hunting knife against her throat. His eyes, so like Alugiac's, gleamed with lust and excitement.

"Deryl, help me!" she squeaked, then shrieked as the knife cut into her cheek.

"Deryl, she's not real!" Tasmae yelled.

Clarissa sobbed louder.

"I know!" Deryl said, but it was almost a whisper. He couldn't tear his eyes off her. "Taz, get Joshua and go!"

"No! We're in this together!"

"Deryl!" Clarissa shrieked.

"Deryl," Tasmae's calm, authoritative voice cut past Clarissa's screams, "let's go. You don't have to—"

Tasmae's words were cut off as the strange tar-like monster, like the ones that had attacked her when Alugiac first appeared, rose from the ground at her feet and enveloped itself around her. She struggled as it immobilized her: legs, arms, shoulders. The featureless mouth surged tauntingly toward her face.

DECIDE, DERYL. CHOOSE THE ONE TO DIE, AND I WILL LET THE OTHERS LIVE. OR GIVE IN TO ME, AND YOU CAN HAVE ALL.

Clarissa had moved so beyond fear she couldn't even scream. Tasmae struggled valiantly, but it was obvious the creature played with her, waiting Alugiac's command. Joshua stirred and groaned faintly, too overcome by the effects of the lightning to help.

CHOOSE.

"No."

Deryl, Tasmae teleped. *You can get us out of here! Just go!*

YES, DERYL. JUST GO. ABANDON YOUR WIFE AND CHILD. RETURN TO "REALITY" WITH YOUR ALIEN LOVER. AND KNOW THAT I WILL FOLLOW. IN YOUR DREAMS AT NIGHT, YOUR IDLE MOMENTS OF THE DAY, WHENEVER YOUR GUARD IS DOWN, I WILL BE THERE. *THAT* IS YOUR REALITY.

"No!" Deryl shouted and a blue haze started to surround him. "I. Will. Not. Be. Your. Puppet!" With each defiant word, shields grew in size and brilliance around him until they blazed with blue light. They crackled and hummed with pent-up power. With the last word, he flung his hands toward Alugiac, and the shield bulged, expanded, and surrounded them both.

Madness Unbound ❖ 371

Clarissa and her attacker vanished.

The monster released Tasmae and dissolved into the mist. Through the blue field Deryl watched her stagger, look his way, and then rush to check on Joshua, helping him sit up. They were real. Now he knew; they were real, and he would never let them be threatened again.

Deryl trembled with fury and power. "You want reality?" he snarled. "Now, *I'm* your reality. I trusted you while you twisted my mind, played with my feelings, tried to forge me into some kind of weapon! You want a weapon? I'll give you a weapon!" The humming of the shields grew louder and higher.

Alugiac, snarling in return, flung an attack at Deryl, but it never materialized. The shields around him reached out and absorbed the power, and it was his turn to scream and thrash as lightning danced around him, pulling energy from him instead of zapping him with it.

"Deryl!" Joshua croaked. "You don't have to kill him. That's not the answer."

"What alternative is there?" Deryl cried, but already, the shields had receded, leaving Alugiac weakened and on his knees, but alive. He grinned smugly at Deryl. Deryl froze. He had to end this, but—

Deryl, beloved, Joshua is right. He is not innocent, but he has been as ravaged as you, Tasmae teleped, sharing with him images of the Alugiac she knew before the battle that had driven him insane. She was crying, and Deryl wept with her.

"Kyrie eleison," Joshua chanted under his breath. Deryl realized that, hurt beyond the ability to think, His friend had reverted to one of the first sung prayers he'd learned: *God have mercy.*

Mercy.

Deryl knew what to do.

"I'm not going to kill you," Deryl whispered, suddenly calmer and surer. He closed his eyes, concentrating. He held his arms out defensively before him.

Triumphant, Alugiac stood again, not noticing the lightning around him taking on a new form: syringes.

"I'm giving you a taste of your own medicine!"

Like darts, the hypodermic needles pierced into him, and the Master shouted in pain and collapsed.

Deryl strode up to him and knelt beside the now-shivering man. "It'll be okay. It's an anti-psychotic cocktail, Alugiac. Some stuff they tried to give me to keep the voices at bay. Your own Realitin, only this stuff will help you see things clearly. Even some Prozac to help you cope. Maybe, maybe you can find your way back to who you really are."

His lips trembled, and he left Alugiac, now just an old and frail heap that lay unblinking in the fog. He walked out of the shields, leaving them protectively around the man. By the time he got to Tasmae and Joshua, he was quaking so hard he could barely walk. He sank down and let himself be enveloped by their arms as he took in their love.

"I want to go home," he sobbed.

"I can do that now," Tasmae whispered as she stroked his hair.

He leaned against her, relaxing into her love as she Called them to the real world.

Chapter Thirty-One

Tasmae awakened back in her own body.

She had just enough time to notice that she'd been moved to a brighter and more cheerful tent than the one Deryl was in, when an overwrought Leinad swooped her into his arms and held her tightly. His concern washed over her.

She was touched—but also very dizzy. Now outside the Netherworld and the influence of Joshua's music, that empty half-complete feeling threatened to consume her, and she teleped a single thought to Leinad: *Deryl?*

When she felt his mood darken, she leaned her forehead against his shoulder and pleaded for his understanding. After a moment, however, she realized his anger was not directed any longer at her human lover, but at himself and at the events that had transpired. While she had been unconscious and in the Netherworld, Terry and the Bondfriend healer had explained to him about the lifebond developing between her and Deryl. For better or worse, what they had started must be finished, and he had been wrong—dangerously wrong—to have interfered.

What you have started, you must complete, he told her, yet she felt his trepidation.

You think this is my will, Leinad, but it is not. It is God's. For whatever reason, the Ydrel was brought to us. To me.

He understood that now, she knew, but the reasons themselves frightened him. He knew the warnings of the Remembrance. He saw some of the most fearful coming true in the Ydrel's arrival. In her.

We face them together, she replied with authority. *I will need your help. The Ydrel has many talents, in the manner of humans, but he needs training. As do I. The Remembrance of Gardianju has opened my awareness to many riddles. The answers may lie in other Remembrances.*

Of course I will help—you and the Ydrel, he affirmed, and she felt his pride. He had first known her as a scared child; now, she was growing into the leader she was meant to be.

A sudden wave of weakness threw off her train of thought, and longing overcame her. Grown or not, leader or not, she was only half-complete without her soul-mate.

Deryl.

Leinad eased her onto the pillows, and she was too weak to resist. Now, he answered her earlier question more fully: an image of Deryl, well enough but asleep, still recovering from the trauma of their interrupted bonding and the terrors of the Netherworld attacks. Joshua, too, slept, though he had regained consciousness long enough to mutter something about light sockets and Jedi before retreating into a more normal sleep. Terry had healed him and reported something had disrupted even the very smallest bits of his body. He had also picked up some of what had happened.

In turn, Leinad's teleped his own one-word question: *Alugiac?*

We are safe for now. She didn't tell him more; the Remembrance Keeper knew Alugiac only by reputation. But a part of her dared to hope, and she wished for Salgoud, who had been one of Alugiac's good friends before the change, to share her hopes. The healers, however, had set up a quarantine shield that prevented her from reaching anyone.

Terry believes what has happened to you is similar to experiencing a Remembrance, Leinad said. She agreed. She assented to his gentle command that she sleep and heal, and give Deryl time to do the same.

She had almost nodded off when a thought struck her. Why was he here in the Bondfriend encampment, keeping vigil over her?

You are the Miscria—and as a daughter to me, came his tender response.

It helped ease the ache in her heart.

Deryl woke up to find Joshua keeping watch over him, with Terry watching over them both. At first neither had noticed him stir, and he lay quietly for a moment listening to Joshua play—or try to play—a kind of flute while Terry embroidered what looked like a vest. Then an intense longing swept over him and he murmured weakly, "Tasmae?"

"Hey, the one-track mind awakes!" Joshua set the instrument aside and smiled at his friend. "Taz is fine, sleeping as much as she can, and just as anxious to see you as you are to see her. However, neither of you is going *anywhere*—in this world or any other dimension—until you're both stronger. Don't even try teleping with her; the healers have some kind of psychic shield isolating you both, particularly from each other. How are you feeling?"

"Like someone put my brains in a blender. Better, though."

Joshua snorted through his nose. "That's better, huh? The bizarre thing is that I know what you mean. In fact, I now know exactly what Luke Skywalker felt when he went against Darth Sidious—and believe me, that was knowledge I could easily have done without."

Deryl didn't bother asking. It must have been a movie reference. "It's over?"

"It's over," Joshua assured. "And before you ask, yes, this is real."

Something about the way Joshua answered seemed familiar. "I've asked this before?"

"About three times. You've been fading in and out most of the day."

Terry set his work aside and moved closer to Deryl. He placed his hands over him and Deryl felt a tingle of energy as the healer psychically examined him. Deryl couldn't help but smile.

Terry smiled back. "You are much healed, and it would do you some good to stay awake for a while. Do you think you can sit up and eat a little?"

Deryl's stomach answered for him.

They helped him into a sitting position, and someone brought a tray of light things to eat. For the next couple of hours, Joshua told him about Tasmae's Amazing Maze and the Bondfriend camp. They didn't discuss Alugiac or what had happened in the Netherworld, either before or after Joshua's arrival, for which Deryl was grateful.

He gladly agreed when Terry told him that he was not well enough to see Tasmae that night or maybe even the next day. Too much had happened, especially in his illusions concerning Clarissa, that he didn't understand yet, and he wasn't sure he could face Joshua's questions—or Tasmae's mind.

Later that night, though, when the camp was asleep, but they were awake and watching the stars through the hole in the top of their tent, Joshua broached the subject. "Deryl? You know all that stuff in the Netherworld? Can I ask you something about Sachiko?"

Deryl's thoughts had been both a thousand miles away and focused on Tasmae's tent, which might as well have been a thousand miles away, and it took him a minute to register the question. "Uh, sure, I guess."

He wanted to add that he might not answer, but held his tongue. That would have started a line of questions in itself.

"Sachiko drink a lot?"

Deryl looked at his friend, surprised. He'd though he was going to ask about her and Malachai. Deryl and Tasmae had run past them, locked in an embrace; Joshua had to have seen them, too. Despite himself, he reached out to Joshua's mind and found that the love-struck human had come up with his own answer. Malachai had hinted to him that he also had an interest in the beautiful nurse, and Joshua had decided the whole thing was a ploy to play upon his own insecurities to slow him down and maybe separate him from Deryl and Tasmae as they'd made their escape. It had almost worked out that way, anyway.

"What brought that up?" Deryl asked before Joshua took his silence for affirmation.

"Before we could get to you, we had to distract the swing shift nurse. 'Ko played jilted lover—and drank an entire margarita to get into character. Swallowed the whole thing like it was water. And back home, at our engagement party, she got a little tipsy, but now that I'm thinking about it, she put away a lot of wine to get that way."

"It depends on what you mean by 'a lot,' I guess. Her family's cultures—on both sides—have a more casual attitude about alcohol than most Americans do. But she's not an alcoholic. I can tell you that. She doesn't have the right kind of personality for that—and believe me, I'd know."

"Good," Joshua said, then fell silent. After a while, though, he asked, "What was all that with the pregnant blond girl—was that supposed to be your wife?"

"Clarissa. Yeah."

"Clarissa?"

Joshua rolled onto his side and raised his brows at his friend. Even in the dark tent, Deryl made it clear with his return look that he didn't want to talk about it.

Instead, Joshua mused out loud, "A fantasy wife and an alien lover. Know how many SF geeks would kill to be you?"

Deryl sat up and glared at him, aghast.

A moment later, however, they both burst into laughter.

The next morning, Deryl felt much better, and after lunch, Terry helped him walk to the falls for a much-appreciated wash. Afterward, he was able to walk on his own back to the tent and spent a wonderful, uneventful, and *painless* hour sitting outside, basking in the warmth of the sun, idly talking about Earth while Joshua outlined to Terry and Ocapo what he planned to do once home.

"A brownie sundae," Joshua said. "Sachiko's brownies, pralines and cream ice cream, caramel and the good spray whip. Then, I'm putting my feet on my table, calling up a movie on Netflix—"

"Netflix?"

Joshua started explaining internet movies while teasing them about what they were missing when something caught Deryl's attention, and his head turned toward Tasmae's tent, like a hound catching a scent. His lips parted in a smile.

Tasmae.

She had clearly recovered more quickly than he, for her steps, while not her usual strong stride, were none-theless lithe and sure. She wore her hair in a loose ponytail and it moved behind her like a dark, velvety cloud. Her obsidian eyes shone as she smiled down at Deryl.

He smiled up at her, mesmerized, feeling his pulse quicken in an incredibly sensual way. She was the most beautiful, most desirable woman he'd ever seen on any world, real or imaginary.

"This could get embarrassing," Ocapo commented wryly.

Joshua started to whistle "Kiss the Girl."

Terry smacked him on the shoulder. "Maybe we should go."

"Maybe they should take it to the Kanaan equivalent of a hotel."

All three young men burst out laughing as Deryl rose, took Tasmae's hand, and followed her out of the camp. So lost was he in her presence that their little comedy routine barely registered with him.

They headed down the forest path. They moved slowly because his legs were still shaky; still, he enjoyed the quiet beauty of the woods, the feeling of movement, and the anticipation.

Where are we going? he teleped to her, though beneath the words lay his real question of whether it was much farther. She glanced back at him a look that was both annoyed and coy, and he felt her impatience growing, too. Again, his heart skipped, and they quickened their pace.

He stopped, however, when she started to take him down a side path. Joshua had told him the trees in the clearings had been trained to attack non-Kanaan.

Tasmae turned and leaned against him, her hand on his chest. *You are Kanaan.*

She kissed him, and as his arms tightened around her, he wondered how he could ever have thought anything less could be real.

Still, when at last they pulled apart, he whispered in her ear, "Do the trees know that?"

I am the Miscria, she responded as if that were answer enough.

And it was. The hanging branches of the willow that covered the entrance like a beaded curtain pulled apart, and Deryl followed Tasmae into a little patch of Eden.

The clearing was dazzling in the afternoon light. Tropical flowers, their brilliantly colored blossoms open to the sun, lined a sparkling pond. Thick, low-hanging branches of trees surrounded the glen, their perfect green leaves unmarred by insect or animal, although Deryl did hear the call of an exotic bird and the chirruping of some kind of cricket. The grass beneath them was thick, fine, and soft as a fur rug. Without thinking, he slipped out of his shoes so he could stand barefoot in it. He turned in a small circle, taking it all in, full of awe for the beauty of the place—and for the woman who created it.

I didn't create it, she corrected him with no false modesty. *I simply made my plans known to God, and He led me in its design.*

Deryl nodded, suddenly thoughtful and a little subdued. He was going to have to get used to the close and comfortable relationship these people had with God—and with the casual way his soul-mate could design so beautiful a trap.

She took his hands and at her touch, his misgivings dissolved. Nonetheless, she reassured him wryly that the trap was only one reason for the glen. Most of the time it was for the enjoyment of the Kanaan.

She leaned toward him, but this time, he pulled back, and spoke in English in an effort to keep her distant from his memories.

"Tasmae, in the Netherworld—Clarissa—"

She pressed her fingers lightly to his lips and the sensation made him dizzy with desire. As his lips played over her fingers, he felt her mind reassuring him. She had felt the times Deryl had slipped away from her; and when she had seen the girl Alugiac called Deryl's wife, she had guessed what had happened. Alugiac had manipulated his mind, used his emotions, but it was not real.

"It felt real at the time," he whispered, suddenly sick and ashamed.

Then she kissed him, and he knew that no matter how it had felt, it had never been real, and that after today, he would never doubt reality again. His shame washed away, and he pulled her closer, while his mind sought hers.

This time, however, she hesitated. Twice they had attempted this, and twice he had been hurt when he let his shields down.

He pulled away before his need made him decide to risk it. He'd thought about it last night and had an idea. He stepped back from her, though still holding her hands, and forced his mind to clear. He found a ley line and reached psychically to pull its power to him and into his shields. Once they were strong, he pushed them outward, past his mind, past his body. Tasmae gasped as they passed through her. Once they surrounded them both, he tied them to a ground, let them go, and smiled at his soul-mate.

Tasmae stared at him in awe as she felt the world, now so quiet, so still, around her. All of the psychic impressions she took for granted had faded. It was if there was just the two of them.

He pulled her close. Their bodies pressed together as their minds flowed into each other's.

Then the two were One.

Chapter Thirty-Two

"Wake up!" Deryl nudged Joshua with his foot. "Time to get you home."

"All right!" Joshua bounded out of the covers, whooping, and hurried to throw on his Earth clothes. "You're sure you can do this right?" he demanded as he slipped on his dress shoes. He shoved the softer leathery shoes the Kanaan had given him into a satchel.

"If I don't, we'll be the first to know," Deryl teased.

"What? Don't even make that joke!"

Deryl laughed, then smacked him on the shoulder. "Come on. Folks want to say good-bye."

They shared one last meal with Terry, Ocapo, and Tasmae—and Salgoud and Leinad. Joshua raised his brows when he saw the Remembrance Keeper, though he was relieved to see the older man looking relaxed and friendly for once.

"Tasmae's talked to him," Deryl said.

"Hope so, for your sake."

As they ate, people came to wish him farewell. Some gave him gifts: The parents of the girl he'd helped gave him a tooth and bone-bead necklace; Ocapo, the flute he'd been learning; and Terry, the vest he'd embroidered. Tasmae gave him one of the elaborately decorated punch daggers she wore in her hair.

"I want to visit your world," Terry said. "I want to learn more about human healing."

Ocapo said, "Spot and I, too. Please?"

"Let me get my life settled first." Joshua laughed. "I'm going to need to come up with an orientation program!"

Then it was time to leave. Tasmae gave Joshua a friendly kiss on the cheek, and shared a far more intimate one with Deryl. Joshua rolled his eyes. "Save it for when you get back. I need him to have a clear head, thank you."

She backed away with a mocking bow. Deryl set his hand on Joshua's shoulder. "Practice run first, to the unicorn fields."

"Sounds good." Joshua took a breath—then they were near the stables.

Deryl smirked. "I think someone's going to be missed."

The entire herd had surrounded them, and as one, they lowered their heads in a bow. Grinning and touched, Joshua returned the gesture. Glory had pulled out nine of her tail hairs, and held them out for him.

"Aw, thanks, baby." He took them, wrapped his arms around her neck, and accepted a horsey kiss. He waved as they ran off.

"You know, despite all the danger and stress, this was a pretty cool adventure," he said as he braided the hairs together. "Not that I want to repeat it."

"No promises. How are you going to explain that stuff?" Deryl asked.

"I'm not," Joshua replied as he tied a final knot and slipped it into his pocket. "If you really get us back to my apartment, I'm going to hide it, first thing. You sure you can get us back?"

"Of course I can. I not only learned how to teleport from the Bondfriends, but I know it first hand through Tasmae."

Joshua shook his head in disgust. "Yeah, right. You should see the grin on your face. I'm sure you spent a quiet evening talking about teleportation."

Deryl's grin got bigger. "Mating on Kanaan is of the psyche as well as the body," he told him mysteriously.

Joshua shrugged casually, refusing to be baited. "Guess that's why they mate for life, then. Well, I'm ready! What do you need me to do?"

Over breakfast, they had decided to take Joshua back to his Rhode Island flat, aiming for Tuesday morning, less than a day after they'd left. Joshua's cover story would be that Deryl had knocked him out, and he'd awakened there. Already, he had shared his memories of the apartment with Deryl, much the same way that he had shared his memories of his grandfather's razor.

Was that really only a week ago? Deryl "heard" his friend wonder, and grinned. So much had happened since then, so many wonders, that he was actually a little sad about leaving.

"Close your eyes and think about your apartment. Picture it in as much detail as possible. Don't think about Sachiko, though, or anyone else—"

"Yeah, you had to say that!" Joshua huffed. "Now why don't you *not* think about a blue monkey?"

"Sorry. Think of your apartment as you left it, empty, the sun streaming in the windows..."

As Deryl led Joshua through the visualization, the picture became clearer and clearer in his mind. When he saw even the dust playing in the sunlight, he concentrated on being there. He felt a stir of wind, a sudden, but more gentle wrenching, then nothingness.

A breathless moment later, they stood in Joshua's apartment.

"Oh, yes!" Joshua breathed, and then dashed to his laptop on the side table.

"What's the day?" He flipped up the monitor and turned it on. While it went through the boot-up sequence, he dashed to the closet, burying the satchel under his dirty laundry, then made a beeline for the fridge. He cheered to find the soda cool and the brownies still good. He shoved an entire brownie into his mouth, moaning with pleasure, tossed Deryl a can of Coke, grabbed a D.C. for himself, and headed back.

He logged in and whooped when he saw the date and time. "Tuesday afternoon!"

Deryl glanced at the apartment and noted the sun coming in from the west. "Wrong windows," he commented wryly, then laughed as Joshua pulled him into a tight bear hug.

Joshua released him, thinking aloud. "Mrs. Radcliffe usually shops on Tuesday afternoons, so we may have some time before anyone notices we're here. Is there anything you want from Earth before you go?"

"A book on orbital mechanics."

Joshua laughed. "You're kidding, right?"

"No, I... I don't know why I said that. I..." Deryl shook his head. "You know my stuffed bear, Descartes? Grab it. Keep it safe. If I return, I'll need it. Got it?"

"What's your bear got to do with anything?"

Deryl cocked a brow. "You think I didn't have an alternate escape plan?"

"What? What's in the bear?"

"Someone's coming!" Deryl interrupted. HIs eyes pinpointed as he concentrated on an outside psyche. "It's Malachai!"

They heard wheels crunching on the rock driveway. There was a familiar knocking in the engine after it shut off. "Why's he driving my car?"

"Your parents are with him—and Sachiko."

"Really? Oh, man! You've got to get out of here. I'll go stall." He turned to leave.

"Josh!"

Joshua turned to look at him.

Outside car doors were opening.

"Tell Sachiko and your parents I'm sorry. And, and thanks, for—" Deryl paused, mashing his lips together against his emotions.

Joshua pulled him into another quick hug. "That's what friends are for, right? Besides, that was definitely the adventure of a lifetime!" He held him at arm's length and regarded him earnestly. "You ever need anything—"

"I know who to come to. And if you need me, just think of me, hard."

"You got it. I'd better go!" Footsteps crunched on the gravel and the car trunk creaked open. Joshua gave his friend a quick squeeze on the shoulder and dashed out the door.

Deryl heard him pounding down the steps, calling out Sachiko's name, then shouts of joy. He looked again around Joshua's small apartment: the wardrobe of clothes, the laptop computer with a dozen messages— he noted with surprise that he could look at the screen now—the paperback lying open, facedown, on the table, the synthesizer on its stand between two window fans. He thought of Joshua outside, surrounded by his family, his boss, and the woman he loved.

So this is a normal Earth life? It felt so wrong. Even the sounds of traffic seemed alien to him.

He thought about a world with mandrakes-on-steroids and everyn and unicorns that could "talk" to you, and about a woman who could change the world with the power of her mind.

He grinned, closed his eyes, and went home.

"Joshua!" Even though Joshua had bounded out of the house calling his fiancée's name, his mother saw him first. She dropped her travel bag and ran, Sachiko and his father looking up and following with shouts of their own.

Joshua jumped the last six steps and threw himself into his mother's arms. "Mom! What are you doing here?"

"What do you mean, what am I doing? You were *kidnapped*!" But she was laughing and crying too hard to scold him properly, and she only released him when he twisted to reach Sachiko. As he kissed his fiancée enthusiastically, his mother leaned against his dad, who held her close, both smiling through their tears.

Malachai, however, was unmoved. "Where's Deryl Stephens?"

Just then, the windows of Joshua's apartment rattled.

"Gone," Joshua pulled away from Sachiko's lips enough to say.

The chief psychiatrist gave him a murderous look and ran up the stairs. They heard him shouting Deryl's name as he searched the tiny flat.

Joshua laughed as he reached out to his parents and tried to hug them and Sachiko all at once. He was going to be in for it when Dr. Malachai came back down, he knew, but for the moment, he didn't care.

He was home.

Epilogue

In the Temple of Eternal Guidance, government headquarters of God's Republic of Barinnin, a robed and bespectacled bishop spoke to the frazzled scientist on the other side of the telephone line. Although frazzled himself after the trying conversation, he nonetheless kept his voice serene as he spoke.

"I am deeply sorry, Exalted Intellect Revluc, but as I have said repeatedly, the Great Prophet can see no one right now. Yes, yes, I understand the urgency of your findings, but he is in even more urgent prayer."

When the annoying man continued to protest—as he had off and on for days now—Bishop Anglin pulled out his last weapon.

"Surely you understand the importance of Alugiac's prayers? Surely you agree that it is only the cooperation of your science with God's will, given to us through him, that we will ever fulfill God's destiny for our people and make the pilgrimage to the next world? I thought so. No, no, I never doubted you, and I do promise to make speaking to you his top priority when he returns to us from his sacred raptures. Of course. God guide you, too."

He felt like a tasmae for what he had just done. He'd all but accused one of the most promising scientists of the Fifth Age of blasphemy and treason—both of which were punishable by the most horrible of public deaths. Had he not seen the Prophet call on the power of the

Ydrel to fling a man across a room in punishment for his continued insolence? The congregation had watched in awe and horror as the wrath of God the Conqueror made itself known upon Counselor Kusel, but stopped before the death blow. Alugiac said it was God's warning, and anyone seeing Kusel's misshapen face should certainly heed it.

Still, I should not have threatened Revluc so, but it was the only way I could think of to get him to leave me alone. Pernicious man!

Bishop Anglin sighed as he rifled through the pile of requests Alugiac had entrusted to him. Such trivialities! Could no one in the entire nation make a decision without the approval of their Supreme Leader?

What was taking Alugiac so long? Could he truly bring the Ydrel to them? Ydrel, Path Forger. Ydrel, Sacred Weapon. Anglin felt a thrill that such holy events would come to pass in his lifetime—but when? Too much, he did not understand, but he knew one thing.: Alugiac must return, and soon. For two weeks now, two long weeks of silence and growing unrest among the order, Alugiac had been locked in his room with the command that no one disturb him.

God help me. I will disobey those orders if he does not return to us soon. Forgive me, Lord Conqueror of All, if that be a lack of faith, he prayed as he turned to the endless paperwork.

Locked in his room, Alugiac, too, prayed. "Oh, God, what have I done? What have I done?"

Is Alugiac cured? Will there be peace for Barin and Kanaan? Read Madness of Worlds and find out. Now on Amazon.

Please Leave a Review

Please take a few minutes to leave a review. It only takes 20 words to share with others what you like and don't like about the book. It helps readers and helps with Amazon ratings which makes author and dragon happy.

Subscribe to My Newsletter

If you want to keep up with my adventures, books, and classes in person and on print, sign up for my newsletter. You'll get a free ebook with a story about Deryl before the asylum!

https://fabianspace.substack.com/subscribe

There's More Fun in FabianSpace!

DragonEye Series

Murder Most Picante
If Wishes Were Dragons
Nun of My Business
Christmas Spirits
Greater Treasures
Siren Spell
Good Intentions
Idol Speculations
Gapman
Plus short stories

Science Fiction

Space Traipse: Hold My Beer Series
The Old Man and the Void
Dex's Way
Discovery
The Rescue Sisters short stories

Neeta Lyffe, Zombie Exterminator

Zombie Death Extreme!
I Left My Brains in San Francisco
Shambling in a Winter Wonderland